21ST CENTURY CHINESE LITERATURE

THE MUD BOOT WEDDING

AND OTHER ETHNIC MINORITY STORIES

FOREIGN LANGUAGES PRESS

First Edition 2009

ISBN 978-7-119-05940-2

©Foreign Languages Press, Beijing, China, 2009

Published by Foreign Languages Press
24 Baiwanzhuang Road, Beijing 100037, China
http: //www. flp. com. cn

Distributed by China International Book Trading Corporation
35 Chegongzhuang Xilu, Beijing 100044, China
P.O. Box 399, Beijing, China

Printed in the People's Republic of China

Contents

21st Century Chinese Literature
— Points of Departure

By Wang Meng

The *21st Century Chinese Literature* series aims to introduce contemporary Chinese literature in English, French and other languages to readers all over the world.

Chinese literature's recent path, along the country's trajectory, may not resemble a smooth highway, yet it is still the main channel toward understanding China and the daily lives and inner-world of the Chinese people.

China has been experiencing soaring development, and its links with the rest of the world have been growing closer. Even if you might not know anyone from China, "made in China" still can now be found in most aspects of your life, or as expressed in a Chinese idiom, "Look up, and see it everywhere." News about China appears regularly in newspapers, on TV and the Internet, trying to tell you what is happening in this remote yet near country called China, and what China is thinking and planning. In this way, peoples of the world have developed their general views of China.

Many of those views are often insightful. Chinese writers, like myself, have also been keeping an eye on the world. We often discuss the US, Japan, Russia, South Africa, Italy and other countries, as well as the interesting or ingenious views about China held by peoples of such countries. But we feel much regret to find

---

Wang Meng is an illustrious writer and China's former Minister of Culture.

sometimes that others' views about China are full of illusions and misunderstandings, more often than not, preconceived, arbitrary and overgeneralized. Thus, my fellow citizens and I have become powerfully aware of how little the world really knows about China, and thus we feel that the world is so near, yet still so remote.

Literature can draw us closer to communicate views and imagination about the world and life, and share each other's joys and sorrows beyond language barriers, different cultures and backgrounds or long distances. It can make you feel that people living afar are like your next-door neighbors, as you perceive and share the secret interiors of their lives and dreams. To illustrate this point, I shall borrow a poetic line from the current Indian ambassador to China, Mrs. Nirupama Rao:

"...making sense of each other,
even as realization glimmers
that, we are little morsels
tossed by the history of these parts."

It elucidates the point of departure of this series. Readers from all over the world, who are used to learning about China through foreign newspapers, TV and the Internet, may now open up these books to see China through the heartfelt thoughts and writings of Chinese people themselves. The many authors of these new short stories, living in this rapidly developing and changing, yet ancient nation, have strived to describe all that is happening in and around themselves, to give genuine dynamic expression to the intricate recent experiences of the Chinese people. Through the power of their words you will be able to catch glimpses of the real, complex and living China, as well as other possibilities for all humanity, including yourself.

The Foreign Languages Press has long devoted itself to enhancing mutual understanding between China and the rest of the world. China followers in every country probably still remember *Panda Books*, mainly published in the late 20th century. Those books collected a wide range of contemporary Chinese literary works. The *Panda Books* series helped many Chinese writers become known to the world. *21st Century Chinese Literature* can be regarded as the continuation of *Panda Books*, though its selection and editing methods vary greatly from the old series. All the volumes of new short stories were edited by Chinese scholars, with in-depth understanding and research in contemporary Chinese literature, whose judgment and views are highly respected among Chinese writers and readers. They accomplished this editing work independently, conducive to this new series better reflecting the highly diversified spiritual quests and artistic creativity of contemporary Chinese literature.

Thus, the other vital impact of this series is to provide international sinologists and Chinese literary researchers with the view from inside, from within the Chinese literary circles widely recognized among Chinese writers and readers. These points of view are likely to differ from the general views held by other countries toward contemporary Chinese literature. It is this very difference that engenders the great potential for new knowledge and discovery.

Modern Chinese writers have been deeply influenced by literature from all over the world. We have been deeply convinced by Goethe's concept of "World Literature." We are committed to the invaluable dream of a "Tower of Babel" promoting mutual understanding among all the peoples of the world. I believe the *21st Century Chinese Literature* series will provide our own enduring great bricks in this skyward "Tower."

Introduction

People, Lives and Times

Shi Zhanjun

Professor Shi Zhanjun, a Ph.D. in literature, was born in 1966, in Tongyu, Jilin Province, his mother from the Mongolian ethnic group. After July 1988 Prof. Shi taught first at the Chinese Department of Jilin Normal University and then at the College of Liberal Arts of Shandong University. In 2001, he went to the Republic of Korea as an exchange professor at Dongseo University. Since September 2007, he has been studying contemporary Chinese literature at the Post-doctoral Research Center of Peking University. Prof. Shi is now an executive director of Chinese Fiction Society and vice-chair and secretary-general of the Shandong Association of Contemporary Literature. He is the chief editor of the four-part, 18-volume literary series *New Spark Writer* and one of the chief editors of *China New Age Literary Research Data*, totaling 18 parts, 24 volumes. His studies won the Theoretical Criticism Prize of the China Federation of Literary and Art Circles and Outstanding Achievement Award of the China Association of Contemporary Literature. At the end of 2007, Prof. Shi was voted "Young Critic of the Year" at the Forum for Young Chinese Writers and Critics co-sponsored by the literary magazines *People's Literature* and *Southern Cultural Forum*. In the same year, he won the support of the New Century Talent Program launched by China's Ministry of Education.

People, Lives and Times

Let's look at the borders on the map of China, starting in the west and moving slowly on to the south, north and east, and then to the regions of sparse population, high mountains and broad deserts. These areas are mostly inhabited by China's ethnic minority peoples, where the economy and science and technology are less developed, but where the pristine beauty of nature and sanctity still persist. These areas may harbor a greater diversity of cultures and literature than inland China. As a developing country, China is moving toward overall modernization. The ancient culture and the old urban and rural structures of China's majority Han people are being drastically remolded by the new economic age, particularly in the 21st century. Although the minority peoples have inevitably been influenced by the general trend of the time, their unique customs and landscape, and the surviving connection between their epic ballads and reality have become an increasingly important subject of Chinese culture and literature.

Recent landmark literary works that have attracted much attention in China, including the controversial best-sellers

Wolf Totem by Jiang Rong and *Tibetan Mastiff* by Yang Zhijun, the esthetic novels *Empty Mountain* by Ah Lai and *On the Right Bank of the Argun River* by Chi Zijian, share a renewed perspective on China's minorities. Two major subjects have drawn the focus of 21st century writers and literary critics, namely, stories of migrant workers, disclosing the progress and consequences of modernization; and esthetic depictions of the ecology in the border areas and the life of minority peoples, providing reflections on modernization and definitions of people's mindsets. In terms of these two dimensions, our general view and habitual impressions may not be basically mistaken, but viewed against such diverse and vibrant creative writing, may be shown to be somewhat incomplete or even arbitrary.

Genuine literature always makes a humane observation of and reflects deeply on the difficult circumstances of others; with minority peoples too, it should not be always admiring or intrusive, but should have empathy for the lives of all individuals.

The writer Lu Yiping from the Xinjiang Uyghur Autonomous Region describes the misfortune of Xiabazi, a man from the Tajik ethnic group in *The Return of Xiabazi*:

"Xiabazi knows that the Tahman Grassland, where the Tajik people have lived for generations, is suffering from the over-grazing of too many herds, which float across the area like white clouds. To keep from starving, the sheep have learned to dig up grass roots from the ground with their muzzles and hooves.

....

"The cow-dung smoke rising from the roof of each *langaili* house, together with the smells of roast *nang* and stewed mutton, mixed with the sweet aroma of the grass in the Tahman Grassland, giving Xiabazi a feeling of warmth. Xiabazi has reveled in the Grassland's charms many times before, so much so that he lived the place with every ounce of his being. Knowing that the beautiful Tahman Grassland couldn't afford to support so many people, he accepted Township Chief Xiren's urging and agreed to leave and move to Markit Plain, a strange area at the edge of the broad desert."

Xiabazi is derided as a fool by a seemingly clever man. What a thought-provoking irony! The real fools are those who are considered to have seen the world but sacrifice their common long-term interest for a price.

Comparisons with mainstream inland Chinese culture are expressed naturally and objectively. Quantities of critiques on the value of minority literature have repeatedly intensified the comparison habit among readers and gradually consolidated their concept of border area and ethnic minority literature.

Actually, the habit of making cultural and esthetic comparisons between the literature of Chinese minority peoples and the Han has misled urban readers. As a result, the average urban reader is interested more in descriptions of virgin landscapes and unusual customs of ethnic minorities in the border areas, than in detailed observations of their lives. Mysteries and legends that seem exotic to inland culture are more appealing than daily life.

Therefore, the importance of writers such as Kim In-Sun and Ma Jinlian is worth mentioning. They do not divorce ethnic literature from daily life, but write about the ordinary. Turning the emphasis away from descriptions of natural scenery and ethnic customs, these writers focus on the normal themes of literature — people, lives and the passage of time.

The young Hui writer Ma Jinlian lives in Xiji County, Guyuan

Prefecture, in Ningxia Hui Autonomous Region, a region known for its arid climate and harsh life. It is the normal literary practice for writers to experience the trials of life here and express sympathy and concern. The representation of ethnic elements is often achieved by means of religious matters or representative characters. *Girl, Wife, Daughter-in-Law* is personal, involved and up-close; it is far from pure observation, still less is it conceptual. Rather than the usual imagination catering to the need for novelty, the story gives us faithfulness to and love for life. The tale recounts the experience of Snowflake from the time she marries to when she gives birth. With her good-natured husband working away in the city most of the time, she has to live with her smart mother-in-law and her calculating sister-in-law. Daily life proceeds in a peaceful and orderly way. Snowflake has a placid, positive nature. Her attitude toward all her toil and the family she married into is one of simple contentment refreshing the notoriously thirsty land.

The virtue of understanding in daily life and the passage of time is vividly expressed in *Ballad of the Bell Flowers* by Kim In-Sun, a writer from the Korean ethnic group. Love and enmity among the older generation are gradually dissolved by the understanding of the younger generation and communication between the two generations. The personality of each character is displayed in dialogue. A feeling of gratitude prevails at the wedding of the younger generation.

This does not mean that ethnic characteristics are neglected. They are not used as stage property, but are revealed naturally in the details of daily life, such as the custom of sweeping clean the *kang* (earthen bed) and taking a bath before giving birth; the absent imam who was supposed to give a name to the new baby in *Girl, Wife, Daughter-in-Law*; and the ethnic ballad, festive costumes and food in *Ballad of the Bell Flowers*. Quietly, without any jarring effect, they exude the pure flavor of ethnic life.

The Remote Hot Spring by the Tibetan writer Ah Lai is an awe-inspiring story, neither embellished by exaggerated ethnic mystery, nor avoiding the modern conflict between the pursuit of material gain and human virtues. The author combines clear self-knowledge, personal experience and understanding of the place he is writing about with his heartfelt emotions, exhibiting the skill and ease of a mature writer. The Tibetan mindset and thinking pattern are naturally reflected in the story, leaving no trace of artificial ornament. At the same time, the story rediscovers the rationality of the Tibetan people through a combined force of history, reality and culture and conveys the magnanimity of the Tibetans to readers. The fast changing scenes are woven through with temptations and depression. However, the story is still dominated by the vigorous dignity and acute cultural perception of the author. It has the same ethos as his previous multi-part novel *Empty Mountain*, which has attracted much attention over the past few years. Only those striving toward creating an everlasting classic can have such incisive, far-sighted vision and discover such an unfailing creative source.

Tsering Norbu's *Killer* and Long Renqing's *The Mud Boot Wedding* were both written by Tibetans, but are dramatically different in narrative style.

"Vanguard Literature" that prevailed in mid- and late-1980s China often used Tibet as background and experimented with new narrative structure and language style based on mysterious imagination. Pioneers of this literary genre included the Han writer Ma Yuan and native Tibetan Tashi Dawa. The masterpieces of the genre they created gained a solid footing in contemporary Chinese literature. "Vanguard Literature" has waned in central China, but a large group of Tibetan writers of "Vanguard Literature" is actively reflecting the inner world through their narratives. At present, Tsering Norbu is the most representative writer of Tibetan "Vanguard Literature." *Killer* has a simple plot of seeking vengeance for previous wrongs. It is not an unexplored area by any means but it is given freshness, psychological suspense and unpredictable twists by the author's treatment. *Killer* poses the question of how to eliminate inner sin and implies rather than spells out the answer.

The Mud Boot Wedding is told from the perspective of a little boy, full of curiosity and longing for adult experiences. In a sense, the story has the nature of "Vanguard Literature." Through a child's feelings it awakens our sensitivity to all living things, using a narrative technique and the unspoiled imaginative power of a child, whilst bringing in Tibetan folk songs, tales and customs that merge subtly into the story. In contrast to the incisive depictions in Tsering Norbu's story, *The Mud Boot Wedding* adopts a child's perspective and reflects a warm and somewhat lonely feeling through his various playful activities. The warm yet lonely feeling is perhaps what we call nostalgia.

The Land of Green, written by Liao Yirong of the Dongxiang ethnic group, is an adult fairy tale about a beautiful woman torn between two men. The courting, slang expressions and observation of physical attraction reveal the love of beauty. The protagonist Yishiha's love for the heroine Jiayina ends in sadness, but without grudges or hatred. The green grass, beautiful sunshine, lovely dreams and generous blessings convey the same warm yet lonely feeling of nostalgia as the previous story.

When "ethnic culture" comes to face with "developed civilization," the unchanging dependence upon nature and the continuous infiltration of external factors will cause ethnic groups to make conscious or subconscious choices about their lifestyle. Therefore, a deep nostalgia for the homeland lies behind the soulful narration of ethnic literature. Hong Ke's *Lake Hanas* about the life of Tuvans, part of the Mongolian ethnic group, and *Golden Ranges* by Sana of the Daur ethnic group, depict this feeling in detailed and graphic descriptions .

Both *Lake Hanas* and *Golden Ranges* flow with poetry and boundless love for ethnic life. However, within the affectionate observation and the longing for tranquility, unspoken worries lurk.

Lake Hanas illustrates feelings of worry in various aspects, including the love affair between the teacher and the "constantly agitated woman" in Urumqi and the relationship between the Tuvans and the hydropower station workers. Nonetheless, no ultimate solution is available to prevent disturbance to the lives of local people, nor their deity culture from being assimilated by modern civilization. Therefore, the story expresses a complicated feeling, an insistent discordance mixed in with the blue theme of nostalgia. Faced with natives and immigrants, with people seeking self-salvation and with intruders aiming at development, Lake Hanas can no longer tolerate or reject them with equanimity; its clarity has been overshadowed by sadness. The story reflects reality in a romantic language.

In comparison, the *Golden Ranges* is simple and well-rounded; it generalizes neither environmental issues nor the contrast between modern and pristine civilizations. Plain but vivid descriptions can be found everywhere in the story. For example, "It had been sunny when we came out, but now black storm clouds were right behind us." Delightful language and subtle depiction in landscape portrayal pack the story with wonderful power and psychological insight.

The well-structured and smoothly told episodes about getting sick and being disappointed in love are natural, substantial reflections of real life. They are without pretension, but they do have metaphorical functions. The grassland climate and lifestyle will inevitably change, and the pains of growing up and mishaps in life will finally subside. Even with the worshiped spirit providing consolation, sorrow, resignation to fate and obedience to the spirits causes tremors in the soul. The author skillfully veils some facts or reveals others as if unconsciously. The connotations are communicated in the grass, sunshine, wind, rain, sky and rainbows. The prettier and more serene the scenery, the deeper the secret worry and sadness.

The ethnic groups enjoy a slow pace of life in quiet, secluded environments, in still partly wild habitats where man and nature coexist. In such a life people search for tranquility amid disorder, a retreat from busyness into peace. There are all the joys and pains of growing up, all the feelings of love, hatred, gratitude and resentment of everyday life. It is like a religious experience, a pursuit of the essential, eternal meaning of life, inspiring awe and giving comfort.

Chi Zijian has produced a series of outstanding works about the lives of ethnic minorities by China's northeast borders; they integrate the history of ethnic life, the experiences of individuals, and ethnic characteristics. Her *Breezes in the Woods,* about the life of the Oroqen people, depicts the appeal of their culture with a humanistic, sympathetic eye. The sexual theme sets this story apart from Chi Zijian's other works: Han people, educated and constrained by their traditional culture and modern civilization, are contrasted with the Oroqens who live in the woods and have a primal passion for life. The contrast imparts a tension to the narrative. Gentle breezes blow in the woods, countless stars surround the moon, silhouetting a horse. Sensual pleasure is depicted more as a gift from heaven rather than the banal grubbiness of an adulterous affair.

A Tale from the Huolin River written by Bai Xuelin of the Mongolian ethnic group, portrays the great maternal bond at the critical moments of life and death, a bond shared by both humans and cows. The heroine and her cows have a moving emotional connection, sharing kind-heartedness, perseverance, sufferings and sacrifices. The "long song" is touching and inspiring, like a hymn of human emotions. Such spirit bolstering the strength for survival is as indomitable and undying as the common faith in the age-old epics.

Many ethnic groups have their own epics, which are the source of their spirit. Today, in the rapid progress of modernization, the cultures of ethnic minorities provide spiritual comfort for countless writers and readers. They are relief and haven for our souls rather than lingering imagination. The epics of Tibetan and Mongolian peoples formed a style of their own, providing rich resources for subsequent literary endeavors. Every literary character embodying the ethnic spirit can be traced to a certain archetype in the epic of that people. The stories in this collection transfer to us the remote, deep esthetic pulse of ethnic cultures.

The Return of Xiabazi

Lu Yiping

Lu Yiping, original name Zhou Rui, was born in October 1972 into a family with Miao blood lineage in Nanjiang, Sichuan. He moved to Xinjiang in March 1990 and traveled extensively around China's west for eight years. He now lives in Urumqi. He studied at the first graduate program for writers in Shanghai, and is a member of the Chinese Writers' Association. In 1992, Lu had his early works published in literary periodicals such as *Kunlun*, *Chinese Writers*, *Shanghai Literature* and *Lotus*. His major works include the novella collection *One Way to Survive*, the novel *The Passion Kingdom*, the documentary *Eight Thousand Hunan Girls into the Heavenly Mountain*, the essay anthology *Book of the Roof of the World* and the travel books *The Golden Outback* and *Yunnan the Paradise*. Some of his works have been translated into English, Russian, Kazakh and Uygur. He has won many literary awards, and his works have been published in *Selected Stories*, *Selected Novellas*, *Novella Monthly* and *Duzhe (Readers)*.

The Return of Xiabazi

I

On the back of his beloved red horse named Wind, Xiabazi looked at the Tahman Grassland and silently wept.

He had cried for the grassland several times. Years ago, he liked singing the old songs about the grassland handed down by his ancestors, but his singing stopped when he first shed tears for the grassland.

Every time he saw the grassland, he felt a dull pain in his heart. Several years ago, he found that the grass was not growing as well and in some places the earth was already exposed before the arrival of autumn. It was ugly. In just a few years, the grassland had aged noticeably. It had been young for several millennia; in just a few years, it had grown old.

In the past, herds of sheep came to wallow in the grassland, like fish in water. And now their hooves were exposed to the herbage on the grassland, which is like the muddy bottom of a waterless lake. Years ago, a herd of sheep could eat their fill in a small patch of grass. Nowadays, however, they ran about the grassland looking for food all day long, like hungry dogs, before coming home half starved.

Xiabazi knows that the Tahman Grassland, where the Tajik people have lived for generations, is suffering from the over-grazing of too many herds, which float across the area like white clouds. To keep from starving, the sheep have learned to dig up grass roots from the ground with their muzzles and hooves.

Herding the sheep that had been running about the grassland all day long, Xiabazi felt as tired as the animals.

He saw the smoke of the cooking fire coming from the chimney of his house, called *langaili* by the Tajik. The house, a square-shaped earth-and-wood structure with a flat roof, was renovated six years ago thanks to the sale of forty sheep. Although it looked shabby on the outside, it was cozy inside.

Xiabazi drove the sheep into the pen and tied Wind to the hitching post, then began to stick the collected cow dung to the wall. Although he would lose all of this in a couple of days, he took great care of the job. After hanging a wicker basket of dung against the wall, he grabbed a handful of dried earth from the corner and cleaned his hands with it. He made a cigarette with Mohe tobacco as he looked at the snow–capped Mt. Mustag in the distance, which seemed blue in the twilight. He felt heavy with gloom.

He sought comfort from Wind. He leaned against the animal and Wind turned and licked his hands.

He took a strong drag from the cigarette and said to Wind, "Since we'll leave here in a couple of days, why am I still collecting the cow dung? This will make others think that I regret leaving here. But I only do this from habit. It's a sin to come across cow dung and not pick it up, bring it home, and stick it to the wall, just like it's a sin to see grains of barley on the ground and not pick them up. I've heard that people on the plains use coal. I was told by the wife of a relative of mine – a section chief in the county government – that

coal stinks and gives off a poisonous gas when it burns. If you inhale too much of the smoke, you'll die. How can it burn better than
dry dung, which lights easily and burns well, and gives off a smoke
that smells like the grassland?"

Wind neighed softly, as if agreeing with him.

"However, in the presence of Township Chief Xiren, a good
friend of mine, I have sworn to Allah that I will not come back
again once I move to the plain!"

Wind raised his head and looked at Xiabazi, then at the blue
mountain in the twilight, and let loose a long, loud neigh. Xiabazi
burst into tears. Now that he was about to leave the grassland, he
was getting as gentle-hearted as a woman.

He leaned against Wind for quite awhile, smoking Mohe cigarettes one after another. He was watching the moon, which was as
divinely white as the snow on the top of Mt. Mustag, rising at the
back of a nameless snow-capped mountain in the west. Moonlight
spilled onto Wind's back, on the fallen gold-colored leaves, on the
red buckthorn fruits – into every corner it could reach.

Wind was standing as still as a statue, the sheep had fallen
asleep, and the shepherd dog named Grey Wolf was squatting at the
entrance of the sheepfold. A thin layer of ice coated the winding
Tahman River and the night wind was blowing. The snow-capped
mountain, together with the lotus-shaped cloud above it, was
drenched in moonlight. Xiabazi thought to himself, for thousands
of years, my ancestors have lived here and looked up at that snow-
capped mountain.

The cow-dung smoke rising from the roof of each *langaili*
house, together with the smells of roast *nang* (crusty pancake staple
food of Uygur and other ethnic groups in Xinjiang – *ed.*) and stewed
mutton, mixed with the sweet aroma of the grass in the Tahman

Grassland, giving Xiabazi a feeling of warmth. Xiabazi has reveled in the Grassland's charms many times before, so much so that he lived the place with every ounce of his being. Knowing that the beautiful Tahman Grassland couldn't afford to support so many people, he accepted Township Chief Xiren's urging and agreed to leave and move to Markit Plain, a strange area at the edge of the broad desert.

II

Xiabazi patted Wind on the back, signaling that he should go back to his house. He opened the door and embraced the comfort. Amansha, his wife, had prepared the milk tea. The cow-dung fire was blazing brightly in the stove, where the family sat waiting for him. The family still disagreed on whether or not to go to Markit. As a native of the grassland, his wife was clearly against the move, but Xiabazi knew she would follow him in the end. The key obstacle was that both his son's and daughter's lovers lived on the grassland. His daughter would go back to the grassland by way of marriage, while his son's lover was unwilling to leave, and the two of them were finding it hard to separate.

Watching the blue blaze of the cow-dung fire with a small piece of *nang* in his hand, Xiabazi accepted the milk tea Amansha gave him. He savored the aroma of milk tea and barley flour. Such pleasures were what made him want to spend his life on the grassland.

He knew that he would face a completely different life on the plain, but he had promised the Chief that he would leave. The Township Chief, who was one of his classmates in primary school, had studied for two more years in a junior middle school before assuming his post. As Xiabazi recalled, shortly after he had returned from the summer pasture to the Tahman Grassland, at dusk on the ninth day, he wanted to graze his sheep a little longer as they were still hungry. Watching the grassland gilded by the setting sun, he suddenly became melancholy and sang a gloomy song:

> *Like Mother's milk, Tahman Grassland*
> *Has brought up our forefathers.*
> *Even in the most desolate winter,*
> *She still gives us endless warmth.*
> *Now she's getting old,*
> *And when I look at her face,*
> *It's as if my heart were cut by a sword.*

The song came straight from the heart. When he finished singing, he noticed someone standing beside him. The man said, "Xiabazi, how well you sing!"

"Oh, it's you, my Lord Township Chief! You made no sound, like a ghost, and gave me a start. I heard that a special car had been allocated for you. Why are you still riding around on horseback?"

They gave hand-kissing salutes to each other on horseback. Xiabazi smelled the cadre's odor, a mix of cigarettes, liquor, mutton and soap.

"You lost yourself in your singing," said Township Chief Xiren, extending a cigarette to Xiabazi. "That thing is a waste of money. The need for a car will lead to the need for a driver, which will take money from the people. It's convenient for a cadre to ride a horse in the pasture region. If I go down to the pasture on horseback, you will still regard me as a grassland inhabitant. But if I go by car, I would be only a township chief who has nothing to do with the pasture."

"It will be difficult to find another official as good as you. You are the same Xiren who was brought up on sheep's milk on our grassland."

"But it's not easy for me to be a township chief, and now I've got a bit of problem."

"What problem is that, Township Chief Xiren?"

"You see, the grassland is not able to support all the people who live there, as the experts tell us, the grassland will become a barren desert in few years if nothing is done to save it. That is why the leaders, in order to move some people down to the plain, have taken great pains to have houses built and opened up more land in the Markit Plain."

He continued, "The people who are moved to the plain are from the poverty-stricken towns. Several waves of those people were moved there, but they all came back when they failed to settle down there. Now set numbers of people who must move to the plain have been assigned to each town, and it's our town's turn to take the lead in the move.

"Three of our households must move, and I have been riding on horseback for two days, unable to find anyone willing to go. I had no choice but to persuade my eldest brother and my wife's brother. They have agreed, but I need one more household."

"This is certainly a hard nut to crack," Xiabazi told him. "What is the Markit Plain like?"

"Very nice. The brick houses are ready for use, and the land has been opened up, too. Each person can have five *mu* (a fifteenth of a hectare – *ed.*) of fields, with the seeds and fertilizer provided by the government. For the first five years, medical expenses and food will be paid for by the government."

"That sounds nice," I said. "So why is nobody willing to move there, and why did the people who did move come back?"

"It's hard for them to leave their homeland. They lived on the highland for generations, and they're having trouble adapting to the different life," he said.

"It's true. Though the Markit Plain is hardly located on the Moon, it's still difficult to pull up one's roots from the Tahman Grassland to go somewhere else." He took a long drag on the cigarette given by the township chief, adding, "Nevertheless, some people on the grassland do need to move, otherwise, the grassland will certainly be ruined."

"Do me a favor, then," the township chief said, extending another cigarette to him.

"How do you know I'll agree to move?"

"I felt it from your song just now. And another thing, you're my friend!"

"All right, I agree!"

Xiabazi made the decision to leave the grassland. But when he went home and told his family about it, they were silent.

Now, the family members seemed to be waiting for him to come home. They wanted to express their feelings to him, the master of the household.

"Up to now, we have been living by following the sheep herd about the vast grassland on horseback. If we move to the plain, everything will change – the light whip will be replaced with heavy farm tools. We'll have to attend the patch of field all the year round just like we attend our ancestors, and everyday we'll have to bend ourselves laboring in the fields."

"More importantly, the Uygur and the Han people, who have been farming there for thousands of years, have a deep understanding of the fields, seasons and climate there. But we know nothing about these things. I'm in awe of the sight of the fields, just as I am at the sight of the snow-capped mountain towering into the clouds. The field exists for the crops, and the seeds scattered into the field should grow of themselves. But someone has to plough and flatten and weed and fertilize the field, which is hard work. If you fail to do this work well, the fields will produce nothing in return. You see how many troubles we have saved living on the grassland!"

"On top of that, I'm afraid that I'll get lost on the plain, which is as flat as a sheet of paper. Moreover, the sky, earth, trees, houses, rivers, canals, roads, donkeys, birds, and even the people are all alike. Everything being alike will make you dizzy! On our highland, however, everything that exists has its own unique appearance."

"I don't like the sky over the plain. I can watch the sky on the highland forever, while I get fed up with the sky over the plain after just one glance. The sky over the plain seems to be sick all the year round."

"There is no grassland on the plain, and we see no herds of horses and sheep there, nor could we enjoy the games like 'sheep scrambling' and horse racing."

"The houses there are not movable, like tents. And it is unimaginable that our descendants would ever grow roots there."

"And what's more, when snow is falling here, sand is falling on the plain."

His son, who was quite funny, said, "The wind there is bad, too. The wind on the highland is nothing but wind, which is so clean that one can swallow it in one big mouthful. But in the wind of the plain there is everything – sand, earth, leaves, and even the sun-dried shit of human beings and animals. There are even tree branches and stones in the wind when it blows. In the face of such a wind as this, you have to cover your mouth with a cloth mask. Yes, I have heard that! If one doesn't wear a mask these things will rush into your mouth and choke you to death!"

Xiabazi stood silent, listening to them talk. The light of the cow-dung fire lit up his face. His milk tea was untouched, and an uneaten piece of *nang* was still in his hand.

He looked at his white-haired mother, who said nothing while the others chirped like sparrows. His mother's thoughts on the matter would mean a lot to him. If she said "We cannot leave here," he would have to listen to her. The reason for that was simple: she was his mother.

Then she spoke. "You'd better not say any more. Since Xiabazi has accepted the township chief's request, we should listen to him. A man ought not to repent today for what he promised to do yesterday. After all, he is the head of our family. Wherever he wants to go, we'll go after him."

She continued. "Nobody is willing to leave the Tahman Grassland, our native land, as our ancestors grazed here. Nowadays, the grassland cannot accommodate the grazing of so many herds of sheep. If we all stay here, crowded together, the grassland will become unrecognizable. Many people can live comfortably in the plain, and so can we. Just as a yak can walk on a zigzag path, and a hawk can fly high in a stormy sky."

Mother's words made Xiabazi grin so broadly that the wrinkles piled up on his face. He dipped the golden *nang* in the milk tea, put it into his mouth, and chewed it with great relish.

When he looked up, however, he found that his mother had more white hair, and that Amansha, his wife, also seemed to suddenly look old. He told himself that since he and his wife were in their 40s, it was high time they looked their real age. The township chief said that people who went to the plain all looked younger. And if that were true, then he definitely wanted to go there. He wanted to see his mother and Amansha look younger. He looked affectionately at his wife, who had reached out to fetch for him a piece of *nang*. She paid no attention to his loving look.

He marveled at the concept of time. They had lived together

there for more than twenty years, but it seemed as if they had come together just yesterday.

III

Early the next morning, all their relatives and neighbors came to see them off. After the guests were seated Xiabazi went around and greeted everyone warmly. He asked them to lie down and rest. Amansha was busy boiling milk tea.

Some people had moved away from the Tahman Grassland, but all of them came back before long. It was unthinkable that a family such as Xiabazi's could move away forever, like a white poplar transplanted to another spot with all its roots pulled up.

Xiabazi suddenly ran out of the house then came back a moment later, dragging a sheep. According to the Tajik custom, he showed the sheep to the guests, who were drinking milk tea. The guests nodded their approval and then Xiabazi killed and dressed the sheep quickly. He wanted to serve the guests one last meal: stewed mutton in clear soup. He deftly cut the mutton into big pieces, put the chunks into a big cauldron filled with clear water, and boiled the mix on the cow dung fire. When the water began boiling, he skimmed the scum from the surface with a spoon, and then let the water re-boil. He didn't add any condiments. The best clear-stewed mutton is cooked that simply.

The enticing smell of the mutton spread quickly throughout the grassland.

Several people were absent; they were Xiabazi's fellow herdsmen who had grazed with him in the same summer pasture. They were annoyed with Xiabazi because he was going to leave their beloved homeland. Since he had agreed to leave, they felt that they, too, would have no excuse to refuse when their turns came. Thus, Xiabazi was reluctant to talk to the group. He leaned against a wooden post with his hands in his sleeves, though he didn't feel cold.

One of Amansha's younger brothers came to comfort him. "Xiabazi, my old brother-in-law, it's said that the plain is as flat as our *kang* where we sleep each night. Is it a good place? Don't worry about anything. I am sure that my sister will go to the plain with you."

Then Amansha's youngest brother said, "I heard that the water of the Tahman River flows into a big river named Yarkant, and when you see the river water, you'll think of the Tahman Grassland. That way, it will seem as if you have seen us."

And Amansha's father said, "It is said that the government has built houses and the fields have been well cultivated. As soon as you move there, you'll live in a ready-built house, which surely will be better than the rough *langaili* here."

One of his neighbors said, "One can grow grapes, apples, pomegranates and figs. How nice! No fruit trees will grow on the highland. Next year we'll come to your new home on the plain and eat the fruit grown by your family until we are stuffed. The fruit we eat now has been imported from the Kashi Plain. It is all so expensive that our entire family must share a single apple. Each one gets a small piece and puts it in his mouth for a small taste."

After listening to them share these thoughts, Xiabazi felt better. "I will grow various crops in the plain," he said, "and I will have an orchard, too. Believe me, I will invite you to my home as my guests."

The mutton was done and Xiabazi placed it on a big plate. He presented the sheep's head to the noblest guest, his good friend, Township Chief Xiren, who had come specially to see him off. The chief accepted the sheep's head and cut a piece of mutton from it, then handed the head back to Xiabazi with both hands. After that, Xiabazi handed a piece of sheep liver with sheep tail butter to his father-in-law, the oldest person among them, and watched him eat it. And then Amansha served each guest with a bowl of thick mutton soup. A bit of salt and some slices of onion were the only flavorings added to the soup. The idea was to dip a piece of mutton in the soup then eat it. In this way, the flavor of the mutton wasn't spoiled, but rather enhanced.

After his father-in-law had finished eating the sheep liver, Xiabazi picked up a knife, extended it to him with the handle pointing out, and invited him to distribute the mutton to the others. The guests were eating the mutton dipped in the soup when Xiabazi began to pour the alcohol. The guests devoured the mutton and drank large quantities of the alcohol, so much in fact, that they had nearly finished all the mutton as well as two boxes of the strong *Kunlun* liquor, with a alcohol content of over 60 percent, before anyone noticed. At that point, Xiabazi's guests began to toast his happy, prosperous life on the plain.

Once they had consumed all the food and liquor they wanted, the guests raised their hands, according to the Muslim custom, to pray to Allah, thanking Him for giving them such delicious food. After the hostess had cleared up and taken away the tablecloth, the guests expressed their thanks to Xiabazi and bade farewell to him. Xiabazi saddled their horses, helped them mount, and handed them their whips. Xiabazi and his guests said "Hush-bur (Goodbye)" to each other, and then he watched them leave.

At that moment, Xiabazi again felt a profound sense of loss. He didn't know how to get rid of his mood, as his love for his family and his home tied him to the grassland. After all, this was his native land, where his forefathers had lived for several generations and were buried. The plain was not his home, because none of his ancestors were buried there.

IV

He sold most of his sheep, together with five horses and seven yaks. He gave five small lambs to his cousin, and kept one ram and three ewes, which he planned to take to the plain. His cousin held out his hand and said, "I'll feed the lambs for you in case you decide to take them back someday, when you realize you don't want to stay in the plain any longer and come back."

Xiabazi said firmly, "I'm sure I will settle down in the plain, but I will come back to see you all. I won't be like those who, in order to return to the highland anytime, still keep a herd of sheep here though they have promised to leave. I asked our township chief yesterday if I could see Mt. Mustag. He said that it stands against the sky like a heavenly mountain, and that it could be seen as soon as I raise my head. As long as I can see Mt. Mustag, I will not miss our hometown too much, and I will be able to settle down in the plain."

He handed his *langaili* over to his neighbor, whose own house was collapsing. The neighbor said to him, "The *langaili,* with its big cooking range, was built by you in great toil, and I'll take good care of it for you. If you don't stay on the plain, come back here and continue on with your life. Then I'll give you back the *langaili,* and you'll feel as warm in it then as you feel now."

Xiabazi looked kindly at his neighbor. "My old brother, believe me when I say that I'll settle down on the plain and not come back. Do come and live there. I asked the township chief, 'Can hawks be seen in the plain?' and he told me that there are as many hawks there as chickens. As long as a hawk is flying above me, it will bless me. Now, I have a favor to ask you. The graves of my ancestors are still located here, and I will not be able to come back, nor will I be able to take them away with me. So please help me and take care of them."

His neighbor held his hands firmly and said gratefully, "Thank you for giving your house to me. Come back for a visit whenever you miss the highland. Your ancestors are as good as mine, and I'll take good care of them for you."

Tulson, a rider and a good friend of his, had ridden over to bid him farewell from a place fifty *li* (half a kilometer – *ed.*) away. Xiabazi gave Wind to him.

Tulson thanked him from the bottom of his heart. "I know that you love the horse more than your wife! First, I'll feed it for you, and when spring comes to the plain I'll ride it back to see you, and than I'll return it to you."

"Wind will be very happy to go with you, a famous rider on the grassland. The township chief said that I would have no place to ride a horse on the plain. Since one cannot let a hawk soar in the chicken coop, I'll not let my Wind plough fields and pull a cart for me on the plain."

"Don't worry. I'll treat it like one of my own brothers."

Xiabazi had arranged everything. The local government gave each family a little small-wheeled truck, which was loaded with furniture and other household appliances to be carried away. Xiabazi and his family went to the main road and waited to start on their journey, which would begin following an address by the county governor.

While they were waiting, there appeared a long caravan of gleaming sedans, each of which held several figures. Xiabazi saw Township Chief Xiren, his good friend, zooming around endlessly like a honeybee. The huge-bellied county governor, who was surrounded by a crowd, marched toward the purpose-built platform before stopping under the red-colored banner printed with a slogan in white characters. The governor gave a lengthy address, with his hands supporting his majestic belly.

Xiabazi had never seen such a big-bellied county governor and couldn't help wondering if the man could swallow a bull whole. Once at the market in the county seat, Xiabazi had seen the governor's wife, who was also a gigantic woman. He was puzzled by something: How did the county governor and his wife, who were both shaped like two balls, make love at night?

Preoccupied by these wild flights of thought, he caught only a few sentences of the governor's address, which went something like this: "Those who are going to move are people of high morals and they are bound to build a wonderful new home on the plain! The people who failed to enter their names for the move so that they could continue to live on the poverty-stricken highland will certainly regret it, and eventually will try to get to the plain." Or something like that.

All the residents of Tahman, faces beaming just like at festival-time, came to see them off. Listening to the wishes for a happy departure, which bore no traces of grieving, Xiabazi's mood brightened. It seemed as if he were like the legendary hero Rostamu, a man who accomplished great feats. A hearty smile spread across Xiabazi's face.

V

The blue in the sky began to fade and it finally disappeared. When Xiabazi smelled the air full of dust and sand, the sky seemed not to be sky any more, but rather a desert hanging down from above. The trucks stopped after a full day's drive. He jumped out of the truck, holding the sheep tenderly in his arms.

Under orders to put the families at ease, Township Chief Xiren, the leader of the team, wasted no time in showing them their houses and fields. Xiabazi caught sight of the brick house that would be his new home, standing at the edge of the Taklimakan Desert. Not far from the house, the sand dunes were the color of gold.

The house had three rooms. At the back of the house there was a sheepfold, a toilet, and a patch of land for an orchard. No one had told Xiabazi that three families in succession had lived in his house; they had moved from the highland and returned to the highland soon after. The badly-worn wall of the house had been brushed white with lime before Xiabazi moved in. The field here was very flat, with the irrigation channels built along its edge. And at the side near the desert stood a row of newly planted white poplars, intended to block the wind and sand.

At dusk, the new home was strangely beautiful, and Xiabazi felt satisfied with it. He looked up at the sky. It appeared clearer and brighter. He saw the waning moon, so very far away. He did not see the towering Mt. Mustag nor did he see any hawks. He thought that the hawks may have nested in a certain tall tree. The Yarkant River, in which was flowing the water from the Tahman River, was dozens of kilometers away. Thus he couldn't see it, nor could he hear it flowing.

The township chief told him that the irrigation water in the field was channeled from the big river. Xiabazi thought that if he had a horse he could ride up to see the river the next day. But he didn't have a horse, and so it would be difficult to get to the river.

VI

The three households settled down here. They lived near each other and formed a small Tajik settlement. Before long, the local Uygur people gave the place a new name: The Three Households of Tajik.

Even the grass here was strange to the families. Thus, to get accustomed to living in the new place they tried to become acquainted with the various types of grass. They didn't know what to call the many species of plants here. All the households were a bit alarmed and bewildered, like babies removed from their mothers. It seemed as if they had floated to an isolated island surrounded by a large, lonely sea.

They called at each other's home everyday to keep from being lonely. They avoided mentioning the highland and the Tahman Grassland, as the wives had burst into tears several times at the mention of the area. Seeing how the women behaved, the men laughed and scolded them at first, then later lowered their heads silently when the tears began to flow.

And then something strange happened to them. They stopped drinking liquor after they came to the plain, yet they felt dizzy and top-heavy all day long, like drunkards. They did not know that people used to living on the high-altitude highland where oxygen is thin can get "oxygen-drunk" when they first come to the oxygen-rich plains.

One day, Bayak, the brother-in-law of the township chief, came to Xiabazi and said to him dejectedly, "Dear Xiabazi, I feel very strange that all my family are gloomy and dreary all day, like drunkards, but we have never touched a drop of liquor. Is there some liquor in the air? I have tried for dear life to smell it in the air, but in vain."

"The same is true in my family," Xiabazi replied. "Even my mother who has never touched liquor all her life feels dizzy. Maybe there are too many people in the plain, and there are a lot of drinkers among them. They have drunk the liquor, and breathed out alcohol into the air. Therefore, there is alcohol in the air. There is so much air around, that's why one cannot smell the alcohol in every place, but alcohol is definitely in the air. We breathe non-stop everyday. So you can imagine how much alcohol you will breathe into your body here! How can you prevent yourself from getting drunk?"

"So I understand. But in the long run, will we all become drunkards because of this?"

Sensing Bayak's anxiety, Xiabazi comforted him. "Don't worry. After all, there are many people on the plain. Only very few of them will be heavy drinkers."

With nothing else to do, Xiabazi tried working in his field . He went there everyday and walked around it several times. Sometimes, he felt a faint sense of the wonder at the field. It seemed unimaginable that he could ever settle down there, and that he could support his descendants through such a field as this. He puzzled on this as he walked around and around the field. He walked for five *li* before consulting Tiyipu, a warm-hearted Uygur farmer with a gray moustache, who lived nearest to them.

But Tiyipu only glanced at Xiabazi and said coldly, "Friend, you'd better not worry about that now. You can stay here for three months, and if you get used to living here, we'll talk about the cultivation of the field!"

"But, my friend, why do you say that? I see you are preparing for seeding the field."

"We are about to sow winter wheat. The reason I am asking you not to hurry is that several waves of Tajik people have come down here. They were very active when they arrived, but before long they couldn't stand to live here any more and returned to the highland, leaving their crops to rot."

"I won't do that."

"That's what they said, in the beginning."

"But I swear that I will settle down here."

"It will be too difficult for you. You have been shepherds for generations, and now you want to come here and be farmers. You should learn everything about farming, taking in new things like a newborn child does."

Tiyipu brightened. "But the good thing is that this is unskilled work, and you can succeed in learning everything about a crop. If you really decide to settle down here, go ahead and sow the field with winter wheat, otherwise, the field will go to waste. Since you came to ask me for help, I will show you how to do farming work."

Regarding Tiyipu as his master in the area of farming, Xiabazi first learned about the usage of farm tools. And in doing this, he made his first friend on the plain.

With the grain supplied by the local government as subsidy, there was no problem getting food. The other two households were still watching and waiting. They did nothing but take turns feeding the two sheep which they had brought from the highland. Xiabazi, however, decided to sow his field with winter wheat. He asked Tiyipu how much it would cost to pay for a day's ploughing. Tiyipu said, "It's fifty *yuan*, but if you want me to do that, you can pay me thirty *yuan*." Xiabazi was very pleased at that, of course.

Tiyipu finished ploughing Xiabazi's field in three days, and then he showed Xiabazi how to make ridges and furrows in the soil, and how to sow the fields. Thus, with the help of Tiyipu, Xiabazi sowed his field with wheat. Seeing the light-gold wheat seeds lying in the brown soil, Xiabazi felt as if a herd of sheep were slowly moving about the grassland. It was on that very day that he saw the snow-capped Mt. Mustag rising against the sky in the distance.

When the jade-green wheat seedlings sprouted out of the brown soil, Xiabazi cried. Almost afraid it was too good to be true, he dug a seedling out with a small branch and carefully put it in the palm of his hand. He marveled at its milk-colored roots. He took it back home and showed it to his family, saying, "This is a wheat seedling from our field."

His mother said, "It, too, is putting down roots in the plain."

VII

One day, Bayak came and looked at him with a long face. For quite a long time, he said nothing, only sighed. Finally Xiabazi asked, "What has happened, my old brother?"

"Oh! What a damned place!" Bayak swore.

Xiabazi tried to console him. "As newcomers, we're bound to have trouble getting adjusted to our life here. But it will be all right in the long run."

But Bayak kept up his tirade. "Our sheep are dead. What's more, they were both pregnant! We haven't cultivated the field, and that's because all of my family members were taking turns going out to feed the sheep. We waited on them as if they were our sacred ancestors, but we would have never dreamed they would become thinner and thinner, and more and more dispirited. Then early this morning, I got up and found that they were dead!" With these words, tears sprang to Bayak's eyes. He was so sad it seemed as if the dead were not his sheep, but his own dear children.

Xiabazi knew that the two sheep were the only property of value that Bayak had on the plain. When the families were preparing to leave for the plain, Bayak saw Xiabazi take a ram with him, so he got the idea that he should replace his own ram with ewes, one of which had been bred with Xiabazi's ram.

"Haven't you sent for a vet?" Xiabazi asked.

He said mournfully, "The day before yesterday, when I saw the sheep spiritless like drunks with hangovers, I ran more than twenty *li* to fetch a Uygur vet. After listening to what I told him, he said that the sheep were just unaccustomed to living in this place, and would be all right after several days. He asked me if I would get some medicine for the sheep. I thought that it was not worthwhile to get drugs for animals that were likely to recover in a couple of days. And then unexpectedly, they were all dead when I saw them this morning!"

Xiabazi shook his head. "You see, my old brother, your grudging of a small sum has led to a big loss. My sheep are also behaving in the way you described. Therefore, I, too, should go and see the vet."

"How can we live in such a damned place as this, where even sheep cannot live?" Bayak then began to curse the township chief, saying that he shouldn't have schemed against his relatives and friends in order to fulfill his assignment to move a certain number of people, because the move had taken them far away from their homeland and turned them into paupers.

Xiabazi knew that Bayak kept all his belongings, including his herds and shelter, back on the Tahman Grassland; in contrast, Xiabazi had disposed of everything he owned there. He listened to Bayak until he finished his angry tirade. He defended the township chief with a few words, and also talked more to comfort his companion. At last, however, Bayak was determined to leave the wretched place and to return to the Tahman Grassland.

Maybe it was due to their horseback riding in the grassland all the year round that made Xiabazi notice that the Tajik people walk lightly on the plain, unlike the Uygur and the Han peoples, who walk with such a heavy gait that the ground trembles slightly. Bayak walked with the same heavy gait that sent the dust up when he went back to his house after vowing that he would return to the highland. But he did not leave right away.

Xiabazi went alone to see the sheep. The condition of the three ewes was just as Bayak had described. He hurried to see the vet and brought back with some medicine that he poured into the mouths of the sheep. Several days later, however, the three ewes died, leaving the vigorous ram running and jumping about. What was the use of keeping a ram without ewes? He held the ram and grieved for awhile, and then sold it in the market thirty *li* away from his home.

When the New Year of the Han people was around the corner, a large group of people led by the township chief, by now promoted to the post of vice county governor, came to give their regards to the three Tajik households, bringing each family compressed tea and cloth. The vice county governor approached Xiabazi as a friend, shaking hands with him and embracing him, without any airs. This moved Xiabazi greatly.

The vice county governor brought Xiabazi a letter from his son's prospective father-in-law. After the official left, Xiabazi unfolded the letter, which, as he had expected, said that his prospective daughter-in-law's father wanted to end the engagement of their daughter with Xiabazi's son. As it turned out, the talk that sheep cannot live on the plain had reached the Tahman Grassland. His would-be in-law wrote, with several incorrect characters, that since sheep cannot live on the plain, how in the hell he could be so hard-hearted as to marry his daughter off to someone who lived there? He hid the letter, not daring to show it to his son.

Azhare, the vice county governor's eldest brother, was 47 or 48 years old. He had a look of misery about him, which made him seem 20 or 30 years older than he really was. Many people mistook him for the vice county governor's father, and thought he was joking when he said that he was but his eldest brother. There were four people in his family. Of the three sheep he had brought with him from the highland, two were dead. The last one, which he raised as carefully as if it were one of his children, was fortunately alive on the plain. He told Bayak that he seemed to be ill, as he was dispirited the moment he came to the plain, and that he would die if he went on staying.

The Tajik Spring Festival was approaching. Xiabazi missed his homeland more than ever, and he often stared off in the direction of the highland.

Two days before the festival, Bayak and Azhare loaded all of the belongings they had brought from the Tahman Grassland onto a truck that they hired even before they came, and said goodbye to Xiabazi. When they talked earlier about leaving, Xiabazi had thought they were just grumbling. He had never thought they would actually go.

Bayak embraced Xiabazi, saying with heartfelt emotion, "I'm used to living on the highland, and even though I came here, my roots are somewhere else. I can't grow roots here. If we leave right now, we can be home just in time for the festival."

Azhare gave his two sheep to Xiabazi, telling him, "I feel that my health has grown worse and worse, so I should go back. Old brother Xiabazi, please accept these two sheep, and I wish you a happy and successful life in the new place!"

Xiabazi watched their truck turn into the white poplar woods and disappear, leaving a trail of dust. He watched until the dust fell slowly down to the ground.

VIII

Xiabazi began to get used to facing the brown earth as a farmer, by the time of the autumn harvest. As a student farmer, he failed to get a high yield from his crops. Nevertheless, he harvested more than 2,000 kilograms of wheat. When he held the wheat grains in his hands, he felt a surge of joy. After all, this was his first harvest on the plain. He was determined to return to the highland with some of his harvest so that his fellow villagers could taste the newly harvested wheat. Also, he wanted to meet his potential in-law to see if there was possibility to save his son's marriage.

When the bus went up to the highland, and when he caught sight of the blue waves of the Kalakuly Lake and the snowy cap of Mt. Mustag, he burst into tears. Going over the Subashy Slope, he could see the Tahman Grassland. He was so excited he could barely control himself. In a low voice he sang:

> O! The golden Tahman Grassland
> Like a bright moon hangs aloft.
> Her beauty is second to none,
> And makes me miss her oft.

He couldn't help nudging his neighbor, a fat man, who had been sleeping on the seat all the way, to wake him up. Xiabazi boasted, "My friend, the Tahman Grassland lies ahead. How beautiful it is!"

Waking up from a dream, the annoyed man said, "Do you think I'm like Xiabazi the Fool? I've passed the grassland at least a hundred times. Do you think I don't know it when I see it?"

Open-mouthed with astonishment, Xiabazi looked at the man and said, "Why do you say Xiabazi is a fool?"

"Aren't you living on the highland? Haven't you heard about the new saying? These days, when the highlanders talk about a slow-witted person who has been cheated by others, they will say, 'you are 'Xiabazi the Fool'.'"

"But why?"

"I can't believe you don't know about this! I'll tell you about it, then. Xiabazi was a man of the Tahman Grassland. Last year he moved to Markit. He was conned into going there by the township chief, a friend of his. In order to become a vice county governor, the township chief persuaded his eldest brother and one of his brother-in-laws to move there. Of course, his friend Xiabazi was urged to move there, too.

"In the beginning, the township chief told his relatives that they would only make a show of moving down to the plain, and that they would move back as soon as he became vice county governor. Then Xiabazi, who knew nothing about it, disposed of his property, selling or giving away everything. Without anything left on the grassland, he moved his entire family down there, including his elderly mother. Now, his household is the only one still suffering on the plain. Everyone says, 'Oh, Xiabazi is such a fool!' By and by, the expression 'Xiabazi the Fool' has come into being and has spread all over the Pamirs."

"Can this be true?"

Thinking Xiabazi was a stranger to the grassland, the man paid little attention to him. He turned his sleepy fat face to the side and dozed off.

(Translated by Meng Fanjun)

The Remote Hot Spring

Ah Lai

Ah Lai was born in 1959 to a Tibetan family in Barkam County, a Tibetan-inhabited area of northwestern Sichuan. He began writing poetry in 1982, and gradually turned his hand to fiction in the late 1980s. His main works include the poetry anthology *Suomo River* (Sichuan Nationalities Press, 1988); the fiction collection *The Bloodstain of the Old Years* (The Writers Publishing House, 1989), winner of the Fourth Ethnic Literary Prize sponsored by the Chinese Writers' Association; the novel *Red Poppies* or originally *The Dust Settles* (The People's Literature Publishing House, 1998) which won the Fifth Mao Dun Literary Prize; the fiction collection *The Silversmith Under the Moon* (Changjiang Literature and Art Press, 1999); the four-volume *Collected Works of Ah Lai* (The People's Literature Publishing House 2001), the essay collection *As So I Bloom* (The PLA Literature and Art Press, 2001) and the novel *The Hollow Mountains* (The People's Literature Publishing House 2005). Ah Lai's major works have been translated into 14 languages and published in more than 20 countries. A member of the Chinese Writers' Association and member of its national committee, Ah Lai is also vice-chair of the Sichuan Writers' Association, vice-chair of the Sichuan Youth Federation and editor-in-chief of *Science Fiction World*. He also enjoys the honorary titles of a distinguished scholar entitled to State Council special allowance and academic leader of Sichuan Province.

The Remote Hot Spring

I

There was no hot spring around our village. What we had there was called a thermal spring.

The steam of our thermal spring was hard to see in spring and summer. Only in winter, when you waded through snow to go to the ravine more than ten kilometers north of the village, would you see its steam rise from among the evergreen firs, cuckoo and chokecherry trees and birches. The thermal mist of the spring froze soon after leaving the water surface, so it lost its upward force and fell onto the yellowish plants and grass, forming a layer of ice. That was how our spring displayed its endless energy to the world.

Back then, when you put your hand into the spring water, it would wrap your cold skin with its slight warmth, giving a sticky feeling to your fingers. Its high percentage of saline plus its strong sulfur smell made the water undrinkable. And the salt, sulfur and various other minerals it carried up from depths of the earth had formed large stretches of rusty red and yellow deposits around the mouth of the spring.

Except for hunters who took rest

there, the locals rarely visited the thermal spring, which was called Dronyin.

Once summer arrived, however, herds of cattle were driven up to the mountain pasture and as soon as our primary school began the summer holiday, we kids were sent to follow the cattle around the pasture all day long to prevent them from wandering off into the dense woods. The cattle loved to drink Dronyin's salt spring water and would dash toward the steamy spring as soon as they had satisfied their hunger with the delicious green pasture grass. The village elders told us it was fine for the cattle to drink some salt water from the spring, but drinking too much spring water would cause digestive troubles and make their bellies bulge like drums. If that happened, they would be unable to eat and would starve to death. Hence, we kids were sent to help throughout the summer, making sure to scatter the cattle after they had tasted some spring water.

I can no longer produce the long, menacing call I used to drive away the cattle, just as I can no longer sing the pastoral songs of my youth. In my silent boyhood years, I sang only to myself and my vocal chords could flutter like the wings of a hummingbird. When I sang a long tremulous tune alone in the mountain pasture, my voice would soar through the small-leaved cuckoo shrubs and crawling cypresses. I could almost see my song floating over the lush pasture and the towering cliffs until it reached the snow peaks on the horizon.

Yes, that was me; always longing for far-off places.

At the time, there were no actual places in my world, just two directions. One was the mighty So-mang River in the southeast, which flowed through the mountains. In the northeast, beyond the jagged snow peaks, was the vast Songpan Prairie.

In the summer, the lush trees shaded us from the sun. The

moss on the rocks clung to our bottoms and crept up the thick pine trees, cuckoos sang nearby. I sat alone amidst all this and soaked my feet in the salty spring water, which cooled my feet. Bubbles rose in the gushing spring water and the smell of sulfur permeated the air. Sometimes, deer and wild yaks came to the spring mouth to drink. The deer were alert to the slightest sound. The careless yaks, however, after quenching their thirst, would lie down and roll in the reddish mud. After the layer of mud peeled off in a few days, the yaks that had skin diseases would have a fine healthy glow. Their hides would shine like satin.

Herdsman Kunpal Sigya would say, "The mud can kill the insects on these yaks and horses. The mud treats disease."

Kunpal Sigya single-handedly took care of a small herd of horses owned by our village. Sometimes he drove his horses to the salt spring, and we would meet him there. When he repeated the advice about the benefits of mud, we kids would laugh and asked him, "Why don't you treat your own disease with the mud?"

The skin on Kunpal Sigya's face was scarred and dotted with big pale patches. Dry skin would constantly fall off his face like dead and peeling birch bark. The village elders warned that kids must try to stand upwind of him or else the skin of our faces would dry up and fall off, too. It was definitely awful for one's face to be that way, and even worse to have to live alone on the mountain, barred from coming to the village. Added to that, no woman would want to live with someone like that. However, back then I believed it would be great if no woman wanted to bother you and you could live alone on the mountain.

The work team stationed in our village divided the villagers into different ranks and stirred up hatred amongst them. Women lived together with the men and bore children one after another. I was one of those kids. For a period of time, I prayed I could live alone on the mountain just like Kunpal Sigya and not be bothered by women.

My old aunt in her 60s suffered from terrible asthma attacks. Her niece, Kelzang Chodron, was one of my numerous elder female cousins and had the most beautiful voice of all the village girls. Even the work-team cadres said they wanted to recommend her to the cultural troupe of our autonomous prefecture. But she was chosen to be the militia platoon head in our village instead.

Filled with power, she began to shout harsh orders outside the stone dwelling of my old aunt, and the tomb-like house seemed to sink deeper into the ground at the sound of her voice. She preferred to shout when the villagers were returning home from their collective work in the fields, the time of day when pale smoke rose from the chimneys throughout our village. As soon as she began barking out her orders, the smoke stopped coming out of the chimney on my old aunt's house. My aunt would walk outside, her face as immovable as stone. She would pull some firewood from her stack and carry it to the small square in the center of our village. The sky was turning from blue to ash gray. The stars were starting to twinkle. Night was falling onto our mountain village, tucked away in a remote corner of the world.

My old aunt started a bonfire with her wood. The villagers gathered in the small square and their faces were lit red — an auspicious color in that era. As the flames stretched and licked at the shadows, my aunt withdrew to a far corner of the square. Some of the villagers, who had once been modest and restrained, became unusually loud and emotional, exaggerating the stinginess of my aunt, who had managed to save her family wealth, saying this was an unforgiveable crime. These men condemned her occasional monetary gifts to villagers as part of a devious scheme.

One recent "schemes" of hers was to secretly send "Motley Face" Kunpal Sigya, who lived alone on the mountain, a small bag of salt and some dried tea leaves.

It was Jamba and I who delivered the salt and tea leaves to Kunpal Sigya. However, Jamba, son of Kunpal Sigya's cousin, later blabbed to the work team about what we had done. The work team leader, who loved to wear an army overcoat around his shoulders, gave the peasant boy Jamba a pat on his skinny shoulder, announcing, "You could become a member of the People's Liberation Army in the future!"

Dropped to the ground by the work team leader's pat, Jamba jumped up at once, too excited to express his enormous gratitude. And on that evening, the resounding order of my elder female cousin again echoed in our village. As ordered, my old aunt once again went to make a bonfire in the square before everyone gathered. Those condemners whose shadows were enlarged by the bonfire became loud once more. It was a puzzle how those under-fed guys could be so agitated and loud in those years.

I looked toward the sky. Some clouds floated by and cast shadows on the moon. A strong blast of wind blew.

The next day, one side of Jamba's face had swollen enormously. Someone said he was slapped soundly by his dad. Others claimed that he was punished by Motley Face Kumpa Sigya. Still others insisted that the slap had actually come from my old aunt. After that, Jamba and I stopped being friends. Someone planted hatred between the two of us, and it lasted until Jamba returned to the village in his PLA uniform and distributed cigarettes to men and candy to women. It seemed that he let go of his hatred against me, but I couldn't get rid of mine.

It was from that time that I began to talk with Kunpal Sigya when I was pasturing cattle. Seated at the lower side of the spring

mouth and letting me sit on the higher side, Kunpal Sigya told me
stories about life in the village. When he told them, the stories did
not sound as evil as they did when they were told at the village
meetings. He did not appear to hate anyone either. Even when he
told me that his wife ran off with another man after his face became mottled, a trace of a smile flashed across his ugly face.

However, when he saw his nephew Jamba, the scars on his face
turned scarlet. He did not say anything to Jamba, but always looked
toward the grand snowy mountain peaks in the distance.

He also asked me about things in the village down the hill. The
cattle were furiously flicking their tails to drive off the gadflies sticking to their skin. I told him I wished I could live alone on the mountain just as he did. A pained pathetic expression crossed on his face.
He reached out to stroke my hair but stopped his hand in mid-air.
I could feel a stream of warmth surge through my body, even from
across the spring.

After a moment he said, "But you don't want to have a mottled
face like I have."

I lowered my eyes and said nothing.

"Actually," he suddenly continued, "if I were allowed to travel
and bathe and wash my face once in the hot spring, I could be
cured. Then I wouldn't have to live alone on the mountain."

This was the first time I had heard about the hot spring.

He told me the hot spring had hotter water than the salt spring
at our feet. It tasted the same but contained no salt. He went on
enthusiastically, "A hot spring can cure many diseases, especially
problem skin. A spring with twin mouths there can cure eye disease
and migraines. Larger springs are so powerful they can cure many
diseases, from rheumatism to tuberculosis. They can even purify
'unclean women'."

I was not clear about the meaning of "unclean women" but I began to long for the hot spring known as Tsona; it became the first destination on my list of distant places to visit. I wished I could see the remote, legendary hot spring with my own eyes. I was not talkative then, and my parents wished I could communicate with people freely — and loudly. I wondered if that hot spring could cure my problems, too.

I asked Motley Face where the hot spring was located. He pointed to the jagged row of snow crested ridges in the west. Some narrow passes could be seen in between the peaks. A highway passed by our village and snaked up one of the snowy peaks. A *Liberation* truck would have to puff for two to three hours along the curvy road to reach the narrow pass atop the mountain. The trucks came from the newly built county seat east of our village and traveled toward the vast prairie to the west. The kids in our village had never been to the east or the west. And the adults, except for a few village cadres, had never traveled anywhere, either. That was why we were led to believe that people did not need to travel far away. However, Kunpal Sigya remarked that people often roamed far and wide in the past, making long pilgrimages to holy hills, traveling for business, searching for good horses and rifles, or galloping off for love or revenge. People also crossed the snowy mountain range on fast horses, carrying bags of delicious food, eager to bathe in the famed hot spring.

"But men are planted on the ground like crops now," Motley Face Kunpal Sigya said with a sigh.

After coming down from the mountain pasture, I went to see the crops planted in the field. Peas were blooming and honeybees were humming among the flowers. Large stretches of wheat gave off a faint scent under the bright sunlight. It seemed only right that the crops did not care about faraway places, but focused instead on their own vigorous growth. A light breeze blew like a whisper over the tender wheat. I knew that I could never be like the wheat, always standing on the same spot, thinking of nothing at all.

One day, driven by curiosity, I climbed up to the narrow pass atop the snowy ridge. Looking east, I could see for dozens of kilometers. The highway snaked up and down along the river valley and I could just make out the county seat — a fuzzy, dreamy outline of a great number of houses. When I looked to the west, I saw the vast prairie rolling with bulges as round as a girl's bosom. That was a distant scene I could identify with: a measurable distance that could be traveled by my own feet, though not in a day's journey. Back then, that was the remote place I dreamed of, and I knew for sure that the hot spring named Tsona was right in the middle of that prairie.

After I came down from the mountain, Kunpal Sigya asked me if I had seen the prairie. I said simply that I had seen the prairie, and that it was just a larger, wider pasture than ours. It just had some rivers and lakes, nothing more.

Kunpal Sigya looked at me skeptically. "I am asking if you could see the hot spring."

I shook my head.

"It's right at the foot of that red rock hill."

I did not see the red rock hill. But I thought I saw a proud expression flickering on his face throughout the day. I sat by the hot spring, suddenly feeling that I could never go to the place he had described and I would never imagine what the red rock hill looked like. Three wild Mongolian gazelles drank from the hot spring and walked away. I felt I was as ignorant as those wild gazelles.

Kunpal Sigya said, "People went to that hot spring for different reasons. Old people wanted to treat their ailments and young men went there to see the world and understand women."

That evening, listening to the mountain wind blast across the top of our pasture tent, I thought about women, like my elder female cousin who was blessed with a silvery voice. Or like my old aunt, cursed with her tragic fate. Unable to fall asleep, I wrapped up in my wool blanket and walked out of the tent. I sat under the starry night sky and saw a single light far away in the river valley. It was coming from the lonely hut of Kunpal Sigya.

Ever since his face became deformed and he lost his woman, Kunpal Sigya had served as the herdsman for our village. By then, the locals considered the horses to be almost useless. The village elders said that ever since a succession of work teams had been stationed in our village, men were nailed to the same place, just as horses are fettered to one spot.

When I was a child, I heard people talk about the hot spring that none of them had visited. The old-fashioned way of locating the spring was to say it was on the prairie beyond the snowy peaks. The modern way was to say that the territory on this side of the snow mountain range belonged to a certain production team, a certain production brigade and a certain people's commune of a certain county. The hot spring on the vast prairie, on the other hand, belonged to another production team, another production brigade and another people's commune of another county.

Boundaries were also drawn for pastures. For example, the cattle herd of our production team was not allowed to go to the grassland behind the narrow pass on the snow-capped mountain range, even if the nomadic locals drove their cattle herds across the mountain pass and relocated their tents each day, until they reached the hot spring a few days later. A large rural fair gathered at the hot spring. Everyone within a hundred square kilometers went there to exchange commodities at the noisy market, and sang and danced at parties. Naked men and women enjoyed the hot spring together.

A young man infatuated by the romantic tales of the herdsmen once made a remark while drunk. As a result, he was ordered to start a bonfire on the small square in the village; then he bowed his head and retreated to a dark corner. That's how it went: those who prepared a bonfire were not allowed to enjoy the fire's bright light.

However, his drunken remark, which had been oft-quoted for many years since, went like this: "The damned production team simply serves as a cattle pen!"

Nobody was sure if this remark was true or not, but the horses that the men back then rode around were put under the care of Motley Face, and they grew fat and lazy from doing nothing all day long. Once in awhile a horse was put to use to haul work team members to the county seat or to bring new members back to the village. Or sometimes a horse-drawn cart would take certain "qualified" villagers to attend various meetings at the people's commune. The cart also was used to bring an elementary school teacher to our village. Hence, we kids were able to learn to read and write.

Occasionally, the horse-drawn cart would be loaded with cloth, salt, tea, enamel basins and bowls as well as checked scarves and scented soaps from the commune's supply and marketing cooperative. With all of these things brought straight to your doorstep, what was the point of uncomfortable long-distance travel on horseback?

Our teacher told us a maxim to remember: "To enjoy a settled life signifies the progress of a society." Theoretically this was sound thinking, but the inner longing for distant places refused to fade away.

Another work team left but the team leader, who knew how to do Korean dances, reneged on his promise to send my elder female cousin to the art troupe of the autonomous prefecture. Even worse, he had made a serious mistake by seducing my cousin. Thus he was saddled with two disgraceful labels: a man with a corrupt lifestyle and a man who had damaged the unity with minority ethnic groups. My cousin was given only one label: a woman who tried to corrupt a revolutionary cadre. She could no longer head the militia platoon in the village. Even my old aunt spat on the ground before her when she walked near. My uncle was offended and said angrily to my aunt, "She just slept with a man, right? You slept with many a man when you were young, didn't you?"

Everyone agreed that the world had changed – and a little too quickly. These were but the things I was thinking about while sitting outside our pasture tent. Above me was the cold night sky, filled with stars.

I watched the lonely light of Motley Face's cabin, feeling in my heart that such a desolate light was worse than no light at all. My elder female cousin slept in a pasture tent, as she had returned to her former position as a village milking girl. In general, a tent would follow a cattle herd on the pasture because it was high on the mountain where the forest ended, while our village and Tibetan barley fields were down in the river valley. Living in each tent was a man who carried a hunting rifle to patrol the pasture and guard against wolves by day; at night squeezed in the tent with him were a number of milking girls. So it was easy for one of those milking girls to become his sweetheart.

During the summer holiday, we kids went up to the pasture to watch the cattle at the salt spring, and almost every night I heard strange sounds coming from the tents. One very cold and windy night I sat outside under the starry sky and thought of the remote hot spring, the noisy rural fair, the wild parties, and the naked men and women bathing in a steamy pool. It made me smile. The night wind grew stronger and began making a strange sound. Wrapped in a blanket I went back to my tent and found the sound was actually coming from under the wool rug of my elder female cousin. While others just moaned quietly, she was quite vocal.

Afterwards, the man known for his good marksmanship returned to his own berth and sighed over and over again. The other two milk maids in the tent began to giggle like a pair of turtledoves. I was told to call that man "cousin," though I did not know why. And I was supposed to call the other two women "aunt" and "elder female cousin," but again no one told me why. It seemed that everyone in our village was related. Even if so much new hatred was stirred up on top of the old grievances, the villagers still greeted one another as relatives. But I was sure that the woman groaning cheerfully under that man was my true elder female cousin, just as my old aunt was truly my aunt.

While my elder female cousin began sobbing uncontrollably, the man I called cousin was soundly snoring. The two women continued their giggling under their rugs. Suddenly I felt sick at heart and walked over to my elder female cousin's berth. I just stood there, at a loss for what to do. Abruptly she reached out and pulled me into her rug. In a flash I found myself tasting all the miraculous parts of the female body. She began to cry out loudly then, kissing me while murmuring "my little brother, my little brother" and rubbing tears and snot all over my face.

The man was wakened by us. He walked over and dragged me away from my cousin's arms. Unable to figure out why she was so sad after all that unabashed moaning, I could only attribute all her sadness to him. No one told me why I had to call him cousin, and he should have never used a flashlight – something very few people in our village owned – to shine its intense beam on my cousin's face and then on mine. I was momentarily blinded.

At that moment all the frustrations that had accumulated in my chest exploded. A burning anger surged through me and I swung out, striking the man in the belly. Then I heard a dull sound like an ox stepping into a mud pit. The man fell back onto the fire pit, and the boiling water in the copper pot that hung from the iron frame splashed onto the embers and on parts of the man's body. It even splashed onto my feet.

The two giggling women screamed, "He is insane!" and my cousin burst into laughter. The man cursed me heartily while groaning in pain.

"You bastard!" he yelled at me. "I want to kill you! Damn! I cannot stand up!"

As the cacophony of his screams and my cousin's laughter faded, I was able to calm down. I wanted to laugh out loud, too. Someone lit a lantern. When I saw one side of the man's bare buttocks squeezed into the pot and the other half in the red ashes of the fire, I burst out laughing.

Unexpectedly, my cousin stopped laughing and screamed at me. "You little bastard! Shut up! How can you laugh at this?" The anger was plain on her face. Her breasts under her half-tied shirt bobbed up and down like two dogs that were tied to an iron chair but trying to dash forward to bite a stranger.

I ran out of the tent, dashing blindly on the mountain pasture in the darkness of night. The grass whipped at my ankles. Cold drops of dew splashed my face and hands. I felt the joy of freedom for the first time in my life. It was not a physical escape as much as an escape from the psychological chains that had bound me to the village: the sounds of the angry voices at village meetings, the complaining voices of my relatives railing against one another because of poverty, the crying, laughter and scolding of my elder female cousin that cheered me one minute and confused me the next.

I continued running, leaving the call of my elder female cousin far behind. I did not slow down until after I ran over a hill and could no longer see any tents or lights. The night dew tickled my feet. I ran through the valley and arrived at the cabin of Motley Face. The light in his cabin was off. I heard his thunderous snoring and smelled the pungent odor of horses from the stable behind his cabin. I sat down on a big log in front of his cabin door and watched the bright moon moving higher and higher in the night sky. My naked body wrapped in a wool blanket was very cold and my feet, which had been scalded by the boiling water, were hurting. But I was too embarrassed to knock on his door. I felt I was an adult already, and a grown-up man should endure pain alone quietly.

It was my uncontrollable coughing that wakened Kunpal Sigya.

I heard him fumble around as he tried to light his lantern, then he opened the thatched door. A warm light embraced my trembling body and his concerned face appeared. When he found me shaking on his doorstep, he was worried but not surprised. With an expression of understanding, he looked toward the tents, where the men and women were making love, then moved aside to let me in. Silently, he gave me some mouthfuls of liquor and wrapped me in a large, thick wool blanket. I fell asleep right away.

When I woke up, the small room was bathed in golden sunlight. Tea was boiling in a shiny copper kettle over the fire. A brown leather saddle leaning against the thatched wall, looking as bright as the copperware. The scene was like paradise to me, so I just lay there, shutting out the reality of the world.

Then the door creaked open and a stronger beam of sunlight burst into the room, dazzling me. A tall figure appeared in the doorway and blocked the light. I could not see the man's face against the strong light but I believed he must be the host of this paradise so I closed my eyes. I realized it was Motley Face and I remembered what had happened the night before. He walked over to me and mumbled something then sat down on the other side of the fire pit. I opened my eyes and watched him pour a bowl of tea for himself. He warmed his face over it and said to me, "Since you are awake, get up."

I had no choice but to get up. I folded the wool blanket and went out to wash my face in the spring. I came back and sat down by the fire pit, face to face with him. He told me to get something to eat. Only then did I realize my stomach was empty and I had a headache. He pointed to the low cabinet behind me that contained bowls and plates for guests, and I became the first guest to use them. As I wiped off the tableware and started to eat, he began to polish his saddle with a big piece of purple flannel. He polished the leather on the bridle, the stirrups hanging down each side of the saddle, and finally the sparkling iron snaffle. His eyes glittered. He was concentrating so intently on his work that he seemed to forget I was there. I coughed softly to remind him, but to no avail. He seemed like an altogether different person from the man I had seen at the hot spring. There, he had spoken with a flattering smile when he asked me about the recent happenings in village.

Now, sitting in his small cabin accompanied by his handsome horse harness, he seemed more real to me. I coughed twice before he stopped and looked up at me.

"Isn't it beautiful?" he asked.

I whispered "beautiful," fearing all its beauty would vanish if I spoke any louder.

"Yes, it's beautiful," he said, patting the saddle. "I went to so many places with this fellow! If I never leave here again, I will die with the horses in this valley, and this saddle and this cabin will all rot here. Now that both the horse and I are able to move, I must leave. I mean it."

"You want to leave here?"

He nodded and put the saddle down gently, like a mother with her sleeping baby. He walked to the doorway and we gazed at the horizon together.

"Do you want to go to the hot spring?" I asked.

"Yes. You don't because you don't know how wonderful that hot spring is."

"Will the hot spring cure your illness?"

"Illness? I was healthy when I went to the hot spring last time. I was such a handsome young man then. Good heavens! I saw so many pretty women there. So many beautiful girls appeared on that prairie, like flowers blooming overnight. Of course now I want to go there to treat this damned illness. If I could bathe in that hot spring, I would become smooth and pure both inside and out."

As soon as we stepped out of his cabin, I regained my senses. I almost laughed out loud when I thought about his bold announcement. According to my limited knowledge at that time, the inside of humans was very dirty and smelled terribly.

So I tried to embarrass him with this comment, and laughed.

He reached out and tried to pat my head, but stopped when he saw the look in my eyes. He sighed and said, "Child, don't you know that humans have two kinds of 'insides'?"

I did not understand what he meant, but I did feel a sense of pity in it – a feeling so strong that it almost brought tears to my eyes. So I stood up and looked off toward the snow mountain range in the distance. Then I left him and headed for the hot spring to watch the cattle.

Jamba was there already. He had slept in another tent on the pasture. When he saw me coming, he looked terrified and leapt agilely to the other side of the spring. Mimicking the work team leader, who stood with his hands on his hips, Jamba questioned me, "So, have you lived with Motley Face?"

I resented his way of talking but I felt inferior to him, so I became tongue-tied.

"It wasn't the first time the belt of your elder female cousin was untied by a man," he continued. "Why did you react like that and run to stay with Motley Face?" Then, just like the bubbling salt spring, dirty four-letter words we generally heard from adults began to flow from his mouth. Those dirty phrases plus his buck teeth reminded me of the awful buzzing the gadflies made around my head in the evening. The noise became louder and sharper until I couldn't stand it any more and I flung a rock at him. Jamba covered his forehead with his hand, swaying like a soldier we had seen in a movie who was wounded by a bullet but refused to fall down. He managed to steady himself. Blood streamed down slowly between his fingers. Finally, he spoke like a normal person.

"Are you crazy?" he asked.

"You are crazy!" I retorted.

"You fool!" he shouted. "Help me stop the bleeding!" I realized he needed help so I ran into the forest to pick an herbal plant known as "blade cut." I chewed the plant in my mouth while running back to him. He was lying under a big redwood, just like our movie hero. His wound was quite small so a small gob of the mushy herb covered it. I tore off a piece of cloth from my sash and bound his forehead with it. As my sash was the purplish-red color of blood, he did in fact look like a hero. A smile played at the corners of his mouth.

"Not bad, you bastard. I can't believe you played such a trick on me." That was the way we talked to each other back then.

He positioned himself under the tree like a wounded movie-style PLA soldier. As soon as I had bound his wound, he stood up and glared at me.

"Stay away from me," he lashed out. "You are stained! You have been with Motley Face. So you are not allowed to return to our village."

My tongue was as numb as a log after chewing the herbal plant so I couldn't say anything. I watched him swagger down the mountain, as proudly as if he had just wounded me instead of vice versa. As I watched him dash down the hill, I knew I just lost a friend. I didn't have many friends to begin with, so I was infuriated by losing even one of them. I picked up a stone and threw it toward Jamba as he ran. But since I was not strong enough, the stone fell to the ground, skipped a few times and stopped at his feet. He turned around to look at me. A snide smile crossed his lips before he turned back and continued down the hill, walking calmly.

*****

Today is April 13, 2001. It is Friday morning. I sit in my room at the New Otani Hotel in Tokyo watching the slowly rising sun, the shiny chrome of this foreign metropolis, and the oriental cherry trees outside my window in the hotel garden. I know I should be writing about what I have seen and felt in this foreign country, but the more I travel abroad, the sharper my childhood memories have become. So, it is six o'clock in the morning, and I am already out of bed and sitting at the computer. Everything seems like it happened only yesterday. The azaleas were blooming everywhere on the mountain pasture. The cuckoos were singing their long lonely songs and the wind was rolling through the grass from the ridge to the valley. I can still smell the strong sulfur of the spring.

A short while after Jamba ran away, my elder female cousin came to the salt spring. I thought she was there to look for me but she had a hateful expression on her face. Refusing to look at me, she remarked, "I just came to watch the damned cattle. There's no need for trouble."

Seeing her pitiful look, I attempted to say something but my mouth was still too numb, so I just sat there motionlessly. She must have wanted me to say something but the herbal plant had thoroughly woodened my tongue. Finally, she raised her head and stared at me.

"Hmmph. You were so fierce earlier. Why are you so quiet now?" Tears streamed down her face. "It's you — all of you. You relatives have ruined me!" Her voice grew louder and louder until she was screaming.

"God in heaven! Look down at us please. See how my damned relatives have destroyed me!"

I thought she was losing her mind.

I fled from the spring. When I returned to Kunpal Sigya's cabin, I saw him sitting on the wooden doorstep, polishing his saddle with the purple flannel. His eyes shone and he looked at me with a dreamy expression. The spell of the herbal plant seemed to disappear.

"My elder female cousin told me not to go back home," I told him.

"Fine," his eyes left his saddle and fell on my face again. "Good. Follow me to the hot spring then."

"We are not allowed to go that far, are we?"

Without answering, Motley Face put his fingers in his mouth and whistled. Several horses galloped downhill toward us, their long manes flowing in the gentle wind. Then Kunpal Sigya said in a low voice: "If I don't go to the hot spring now, I'll never be able to cure my illness. And these horses will grow old also."

He looked at his horses tenderly and caressed his saddle. The sadness on his face gripped at my heart. "These horses will be too old if we don't go now."

I pretended not to hear him and looked away toward the snow-capped mountain range.

Suddenly, he said cheerfully, "Hey, son. Want to ride a horse?"

Of course! I had never ridden a horse, even though our production team owned a whole herd. Kunpal Sigya began to saddle a horse while telling me, "Maybe a smart kid like you would want to go with me when I start off to the hot spring. We have to ride horses as we cannot afford a bus trip. Besides, everyone goes to the hot spring on horseback. And we can't go against the rule."

Then he hoisted me up onto the horse and shouted gleefully as he put the reins in my hands. The horse dashed forward. My body jerked backward then jolted forward and I screamed. Instinctively I hooked my feet in the stirrups and held onto the reins with all my might. All I could hear was the pounding of horse hooves and the wind whistling in my ears. All the familiar scenes such as the grass, the azaleas, the crawling cypress bushes, the creeks, the large bushes bordering the pasture, and the giant rocks flashed before me and then disappeared behind. Everything looked strange and fresh. Only the snow peaks towering in the distance seemed calm and still.

The horse galloped on. I gradually relaxed and my breathing began to echo the heavy puffing of the horse. I thought that if the horse continued to run I would soar into the air, into the sky, even higher than the snow-crested mountain range. I, a descendant of equestrians, had experienced the joy of riding for the first time. As long as the horse galloped on, I was free from my suffocating life.

But Motley Face gave another sharp whistle and my horse

made a sudden sharp turn. I was almost thrown off, but I managed to cling to the horse with my legs and that wonderful feeling of freedom made me yell happily. Imitating a veteran rider, I bent closer to the horse to let the wind fill my ears. But when the horse finally stopped abruptly, I was thrown forward over its head. I landed heavily on the grass. I laid there for a moment, trying to recover from the impact. Ignoring my pathetic state, Motley Face mumbled something to his horse while removing his beloved saddle. I heard footsteps coming close. I just looked up at the sky and murmured vaguely, "I want to go over the snow mountain with you."

I closed my eyes but could sense someone there. I murmured again, "I want to ride to the hot spring with you."

A cold, dignified voice came from above. "Get up and come home with me." Then I saw the face of my father looking down. When I stood up, he wiped the grass off me, with some tenderness. But like the other adults in the village he refused to talk to Motley Face. He took my hand to leave. Motley Face just stood there, silent as a log. I turned around to look back at him and Dad saw that. "Okay, go say good-bye."

Dad just stood there and watched me go to Motley Face. I walked back to him but found no words to express my feeling. He started to speak, but stopped. "Don't even think of going to the hot spring with me again. I can go there anytime I like."

At this cold remark, my words were caught in my throat. I opened my mouth but couldn't speak. I turned around and walked back to my dad, and Motley Face repeated his curse to my back. "You will never go to the hot spring." And he was right. There was no way I could go to that fabled hot spring in my lifetime, that remote spring behind the snow mountain. Perhaps Jamba could become a PLA man and perhaps my elder female cousin could get her good

luck back and become a member of the art troupe in our autonomous prefecture. But as soon I came down the hill with my dad and
saw our lifeless village, my heart was gripped with total desperation.

Maybe it was something in my eyes that touched my dad because he reached out somewhat clumsily to stroke my head, but I
shrank away. He sighed heavily.

What else do I remember about that year? I recall that the winter came quickly, but the summer and the fall before are a blur. It's
not that I have forgotten that time, just that there was nothing special
to remember. Although life in the village seemed to be increasingly
busy then, my heart seemed to sink deeper into a bottomless pit. I
can remember only three things from the year I entered grade three
in the village elementary school till the time I left for high school.

My elder female cousin was married in the autumn of the next
year. She married a young man in our village after giving birth to
a child. She was distributing candies to celebrate her wedding, and
when she came to me, she kissed me on the cheek and whispered
into my ear, "Younger brother, I love you."

Sharp-eared villagers laughed out and asked, "Do you love him
as a child in your bosom or love him as a man?"

"I love him as my own younger brother," she replied.

My old aunt walked up to give her a kiss, too, saying, "Child,
the curse on your mind has been removed." Soon after her marriage, my elder female cousin, who had not sung for a long time, began singing again. When the sun was bright on winter days, women
in the village gathered in the small square and my elder female
cousin would bare her plump breasts to nurse her second child. After the baby was fed, people would urge her to sing a song, so she
would open her mouth and sing happily. As many old songs were
forbidden by the work teams in the village, she sang the quotations

of Chairman Mao taught by the work team members. However, the Mandarin words in the songs became indecipherable and the tunes became long and drawn-out. So her listeners just took them as melodious folk songs.

Just now, after I wrote these past paragraphs, I stood up and walked to the window to smoke a cigarette. Outside is not the cityscape of Tokyo but a lush and colorful garden of the New Otani Hotel. Dusk has fallen. A light breeze passes and my heart is stirred. I can remember another story.

One day when my elder female cousin was singing in the square, the horse-drawn cart of our production team came back from the commune and a young man in a new PLA uniform jumped off the cart after the work team members. It was Jamba, who had just enlisted in the People's Liberation Army. Although the work team reneged on their promise to my elder female cousin, they did fulfill their promise to Jamba. A little uncomfortable because of his new uniform but still spirited, Jamba followed the work team members around. A new order was announced by the work team, and several old men and women in the same condemned status as my old aunt began to set up a bonfire in the small square. Only instead of retreating to a dark corner to listen to condemnations, they were told to "behave and go home obediently" that night.

Then a celebration got underway. Jamba stood before the bonfire, with a big red flower on his chest. Another red flower was hung on the low gate of Jamba's home. The work team leader watched while others pasted a red paper on Jamba's gate and made hand-painted slogans on red papers all over the village, bearing the big characters of "Glorious Home of a PLA Man."

Even after Jamba became a PLA man, most villagers still regarded him as a treacherous young fellow. They said Jamba liked to hide in a crowd and immediately report everything he heard, even petty things, to the work team. So, when bonfire gathering ended that day, the little square was left with lots of phlegm stains. But we kids envied Jamba. He was only two years older than I was but he had become a PLA man at the age of fifteen. It meant that he would have a very bright future in this new age and he would never again have to return to live in the village. Even if he was demobilized from the army one day, he could put on his faded uniform, tuck a pistol in red silk on his belt and join a work team in another village. He could even become a prominent work team leader.

Many village elders said I was not a good boy either, especially because I did not talk to others and was impolite to the elders. The work team members agreed with them. They had hoped that somehow the students who could write the Han Chinese characters in the village could become closer to them. But I was unable to live up to their expectations. My dad asked me sadly, "Would it be so hard for you to call the team members uncle just once?" But I turned dry-mouthed whenever I stood before them. Nothing could be done about it.

When the annual event of electing outstanding young pioneers in our elementary school began, I made an effort to do my homework as neatly as possible. Every day after classes I stayed behind to clean the classroom. I even stole ten cents from home to give to our teacher. But the teacher seemed to ignore all my efforts. We were thirteen and fourteen at the time, soon to graduate from the village school, but I still could not wear the red scarf of a young pioneer around my neck. Desire burned in my chest when the important election day arrived each year. Noticing my eagerness, our teacher told me, "You can write a composition so well, why is it that you can't talk normally to people?" He tried his best to coach me for a while before he took me to see the work team members. On the way there I attempted to run away several times, but my wish to be a good youth overcame my timidity.

We entered the stone fortress where the work team lived temporarily. The team leader was watching others play Chinese chess. He crossed his arms at his chest and adjusted his shoulders again and again to hold his coat in place. Whenever his subordinates made a move, he would say with a nasal voice, "Bad move."

My teacher nudged me to speak but I was unable to find an opportunity. When the team leader glanced at us, he appeared to look straight through me to something on the other side. When someone looks at you that way, it shows that you are but a ghost and nonexistent to that person.

My tongue felt numb and all of my fingers and toes felt stiff. I knew I had to say something before it was too late because I might never get such an opportunity again, and the red scarf of the young pioneer would flutter on someone else's chest. Eventually, I spoke, but my voice was so soft that no one could make out what I was saying.

The work team leader turned around abruptly and remarked, "Ah, even the stone Bodhisattva opens his golden mouth now!"

Some more rumblings came from my throat. If God had taken pity on me he would have taken the numbness away from my tongue. But apparently he chose not to, because the numbness filled my mouth.

The team leader looked past me and told my teacher, "This boy cannot smile even when he is begging for help."

Our teacher had taken me there in the hope that I could express my wish for advancement, not to beg for help. But I sensed the visit did in fact amount to begging, which explained why my tongue remained wooden. The team leader's comment hurt me so badly my eyes welled up with tears. I did not want him to see me cry, so I turned my face away.

But those who wanted to crush my last ounce of self-respect showed no mercy. The work team leader started in on me. "I didn't hear what you said just now. Say it again. It seems I must pay very close attention when you speak." Behind me I heard the giggles of Jamba, my childhood friend who had on a PLA uniform now. As the burning tears rushed to my eyes, I turned and ran downstairs. My teacher came down after me. The chilly winter wind whipped at my face.

Our teacher sighed and walked with me through the small square back to the school. Suddenly I broke away and ran up the hill. I could not bear to live in the village any longer. My once good friend Jamba found a shortcut to escape, but I knew of no way out. I could only flee to the mountains surrounding the village. Crossing the woods dotted with patches of late spring snow, I dashed up the hill. I could see Dad following me in from the distance. When he finally caught up with me, my tears had dried and I sat on the snow and announced that I would never go to school again. I wanted to live alone on the mountain just like Kunpal Sigya and I would give every cent I made to my family.

Father said nothing but I could see the anxiety for his son on his face.

After a long silence, he said, "Let's go and pay a visit to Kunpal Sigya."

That was the last time I saw Motley Face, and by then I did not recognize him. When we pushed open the creaky wooden door, some snow that had piled on the cabin roof fell off. The light reflected from the snow shone into the cabin and danced off the brightly polished saddle. Its wooden bridle and leather pads, its copper stirrups and iron bit all gleamed. I called out to Motley Face when I saw him, standing with his back to the door. But there was no response. I walked in and called him again but he said nothing. At that moment, I sensed a cold cloud surrounding him like a thick layer of ice.

Death. The word jumped into my head.

Father must have had the same thought because he pushed me behind him at once. Motley Face was leaning sideways against the saddle, two liquor bottles at his side. His face was down in the fire pit, but the fire was long extinguished and the fine ash was icy cold. Dad tried to straighten Motley Face's body but he plunged forward as soon as dad let him go. Dad sighed, mumbled something, and tried again to lean him up against his beloved saddle, the saddle that could carry him far off to the hot spring behind the snow peaks. In that moment, I had witnessed death, coming face-to-face with the cruel truth for the first time. His face was a charred mess.

As I write this, the Japanese TV station NHK is broadcasting the news that a Buddhist temple in the country has been burned to the ground. A wooden face of a Buddha statue burned beyond recognition was just shown on the TV screen. It reminded me of the charred features of Motley Face.

And that was my last image of Motley Face Kunpal Sigya – leaning against his sparkling clean saddle with his burned, unrecognizable face. Dad and I backed to the cabin door slowly, and Dad closed it. That face disappeared from our view forever.

We paused for a moment on the steps outside the cabin, which was half-buried in knee-deep snow. Dad chopped off two large pine branches and we used them to sweep the snow from the cabin roof. The log cabin was built into the slope of a hill so it was easy for us to reach the roof from a higher place on the slope. Chunks of snow fell off and the thick cedar roof soon appeared.

A single match started the fire that swallowed the log cabin.

Flames rose and the dry logs burned with a crackling sound. The heat from the fire scorched my face and melted all the snow around, but I still felt a chill up my spine. The cabin roof began to cave in and finally collapsed, consuming the body of Motley Face. The fire twitched and danced in the wind, and blue smoke rose into the sky. Now that his soul had been set free from its mortal shell, it could rise freely up to heaven. I raised my eyes to the blue sky. The snow crests glittered. The tranquil blueness seemed endless.

At the foot of the hill, the villagers saw the fire and climbed up for a closer look. The militia platoon, consisting of village youths led by the work team members, arrived first. Jamba in his new PLA uniform dashed up, too. He was trying to appear courageous in the face of such a tragedy, but the fire was nearly burned out. Finally almost everyone from the village was there. They watched the fire slowly burn out with a feeling of sadness tinged with guilt. The look on Jamba's face changed, too.

On our way back down the hill, Jamba joined me. I didn't want to talk to him but he hemmed and hawed and finally said, "You should try to join the PLA, too."

"Why?" I asked.

He lowered his voice. "You are just like me. You want to leave this damned village."

He stopped and looked at me directly. I felt he had seen my innermost feelings. It was not up to me to get away from such a miserable lifestyle, but you couldn't get to heaven on only a wish. Motley Face was freed forever and Jamba had also escaped. He stepped into the new pair of leather shoes that would carry him away without question. But I could never leave this gloomy village. My eyes welled up with shame when the harsh reality dawned on me.

The look on Jamba's face was hard to read. He tried to be aloof.

"You're like a kid who can't grow up," he tried to joke.

Then, he went ahead of me on the snowy trail to join the noisy crowd, leaving me behind. I looked back to the place where Motley Face had died. The horses under his care came down from the mountain pasture and gathered around the spot. They stood there like an image in a dream.

And I had a dream that night. I saw Motley Face leading his horse with the lovely saddle. Behind him was a blooming wild cherry tree covered with snow-white flowers.

"I am leaving," he said.

He raised the horsewhip and the snow-white cherry flowers scattered around like snowflakes. He pushed through the snowflake curtain and came up to me, saying "I am leaving for the hot spring."

In the dream, I felt so desperate that my heart started to ache. I told him, "You are lying. You cannot go. There is no hot spring behind the snow peaks."

He looked sad when I said that. He lowered his eye, resembling a beautiful woman weighed down by sadness or a Buddha who could no longer bear the sight of mortal suffering on earth.

Shortly after Motley Face died, several trucks arrived at our village. The horses of the village were driven downhill. They had become useless with the emergence of the automobile. Each of them was bound with heavy ropes and driven into a small stall separated with wood planks on the truck. These once-dynamic creatures that used to roam freely at the foot of the snow peaks looked terrified and dejected. Many villagers sobbed when the trucks rolled off. We would never again see horses in our lives.

A work team member tried to comfort the villagers, saying that the horses had been sold to the PLA to be trained as military horses. They would follow the bugle tunes as they ate their meals, practiced drills and galloped on the battle field.

But the work team leader snapped, "Nonsense! This is the era of socialist development. The horses were idle here, doing nothing. Do you know how many places still have men pulling ploughs?" At this, we realized that the horses had been sent to work on farms. In our lives, however, a horse was an invaluable means of transportation and a loyal companion to travelers. Hard field labor such as pulling a plough was meant for cattle, which were stronger than horses.

After discovering the fate awaiting their horses, many villagers began to cry. They sang ballads of horses on the prairie. I heard my elder female cousin's beautiful voice above everyone else's. When telling stories about our origin of civilization, the elders loved to start out by saying, "In that barbarous age, the work horses were separated from the wild horses." Well, this time the horses had been separated from their riders in our new, civilized age.

The horses were gone and in their place came the small, booming, smoke-spitting walking tractor. Instead of being used to plough fields, the tractor was used by villagers for transportation. Its first task was to send off groups of work-team members and bring back others. Jamba left with the work team. On the day of their departure, all the villagers went to stand at the intersection to see the tractor noisily climbing the hill trail, spewing out black clouds of smoke before it disappeared.

* * * * *

Time seemed to stand still, but it did move on. The near-suffocating days started to change, too. Several years later, I entered high school, graduated and returned to the village. When I received the admission to high school, Dad had told me, "If our village remains as it is, do not come back."

He said this as he was replacing the soles of my boots. He also told me to go uphill to soak my smelly feet in the brine spring. The wrinkles on his face smoothed out when he said this. "Go soak your feet thoroughly in the spring," he said. "You don't want to smell like a 'barbarian Tibetan'." That was what some outsiders called us. When Dad was in a good mood, he used that epithet jokingly.

I went uphill and soaked my feet in the brine spring. I put my feet into the icy water and then stuck them into the soft mud at the bottom, which felt wonderful. I did not really believe that it could get rid of the odor of my feet, if it was indeed true that my clansmen and I were born with that smell. Then I pulled my feet out and looked over to the spot where the log cabin once stood. There was nothing left now but a plump shrub of Chinese rhubarb, an herbal plant used for treating fever. I stood before the plant for a long time and then walked around aimlessly, when something caught my eye. It was a human skull, glaringly white, a horrifying smile formed by its two rows of teeth. But the two black holes of its eye sockets looked vacant.

A blast of cold air smacked my face. I sucked in the cold air and blurted out, "Motley Face?"

No answer.

Of course, no answer.

I knelt down before the skull. The cold air snaked down my spine. Instead of running away, I chose to face the skull squarely. The valley appeared so empty and dead without the horses.

I shouted, "Motley Face!"

A gust of wind blew past. The lush greenness around me started to sway and the skull seemed to shake. It must have heard me, so

I told it, "I am leaving. Your horses are gone." The skull remained silent and my fear dissolved as I sat on the muddy ground. I pulled some leaves off the Chinese rhubarb shrub and wrapped the skull in them, telling it, "It is cold and wet here. You can see nothing from here. Let's find you a better place."

I found a large cypress tree with a majestic crown, and perched the skull onto a large branch where it would be protected from rain but still able to enjoy the sunshine. This position would also enable Motley Face to look south, like a dignified personage. If he chose, his big eye sockets would allow him to see both the east and the west without the need to turn his face. Of course, there were also the snowy mountains in the west and the vast prairie behind the mountains. And in a remote spot on the prairie, there was the legendary hot spring that purified and beautified all creatures.

II

Who could have imagined that I would become a traveling photographer ten years later?

Not as a journalist, nor a studio technician nor a photographic artist: I was on the staff at the People's Art Center of our autonomous prefecture. Wearing a photographer's vest, I went around taking pictures at meetings, villages, factories and scenic sites in our prefecture. I was responsible for the three display windows set up outside our office building, the stadium and the square in front of the cinema beside our center. The minister in charge of publicity work in our prefecture cited the same sentence that appeared in the government documents: "Change; we must reflect the great changes of our great era."

But it was no easy task to reflect those changes.

For example, the leaders sitting on the rostrum during meetings loved to see their photos hung in the display windows. The same large portraits of our leaders sat in our display windows for years. No change seemed to occur in the way the peasants cultivated their fields, either. Tractors had appeared on farms ten years earlier. Ten years passed, but the tractors just got rusty and lost their original freshness. Then the modern hydropower stations were constructed, sending electric light to every household. But how much change could the solid power stations demonstrate? So the best we could do was to use different scenic photos to enliven the staid look of our display windows. Consequently, various landscape photos were put in our windows to meet the leaders' requirement that we must reflect the great changes of our era.

And the scenery worked wonders.

It was really a delight for me to view these landscapes from behind the camera lens. I carried the cameras that the government bought me and traveled around taking photos on meager business trip expenses. Some other guys also went around with their office-reimbursed cameras, taking similar-style pictures. So in the process of traveling and photographing scenery, many of us began to regard ourselves as photographers or potential artists.

Encouraged by the three display windows under my charge, I became a rare, authoritative figure on photo publication in our small town. A lot of photos were sent to me from all over, so I began to acquire new status as an editor and an amateur critic of photography. My three display windows grew increasingly influential and fashionable. In those years, the government officials became younger and younger, their diplomas more and more prestigious, and their fashion sense increasingly tasteful. Those young, fashionable leaders all regarded cameras as basic necessities, next only to automobiles — just like the status of cell phones and laptops today.

Naturally, I was befriended by many leaders. It was advantageous for them take me along in their fancy cross-country jeeps when they went out. On the way, we could select scenes and take photos together. Coming back, we could publish our collective works in my display windows. I became a highly popular figure in our small town and the artist friend of many leaders thanks to my display windows.

Some bold girls even sought me out, asking if I could take some illicit photos of them. They would come to me with albums of nude photographs and say shyly, "I want pictures like these." They claimed such photos would be valuable memories for them when they were old.

When decorating my display windows, I was accustomed to the small crowds that gathered to watch and admire my work. Actually, the admiring eyes were not all on me, although I managed to arrange the photos artistically and match them with beautiful captions using various fonts and colors. Most of the onlookers seemed to recognize and appreciate the familiar faces in the photos rather than the quality of the photos themselves. They would sigh admiringly and say, "Ah, so-and-so bureau chief!"

"Look, so-and-so director!"

One day, I had filled half a display window when I suddenly began to doubt the significance of my work. So I ordered a bottle of ice-cold beer from a small shop across the street and sat down in the shade of a locust tree for a short rest. It was May, and the days had turned hot by noon. The thick fragrance of the luxuriant white locust flowers made me sleepy.

Under many envious eyes, I titled a photo "Remote Hot Spring" and scribbled it on a piece of paper. Two or three sensual female backs soaked in a steaming hot spring. The female figures in the photo were intentionally shot out-of-focus to look blurry. It was the first time I had put up such a controversial photo in my display window. I was drinking with a leader the night before and listened to him describe the marvelous scene he had witnessed of men and women bathing together in a hot spring. A Tibetan too, the leader sighed, "We were all degenerates. When the bathers called me to join them, I peeled off everything but my underpants."

"Those in the pool laughed at me, calling fishy-minded. When I think about it, I did have fishy thoughts." The leader who shot this photo was a little drunk the night before. He asked me, "Buddy, guess what I was fishy about at the time?"

I had no idea.

"The girls in the hot spring looked so healthy and pretty," he admitted. "I feared I might be stimulated physically so I had to have my underpants on. And I had to get far away to shoot these photos with a telephoto lens." Some of his photos were much better focused but after some hard inner struggle, we ended up choosing that blurred one for the display window.

I drank the beer under the locust tree, scribbled down the photo caption and pulled the photo from a big Kraft envelope. The fuzzy pink shades in the photo caught people's attention immediately and made them want to take a closer look. Although the Xinhua Bookstore nearby was openly selling albums of nude body art and video stores were semi-openly renting X-rated films from Hong Kong and the US, the blurred fleshy shades still attracted a lot of attention. However, my decision to display the photo in my hand was shaken by the enthusiasm of onlookers. I did not have to be responsible for the moral standard of our city but any small careless slip might cause me to lose my official friends who made my life there as pleasant as possible.

So I put the photo back into the envelope and the paper bearing the caption was torn up. I took another big gulp of cold beer when I saw a government official in a black Western-style suit and a well-kontted tie open a folding chair and sit down beside me.

I knew he was a government official because of his attire and his bold confidence when he grabbed the chair and seated himself. He smiled and said, "Buy me a beer." I poured away the cold tea left in my mug and filled it with beer. I was tired but tried to smile attentively.

"You don't remember me?" he asked.

I shook my head. "No, I don't think so. But I guess you are at least a deputy county head."

"Good eyes," he commented. He was a deputy head of a certain prairie county.

"You will become a county head soon then." According to my years of experience, I knew there were two kinds of people who loved to hear false praise. One kind was the women who loved to hear they looked younger than they actually were. The other kind was the officials who had not gone far in their careers. They loved to hear about a promotion coming their way soon.

He laughed and took a big gulp of beer. "People like us do have a special smell." he said. "Those with a dog's nose could tell right away."

"Did you just call me a dog?"

"I was referring to both of us."

He was right. He was poking fun at both the officials and those with a special sense for them.

"I know you," he said.

"Who besides me would photograph you people sitting on the rostrum at every meeting except me? Of course you know who I am."

"Once you went to our county. I meant to go to see you and

take you to the hot spring you dreamed about seeing. But you had already left when I came back."

I was a bit annoyed at the mention of the hot spring. Seeing that I showed no reaction to his hint, he took off his sunglasses and leaned forward across the table.

"You little…, You really don't remember me?"

I thought his eyes looked familiar, but the memories of the hot spring years were long past. I shook my head again.

He was a little disappointed and a bit upset. "You bastard. I am Jamba!"

Good heavens! Jamba! I had engraved his face in my mind but hadn't seen him for many years. And when I finally managed to erase him from my memory, he showed up. My former recollection of him was accompanied with some pain, but when he disappeared from my memory, my hatred left as well. He had chosen a good time to show up again. Heaven must have helped him all along, I thought.

"Jamba!" I cried out, as if I had been reunited with a long-lost family member.

He remained calm and poised in spite of my excitement. Patting my shoulder and then checking his watch, he said with that authoritative tone of officials, "I must go say good-bye to the prefecture office. Finish what you are doing here and go home to get your cameras. I will come here to pick you up in two hours."

He talked while walking toward a Mitsubishi jeep parked across the street. His secretary stepped out and opened the jeep door for him. I could not help but follow him to the jeep. He got in and said, "Be on time. We have a long way to go."

Still astonished by the sight of him, I repeated excitedly, "Sure. Sure."

Not until Jamba's jeep rolled off in a cloud of dust under the high noon sun, did it dawn on me just how this guy had ordered me around! How dared he, a mere deputy head of a small prairie county with a population of no more than several tens of thousands, talk to me with that authoritative tone? And I followed his direction obediently! More automobiles were speeding by, raising up dust behind them. It choked me and a violent fit of coughing forced me to bend over. After I recovered, I hurried back to my display window to finish my work. Then I went back to office, took out my three cameras from the cabinet and got them ready. I loaded my big bag with films of various speeds.

The director of our cultural center was not in his office. I waited there for a long while, then finally put a note on his desk and left. Out on the street, I thought of the past. That damned Jamba! He seemed to forget all the unpleasantness between us from more than a decade ago. But the fact that I still felt so much anger showed that it was still stuck in my heart and had the power to prick me. But I hadn't said no to his invitation. If we could have gone back in time to a decade before, I believed that the stubborn lad I had once been would have refused. But now, a decade later, I wasn't so brave.

Was it because of that hot spring where men and women bathed merrily under the blue sky?

I reached the display window in front of the gym. Jamba's jeep was there already and Jamba came up to me with a broad smile. But as soon as he opened his mouth, his official tone was back.

"I thought you would be late."

"You thought?"

"You guys in the literary and arts circles are always carefree," he said condescendingly.

I was a staff member at the cultural center of the prefecture, but it wasn't clear if that placed me in the literary and arts circle.

Jamba hugged me warmly as if we were close friends, as if our separation before had been very pleasant. He told his secretary to take over my two camera bags and put them in the trunk. When I was seated in the jeep, he turned around from the front seat and asked with a smile, "Shall we go?"

The fragrance of the locust tree flowers in the sultry summer sun filled the air. I nodded my head.

The jeep was started. Jamba was comfortably perched in the front passenger seat. His secretary and I sat in the back. I watched the back of his head, feeling the old hatred, now mixed with some envy. Then, in the rear view mirror, I saw his eyes. He looked confident but not without some uncertainty. I had taken photos of myself, just as great artists paint their self-portraits from mirrors. I had seen a similar ambitious look in my eyes, too. I was startled at first because I had thought I was an easygoing guy, taking things as they come. But the gleam in my eyes revealed what I actually longed for. I thought to myself that the man sitting in front of me must be like me: a man with aspirations and lofty ideals who is just trying to escape the confusion of an uncertain future.

Jamba finally spoke. "I can see that you are doing well."

"Far from what you are," I answered.

"A mere deputy head of a county. Who knows when I will have to step down."

"But I have no idea what that feels like."

He changed the subject. "After I heard you do photography, I thought you would come to shoot photos of our hot spring. But you never showed up."

His words reminded me of Motley Face Kunpal Sigya, who had died many years before. The hot spring, as well, had faded from my memory with the passing of time.

Jamba watched me in the rearview mirror and said, "I mean the hot spring Motley Face told us about a long time ago." He sighed. "If Motley Face were alive today, he would be free to go and see the hot spring, too."

"But Motley Face is dead," I said. I stared into his eyes in the rear view mirror. "He died so tragically." My tone hinted that he had something to do with Motley Face's miserable end. But he didn't seem to be affected by that.

"Who didn't suffer in those years?" he said.

In my mind I could see the sad image of Motley Face bending over the fire pit, his face a charred mess. Was that skull still on the cypress tree branch? The cherry tree would be in bloom now, with dense, snow-like flowers. When the wind blew down from the snowy peaks, the cherry petals would fly everywhere like snow-flakes.

I was irritated. "Let's not talk about people who died a long time ago."

"But we must not forget them," Jamba said. "It was the error of an era." Jamba mimicked the tone of the government documents. The jeep roared on. The landscape outside the windows flashed by: a tree, stones in a shrub, a bush of colorful wild flowers were thrown behind – instant memories. What a vast world was the human memory! So many things were thrown into the mix of memories, layer upon layer. I wished the stones and flowers on the prairie could bury my gloomy recollections but the damned memories struggled to burst out from the deepest corners of my mind. My memories were more stubborn than my will.

Jamba mentioned the hot spring again. I pointed out to him that he seemed to use two different tones when talking about the hot spring. One was the official tone, used when he discussed the hot spring as a tourist attraction and how it should be developed.

He touched on the budget needed and the culture involved – the damned culture everyone seemed to be so interested in. But when he talked about the men and women bathing together, he used a very different tone, bordering on obscenity. He mentioned breasts, buttocks and body hair. The asceticism in our teenage years gave our generation an abnormal view of sex that enabled us to sense obscenity and suggestions of immorality in even the most innocent things.

Not at all offended by my sharp comment, Jamba laughed and patted the shoulder of his chauffeur. "Yes, yes, two tones. The official's and the man's." He twisted it into an undeniable fact that he was both an official and a man. I decided not to talk about it anymore.

But his eyes were shining with an odd gleam and he continued.

"Don't tremble when you hold your camera there. Make sure to focus your lens."

I remained silent.

"I know what you're thinking. You just want to satisfy your own desires and you don't want to share the scene with others. You'd better take good pictures there or you won't be allowed to see the place again."

I was staying overnight in the county seat and Jamba invited me to his home. His wife was a sickly woman who smelled of medicine from head to toe. She had the dignified air of a county head's wife and put on a poker face when visitors came to her home. Feeling uneasy about her coldness to me, Jamba reminded her, "This is my old schoolmate, my fellow villager."

But her face became even longer and she mumbled something to herself.

I teased her. "I am just a poor relative from the countryside."

Her poker face became a little more natural. She sized me

up and down and said, "Too many poor relatives come from your village."

That surprised me, so I asked, "They all come here?"

She was sitting on a brightly colored mattress with her legs crossed, holding a fine wooden comb. "They come here to bathe in the hot spring."

"I came here for the hot spring too," I said.

Jamba interrupted us. "He is a photographer. He is here to take pictures of the hot spring. We plan to make good use of this tourist hotspot of ours."

The poker face loosened even little more. She looked at me but addressed her husband. "Tell the county office about his visit. Tell them to take good care of him." After saying that, she seemed to have accomplished an exhausting task. She sighed, tapped on her waist with her fists, and went inside.

Actually, Jamba had already arranged my accommodation at the county guest house. Concerned that he might be embarrassed about his wife, I tried to avoid his eyes. He walked me downstairs and explained, "She is different from us. Spoiled from her childhood. Her dad is my top superior." He said his father-in-law's name somewhat smugly. "She is his daughter."

Certainly, the name was very well-known.

It was getting late. The pale yellow streetlights failed to illuminate the ground but blurred the stars in the prairie sky. Jamba asked me about my wife so I told him she was a high school teacher.

"Teaching is not an easy job," Jamba said.

"No job is easy," I told him.

He laughed, than patted me on the shoulder and saw me out of his courtyard. The street outside was deserted. A gust of wind blew past, rolling some dust, scraps of paper and plastic bags. The pungent odor of horse dung and dirt filled the air. The distant sound of barking dogs and the dim starry sky pressing down assured me that I was on the prairie.

Jamba did not show up the next morning.

The office director of the county government came over to accompany me to lunch. Smiling politely, he explained that Jamba had a busy schedule of meetings that involved reviewing the plan for the county's tourism development and various other issues. I answered politely that I did not mind.

After lunch, I went outside for a walk. Many small shops lined both sides of the main street and there were quite a number of open-air billiard tables. Some young monks were playing billiards with a few street youths. The balls hit each other with loud clacks. Herdsmen passed by on languid horses under the noon sun. During my hot stroll I learned that the hot spring was thirty kilometers from the town. After watching the billiard game for awhile, I saw a herdsman ride by, followed by a second horse. I raised a thumb at him like the hitch-hiking Americans standing by the highway in the movies. The herdsman and his horses paused before me. His tall figure bent forward and asked, "Buddy, are you going to the same place as I am?"

I told him the name of the hot spring.

He laughed and jumped off his horse. He patted my bottom and said, "You ride the horse that has a saddle. Go!" He gave me a push and I was hoisted onto the horse's back high above the ground. All the billiard players watched me. The rider jumped on the bare back of his second horse, gave the rein a quick jiggle and the two horses trotted on side by side. Soon we were out of the town and after crossing a hill pass, we saw a vast prairie stretching before us.

The sight made me gasp.

Then, by flicking the reins, I directed my horse to trot off the highway toward the lake. Once we reached the lakeside, I loosened the reins to slow my horse down on the soft trail around the water. Water birds warbled noisily above. The herdsman caught up with me. He smiled and went on ahead. He controlled the speed of our rides all the way. A reddish rock cliff towered before us on the prairie, and the herdsman said the hot spring was at the foot of the cliff. The reddish cliff with green saplings bursting from its cracks reminded me of a volcano. There must have been a volcano eruption there centuries before. I said this to my companion and he replied, "You sound like a geological team member."

"I am not from a geological team."

The two of us were chatting when a jeep roared up from the prairie. Its wheels stirred up a cloud of dust. My companion coughed violently and I teased him, "Don't tell me that you are choked by a little dust!"

He stopped coughing and looked at me earnestly. "It's not just me. Our whole prairie is choked."

We tried to keep a distance from the highway. As we went on, the herdsman told me, "Don't drive when you come here again."

I told him that would be impossible because I came from so far away.

He waved his hand impatiently. "Don't give me that. Did your elders ride here in a jeep to bathe in the hot spring?" He had a point. None of my elders had come to the hot spring in cars. Furthermore, they lost the capability to roam around after the automobile appeared. Although they gained back the right to travel around freely again, after being confined to the same place for so long their souls had become as sedentary as the rocks on the hills.

"I know how you feel," he continued. "I mean, if you really want to see the hot spring and enjoy it as your elders did, you should leave your jeep at the county seat and ride a horse to see the hot spring."

"Like we are doing now?"

"Right, like we are doing now."

By the time the jeep whizzed pass us on the highway, we had reached the reddish cliff. We looked up and saw flocks of pigeons and swifts swirling around their nests on the high cliff. The herdsman said, "My name is Lobsang."

Watching the swifts soar nimbly across the sky, I did not hear what he said right away but I soon turned my attention back to him and apologized.

"I should have asked you earlier," I said.

We both jumped off our horses and led them along, walking side by side. "You should tell me your name," he said.

I apologized again and told him my name.

Lobsang laughed. "Are you always this absent-minded?"

"My mind is on the hot spring all the time," I explained.

He glanced at me, momentarily surprised. "Ah, the hot spring, the hot spring! Well, buddy, you are right at its door now."

The grassy trail under our feet ran around a number of huge rocks that had fallen off the cliff. The sun was setting and a chilly evening wind blew over. But after we passed through the shadows from the cliff and back into the sun, warmth bathed us again. And there, suddenly, a dazzling light reflected from the surface of the water.

The hot spring! The remote Tsona Hot Spring! The spring that once seemed untouchable to me was right before my eyes!

My feet were nailed to the ground as the glistening light of the spring mesmerized me. A strong smell of sulfur floated in the air. I stood there for a long time, entranced. As soon as the sun receded more fully, I could see everything clearly. The water was gushing out from several spring mouths in the cliff cracks and on the grassy slope, spilling in all directions and forming small lakes one after another. It was those small lakes that had caught the last sunlight of the day.

I handed the horse's reins to Lobsang and stepped onto the bank of a hot spring mouth. The sulfur smell became stronger. The spring water gushed into a small lake and then seeped off into another lake, snaking pleasantly along.

I sat down dizzily as if returning to the brine spring on the mountain behind my home village years before. The songs of the birds were familiar, and the sulfur odor was familiar, but there was no forest or snow mountain here, only a reddish rock cliff towering behind me. A vast, boundless prairie stretched all the way to the horizon in all directions.

Lobsang switched his whip against his boots, interrupting my trance. He sighed. "Every time I am here, I feel as if I'm seeing it for the first time – like visiting a fresh young girl."

"But this is not the hot spring I dreamed about," I said.

I began to tell him the hot spring Motley Face Kunpal Sigya had described to us. Rather than being tranquil and quiet as it was now, it had a large rural fair around it, with a lot of tents, stalls, food booths, singing and dancing, many splendidly decorated horses and an endless flow of people coming from everywhere. They came to the spring, took off their festival clothes, both men and women, and stepped into the water to wash the dirt off their bodies and the fatigue and disease from their insides. Many an attractive or unattractive body soaked in the warm water of that hot spring.

Perhaps the reality had never been as innocent, free and relaxing. The portrayal of the hot spring by Motley Face and other village elders who had been here had created a dreamlike image for me throughout my childhood. Now, when I finally stood before the wonderland that had appeared time and again in my dreams, it seemed as if it had been forgotten by the world. The lush grassy slope stretched out under the vast blue sky. Its sulfur smell spread to the path like the sweetness women brought to our hearts. A herdsman named Lobsang was looking after two splendid horses. The horses stuck out their tongues to chew the tender grass on the lawn.

I remained sitting by the hot spring. I have no idea how long I was there, but I sensed the weakening of the heat from the setting sun.

"Somebody is coming this way," Lobsang suddenly said behind me.

A guy was walking up the slope. The visitor was a rural mailman. He stopped before us and greeted only Lobsang. Lobsang placed a bottle of liquor on the ground followed by a chunk of meat. The postman took a big hunk of fresh cheese from his bag. The two of them then peeled off all their clothes and jumped in the spring. I followed their example, plunging headfirst into the warm water that gently enveloped me. I closed my eyes and was consumed by a humming darkness. Then I opened my eyes and saw a rippling of bright dots. This must be what we saw in our mothers' wombs, I thought. The Buddhist scriptures claimed that the world was destroyed and born again repeatedly. So the world must be like this every time it is reborn.

Lobsang and the mailman sat in the warm water and leaned against the grassy spring bank, letting the spring water caress their bodies while enjoying the delicious food they had brought: the meat, the cheese and the liquor. But I just kept plunging my head into the water, emerging only when I had to spurt out the water in my nose. Then I would take a deep breath and dive under again.

I plunged into the water tirelessly as if there was nothing else in my life. The water embraced me with its gentle, caressing fingers. My life became so simple then; I could forget pain and be relieved of the gray suffocating memories. What a simple, solid pleasure! Then a smart spank from Lobsang ended my joyful game.

None of the small lakes formed by the spring water were deep, and so it was easy for Lobsang to see his target: my buttocks. Seeing my bewildered look and trying to cover my nakedness, the mailman let loose a resounding belly laugh. Never had I imagined such a sound could be uttered by a short guy like him. His vibrant laughter embarrassed me but the liquor Lobsang offered me helped relieve the situation.

The liquor, plus the cheese and the oncoming dusk began to narrow the gap between my first sight of the hot spring and my long-held expectations. The alcohol had started to have an effect, too. So I blurted out, "If only there were some girls, beautiful girls as naked as we are."

This made my two companions laugh heartily. "Ah, girls, girls!"

"Aren't there any girls at the hot spring anymore?"

They continued to laugh.

Many years later, at a banquet held for us by some Japanese writers in Tokyo, the topic of our conversation turned to the hot springs in Japan. I asked Mr. Kuro Kenji, an elderly writer who kept filling my wineglass, if there were still mixed-sex springs in Japan such as the one portrayed in Kawabata Yasunari's novel. He smiled.

"If Mr. Ah Lai wants to see sincerely, I could be your guide, only you will have to hear my story first." He said he was in his 40s, the same age as I was then, when he left his noisy city to travel in Hokkaido. One important purpose of his trip was to enjoy the famous hot springs in the Hokkaido area. He also hoped that he could find a mixed-sex spring there. Many outsiders had thought all hot springs in Japan were mixed-sex but once you entered Japan, you would be told such a thing was only to be seen in Hokkaido. However, once you arrived in Hokkaido, the locals there would say that you had to go to a remote corner in their area before you could find a mixed-sex spring.

At least that was what Mr. Kuro Kenji was told. He lived in a famous hot spring hotel in Hokkaido at the time, and there was no mixed-sex spring in his hotel. After asking around, he finally located one. However, after making the long journey to get to the place, Mr. Kuroi Kenji said, "I saw only retired silver-haired grannies. They commented, 'The poor young man who had never seen the world and had come there to open his eyes'."

His story brought a hearty laugh from the other diners at the banquet. He poured more wine in my glass and said, "Mr. Ah Lai, I don't mind telling you where that mixed-sex spring is. Only, those grandmas will be even older by now. A man in his 40s like you will be a mere kid in their eyes." People burst into laughter again.

Back at our hotel in Tokyo, I began packing because we were to leave the next morning for Ueda City in Nagano Prefecture, known for its multiple hot springs. The hot spring on our Tibetan prairie came to my mind again. On that tranquil, faraway grassland, the hot spring water sparkled like diamonds. Birds sang all around. The light of the spring water changed colors at different times during the day.

I recalled the first time I bathed in that hot spring on the prairie.

I recollected that I had blurted out, "If only there were some girls here!"

Lobsang and the rural mailman told me if I would just be patient and wait a little longer, I might bump into what I longed for. But in the description given by Motley Face and other village elders, the hot spring was surrounded by a clamorous rural fair every day from late spring to midsummer. Naked bodies crowded in the steamy spring water, relaxing in the open air just like the clouds under the sun. Pretty girls spread out their long hair in the water, their eyes dreamy, their breasts fair and their songs soft and lingering.

But when I actually soaked in the hot spring, all the stories I had heard were as far-removed from reality as a dream of paradise. I told this to the two men at my side in the spring. We were all half-drunk so no one said anything; we just sat in the warm water, listening to our own thoughts and watching the stars in the night sky.

Lobsang addressed my disappointment. "That kind of thing does not happen anymore. The custom has been prohibited for many years now. The pretty girls who bathed here then are all old now. Today's girls have learned to wrap themselves tightly and show nothing for others to see. Men also were bound to their cattle herds, unable to ride horses with their women or to roam around. If a horse is shut in for too long, it doesn't know how to gallop after it is set free."

"Only I can roam on the road every day!" the mailman said smugly.

"Oh shut up!" Lobsang cut him short.

Refusing to shut up, however, the short mailman bragged on. "I get to walk around every day and see different women." His two golden teeth twinkled in his mouth.

"Shut up!" Lobsang snapped again.

The mailman took a gulp of liquor and continued to boast to me, the stench of his breath rushing to my nose. "Buddy, I am a government employee. Women like us because we earn a guaranteed government wage every month!"

"A wage," Lobsang mumbled. He soundly slapped the mailman's cheeks. The mailman grabbed his face and jumped out of the water, his short silhouette swallowed by the dark night. He laughed despite the slaps and said to me, "That son of a bitch is upset because he is jealous that I attract so many women."

Lobsang jumped out of the water and the two naked men chased each other around the small lakes under the night sky. Suddenly a light came shining from the roadway and a jeep roared toward the slope. Its bright headlights caught the two naked men – the robust Lobsang and the short mailman. Blinded by the strong beams of the jeep, the men raised their arms to cover their eyes. The jeep screeched to a halt at the men's feet. A man jumped out and walked into the beam. The mailman put down his arms and murmured, "County Head Jamba."

Lobsang groaned as if he had a toothache.

Ignoring the mailman, Deputy County Head Jamba asked Lobsang directly, "Where is my friend?"

"Your friend?" Lobsang asked, puzzled.

"Here I am," I said from the water.

Jamba looked in my direction. "I was waiting for you in the township government office, believing you would go there."

"I came here to see the hot spring," I said. "Why did I have to go to the township government office?"

"Why? To arrange for your accommodation and meals!" Jamba said.

"Why can't I sleep and eat with these people?"

"Put on your clothes and let's go," he said. Then he turned to Lobsang. "A man like you would be smart to stay away from my friend."

"Your High Majesty County Head, it is your friend who raised his thumb asking to come with me." Lobsang took another gulp of

liquor and turned to me. "So you turned out to be an important figure. Leave with your friend now!"

By that time the mailman had quickly gathered up his clothes,
snatched up his canvas mail bag and disappeared into the darkness.

Jamba pulled me toward the jeep but Lobsang grabbed me,
too. I thought he changed his mind and wanted me to stay with him.
I knew I would say yes if he asked. But he said to me, "Are you just
leaving like this? Isn't a government cadre supposed to pay a common man after riding his horse?"

I was still naked. Jamba threw a 50 yuan bill to Lobsang who
glared at us. The bill floated on the water so Lobsang reached over
to get it. I put on my clothes and got inside the jeep. I felt relaxed
after soaking in the hot spring but my mind was churning from everything that was happening. The jeep roared to a start and its headlights swept across the trees and rocks, lighting them up for a flash
before they went back into darkness. Then the jeep swayed onto the
highway and began to roll steadily down the road.

Jamba turned around in his seat and the polite expression
he had worn for the past few days vanished. The old mocking
look from his youth – before he enlisted in the PLA – reap-
peared. "Have you photographed naked women? My goodness,
how times have changed! Wouldn't you agree that that is a backward custom?"

"No, I think that is a wonderful custom."

The jeep jolted and Jamba bumped his head against the ceiling.
He was furious. "You writers regard these backward things as being
somehow admirable. You take your pictures and win prizes but it is
our faces you are throwing in the dirt."

I was speechless. What could I say to that kind of logic? This
was the official line of thinking repeated in the newspapers, TV

programs and government documents. Even people in a remote prairie area such as this would give self-righteous lectures about it.

I ignored Jamba and my mind flashed back to the hot spring with its steady streams of pearl-like bubbles. I thought of the prairie illuminated by the sun, the clouds flying across the sky. Pretty, healthy prairie women sprang up merrily from the spring water, their brass-colored Tibetan skin gleaming and their full breasts glistening. Crystal water drops fell from their black body-hair like strings of jewels.

I didn't bother to ask Jamba why such a beautiful thing was backward in his eyes. I was mesmerized by the images in my head. Dreamily, I fancied falling in love with one of the pretty girls. My body was relaxed after soaking in the hot spring and I knew I would fall asleep soon. But just then the jeep's headlights fixed on a red brick single-story house. It was the township management office of the hot spring, our accommodation for the night.

Seeing their county head get out of the jeep, the township leaders, including the party secretary and the deputy party secretary, the township head and the deputy township head, and the directors of the women's and youth federations, all looked a little excited. The conference room was ready and big plates of mutton and freshly brewed Tibetan barley liquor were laid on several long, low Tibetan-style tables. The township head ordered someone to go notify the town's small hydropower station, which was scheduled to shut down at midnight, to continue its operation till morning. People were raising liquor bowls in toasts, drinking and singing Tibetan songs.

In such a small prairie town with no more than a dozen houses like the one we were taken to, half of the residents were wakened by the loud singing in the township office. A number of the locals peered at us from the windows, their faces squashed against the glass like pancakes. Some shy but curious girls were invited in. After being offered some liquor, they joined the officials in the singing and dancing.

I wished the girls would not giggle so foolishly but they did, and they would not stop. I also wished that they wouldn't wear that pleased expression that comes from being singled out, but it was clearly on their faces.

I wanted to tell Jamba that this sort of behavior was a truly backward custom, but he was accompanied by two girls who kept toasting him and he was getting drunk. He gestured authoritatively for me to join him. The two smiling girls looked at me. After I sat down at their table, Jamba gestured with his lordly chin and the two girls poured two bowls of liquor down my throat. They were clinging to me in a seductive way and I could feel their heavy breasts bumping against my side. Jamba grinned broadly, "Isn't this better than dreaming about the mixed-sex bathing in the hot spring?"

The two girls laughed right along with him. Their laughter sounded phony and crude to me. But this is all it was: easy laughter, bodies timidly touching.

Jamba whispered to the girls, "This guy is my buddy. He has super cameras with him to shoot pictures of women bathing naked in the hot spring." This brought another round of raucous laughter and some more touching – bolder this time, but still controlled.

Certainly, the three behaved more flagrantly than I, but still did nothing more than flirting and joking. If no one ended up undressed (though I did see some hands groping along female curves), the flirtation did not amount to anything serious. When the girls eventually left, the day was almost dawning and our heads were heavy with fatigue and too much liquor. It was arranged that I would stay in the same guest room with our deputy county head.

Before we went to bed, Jamba gave me a friendly punch, reminiscent of our childhood days. After we got in our beds, he started to laugh. "What I can say about you!"

"What about me? What do you mean?"

But he started snoring lightly. My eyelids became heavy. I realized after I woke up that I still had my clothes on. What a sound sleep! The sun was bright outside our window and cows were mooing lazily somewhere. Jamba was gone. I pushed the door open and the brilliant sunshine spread through the courtyard like a gleaming roll of satin. The courtyard had lush lawns but the several willow trees standing along the wall were thin and small. Outside the dirt wall, the vast prairie stretched into the distance.

The guesthouse chef fetched a basin of water for me to wash my face and then brought my breakfast on a tray: steamed buns with beef filling and a pot of milk tea.

"Just a light breakfast," he said. "Lunch will start soon. The township leaders are reporting the progress of their work to our county head right now. Lunch will begin as soon as their meeting is over."

I had a slight headache so I drank only two cups of milk tea.

Standing in the courtyard with the milk tea in hand, I heard voices from the conference room. The tone of the speaker was noticeably different from that of the common people. That type of dramatic tone was prevalent across the country.

I strolled out of the guesthouse courtyard.

The town looked no different from other prairie towns I had visited. Some red and blue brick houses were scattered along the roadway. The dirt road was extremely dry, so dust would cloud around your footsteps. And when the sun was beating down, small whirls of wind would often rise for no reason. Whenever a truck rolled by, the town would be shrouded in a large yellow cloak. The dust-covered houses were all huddled together. The green grass of the vast prairie stretched farther than the eye could see, but these houses could go nowhere; they were covered by dust day in and day out, deserted in this remote corner of the world.

Walking down the dry dusty road, I came to the small supply and marketing cooperative shop in the town. Once inside, I could see nothing for a moment, and felt only a whiff of cool air brush over me, followed by the familiar giggling of a girl. When my eyes adjusted to the dimness inside, I saw the face of a girl standing in front of a shelf of cigarettes and beer. She was one of the girls who had been singing, drinking and dancing at our banquet the night before.

"Beer?" she asked.

I shook my head. "Cigarettes."

"Some men like to drink more liquor to sober up," she said, putting a package of cigarettes in front of me. I paid her and lit a cigarette but did not know what to say. She giggled again. Someone had told me her name the evening before but I did not remember it. She laughed and asked, "Do you really mean to take pictures of the hot spring?"

"I took pictures there yesterday."

"You take pictures of women without their clothes on," she said, blushing.

I nodded, a bit embarrassed.

"Take my picture," she said suddenly, covering her face with both hands. She walked out from behind the counter and nudged me with her shoulder. I felt the tender, warm touch of her body. She nestled up to me intimately. "Let's go," She said, her warm breath tickling my ear.

We walked outside into the scorching prairie sun. She locked the door of the shop and tickled my ear with her warm breath once more. "Let's go, photographer."

I was startled when she called me that, but she explained, "That's what county head Jamba called you."

As we walked across town, I sized up this local beauty with my photographer's eye and decided she was a bit too plump around the waist. Her tight clothes tended to wrinkle unattractively when she walked. But her laugh was loud and carefree, and I felt somewhat like a captive as I walked behind her. We finally arrived at the elementary school, which consisted of three single-story buildings surrounding a small open area for drills. In one classroom the students could be heard reciting an ancient Chinese poem in Mandarin; in another room the kids were spelling Tibetan words in unison. Soon the shop girl who laughed heartily but loved to whisper put her mouth to my ear again. "Wait here. I will call Yeshe Drolma out."

So I waited at the flagpole under a fluttering national flag and saw her go into one classroom. The chorus of Tibetan spelling stopped abruptly and soon she led a young female teacher out to where I stood. Teacher Yeshe Drolma, the name I had learned a minute earlier, was a real beauty. She stood before me a bit timidly, her eyes shyly darting into the distance and then back to her feet.

The girl from the shop whispered something in her ear. Yeshe Drolma exclaimed reprovingly, "Akyi!"

So I knew the name of the shop girl was Akyi.

Akyi put her plump, red lips to her friend's ear again. Yeshe Drolma glanced at me, blushed and reproved her friend again before she went back to her classroom.

Akyi turned to me. "Come!"

She pulled me into a clean dormitory room. The bed, the stove in the corner and the kettle on the stove were all neat and polished. The lake-green window blinds and the natural wood floor looked cool and pleasant. I sat down on a chair and saw many photos of Yeshe Drolma pressed under the glass plate on a desk by the window. To my eyes, none of the pictures truly reflected the beauty of the shy female teacher.

While I was studying the pictures, Akyi came up behind me and brushed the back of my head with her breasts before she bent over my shoulder and placed a book on the desk before me. It turned out to be an art book of nude photos, so I fingered through its pages casually. One after another, smooth female bodies of different skin colors flashed before me. They were stretched out or in curved positions, their faces showing seductive or innocent expressions and their private parts outlined boldly or indistinctly by the skillful arrangement of light.

Just then, the bell rang for the end of classes and soon the dorm door was pushed open. Teacher Yeshe Drolma came back after her class. She patted the chalk dust off her clothes. When her eyes fell on the album I was viewing, her pretty cheeks turned pink.

I could hear the thumping of my heart.

Akyi made a naughty face to Yeshe Drolma and bent over my shoulder again. She flipped through the familiar album pages until she came to a page showing a beautiful black woman whose body was covered with water drops. Akyi said, "Yeshe Drolma wants to be photographed like this."

Yeshe Drolma pinched her friend hard. Screaming, Akyi and her friend playfully wrestled and giggled. When they were finished romping, Akyi laid down on the bed to rest. Yeshe Drolma straightened her dress, came over to me and pointed to the album page. "Can this effect be created by walking out of the hot spring?"

I could not explain why I nodded, as I was not quite sure if indeed that same water drop effect could be made on a girl walking out of the hot spring.

"I don't have class in the afternoon. We … could, go to the hot spring…," she said shyly.

Was she like this when she was standing on the platform facing her class? Akyi asked me if I wanted her to bring some beer with us. I said yes. She asked if we would like some canned fish. I said yes again. So she went to her shop to get the food for our picnic. After Akyi left, Drolma and I fell silent until I said, "Now you look like a teacher again."

"I borrowed this photo album from the library of my college but failed to return it before my graduation. So I brought it here." I started to say something but she continued, as if she were lecturing her pupils. "You could go and pick up your cameras. We will wait for you."

I returned to the township government building and found their meeting was still going on. I slung the camera bag over my shoulder, wondering what kind of picture I wanted to take at the hot spring. My heart would not stop pounding.

The two girls posed on the green grass for photos, giggling foolishly whenever they moved into a new position. Sometimes Akyi would lean over to give me a quick kiss. Later she started to push me toward her friend to get a kiss from her, too. Drolma was extremely shy but once my lips approached hers, her mouth opened slightly and her trembling lips simply stupefied me. My original plan for hot spring pictures was long forgotten. The two girls from that small town on the prairie were adventurous, even though their clothes were a little rustic. Nevertheless, with all their clothes and ornaments removed, their naked bodies writhing in the water, gleaming like mermaids in brilliant sunshine, were almost too stunning for me to look at – but I couldn't look away.

They kept diving in and leaping out of the water, making various poses on the grass while my camera shutter continued to click, accompanied by the strong beating of my heart.

I could not deny my natural impulses. In fact, I did feel a strong reaction to the situation. They must have sensed this, because they began to hide in the water.

"Why don't you take off your clothes?" they giggled. "You don't dare take off your clothes, right?"

As there was really no necessity to pretend in front of women who knew a man's secret, I began to peel off my clothes. But as soon as I unfastened three shirt buttons, they shrieked, "No, no stop!" and acted like they were offended. When they saw I was irritated by their behavior, they splashed water at me and then leaned provocatively against the lakeside, lifting their faces with pouted lips. "Have a kiss. Come on!"

I did kiss them, with passion. However, as soon as my lips touched Akyi's, she acted as if she had been burned and then slid from my grasp. Drolma was no different, except that she would linger a little longer in my arms to allow me the luxury of sensing her trembling lips and torso. But she would soon follow the example of her friend, letting out a scream and slipping away. Then both of them would squat in the shallow part of the spring with the same expression of purity and innocence. When I could no longer bear the situation, I turned around and walked up the hill by the hot spring.

I sat on a big rock and let the cool clouds floating by quench the burning desire in my body. Sadness filled my heart. By the time I walked back down the hill, the two girls had already put their clothes back on. They unfolded a blanket on the grass, and put beer bottles and fish cans on it. A bunch of chrysanthemums were placed in the center and the pretty glasses they had brought completed the picturesque picnic setting. But the atmosphere was a little uncomfortable. I must have looked miserable – as if they had wronged me and owed me something. It made them smile at me in a flattering way. Then we heard a car coming and saw the yellow dust clouds rising up from the prairie.

Before long, Deputy County Head Jamba flanked by his team of township officials appeared before us. The expression on Jamba's face was inexplicably grim. The two girls smiled brilliantly at him but could not hide the fear in their eyes.

Ignoring our invitation to sit down, Jamba strolled around the picnic we had spread on the grass. He circled around the three of us with his hands clasped behind his back. The township officials simply watched from a distance with their arms crossed before chests. Seeing the fright on the girls' faces, I began to feel guilty, as if we had stolen something.

Jamba finally opened his mouth. He turned to the township head first and said, "I can tell there is a big problem in your management. Your employees could quit teaching and close the shop and the government would never know it." He shot an ominous look toward the two girls.

Jamba stared at them while they hurriedly wrapped up the picnic things. He spoke to the township head again. "It is your lousy management that has led to this sort of situation."

He walked up to the girls and said, "It is no big deal actually. Just try to work better in the future. I will give you two a vacation day today. This photographer friend of mine hopes to take some pictures of our hot spring. So let him do his job, of course." He smiled at them, seemingly sincere.

"Maybe I'm out of line here, as you may have already finished this job," he said.

The two girls swore that nothing had happened; really, nothing.

"Take the photos after we leave then," Jamba said. "There will be plenty of time in the afternoon."

The two girls shook their heads "no."

The deputy county head smiled kindly. "In fact, nothing is wrong with taking pictures. We could publish the photos and they would be good advertising for us. We have been wanting to develop our tourism resources, haven't we? It's a pity that this is China. If you were in a country like the United States, the nude photos you took in the hot spring could be posted everywhere to use as advertising for our Tsona Hot Spring."

At this ominous suggestion, the two girls fled, too scared to take the food and glasses with them.

Jamba sat down on the grass and helped himself to the abandoned picnic, eating in a lordly manner, full of the same arrogance he displayed when extracting various favors from the work team in the village. Refusing to join him, I peeled off all my clothes and got in the hot spring.

The soft, smooth spring water quickly eased my tension and I sat back in the water. At a hot spring resort called Pine Hut in Ueda City, Japan, I laid down slowly in the spring in much the same way. The small spring was surrounded by carefully arranged stones and a Japanese maple tree. Some branches with early sprouts twisted above me. There was no moon that night, but the dim lamplight through the window had the effect of moonlight. The pool was really small and I could hear women's checked giggling and lively splashing from behind a bamboo screen. Following the example of the bathers, I soaked the small towel provided by the resort and then put it on my head. A tray containing sashimi, sushi, pastries and a small bottle of sake floated before each of the bathers. Though not a strong liquor, the sake lifted everyone's sprits. When I heard the splashing sound from the other side of the bamboo screen again, I asked Mr. Yokogawa, who accompanied us during our visit in Japan, "Are there women bathing on the other side?"

He smiled. Sipping sake from his cup he looked at the screen wall and said, "Those are all older women."

But it seemed to be one of the hot springs that Kawabata Yasunari had bathed at and written about. One of his neat calligraphies, the title of one of his novels, *Waltz of Flowers,* was hung inside the exhibition room of the hot spring resort.

Mr. Yokogawa's answer reminded us of Mr. Kuro Kenji's story of his mixed-sex bathing experience. We all chuckled softly. When everyone fell quiet again, I thought back to my own experience of bathing in the hot spring on the prairie.

While the annoyed deputy county head sat by the hot spring and made a pig of himself, I soaked in the water. The leaders of the township stood there, neither eating nor bathing. They were trying to figure out this strange relationship between their superior and his friend from afar. Therefore, when I asked for a beer, I got it. Soon the warm spring water plus the alcohol relieved my tension. The township leaders were still ruminating. Was all this just about some pictures of girls bathing in the hot spring? Were there even any photos taken?

After his majesty finished eating and drinking, he turned to me and asked, "Have you soaked enough?"

I put my clothes on and everyone started off. The Beijing jeep owned by the township government followed ours. When we got back to town, Jamba told his driver, "Don't stop. Drive back to the county seat."

The driver pushed down on the accelerator and the imported jeep with its flashy features sped up at once. A large cloud of yellow dust behind our wheels soon enshrouded the prairie town. The two prairie girls left their beautiful bodies on my film and some of their hard-to-explain desires in my heart as well. The town government jeep followed us in the dust for awhile before giving up in frustration.

Jamba coughed and said, "The township official must be choking to death."

"That may cure his 'bronchitis' (homophonous to the Chinese phrase meaning 'henpecked' – *ed.*)," the driver replied.

Jamba grew angry. "His working ability is lousy. Think about it. The cadres in his town went on a picnic during work hours."

His mean-spirited words were a challenge that I had to meet. So I opened the door to the conversation he was waiting for.

"Okay, your majesty, I invited two girls to help shoot a few pictures. I don't see how that could offend you so badly."

He just hummed.

I felt bold now. "Are you the king of the prairie and those two girls your concubines?"

"No matter how hard we have tried," he retorted, "stinking writers and artists like you always come here to search for proof of our backwardness."

"Do you call it backwardness when people take off their clothes and bathe in the hot spring?"

"Must the men stay when women bathe?"

As I really had no answer to that strange attack, I looked away and watched the beautiful prairie outside the jeep window. While

I enjoyed the scenery, my ears suffered as if a swarm of flies were buzzing around. The deputy county head kept up his self-righteous lecture until his face glowed with excitement.

I had had enough. "If you don't shut up, I will get out now."

He looked at me with pity. "Do you know, you bastard, that your stinking personality has not changed a bit after all these years?" He sighed. "We are organizing a tourism bureau in my county and I had thought to bring you here to be a director or something for the new office. But who would have imagined that you are still the same old character!" He sighed again. "Your destiny is to put up photos in those dusty old display windows."

"Let me out!" I said again.

"You can get out, but not here. I will let you out once we are back to the county seat. Otherwise, as soon as you get back to the village you will tell the villagers that Jamba bullied you and deserted you on the prairie." He paused for a moment, and then said, "To tell the truth, what do those villagers know? I don't give a damn about what they say about me. They never said anything good about me, but look at me – am I not healthy and happy? I am doing better than any of you!"

Our effort to restore the friendship of our childhood was doomed, and it depressed both of us. But Jamba, who regarded himself as a giver, had a great amount of unresolved anger in his heart, while I was just disappointed in human nature. And another thing, I did not believe that I failed to find inspiration from human nature in other places in the world.

I left the prairie county the next morning and Jamba did not come to say goodbye. As the car sped through the grassland, my good spirits began to return. Instead of feeling upset about missing the opportunity to become the head of the new tourism bureau in

that county, I felt relieved to be able to see the breathtaking landscape of the vast prairie and feel the sensation of riding in a speeding automobile.

I was also eager to go back to my office so I could shut myself
in the darkroom to develop my film. It was dusk when I arrived in
the prefecture seat. It was a Saturday, so the streets were crowded
with people taking evening strolls. I sneaked into the darkroom.
Surrounded by the control panel, the irritating yet refreshing chemi-
cal smell and the low humming of the processor, I saw one after
another photo developed. But my mood was low because the two
girls in the photos were much less attractive when seen through my
lens. Without all the enticing sounds and colors, the glaring sunlight
and the pulsating waves of the hot spring, their images became little
more than unimpressive shapes of flesh.

I tidied up the darkroom and walked out onto the street, feeling
a bit empty. The night wore on. The rows of streetlights stretched
into the distance, giving the short street some perspective. Throaty
singing from two music halls spilled onto the street. The locust trees
were still blooming but the thick fragrance of early blossoms had
already dissolved. When the soft night breeze blew, many withered
petals floated down to the ground. When I got in bed, some petals
that had fallen on me earlier dropped onto my bed.

I laid back and sighed. "Motley Face, you lied! The hot spring
is not as wonderful as you described." I was not sure if I was talking
to him in a dream or when I was still awake.

If it was a dream, why didn't I see him when I was blaming
him for lying? But if it wasn't a dream, I wouldn't have said such ridiculous words, no matter how frustrated I felt.

The two girls in my photos did not look as attractive as the
ones in the photo album; they did not photograph well enough

and my craftsmanship, which couldn't compare with the masters, didn't help. And the hot spring was totally different from Motley Face's description.

I put my hot spring photos in a big envelope and locked them in a drawer of my filing cabinet. Also sealed inside that big envelope were my dreams and youthful memories of the remote hot spring. I added a second lock to that drawer.

It was easy for me to forget Jamba, my childhood friend and to let him forget me. However, he seemed reluctant to leave me alone. When I went to the office the next morning, my colleagues asked me when I would leave for my new job as head of the new tourism bureau in the prairie county. The director of our cultural center even told me I could use our three display windows for a special showing of the photos I had taken on my trip, to use as tourism advertising for the prairie county.

I found it hard to explain the situation to our director.

The director told me our unit was glad to show so much good will about my promotion. And I told him I would not take the job of the tourism bureau director.

He smiled and patted my shoulder. "It's really unfair for a talented guy like you to be stuck here with me. To be honest, I have been meaning to tell my superior that I want to quit and let you take my position. But now, well, forget about that. Hey, I may need *your* help in the future."

His remark made it awkward for me to explain why I didn't want to go. Even worse, I wasn't very interested in being the head of the prefecture culture center, either.

After a few months, I found my colleagues were looking at me with pity and some amusement. After a reorganization of his county government, Jamba became its full county head and the new

tourism bureau was set up under him. A written invitation was issued by his county government to invite our newspaper and TV station reporters to the opening ceremony of the new tourism bureau.
Vehicles were sent over to take the ceremony attendees. Thanks to
our display windows, my cultural center received an invitation. Since
I had refused to serve as director of the new tourism bureau, my
name was excluded from the guest list. A colleague of mine showed
me the list and I saw his name was on it.

"You should go. Your photography skills are better than mine,"
I told him, and I meant it. He indeed took better photos than I did.

Seeing my calm reaction to the whole thing, my colleague
sighed. "I just don't understand what you want."

To tell you the truth, neither did I. Sometimes I seemed to be
as inscrutable as the characters in the novels I wrote. And ever since
the opening ceremony event, I was not considered for any of the
perks and promotions at our center, such as transfers to better units
and prizes and commendations. People seemed to forget I existed.
When I thought about it, what could inspire a man to do a better
job if he was uninterested in the director's position? And all this reminded me of the powerful presence of my childhood friend Jamba.

When he told me about the possibility of getting me that
promotion, he had actually already destroyed my chance of getting it. But he chose to spread the news until everyone around me
knew about it. He lured me in with desirable bait, assuming I was
starved for it. Then once I was on the hook he told me at the last
minute that I almost had the job but had ultimately failed because
I didn't deserve it.

How could I ever explain such a complicated issue to those
around me? I could only pretend to be deaf to everything. If someone tried to bring gossip to my ears, I just glanced at the filing cabi-

net to remind myself of the drawer with two locks. And I would turn a bright smile on the gossiper. When I recalled those two girls, my smile became more dazzling.

When another county sent a similar invitation to our cultural center asking us to photograph their opening ceremony of a newly built hot spring resort, people noted that I had not been on a business trip for at least two years. So the director of our center gave the opportunity to me, not without first taking a vote by applause at a staff meeting.

On our way home after work that day, the director gave me a brief introduction of the county I was to visit. He said the head of that county was one of the two young county heads in our prefecture. The other was my fellow-villager Jamba. Both highly promising and ambitious, the two were rivals in every aspect of their work.

"When your fellow-villager founded that tourism bureau and tried to develop the hot spring in his county, the first young county head chose to work quietly and put together his hot spring resort alone. Your photography could help give his project some good publicity."

His words seemed to hint that I would be able to get my revenge on Jamba. At least, he seemed to believe our display windows had given us great power to do so. But he meant well and so did my colleagues. I did not know what to say.

The new hot spring resort was in a county farther than my native county and a hundred kilometers closer than the prairie spring. Oddly, no one in our village had ever mentioned this hot spring.

The host county sent a cadre from their publicity office to accompany me and a group of reporters to the town. I asked him when his county had discovered their hot spring.

"Discovered it? We just developed it," he said.

"How come no one has heard about it before?"

He became a bit impatient. "Well, you've heard about it now."

Our vehicle made the 100-kilometer trip to the county seat. We were scheduled to stay in the county's guest house for the night. When we set off again early the next morning, we joined a long motorcade of nearly a hundred vehicles headed by a police car. It was September. It had rained the night before in the river valley and snowed on higher places, the flakes glittering and dazzling under the sunlight.

The motorcade rolled slowly through the magnificent landscape for more than ten kilometers before we saw a memorial arch decorated by pine branches before us. Merry music and resounding drumbeats filled the air. Beautiful girls in colorful minority costumes were holding bowls of wine and white khatag by the roadside. Our motorcade stopped and officials stepped up on the rostrum, decorated with a red rug, in front of the memorial arch. After giving speeches, they used scissors to cut the red silk ribbon across the road.

We all entered the shiny new hot spring resort. After another red ribbon hung across the gate was cut, a stream of water gushed from an iron pipe into the swimming pool located in the center of the resort. Water splashed onto the pool bottom, which was lined with ceramic bricks. The unique sulfur smell of a hot spring permeated the air. A new tourist resource had been launched with great success. My camera and many others were help up and shutters were clicking furiously.

By the time the banquet had drawn to an end, the swimming pool was filled up. Many people changed into swimming suits and trunks and jumped into the pool. Because there were so many visitors, only leaders could use the guestrooms that were each equipped with an exclusive spring-water tub. As I hadn't brought a pair of swim trunks and I wasn't qualified to use a guestroom, I gathered together a number of people in a similar situation to walk along the pipeline of spring water that went up the hill. The pipe was buried underground after it entered the woods, but we were able to trace the direction from the newly filled black dirt winding up the slope.

We climbed through the wood full of birch, beech and pine trees, birds singing here and there, and soft, moist moss underfoot. Soon the wind blew a strong sulfur smell our way. After crossing the huge decaying trunk of a spruce tree, we saw the source of the hot spring in a creek valley.

The spring burbled out from beneath a rock that was wedged under a yellow birch, and splashed into a concrete pond. From there, the spring water went through a drain filter before flowing down an iron pipe to the resort downhill. Thick clusters of fallen leaves had accumulated at the filter opening and this helped further sift the dirt particles from the water. Of course, the purpose of our hike was not to see the cement pond but to find the natural source of the spring.

The creek valley where the spring water once flowed was dry. Many moss-covered rocks were scattered between some puddles in the creek bed. Obviously when the spring water flew freely through the creek, these puddles were natural bathtubs for bathers. Although these puddles were cramped compared with those at the prairie hot spring, several bathers could still fit into a single puddle.

After sitting there for some time, our sweat-soaked clothes had grown cold on our backs so we stood up, felt our wet bottoms and took another look around before we walked down. None of us thought to take out a camera to shoot a picture. A hill trail wound down from the spring mouth along the creek bank through the woods. It was easy to follow. After we hiked around two bends in the hill, we came upon a small log cabin. A whiff of blue smoke curled up from the chimney.

Inside, a meat-filled pot cooking above the fire pit filled the room with a delicious smell. There were three people in the cabin. A little girl fed the cooked broth to an old woman whose eyes were covered with a wet towel. An old man sitting next to them smiled vaguely and smoked tobacco. The old woman with her eyes covered smiled in our direction and asked, "Are there newcomers? Are you here to treat your disease too?"

As I appeared to be the only one in our group who could speak the Tibetan language, I responded, "We are here to see the hot spring."

"The hot spring is wonderful," the old woman said. "After washing my eyes for a few more days, I will see again."

She pushed the broth bowl away from her mouth, took off the wet towel over her red, watering eyes and told the girl, "Daughter, make some space for the newcomers. We will have three families here tonight."

Her daughter told her the newcomers were but cadres come to see the scenery of the hot spring. Sounding a little disappointed, the old woman laid down on her makeshift bed on the ground and put the towel back on her eyes.

We left the cabin and saw a rock nearby. Two thin streaks of spring water spilled from the cracks in the center of the rock and gathered in two small hollows, reminding one of two crying eyes. The little girl walked out of the cabin and rinsed her towel with the water on the rock, and then filled a copper jar with fresh spring water. She soaked her towel in the jar and walked back to the cabin.

I saw then how people used the spring water to treat ailments.

Then I heard someone vomiting violently from behind a grove. A few steps farther and we saw another spring mouth and a man bent over, vomiting. A woman who appeared to be his mother held his shoulder with one hand and patted his back with the other. After struggling to vomit, the man straightened up and gasped for air. When he saw us, a weak smile spread over his thin young face.

"I heard it was bustling downhill today," he said.

I nodded and asked him, "What are you trying to treat here?"

"Stomach trouble," his mother answered for him. "When my son was healthy, he could carry a calf around but look at how bony he has become."

Looking extremely frail, the young man managed to speak. "I am here to drink the spring water to wash my stomach. I drink and vomit, drink and vomit until I can get all the impurities out. Once my stomach is cleansed, I will be cured."

Then one of my companions asked insensitively, "Why don't you go to a hospital? If you want to cure your stomach trouble with the water here, you could go and live downhill. Don't you know that the new spring resort has both meals and accommodations?"

What a callous suggestion! Anger rose in me but the pale young man continued to smile and answered simply, "We can do it free here."

Then he bent over to swallow a big gulp of spring water. We turned and walked down the hill. We could still hear him vomiting again behind us. I began to walk faster to get away from that terrible sound.

Because of that sound, I lost my appetite and couldn't eat any of the sumptuous evening banquet. I didn't want to dampen the high spirits of the others so I went outside. A giant billboard listing all the valuable mineral elements in the spring water stood at the resort entrance. It advertised how the spring water could treat rheumatism, skin diseases and have cosmetic effects. I looked toward the woods and remembered the people at the hot spring mouths uphill. They all believed in the omnipotent power of the spring because of the magical influence of their folk legends. And the ad on the billboard beside me was based on information from authoritative medical establishments and the scientific testing they had done. Of course, around here, one would need a lot of money to enter the gates of science.

Part of the opening ceremony began in the resort. After several singing and dancing performances, fireworks streaked high into the sky with sharp hissing sounds and dispersed brilliantly into the night, blocking the light of the stars. The second half of the party was a dance. Attractive actresses were shuttling through one after another leader's arms.

I went out of the resort to take a walk. The night was cool. The stars filled up the sky again and the mountains sank into a solid sleep. I wondered if the people at the hot spring mouths uphill would be able to sleep as soundly as these mountains.

It seems to be a rule that unless you choose not to, once you go to a place, regardless of how far away it is, you seem to make an agreement with it that you will go back again and again. That's what happened to me with the hot spring resort.

Sometimes, we stopped and washed our car in the waterfall splashing down a nearby cliff before we went to bathe in the outdoor swimming pool of the hot spring resort. Since people always had a fine appetite after bathing in the hot spring, I was not surprised to see more and more new restaurants springing up outside the resort. Sometimes, our vehicle sped by the resort. Even a quick glance showed me that one small bungalow after another had mushroomed up around it. In just a few years, a thriving town had developed there. Eventually, the new town even had a new spring water factory. The shops along the roadway there all sold its products.

One day, when I was talking to my companions about the dramatic changes that increased tourism had brought to the remote county, I remembered my childhood friend Jamba and his ambition to open up that attractive spring in his county. The reddish rock cliff and the vast grassland decorated his hot spring so beautifully. They would make that prairie hot spring an even more flourishing tourist hotspot. Since I was taking a documentary film team around as its guide and consultant, I pulled out the map and told the film director that we needed to add a special spot to our itinerary. He asked why.

"To see a hot spring," I said.

"A hot spring?" he looked at me, puzzled.

"Yes, a hot spring," I confirmed.

"Damn it, you want to stop just for a hot spring? Well, you must have a good reason."

I smiled.

The director smiled too. "I know your reasons are generally good."

In fact, I was beginning to realize that about myself, too. As a result, I began to write down my inner feelings – often appearing unreasonable in others' eyes – in my novels. When I had earned a little fame by writing, I stopped shooting or puting up photos for those display windows.

Two days later, the film team was stranded in a nearby county seat. The director stood in the doorway of his hostel room and looked up at the sky with knitted brows, worrying about his travel budget. Bored stiff, I laid on my bed and picked up the phone. I dialed 114, the inquiry number, and got the phone number of the county government offices in the prairie.

I called them. Without mentioning the name of their county head, I said I wanted to ask about their tourism development.

The person on the other end sounded a little nervous. "Who are you?"

I gave him the name of a travel agency and said, "I heard your prairie is very attractive, and your hot spring, too." Sounding relieved, the man gave me a phone number to call, and I dialed it. A pleasant voice answered.

"Hello, this is the tourism bureau of the county."

"I would like to find about the development of your county's tourism resources."

"In which aspect?"

"Oh, how about … your hot spring."

The person on the other end covered the handset. After a long wait, a different voice came on the line, sounding eager. "Could I ask if you are interested in making an investment?" It was Jamba! He sounded very, very excited. "Our Tsona Hot Spring is a great project for investment!"

"Sorry, I am just a tourist and wish to travel to your county."

Not recognizing my voice, Jamba hung up the phone at once. Obviously, this ambitious man was not having a good time these days. The other young deputy county head, who had made a great success in developing their spring resort, was promoted to the head position of the county and had recently been sent on an inspection trip to Italy. Everyone said he would be promoted again after he returned from overseas. However, Jamba remained in the county tourism bureau to wait for investors' calls. Most likely, his buttocks would be glued to a county head's chair forever.

Ten days later, after the vehicles of the film crew drove out of the last canyon, a vast prairie spread out before us.

We hurried to the Tsona Hot Spring that afternoon. The reddish rock cliff towered under the blue sky, a splendid backdrop for the prairie. But when the hot spring came within view, I was shocked beyond words. Everyone on the film team was disheartened as well, because the stunning scenery I had described to them along the way and held tenderly in my heart had vanished. The small lakes linked together by the spring water creek were all gone. The prairie was half dead. The pebbles that were once wrapped in moist gray or reddish moss and caressed by the spring water were dried up and pathetic now.

All that remained were some cement houses scattered over the original site of the hot spring.

Although the houses seemed to be no more than five or six years old, they looked as dilapidated as 50-year-old homes. Large pieces of plaster fell off their exterior walls. Weeds stuck out from the front steps. Cracked wooden doors tilted this way or that. Inside, the rooms were narrow and the wooden benches built against the walls had begun to rot. A cement pool dug into the ground occupied most of the space and the rough walls of the cement bath pool had cracked off. Rotten; it seemed as if everything around us was rotten. Even the air had an odor of decay. Rusty water leaking from shabby pipes had killed off the grass outside and turned the whole place into a big muddy swamp.

Walking farther up, the source of the hot spring was now hidden behind a high circular wall. A set of stone steps was built at its entrance. It turned out that the developers had constructed an outdoor swimming pool on top of the spring source. A grandstand was built around the pool. The cinematographer in our team put down the camera on his shoulder. Mumbling angrily, he sat down on the cement stand.

Everyone on the film crew cursed the place.

A bathhouse in ancient Rome abruptly came to mind. But the bathing pool encircled by a grand spectator stand in front of us featured neither attractive marble nor delicate sculptures, just a cracked cement floor. I wondered if it was the builder who had had the nerve to construct such an ugly, formless structure. After a sad laugh, I sat down on the cement stand, too.

The film director handed me a cigarette and asked indignantly, "Didn't you say this place was the most marvelous spot of all? Where are the strings of pearls on the grassland? Where are the beautiful bathing girls? Damn it! Look at this place!" With a willow stick, he lifted up a dirty pair of pants someone had discarded in the mud, and then walked to the side of the pool to poke at the grease and hair clinging to the pool wall. This would have decomposed shortly among the grass, soil and pebbles thanks to the rich chemicals in the soil at the former spring site. However, the chemicals would not survive in a cement enclosure, so the grease and hair would be preserved there for eternity.

An even more puzzling phenomenon was that there was not a single maintenance person around to keep up such an expensive site. Alone, this manmade monster was decaying amid a powerful sulfur smell. I had heard about things decaying quickly in the world, but I had never thought I would see it here with my own eyes.

I recalled how Kunpal Sigya had described this hot spring as a paradise. If he had seen the horrible scene before me now, what expression would appear on that motley face? Fortunately, he would never know. He had bemoaned back then that people were nailed to their tiny spaces and lost the freedom to roam, and that they would forget the hot spring. Sadly, he had been right. But he never would have imagined that Jamba would become a county head, not to mention that County Head Jamba would want to make money from the hot spring but would end up destroying it.

We sat on the grassy slope by the deserted spring resort, too depressed to speak. Then, we saw two passersby at the foot of the hill. A small lake had formed in the bushes down the valley, where the spring water flowed through the cement construction and then a temporary bridge. The two passersby paused, took off their clothes and jumped in the small lake to take a bath. From our secluded position a far distance away, we could see a man and a woman. We all stretched our necks, hoping something interesting might occur. But nothing happened. The man and the woman bathed, got out of the water and put on their clothes. They picked up their bags and left, with the characteristic bowlegged steps of prairie herdsmen.

I ran downhill and stood by the small lake. I felt the water temperature with my hand; the heat of the spring water was basically gone. But the lush grass and especially the clumps of small leaf cuckoo flowers adorned the small lake most pleasantly. So we settled down at the bank and our photographer turned on his camera. Suddenly the sharp shriek of a car braking sounded from the roadway above and a large cloud of dust swept toward us. After the dust passed, a group of people appeared on the roadway and ordered us to come over and answer their questions.

We did.

The interrogators were from the government of that township. In a menacing way, they asked who had allowed us to collect news in their area. I told them we were there to shoot a documentary film, not to collect news. They said they did not see any difference between the two. In fact, they prohibited any filming of their hot spring.

There was nothing glorious about turning such a scenic site into that terrible mess. I told them with some irritation that our intent was only to photograph some beautiful scenes. Why would we want to shoot such ugly sights for our film?

"Why are you here then? And why have you stayed for around for two or three hours?"

I said I had been there before. It had been a beautiful site in my and many others' memory. The reason why I could stay there for two to three hours was that I was devastated to see how such a pretty site could be so completely ruined! And the last time I was there, I had been invited by County Head Jamba.

One guy in the group recognized me. "Yeah, right. You and two girls. That's right! Okay, go to our township office please. We will notify County Head Jamba about your visit. He may choose to see you. You and he are fellow villagers, aren't you? "

They arranged for us to stay at the government guesthouse in town and treated us to a sumptuous meal. But everyone around us seemed to be on their guard. I smiled to the town head at the dinner table and asked him, "I feel as if we are under house arrest."

He just smiled and said nothing.

I could no longer control myself, so I asked him how they had managed to mess up their hot spring so badly. He thought for a moment, took a big gulp of liquor and said, "You'd have to ask your fellow villager. He will be here soon. But you'd better not touch on that topic. The hot spring is an open wound for him. Heaven only knows when he will recover from it."

Later, when we were out for a walk on the street, the town head sighed and spoke again. "I am here to take the blame for someone else. Seeing the hot spring has been ruined like that, the locals are cursing me up one side and down the other."

I asked him if Jamba was in charge of the construction of the hot spring.

"Who else? He set up the tourism bureau in the county single-handedly and this is the first and most important project of that new bureau."

"But that doesn't give them right to turn the hot spring into a disaster!"

The town head said gloomily, "The county has invested a lot of money in the place and our township threw in all of our savings, too. But the result has been that no one comes to the resort now, neither tourists nor the local people. Once it turned into such an eyesore, no one wanted to put money into it again. I heard with my own ears an investor claim that neither County Head Jamba nor his subordinates are able to manage this project properly."

As I had no way to figure out who was at fault in all of this, I asked about the two girls I had met there last time.

The town head said, "All gone. That teacher ran off without a word. I hear she is in Shenzhen now, singing and dancing at a folk culture village there. The girl in the supply and marketing cooperative quit her job and left with a medicinal herb salesman, who is doing business somewhere now." He smiled, somewhat embarrassed. "You see, no one wants to stay here if we are unable to produce any significant development."

It didn't seem to be the purpose of my trip there to hear his elaboration. We passed the veterinary station and saw two vets busy in the courtyard. One was grinding herbs using an iron roller and the other was boiling cypress bark in a pressure cooker. People said a Buddhist monk who was an expert in traditional medicine here had developed several effective medicines for livestock. When I asked them about the monk and his medicines, they said they were preparing medicine based on the monk's prescription. I sat down and listened to them tell me which herbs were used in the various concoctions. When they cited a particular medicinal herb, that plant with its blossom and seeds would appear in my mind. One of the herbs they named was "gentian" and I could visualize it, swaying with its blue flowers.

While we were chatting, someone came in to tell the town head that County Head Jamba had just arrived from county seat, and so the town head left in a hurry. Feeling no need to follow suit, I stayed in the veterinary courtyard and continued my conversation with the two vets, who also appeared indifferent to the departure of their town head. They brought out a big volume of pharmacopoeia they had written themselves. The pharmacopoeia was hand-written on the heavy paper used by temple monks to copy religious transcriptions. The vets had illustrated every prescription in the book and clamped herbal specimens to some of the pages. They told me the prescriptions were left by that great monk master. One of his last wishes, they said, was to build a modern plant of veterinary medicine. But no one in their county government cared to help them. A number of businesses had offered to buy their pharmacopoeia at a high price. I thumbed through the huge volume. The herbal specimens clamped to its pages gave out the scent of plants.

A resounding laugh could be heard in the courtyard of the veterinary station. If that laughter had occurred on a theatre stage, it would have signaled that an important figure was about to make an entrance. Sure enough, the broad figure of County Head Jamba with a felt overcoat hanging from his shoulders emerged in the narrow doorway of the courtyard. He stood there laughing, braving our silent, cold stares for quite a while. He finally stepped in and shook hands with the two vets, who stood up to greet him.

After shaking hands with Jamba, the two vets stood aside, at a loss for what to do next. Just then the pressure cooker began to shriek like a steam whistle as its internal pressure reached the preset level. The two vets seized the opportunity to excuse themselves and returned to their work. Jamba grasped my hand. "So, you have come here without registering with your fellow villager? Are you worried I will not provide you with meals?"

His behavior surprised me. I had assumed that he would feel a bit ashamed by the ruination of the hot spring, but he didn't show any trace of discomfort. The town head, who had been displeased with Jamba a minute before, followed Jamba with a broad smile now. Before I had time to respond, Jamba turned around and asked the town head, "Did you mistreat my old buddy?"

"We took good care of everything, everything," the town head said quickly.

"Your town head is faithful to his duty, keeping a close watch over the hot spring so that no one will ever bother it."

Jamba patted my shoulder. "My good fellow villager, you have no idea how hard it is to manage a county. We did make some investment in our hot spring project, but as I often said, being an official heading a county government, I must not limit our vision to such small issues only."

He jiggled his shoulders to keep his overcoat from falling off his back. When he spoke again, his tone slid back to that of an official giving a report at an important meeting.

"Have you seen the bathing rooms we built with the very limited budget? It is true that we are short of our anticipated target economically, but, the way we separate the men's and women's bathing rooms signified a remarkable transformation of the old backward custom. Therefore, we must realize the huge impact we have made on reforming our old habits. Many of our comrades have set their sights on the economic side only, turning a blind eye to the significance of our reforming effort and its great effect on our construction of ideological civilization. Furthermore, if we regard things with a far-reaching perspective, we will see that to reform the backward life style is also to improve our environment for investment. We will definitely get the investment needed for our development!"

I had meant to say something consoling about the hot spring or our shared dream for the spring in our teenage years. But after listening to him speak in that formal tone, I didn't bother to open my mouth. I was not a government official, but to quote a fashionable saying, I was inside the system, and it was pretty normal for me to see such exaggerating, lying officials at high or low ranks. So I wasn't too surprised by his behavior that day. But because of the hot spring and our shared boyhood in the village, I wished he would show at least some sign of sadness or regret.

A glow lit up his gloomy face as he turned his back on me and started to lecture his subordinates in the township government. His eyes glittered and his tone turned passionate.

"No, our hot spring project is not as successful as we had expected because of some obstacles in our path, such as the budget shortage and the challenging custom of local peasants and herdsmen. However, these are minor problems. The primary obstacle is conservative thought. Now that our reform and opening-up policy has been in place all these years, and the hot spring was lying there all these years, why did no one ever think of taking action to develop it before? No one even made a suggestion! That was why I decided to do it. Well, soon the investigator arrived. Then gossip and rumors started. Many did not vote for me at the county head election. But why has no one ever considered the positive significance of our spring project?"

Jamba seemed to cheer up his cadres with his confident speech, a bravura performance based on his years in the vanity fair of officialdom. From that moment on, this county head defeated by his disastrous hot spring project would parade himself as a daring pioneer of reform, a tragic martyr willing to risk his life in a fatal minefield.

I could no longer bear his nonsense. I was there to see the remote hot spring – my symbol for freedom and the romantic ideal of my teenage years. After traversing considerable time and distance, I had gone there to see the heavenly landscape of my imagination. However, the hot spring in my dreams had been obliterated by the man who had shared my dream for the Tsona Hot Spring. And all because of his unspeakable ambition.

With the barbaric, ugly cement blocks and decaying wood, he had destroyed everything.

I left those officials as well as my companions to drive to the reddish rock cliff for another look at the hot spring. The sun was sliding behind the mountains. The temperature dropped rapidly, stirring up a sudden whirlwind, swirling the dust on the dirt road and throwing it onto the thoroughly defaced, lifeless hot spring.

If Motley Face had been alive to see what had become of the hot spring and what that shepherd boy Jamba had become, he would have been shocked beyond words. He would not have understood how a person could so easily lose his natural admiration for the beauty of nature. How could any normal person with a reasonable perspective pile up all those cement blocks and ugly decaying wood to suffocate the pretty Tsona Hot Spring, the unforgettable Tsona Hot Spring that had seen so many prosperous days?

Fortunately, common sense consoled me that the spring water would never decay. After everything that was corrodible fell apart and eventually disappeared from the earth, the spring water would bubble up from the ground again and again, fueled by its thermal energy. It would take an extremely long time and be out of the control of us short-lived humans, who never give up our pathetic desire to leave our mark on this world.

At the thermal spring in my home village, Motley Face Kunpal Sigya gave us a yearning for beautiful things, an aspiration for lovely landscapes, and the romantic imagination to appreciate a bygone way of life. Exactly because we could not walk freely on the earth at the time, our deepest desire was to be able to roam around unchained. When that right was returned to us, the desire transcended into a poetic longing for happier times past.

Perhaps Jamba had seen through the unrealistic nature of those aspirations. That was why he destroyed the very source of all those sentimental dreams with his own hands.

I sat down and watched the decadent scene before me. In a daze, I felt I was looking at the wild chokecherry blossoms at the thermal spring by my village, and at Motley Face Kunpal Sigya, now just a chalky skull wedged into a tree branch. And I was no longer that naive schoolboy but had grown into a dissolute man roaming with Motley Face to many places under the sun. He was asking me to tell him what happened to the hot spring after his death. I heard myself say, "Buddy, there is nothing now. Jamba has destroyed it with his own hands."

He did not push me for a reason, but I knew my words saddened him.

His empty skull could not shut its eyes. So his sadness would deepen and for a moment, the sky would grow dim. Then the skull

I had placed on the tree branch dropped to the ground and shattered into dust, from which a wisp of ash rose, like a long sigh.

(*Translated by Ji Hua & Gao Wenxing*)

Girl, Wife,
Daughter-in-Law

Ma Jinlian

Ma Jinlian was born in May 1982 to a Hui family in Xiji, Ningxia and graduated from Guyuan Teachers Training School in 2003. Ma began writing in 2000 and mainly writes short stories. Many of her works have been selected for literary journals such as *Hui Literature*, *Yellow River Literature*, *Shuo Fang* (The North), *October* and *Prose and Poetry*. Some of her works included in *Fiction Monthly* and *Selected Stories*. Among her representative works are *The Lamp-Holding Woman*, *The Spring Breeze*, *Father's Snow*, *Glutinous Millet* and *The Farming Season Again*. She also has stories included in fiction collections: *Flowers Blossom in June* and *The Ink Marker* were both in *Selected Works of Ningxia Writers*, and *The New Wife* in *Short Stories of 2008* published by Lijiang Publishing House. Ma is a member of the Ningxia Writers' Association and one of the first commissioned writers of *Yellow River Literature*. She is also a member of the Ninth Chinese People's Political Consultative Committee of Xiji County and works at the county's Xinglong Town government.

Girl, Wife,
Daughter-in-Law

As she calculated the days, Snowflake knew that it was time to give her room a thorough cleaning.

She set to work as soon as breakfast was over. Her room was not large and there were not many pieces of furniture in it, but it was going to be a big challenge. In the past, it would take no more than half a day to clean the room and tidy things up. It was more difficult now. Heavy and clumsy in her present condition, she had lost her usual dexterity. Push herself as she might, she just couldn't move any quicker. According to her plan, she was going to unpick the cotton lining of the quilts and mattresses and wash their outer cases, as well as the pillowcases and bed sheets. She would take down the curtains and the door drape and wash them too, along with the TV cover. It was better to wash everything now, she thought, for it would be at least a month before she could do any more washing, and one could imagine how dirty things would get over such a long period. After she had gathered everything she saw that the washtub was piled with laundry. It looked like the washing was going to take the whole day.

The next day, she started to clean the *kang*, the heated earthen bed. First she removed all the bedding and then she rolled up the reed mats, exposing the adobe bricks beneath. She carefully swept them with a brush. It was surprising to find them covered with such a thick film of dust, which, when stirred up, irritated her nose and throat and made her cough. She clearly remembered her last sweeping not very long ago. How could dust have accumulated so fast? Where did it all come from? When did it slip under the reed mats and gather into such a dense layer? As she swept into the corners, the memory of her first day with this family rushed back to her.

It was on her wedding day that she saw her husband's home for the first time. Cheered on by the guests, her husband lifted her to his shoulders and carried her through the gate, into the bridal chamber and onto the *kang,* where he lowered her down into the far corner. The first thing she noticed was a pin-up of a woman smiling at her with bright red lips. Without even thinking, she reached out and tore up the picture. Her married girlfriends told her that stuck in the corner of the *kang* there should be a square piece of paper bearing the character of "happiness" in red ink. According to custom, the bride should grab the character and quickly tear it up before the bridegroom could get it, because it was commonly believed that the spouse who got the larger part of the character would get the upper hand in domestic life.

Snowflake had kept that tip in mind, but instead of the character of "happiness" she found the picture of the woman. Her husband's family must be awfully careless, she thought, or how else could they have made such a slip? Nevertheless, she tore the seductive photo into pieces, then sat quietly in the corner of the *kang*. In the past, the bride traditionally had to remain in the corner, but nowadays this was not strictly observed, especially not by girls who had been to school and had worked in big cities. Since they had seen the world, they were more knowledgeable about life and did not like to remain in the corner of the *kang*. As they saw it, women didn't need to be bound to their *kang* all their lives; this would be tantamount to tying themselves down at the feet of their men and children. To demonstrate their independence, many brides instead sat on the edge of the *kang*, or even got down from the *kang* and sat on the sofa, disregarding the notion that brides should act coy. But Snowflake stayed in the corner.

Snowflake had attended school for a couple of years, but she dropped out before the end of the third year and started to work in the fields. She had also worked in the city. A cousin had taken her to a city in Xinjiang Uygur Autonomous Region, where she found a dishwashing job at a restaurant. She came home after several months and never set foot out of her hometown again. She had the impression that the outside world wasn't as big as she had imagined, and nothing there was especially appealing. She couldn't erase the memory of the greasy smell of dirty dishes that could never be washed clean. City life wasn't as wonderful and colorful as others had made it out to be. She couldn't understand why those girls who had worked in the cities tended to dress up in a glamorous fashion, and why even the way they spoke and walked changed dramatically. Even the young ones liked to flirt with men.

Snowflake was more traditional. She didn't like the work that left her tired all the time and made her so sleepy that her head seemed heavier than her feet. After returning from Xinjiang, the scenery of her homeland looked more attractive and beautiful to

her. She sometimes wondered why she had never noticed her sur-
roundings before. In summertime, the land is covered with the lush
green of crops or grass. Their drinking water came from a bubbling
clean spring. Every day she walked to the spring at the bottom of
the vale, with two pails dangling on a shoulder-pole, along the path
cut in the yellow earth rubbed to a shine by thousands of feet. The
shimmering surface of the water reflected the dazzling blue sky and
the cottony clouds. The reflection of her face in the water made
her feel clean and cool. Often she drank a big ladle of the fresh
water, which sent a refreshing chill through her body. Where could
you get such sweet water in the cities? The tap water there had an
ambiguous and inexplicable taste.

One day when she was carrying water home, she found a
matchmaker sitting on their *kang*. Her mother beckoned her aside to
have her opinion. "It's a son of Ma Shouyuan," Mother whispered in
her ears. "Your grandpa has long heard of that family. They're solidly
established and quite well-off. The young man himself is said to be
handsome. Married into such a family always means an easy life."

Her mother's delight was clearly written on her face, as if
the proposal had been accepted already. Snowflake felt faint and
her cheeks were burning. She held tightly to the shoulder-pole for
support. Up to that moment, she had never realized that marriage
would be an urgent issue for her to consider. Her hand slipped to
the middle of the shoulder-pole. It was still warm from her body,
and she had a pain in her back where the pole had pressed into her
skin. When she first learned how to adjust two pails on a shoulder-
pole, she had barely stood as tall as an adult's shoulder. And now
she was grown up. How time flies, she thought.

The pleasure on her mother's face affected Snowflake. She
felt happy, too. But happy about what? She didn't know. At the

same time she felt a twinge of sadness, just a tiny bit of unnamable sadness, tearing at her heart. What was it? She couldn't tell.

Shortly after that, the matchmaker arranged for her to meet her future husband for the first time. In fact, they got no more than a glimpse of each other. The man was of medium height. He had a round face, a face that looked honest and candid. Though she didn't dare stare, his honest looks reassured her and she nodded her agreement. The days rushed by and soon it was winter. After the first dusting of snow she was married and became a member of the Ma family.

Her retrospection did not interrupt her work this day. She swept the *kang* carefully, stroke after stroke. She understood that this kind of cleaning should be done without attracting too much attention. So she closed the door before she started. She cleaned the room section by section. The *kang* was the most difficult place to clean. She had wrapped up the newer quilts and mattresses and would store them on the top of the clothes cabinet until the first month after her pregnancy. For now, she would leave only a couple of worn blankets on the *kang*. She briskly swept the four corners, leaving not a speck of dust behind. As she watched the dust rise up into the air and float there a while before it slowly dropped to the floor, a thought also floated up in her mind. At first it was vague, but it gradually took shape. With a mixture of self-pity, she saw herself as a heroine in a tragedy.

Her sister-in-law, the wife of her husband's elder brother, was calling out for her children in the courtyard. Sometimes loud, sometimes soft, her voice gradually moved closer and then stopped outside Snowflake's window. Sister-in-law was probably peering in through the panes. Snowflake lowered her head and continued her work, pretending not to notice. It was Sister-in-law who had told her that a thorough cleaning was necessary before childbirth. Of course she didn't say that directly to Snowflake's face; Snowflake figured it out through their daily chitchat, for Sister-in-law liked to talk about the most intimate details of her two deliveries. She told of how she suffered from morning sickness and nearly vomited to death, how she gave birth, and how she washed and fed the children and brought them up. It was her conclusion that it wasn't easy to be a woman, and she had endured much hardship. There, too, was a hint of complaint in her chattering that her mother-in-law didn't treat her well. When the daughter-in-law was suffering so much for the family, shouldn't the mother-in-law take on some of the responsibilities? She certainly should; in fact, she should shoulder most of the responsibility! As Sister-in-law talked and sighed, Snowflake listened and stored up many useful tips. Sister-in-law had been married for several years and had lived much longer under the same roof with Mother-in-law. So she understood and knew how to cope with the complicated relationships in the family. These valuable bits of wisdom and experience were exactly what Snowflake lacked.

When she first became a member of the Ma family, Snowflake was nearly scared away by their many do's and don'ts. Her husband's family was a big one: a total of ten people lived together, for the married elder brother did not live separately. This was quite different from Snowflake's maiden home, where she was the only daughter and pampered by her parents. Once she married into the Ma family, she felt like an undomesticated animal suddenly put into a bridle. She couldn't say or do anything without first considering the consequences and what others would think. She was afraid that others might laugh at her, afraid that she might innocently offend her parents-in-law, and afraid of many other things. She often regretted that she had married so early, but she couldn't share this with anyone. She had to store it in her heart and wipe it off her face. Never, never should she mention this to any member of the Ma family, especially not to Sister-in-law, who not only had a sharp tongue but was also smart and shrewd.

Snowflake rose out of bed very early on the second day after her wedding, for she knew that a new bride was expected to get up early and do the housework. She should show the countless pairs of watching eyes, both inside and outside the family, that she was a diligent and competent wife. The first thing she did was to go to the main house to pay her respects to the elders. Then she returned to her room to wash herself and comb her hair. After cleaning up her own room, she went over to clean her mother-in-law's. Then she donned the apron she had brought from home and went to the kitchen, where she found a woman was already busying about. The woman didn't speak when she entered, just looked her over from head to toe, and then from toe to head. The staring made Snowflake uncomfortable, as if numerous caterpillars were crawling all over her back. How could one person greet another this way? She was offended, and yet the woman seemed even more offended despite the slight twinkle in her eyes. After a moment the woman turned aside and snorted. Snowflake was bewildered, for she couldn't understand how she could have offended this narrow-faced woman at first sight.

It was only later that she learned the woman was her new sister-in-law, the *de facto* domestic mistress of the house. Since her mother-in-law was old and seldom came to the kitchen anymore, responsibility for the kitchen fell to Sister-in-law. The work entailed preparing not only the family's three daily meals but also tending to its everyday affairs. As time went by, Snowflake came to see why Sister-in-law had behaved like that on the first day; her standoffishness was intended to demonstrate her position and power in the family.

Gradually, Snowflake learned how to put up with it, learned to restrain herself and be careful with everything she did or said. Sister-in-law had been ordered around by Mother-in-law for years and so it seemed she deserved this hard-earned opportunity to order others around. Only then did Snowflake realize why the young wives so often demand to live separately from their parents-in-law. In fact, Snowflake had also thought of living independently, but she didn't dare to be outspoken on the matter with her husband. Beating around the bush, she learned that it was impossible to do this in the foreseeable future, for the family hadn't yet paid off the debt they had contracted from their eldest son's marriage, and they had run deeper into debt when they borrowed for the marriage of their second son, her husband. Her parents-in-law had four sons and it wasn't an exaggeration to say that due to the two weddings, the family's savings had been "licked clean by the dog." Their third and fourth sons left home to find work in cities. They were both of marrying age.

Her father-in-law was an easygoing man, but her mother-in-law was a shrewd housekeeper. Her sons were submissive around her, out of both fear and respect. She had made it clear that the big family could not split up before all its debts were paid and enough was saved for each of the two younger sons to get a wife. As the sons were all obedient boys, they dropped everything and went dutifully to the cities to make money. Since the two younger sons were not married, it was no problem for them to leave home, but with wives and children it was obviously more difficult for the two elder sons to go. Added to that, Snowflake and her husband were still on their honeymoon.

Although Snowflake was reluctant to let her man leave, she didn't dare utter a word of objection, and managed to put on a happy face in front of her mother-in-law. Sister-in-law also found this separation hard to bear. As she couldn't reveal her displeasure to her parents-in-law, she focused her anger instead on the kitchen utensils, knocking them around when she was cooking as a way to vent her feelings.

By and by, it became clear to Snowflake that even before she was married into the Ma family, Sister-in-law had laid out her plans and Snowflake had walked unsuspectingly into her trap. Snowflake had a docile character and spoke softly, treating everyone as she did at her maiden home. She didn't know how to manipulate people. But Sister-in-law was different. When she spoke to you, you didn't realize she had ulterior motives. If you were observant, you would notice there was often a catch in your dealings with her.

Mother-in-law knew this, and from time to time she gave Snowflake advice behind Sister-in-law's back. For example, she told Snowflake that one could not afford to be too simple and trusting. Snowflake knew what that meant, but she didn't know how to change. To be artful and calculating was quite beyond her.

As a result, the responsibility of preparing the three daily meals for a family of a dozen mouths was placed on Snowflake's shoulders. Her life seemed tied to the kitchen. She was always there, attending to the stove, kneading dough, and washing up the pots and pans. In all but name she had become Sister-in-law's maid.

Luckily Sister-in-law's shrewdness wasn't bullet-proof, for she had one fatal weakness: she talked too much, as if she had a bellyful of complaints. Nothing could be done to her satisfaction and she had the habit of grumbling. And as everyone knew, the more you say the more vulnerable you become, for a slip of the tongue may let out the most carefully guarded secret. As Snowflake was a good listener, little by little she learned many things about her husband's family, and also learned what it took to be considered a good daughter-in-law.

Sister-in-law once mentioned that many women liked to show off their pregnancy by pretending to be sick in front of others, and in her opinion that showed a lack of shame. So Snowflake figured that even if one was suffering from morning sickness, one should hide it from others and certainly not throw up in public. Actually, Snowflake hadn't suffered any morning sickness. She didn't even notice she was pregnant until she felt a tightness around her waist. Without telling anyone, she and her husband went to the clinic, and she was happily surprised when the doctor told her she was in the family way and should not be alarmed if she noticed a growing appetite.

Yet despite her happiness, she was worried. Why didn't she have any morning sickness? Mother-in-law had talked about Sister-in-law's strong pregnancy reactions and said that Sister-in-law had made it a point to throw up in front of the family. She would squat in the courtyard and vomit even though she had nothing to throw up. For a fortnight she was unable to cook for the family. She vowed that she had no appetite and would spew up whatever she ate except for eggs, which she could take without getting sick. Therefore she ate two eggs a day.

It was obvious from Mother-in-law's tone that she didn't like this turn of events. In her opinion Sister-in-law's behavior was nothing but attention-seeking. Wasn't it natural for women to give birth? And morning sickness was nothing unusual. Her conclusion was that Sister-in-law was pampering herself. Therefore Snowflake had made up her mind that when she felt like vomiting she would hide from others, and she certainly would keep her food preferences to herself. But three months into her pregnancy, she still had not gotten sick. By the fourth month her belly became too conspicuous to conceal and Sister-in-law's sharp eyes didn't fail to notice the signs, though she didn't say anything. By feigning ignorance, she could still be picky about doing kitchen work. During all that time, Snowflake did most of the heavier jobs, as usual.

Sister-in-law said that as a rule, if it's a boy in the womb the mother would have a craving for sour food, and if it's a girl the mother would prefer spicy food. So she asked Snowflake about her preference. The question gave Snowflake a start. She preferred spicy food, and her mouth watered at the very thought of it. But rather than answering, she put the question back to Sister-in-law. What, she asked, did you prefer when you were pregnant?

She loved sour things, Sister-in-law replied. Even in the depth of winter she had a craving for green apricots. She swallowed hard as she spoke, as if she tasted the sourness in her mouth. Snowflake also swallowed hard, her heart aflutter with anxiety. Sister-in-law had been pregnant twice and both times had given birth to boys. Because there was a strict family planning policy that each couple could have no more than two children, Sister-in-law was considered a fortunate woman to have two sons. Compared to those women who gave birth to one or even two girls, she was a big winner and enjoyed a great social advantage. Her smugness was palpable in her talk and actions, which only made Snowflake feel all the more humble. Comparing her pregnancy with Sister-in-law's, she just knew that the child in her belly was a girl. And yet she didn't dare tell anyone. This made her miss her husband more than ever. If he were home, she wouldn't feel so lonely.

Having swept the *kang* clean, she sat down and leaned back against the pile of folded quilts to rest. As her eyes fell on the full dustbin, she wondered how there could be so much dust. At the same time the uneasiness in her heart was relieved by her work well done. She had washed everything that needed to be washed, the ashes in the stove chamber were removed yesterday, and now the room was clean. So in the days that followed all she had to do was wait for the baby to come. Suddenly it occurred to her that she should give herself a wash, too. Although it hadn't been long since her last bath, she decided to take another one. Only when she had washed herself clean could she rest easy, for to a woman, giving birth is no less than venturing through the gate of hell, or, more figuratively, attempting to ride a horse along the slim edge of a water vat.

Before one gives birth, one should sweep clean the *kang* and take a bath, she reminded herself. That was what she had learned from Sister-in-law's endless ridicule of other women. Snowflake had come to understand that a virtuous and diligent woman should get everything in order before she gave birth, just in case the worst should happen. Should she fail to catch her breath and give in to the fickleness of life, her *kang*, her bedding and everything about her, everything she had done and everywhere she had been, would be placed under the scrutinizing gaze of everyone. Her neighbors and relatives – both her husband's and those from her maiden home – who would come to her funeral would see what kind of woman she had been when she was alive.

As she thought of that, a feeling of sadness grew in her heart and tears gleamed in her eyes. People say life is hard for women. There was truth in this. Indeed life was hard for women: giving birth to a child was just like betting with your own life. Men bet with money; women can only bet with their lives. Such thoughts could bring bad luck so she tried to shake them off. She was still young, in the prime of life, she reasoned. But once such thoughts had occurred, they seemed to get out of control, like a smoldering fire that had burst into flames. She caught herself yearning for her maiden home, for the little courtyard surrounded by earthen walls, the limpid spring at the bottom of the vale and the meandering steps that lead down to it, her mother, and her last visit home when she was six months pregnant.

Recently she had felt heavier by the day. Although she had been thinking of going home to see her parents once more, her clumsiness prevented her from walking that far. It would be easier if her husband were home, for he could give her a ride on his motorcycle. She realized that she was thinking of someone other than her parents. Her husband had been away for ninety-four days at a construction site in the county seat. He had called home several times, but it was always her parents-in-law who picked up the phone.

She went into labor the day after she swept the *kang*. Although the quilt cases and bedding she had been washing were not thoroughly dry, she managed to carry them in. The pain in her belly intensified every moment as if a knife were making sharp cuts into her. Sister-in-law had made it clear that a woman shouldn't holler as soon as she felt labor pains. That would throw the whole family into panic and everyone would be worried and flustered, but no one would be able to do anything to help. Rather than embarrassing and worrying others, it would be better to keep the pain to herself until the baby came. Then she could call others for help.

The labor pains started around midnight when Snowflake got up to go to the toilet. At first it was a dull pain, which she was able to endure. She curled into a ball and fell into an uneasy sleep. At daybreak she got up to add some dried cow dung into the *kang* stoves in her room and her mother-in-law's. Then she swept the doorstep and went into the kitchen to prepare the family's breakfast with Sister-in-law. They were having steamed buns and rice gruel.

While others were loudly slurping the gruel, the cramps in her middle made her suck her teeth in pain. She couldn't swallow any food and lost her appetite. By noon, she couldn't even walk. She shut herself in her room and sat on the floor, not daring to move.

How nice it would be if her husband were home. Although her dark-faced man didn't have any great capabilities, his presence would be a comfort, and at least he could let his mother know about her condition. But damn him! Once he got away from home he forgot all about her. When they first found out she was pregnant, he said excitedly that they would go to the county hospital to have their first-born delivered, like those people who have money, and it all would be fast and painless. Snowflake only smiled at his idea. She said that it was unnecessary to go to the county hospital. An obstetric nurse from the district clinic would be good enough and this would save a bundle of money.

Deep in her heart, however, she felt a fear which she couldn't put into words. What if it was a girl? What would people think? No doubt they would laugh at her. How could she travel that far and spend so much money just to have a girl delivered? Had she mistaken herself for a queen? Such ridicule was not new to her, for she had heard Sister-in-law ridiculing a woman from a neighboring village. It was the woman's first birth and she had had trouble. Her family took her to the county hospital and spent a thousand *yuan* just to get a baby girl! Even Mother-in-law considered that absurd.

Since Snowflake knew Mother-in-law's opinion of such matters, she could see how unrealistic her husband's idea was. Sister-in-law was rather keen on matters of appearances, and yet she gave birth to both her children at home, with Mother-in-law serving as the midwife. If that was good enough for Sister-in-law, Snowflake couldn't hope for anything better.

There was one thing that worried Snowflake now: the baby's clothes were not prepared. She had been spoiled as a girl and had never learned how to do needlework. And now that this was her first child, she had no idea how to make or where to get the small baby clothes. She thought of asking Sister-in-law, but she was afraid that rather than getting help she would only receive scorn and mocking. In that dilemma she remembered a story she overheard Sister-in-law tell some neighbors. They were joking about a young mother in the village who had prepared a stack of small clothes, including diapers, for her firstborn. When she took them out after the baby was born, her mother-in-law's face clouded over and she commented sarcastically that she had a smart daughter-in-law, smarter than she herself who had given birth to a number of children. The prepared baby clothes only proved how old and useless she must be.

Snowflake thought about this and decided to sit and wait, as if she had no idea that the baby would need small clothes. But as far as she could recall, she had never seen Mother-in-law pick up a needle to do the sewing. She couldn't help getting worried and had intended to ask many times. After all, it was her baby. If Mother-in-law hadn't made any preparations, what would the baby wear and what would she wrap the baby with? This sort of negligence sometimes happens when one woman is expecting the other to do a job.

Nevertheless, at the onset of her labor pains she was surprised to see Mother-in-law hurry over with an armful of clothes. As Mother-in-law laid them out on the *kang* one by one, Snowflake saw that everything she needed was there: tops, pants, quilts, diapers, and even the gauze to tie up the umbilical cord. Surprised by Mother-in-law's quiet efficiency, Snowflake momentarily forgot about the worsening cramps.

It's a girl, she heard Mother-in-law say in an even voice that reflected neither delight nor disappointment. Snowflake felt her head growing heavy. So, it was a girl. Although she tried to persuade herself that boys and girls are the same and no matter which, the child was a part of her, Mother-in-law's unenthusiastic voice gave her a chill, a heart-freezing chill as if she were sitting in cold water and the coldness was seeping in and spreading through her body. Sister-in-law dashed in and out of the room with unusual excitement, busy as a bee. Watching her bustling body, Snowflake closed her eyes.

The door opened and Mother-in-law came in with a bowl of gruel. Her footsteps were light; she didn't want to wake the baby. Hurriedly Snowflake sat up on the *kang*. Mother-in-law had talked about Sister-in-law's postnatal confinement, when she had waited on her and brought her three daily meals to her room. Looking in through the window before she entered her room, she thought she saw Sister-in-law sitting on the *kang*, but when she pushed open the door she found Sister-in-law sleeping with her face turned toward the wall, snoring noisily. What a mother-in-law she was! Just a humble serving maid! Mother-in-law had concluded.

Snowflake remembered how, just then, Mother-in-law had uttered a sad sigh. That was the first time Snowflake had noticed the sore spot in Mother-in-law's heart, a scar left by life. Given the kind of tough woman she was, such soreness seemed all the more astonishing. So even before Mother-in-law had reached the side of the *kang*, Snowflake was sitting up on her knees and stretching out her arms to take the bowl from Mother-in-law's hands.

The baby didn't have a name yet. Names are usually given to babies by the imam or the head of the family. But the imam was said to have gone home for a short visit. So the naming was put on hold for the time being. A day or two wouldn't have mattered, but it had already been ten days now, and Snowflake could hardly contain her growing unease. She felt as if she had been abandoned; both she and her child had been slighted. Sister-in-law had told her that the names of both her sons were given by Father-in-law. If so, why couldn't he give a name to his granddaughter? Mother-in-law also seemed to have completely forgotten about this. Since Snowflake couldn't read the minds of her parents-in-law, she decided to let it go.

Sister-in-law, however, wouldn't give up. She often dropped in to sit awhile, bending down to look closely at the baby while making such comments as, "She has the eyes of so and so, and the nose of so and so…," and cleverly she would bring up the question of giving the baby a name. The child was about two weeks old, Sister-in-law said. How was it possible that she still didn't have a name? Was Grandpa too old to remember her? Although she was a girl, she was a member of the Ma family. Why shouldn't she have a name? When her sons were born, Grandpa was standing outside the window and he gave them names on the spot.

Tears formed in Snowflake's eyes as she listened to Sister-in-law's chattering, but she knew full well that it wasn't time for her to pour out her dismay to anyone, least of all to Sister-in-law. She bit back her agony and said there was no hurry and the naming could wait. It wasn't a big deal.

As she pondered over the matter at night, she came to see that she had placed too much significance on the naming, which was merely fingernail big in consequence compared to the fullness of a person. She shouldn't fall for Sister-in-law's trap. That realization soon put her mind at ease.

The baby was always sleeping. How could she need so much sleep after sleeping nine months in her mother's belly? She often woke up at dinner time, her dark eyes staring around the room. She nursed at Snowflake's breasts and urinated, then quietly went back to sleep. The next morning she would open her eyes again and gaze at something. If Snowflake left her alone, she would fall back to sleep before long. Her nostrils were very thin, almost transparent, and with each contraction and expansion there came a soft snore. Fancy that such a small baby could be snoring! When she watched the baby, Snowflake's heart became even more tender. She could almost feel that the baby was still tied to some part of her body, its breathing pulling at her as if they were one.

A bright red sun had risen. There were many sunny days in winter, as long as it wasn't snowing. The sun poured its heat on the window, but the curtain was pulled tight. In addition, a large bed sheet was hung up to shelter the *kang*. The whole room was enveloped in a hazy coziness. In fact, a woman usually spends the first month after giving birth sitting on the *kang*, where she is protected from the slightest brush of wind. In this month, she is relieved of all the household chores and work in the fields. She can't even let the wind touch her.

Mother-in-law had told Snowflake that she should stay in bed and not worry about anything. So Snowflake was wholeheartedly enjoying the leisure time. She didn't have to get out of bed at daybreak and sweep the courtyard, add coal to the fire, remove the ashes, and prepare breakfast before her parents-in-law were up. In the past, she would be busy from sunup to sundown without a moment's rest. Although housework was not backbreaking work, it was an unending cycle of chores that literally tied a person hand and foot to the house. Busy as one might be, one could hardly feel any sense of accomplishment. Sister-in-law made a perfect analogy: Once you become somebody's daughter-in-law, you're turned into a donkey at the mill, churning around in the kitchen and waiting on others for the rest of your life.

Throughout her life, the month after giving birth may be the only time when a woman can take a break. As Snowflake knew full well that this was a hard-earned opportunity, she tried to push all annoying thoughts out of her mind. With her baby, she slept through the days as well as the nights, trying to make up for her sleep deprivation of the past year. What a year it had been, being a daughter-in-law! She had made up her mind to get some compensation.

She often dreamed, and in her dreams her husband came home. Side by side they worked in the bean fields, pulling out weeds. Or they cut wheat together. Suddenly her man grabbed her in his arms in front of many people. The embarrassment of this nearly shamed her to tears. She could feel his breath hot on her ears as he whispered: Don't cry, don't cry. We're young and we have time. We will have a son. That made her laugh, and she sometimes laughed herself awake.

Her daughter was still asleep beside her. It was very quiet in the room, but she could hear the noise of children playing and chasing each other outside. She sat up in bed, and after watching her baby for a while she laid down again with a smile on her lips, for she had already chosen a name for her child. She no longer needed to wait for others to do it for her. She murmured the name to herself: Tina. Let her baby be called Tina, for she was so small and delicate. Snowflake put her mouth close to the baby's ears and whispered the name. The child was sleeping soundly, one arm peeking out from under the sheets, her little pink hand curled in a tight fist.

Mother arrived late in the afternoon, bringing with her several dozen eggs and some small clothes for the baby, including a bonnet, shoes and even little socks. Snowflake heard people speaking close by. She sat up and saw her mother standing beside the *kang*. The sight of Mother brought a lump to her throat, and all of a sudden her passions poured out uncontrollably in loud sobs. Only after she herself had been to the gate of hell could she know how difficult it was to be a woman, and more so, to be a mother.

Mother stood silently by the *kang*, smiling at her. Mother-in-law followed close behind and was disturbed to see the tears on Snowflake's cheeks. What's there to cry about, she asked. Everybody in the family cares for you. If your mother sees you crying like this, she might think we've mistreated you.

Snowflake quickly wiped her tears away. Honestly, Mother-in-law had been quite nice to her. She personally cooked her three meals a day and brought them to her room. No meal was ever missed. In fact, if it weren't for this month-long rest, she might never have had an opportunity to get Mother-in-law to cook for her. However, the melancholy lingered. Humans are really strange beings, she thought. It was a once-in-a-lifetime chance to sit idle like this, and yet she was depressed, as if she had suffered a great, unspeakable wrong.

Young people nowadays are very lucky, she heard Mother and Mother-in-law saying to each other. Things weren't like this when we were young, they agreed. They couldn't sit on the mat, much less a mattress. They had to sit on the bare earthen bed and even before the first month was over they had to go to work in the fields again. Just think how much they suffered! Nowadays young people know nothing of that. Their conversation was punctuated by sighs and sobs, and Mother-in-law's occasional glances in her direction. Snowflake did not fail to catch the hint that she should consider herself fortunate and not complain.

A smile spread across her lips. After being married and living with her husband's family for a whole year, Snowflake had learned to be resilient, to speak less and work more, and to bear unfairness in silence. It is only when you've become a woman that you can truly comprehend the meaning of life.

As she cradled her baby in her arms, Snowflake thought it was not all that bad to be a woman, especially in this postnatal first month, during which all toils and troubles were left behind. She might become lazy and sloppy, but she had acquired peace of mind. With her daughter sleeping next to her, she felt like she had the whole world on her side. All worries and troubles were shut outside, and now her thoughts were concentrated wholly on her daughter.

Things were different before the baby was born. Snowflake often felt empty and unsure in the dark of night, as if she had lost something. Something was missing from her heart and nothing could fill the void. Her husband was away most of the time. Even if he came back home, his stay was so brief that he barely had time to warm the bed. She often stared vacantly at the impression he left in the mattress, remembering again and again the times he was there. But this only stirred up sentimental thoughts. On the one hand, she hated him for leaving her and wished he would come back; on the other hand, she would rather he had never made those brief visits, which only excited her steady heart and made it float in midair, devoid of any solid landing.

Now that she had a daughter, those floating dreams seemed long ago and far away. She now believed that it was a correct decision to have a baby right away. At first her husband didn't agree with her. He proudly proclaimed that he was saving money and they should first travel and see the world. A baby would be an encumbrance. He was quite earnest when he said that, and Snowflake couldn't help laughing every time she recollected his unrealistic dreams. He was just a big, foolish boy, and yet that was what made her love him.

But like the many women whose husbands were working in the cities, she couldn't keep her husband by her side, for the whole family depended on his income. If you wanted cash to buy rice and flour, cooking oil and salt, and all sorts of daily necessities, he had to go away, and you had to watch him disappear into the distance. Once it is decided that they will do this, men simply pack up and go, leaving their warm beds and tearful wives behind. Men cannot stay home. If they do, they are bound to be poor. But the babies will stay. When the women see their children around them, they feel that they have their husbands' likeness close by. When they watch their children, they feel that the empty places in their hearts are filled.

Snowflake was becoming like the other women. She had acquired the habit of talking to herself about such trivial matters as diapers, milk, and so on and so forth. She liked to discuss household matters with other married women. Their main topic of conversation was almost always their children. Snowflake even worried that her daughter's eyes were too small and she might not grow up to be a beauty, and later blame her mother for not making her prettier.

Snowflake found that it was snowing. Mother-in-law had brought her dinner in and the bang of the door woke her up. She had slept through the day and now it was nearly dark. It's snowing, Mother-in-law said, and from the delight in her voice it was not difficult to tell that she was already envisioning the spring plowing and planting. A good snow always brought joy to the heart, for it added moisture to the soil and made it ready for sowing. As soon as Mother-in-law was out of the room, Snowflake slid down from the *kang* and went to the window in her bare feet to watch the falling snow.

Big flakes of snow were falling thick and fast, one upon another, from the depths of the clouds. Wasn't the falling of snowflakes like marrying off a daughter, who, led by a matchmaker, would land in a strange new home? Midway down the sky, snowflakes seemed to hesitate, as if they would like to linger awhile and play in the air before falling to the ground. There they would melt and blend into the earth, and start a completely new life.

This, Snowflake said to herself, is the first big snow of the year.

(*Translated by Zhang Guangqian*)

Breezes in the Woods

Chi Zijian

Chi Zijian. Born in Mohe, also known as "North Pole Village," during Lantern Festival in 1964, Chi Zijian spent her childhood by the Heilongjiang River. In 1984, she graduated from the Greater Xing'an Mountains Normal School and went to Beijing Normal University for graduate courses, and in 1987 she studied at the Lu Xun Literature Institute. After graduation in 1990, Chi Zijian worked with the Heilongjiang Writers' Association.

Since 1983, Chi Zijian has published more than forty separate books. Her major works include: the novels, *Under the Tree*, *Morning Bell Resounding at Dusk*, *Puppet Manchu State*, *Sunshine Penetrating the Clouds*, and *The Right Bank of Ergun River*; the short-story collections, *Bathing in Fresh Water*, *Fairytales of North Pole Village*, *Graveyard Covered in White Snow*, *Travel through the White Night*, *The Flow of Water*, *Bayina Village*, *Bullpen on a Misty Night*, *Moonlight Andante*, and *All the Nights in the World*; as well as the collections of prose and informal essays, *The Beauty of Sorrow*, *Listening to Time Flying*, *My World Is Snowing*, and *Informal Essays of Chi Zijian: A Self-Selection*.

The Collected Works of Chi Zijian (four volumes) and *Essential Collected Literary Works of Chi Zijian* (three volumes) won her the first, second and fourth Lu Xun Literary Prizes, the seventh Mao Dun Literature Prize, and the Australian James Joyce Foundation's literary "Suspended Sentence Fellowship," to name but a few. Some of her works have been translated into English, French, Japanese and Italian, among other languages.

Breezes in the Woods

The light fixtures at the Luoliqi Health Clinic were all of the white incandescent bulb type, hung in the middle of the room from the ceiling. When turned on at night, they looked like overripe pears on a neglected tree. An accumulation of dust and insect droppings had gradually dimmed their innate brightness and reduced their brilliance. There was a sole exception – the lamp in the reception room. This one had a hexagonal shade made out of birch bark. The whitish, fuzzy side of the bark faced inward, so that when the bulb was lit, the light had the effect of shining on snow-covered rolling hills, invoking a cooling sensation. The smooth side of the bark faced outward and was painted with colored birds and white clouds. The deftness and elegance of the lamp captivated everyone who came to the clinic. People assumed it must have been the handiwork of some Luoliqi women: they were famous for their craftsmanship with birch bark. In fact, this particular lamp had come from the dexterous hands of Fang Xuezhen, a nurse at the health clinic.

The clinic had a staff of just seven doctors and nurses. Xuezhen had two nightshifts a week, which she loved. During those nights, she could admire her beloved birch bark lamp to her heart's content, as well as enjoy the beautiful night scene outside the window.

Luoliqi had a population of about fifteen hundred, half Han Chinese and half Oroqens. By any measure, it was a very small town. But as the saying goes, even the smallest bird still has all the organs necessary for life. Luoliqi had everything you'd find in a big town: a clothing store, grocery, drug store, restaurants, barber shops, even a store selling mourning apparel. Needless to say, most of the business went to restaurants. Not only were these the usual hang-outs for local drinkers, they also attracted lots of out-of-towners who were on the road. Luoliqi was situated midway along the highway connecting Tali and Huyuan, the two major cities in the area. Together, they were like two pearls tied at each end of a silk ribbon, and this fortuitous situation spelled prosperity for Luoliqi. On top of its enviable location, Luoliqi was also blessed with unmatched natural beauty. As might be expected, it was a most popular rest area for drivers and passengers alike.

Luoliqi Health Clinic was located at the foot of the eastern slope of a mountain range, in a south-facing red brick building. It wasn't big. It was limited to internal medicine, minor surgery, pediatrics and gynecology, and had just enough space for ten beds for occasional inpatients. It had never been full; the highest occupancy – six beds – had been reached only once, a few years back, when six people got a bad dose of seafood poisoning at a local restaurant and were forced to get emergency treatment locally. Ordinarily, the beds were vacant; patients with severe conditions would be referred to hospitals in Tali or Huyuan. Locals with a cold or headache would come to the clinic to get shots or medicine. The Oroqens hardly ever came, for they kept to their traditional way of treating illness, namely, getting a Shaman to perform dances to dispel spirits and cure diseases. So, all in all, doctors and nurses at the clinic enjoyed a rather undemanding workload.

It was just before *sanjiu*, the third nine-day coldest period following the winter solstice. This year, the big chill seemed to have arrived earlier than usual. The mountains were already thickly coated with white snow. Xuezhen, sporting a purple padded jacket in soft silk, and a white rabbit fur scarf around her neck, was walking toward the clinic. It was her day for nightshift duty. She loved walking on snow-covered roads, loved the sound it made against her shoes, as if it was sharing a secret with her. A clear winter night is distinctly different from a clear night at other seasons: not as soft and gentle as in spring; not as lazy and idle as in summer; nor as deep and unfathomable as in autumn. Clear winter nights defy simple description. When the moon is full, the night is crisp; the shadows of mountains, people and houses are as clear as in broad daylight. A clear night at half-moon is a melancholic one; all seems to be veiled in a cold mist, making it difficult to tell the real from the unreal. When the moon wanes to a crescent, it renders a clear winter night extraordinarily auspicious and elegant, thanks to the bright stars packing the heavens and the starlight showering down to earth, as if sprinkling the snowy ground with bubbles, and making you feel you are soaking in a fragrant bath.

Dr. Zhang was already at the clinic by the time Xuezhen arrived. He was a man in his late fifties, with sunken cheeks and a crisscross network of gullies on his face. The only thing he seemed capable of doing all day long was yawning. One time he managed to fall asleep while listening to a patient's lungs with his stethoscope, and for this he garnered himself the nickname Dozy Zhang. Xuezhen was always paired with him on their nightshifts. By any measure, Xuezhen was an attractive woman. Even though she was nearing 40, she had a beautiful figure. With her white skin, smiling almond eyes and upward curving mouth, she was actually very lovely. But Dr. Zhang hardly looked at her, and avoided conversation with her whenever possible. During their shift, he would say to her, "I'm just going to doze off a bit. Wake me if anything crops up." He'd pick an empty bed in the inpatient section of the clinic and fall fast asleep in it. His "doze off a bit" usually translated into "sleep all night." Even when there was an emergency, if Xuezhen could handle it herself, she wouldn't bother waking him. At first, she didn't know why she was always assigned to do night duty with Dr. Zhang, and then one day in a casual conversation with Director Wang she happened to discover the reason. "Your husband told me that only when you take your nightshift with Dr. Zhang can he feel at ease," he said with a smile. Xuezhen blushed and said fondly, "I didn't know he was so thoughtful. He never told me."

"Strapping young guys like myself don't get lucky enough to work nightshifts with you," teased Director Wang, "Guess the old derelicts are better off than us. No risk of affairs or tongues wagging."

Since that conversation, whenever Xuezhen was alone with Dr. Zhang, she recalled the words "old derelict." Sometimes she imagined Dr. Zhang was a dead tree trunk that could decompose into nothingness under the right conditions.

Dr. Zhang shot a cold glance at Xuezhen as she walked in. With him, that passed for a greeting.

Xuezhen said as she changed into her white uniform, "Dr. Zhang, why don't you go rest. I'll call you if I need you."

Dr. Zhang said, "I already checked the patient in Room Three. His pulse and blood pressure are normal, and his condition seems stable. Give him a shot of tranquilizer in an hour's time. He needs a good rest."

Before Xuezhen could say anything, Dr. Zhang had already vanished like a wisp of smoke and gone off to bed.

The patient in question was a man admitted to the clinic about a week ago after suffering a sudden stroke. On arrival, his eyes and mouth were drooping to one side and he was unconscious. Thanks to Dr. Zhang's rescue efforts, the patient was now out of danger. The caregiver was his wife. The couple had children, but they had made only a perfunctory visit, and at night there was only his wife at his bedside. Xuezhen opened the door to the room and saw the old woman holding the old man's hands in hers, her head leaning against his shoulder. She was deeply moved.

After performing her duties in the patient's room, Xuezhen went back to reception. She took a piece of moist cloth, stepped on a stool and started wiping the hanging birch bark lamp even though there wasn't a scrap of dust on it. She just had to do it as part of her nightshift routine. She knew why she liked dusting the lamp – it was her chance to get close up and appreciate her beautiful lamp, with its brightly colored birds and interesting cloud patterns.

She had painted a dozen birds in total. To suit the lamp's hexagonal shape, the twelve birds were arranged evenly over its six sides, one pair to each face. Each bird had its own unique expression and pose: some were perky and confident with heads held high, others were pretty, irresistibly shy and lovable. No one at the clinic could tell what kind of birds they were, and when they asked Xuezhen she said she couldn't put a name to them either, and suggested they just call them "heavenly birds." Hence the joke around the clinic that Xuezhen wanted to be the great Creator so she'd created these unrecognizable birds to scare people.

The fact of the matter was that Xuezhen hadn't copied any specific type of bird when she painted: no thrushes, no sparrows, no swallows, no golden orioles, no nothing. They all sprang from her imagination. Their feathery bodies were clothed in extraordinary combinations of colors: dark red, aquamarine, emerald green, silvery white, orange yellow, burnt ocher, and so on. But the heads were in one solid color: pure yellow, pitch black, or pure red. Illuminated by such an unusual lamp, even on cold winter nights the reception room had a spring-like, bird-animated freshness to it.

After admiring the lamp, Xuezhen pushed the stool back to its original position and stationed herself by the east-facing window to relish the serene night outside. The moon had risen, just barely it seemed, since it still looked a bit lazy. The snow-coated mountain forest seemed indistinct in the moonlight so, figuring the bright light inside the room might be dimming the otherwise brilliant moonshine outside, Xuezhen switched off the lamp. Now, standing in complete darkness she looked out again onto a different world, a miraculous transformation. The moon was limpid, lustrous, inviting. All its sluggishness of a moment ago had just evaporated. The woods, the mountains, and the snow-covered ground were sharp and distinct, with a silvery sheen to them, as if someone had frosted them with egg white. Oh yes, it was so much better to appreciate the beauty of night scenery in complete darkness, with no extraneous illumination.

Xuezhen and her husband Chen Kui had been classmates in middle school but after graduating they had gone their separate ways, he into teacher training, she to a nursing school. By coincidence however, they had both got jobs in Luoliqi two years later. It was as if someone up there wanted them to get married and live together forever. Teacher Chen Kui and Nurse Xuezhen were now a couple with a son of twelve, a perfect happy family of three and the envy of all Luoliqi. Chen Kui was of a somewhat delicate constitution, so it fell to Xuezhen to perform most of the household tasks. At the start of their marriage, Chen Kui had been a healthier and more spirited man. But ten or so years on he was a different person: lethargic and negative, he was barely holding down his teaching job. Students often complained about his behavior to the principal, saying his voice was such a soft drone they could barely hear him. Lately, he had started going out to bars, drinking with a couple of colleagues and this troubled Xuezhen a great deal.

The moonlight poured into the room through the window lattice, glossing the white walls with a film of pale yellow. Xuezhen stared blankly out of the window and sighed. After a while, she turned the light back on, prepared the syringe and the tranquilizer as requested by Dr. Zhang for the patient in Room Three. Once she had given the injection, she came back out to reception. Lately, she'd been feeling a little bit listless and forgetful herself. She couldn't remember how many times she'd overcooked the noodles to a complete mush, or had ruined a dish by absent-mindedly salting it twice. And there was the time too that she had even squeezed the toothpaste onto a shoe brush. Her son had caught her and teased, "Mom, do you want your shoes to clean their teeth?"

The thought of their son soothed Xuezhen a little.

It was midnight and the moon was now very high in the sky. The clinic was still and quiet. Xuezhen felt a little tired, so she sat on a chair facing the door and dozed off.

Some 15 minutes later, a sudden tremendous banging on the door woke her from her dreams with a rude jolt. She opened her eyes to see a man dashing into the clinic, his face a mass of blood. Panicky and breathless, she thought for sure she had encountered a ghost; her legs felt like jelly and she couldn't stand up for what seemed like an eternity.

"Nurse," the man shouted, "stop the bleeding for me. Now!"

Xuezhen recognized the gruff, raucous voice of Meng Hezhe – an Oroqen. He raised horses and hunting dogs and often took them when hunting in the mountains. He loved to drink, but not in bars, only in the mountain forests.

"Hey, you stupid woman, why aren't you stopping my bleeding?" he bellowed.

This seemed to finally register with Xuezhen, who was still struggling to get back to her senses. She examined his wound and saw a two-inch long gash on his right temple. Blood was still seeping out from it. "I need to stitch this. Let me give you a local anesthetic."

"Skip the local," Meng shouted, "Just give me the stitches"

Xuezhen did as he said and started sewing his wound ever so carefully and deftly. Not once did the man moan. Amazed, she wondered whether perhaps his nerves had been so badly damaged he'd lost all sense of pain. Once she'd sewn up the wound, she applied antiseptic and dressed it carefully with a bandage. Then she started cleaning off the blood from his face with rubbing alcohol. She used up a full tray of cotton balls before she see could see his face clearly. It was round and flat. Planted prominently in the middle of that face was a big nose, like a confident and fearless frog sitting on a lily pad. He had a big mouth too, and his lips drooped slightly. Like most Oroqens, his eyes were small and heavy lidded.

"You done?" he asked.

"All done."

"My horse is still outside. I'll bring you a couple of haunches of venison in a few days." Then he left, no mention of fees and he forgot his hat as well. Xuezhen ran after him, hoping to give him some aftercare advice. But he was already long gone. The shadow of Meng astride his horse looked like an arrow on a shield, the horse being the shield and Meng, without a doubt, the arrow.

That day happened to be the second day of Xuezhen's period, and normally the heaviest. But that night, the bleeding mysteriously and abruptly dried up. She put this down to the big scare she'd had and so didn't pay it much heed, assuming it would come back next month. A few days later, Meng rode by to give Xuezhen the two haunches of venison but left without even dismounting. She later heard from Chen Kui that the night of the accident, Meng had been out riding in the mountains and a gigantic bird nest had fallen from a tree he happened to be under, hitting him on the forehead. Some said Meng must have offended the tree god and that this had been his payback.

Sanjiu passed and Spring Festival arrived. But of Xuezhen's period there was no trace. This went unnoticed by Chen Kui, whose love life with his wife was getting increasingly sporadic. Xuezhen, on the other hand, was getting increasingly uneasy. But she just kept it to herself. Spring Festival came and went, followed by two more months of anxious, fruitless, waiting. Spring was nearly there before her anxiety finally made her confide to her husband, "It's been several months since I had a period."

"No wonder you've been so frigid" was his response. Xuezhen then told her husband everything that had happened on that shift – the nap, the tremendous banging on the door, the bloody face … the lot. Chen Kui's face dropped. "Shit! Why didn't the goddamn bird nest just kill the bastard!" He wanted to get even with Meng.

Xuezhen restrained him, "Don't you know this guy? Nobody screws with him! The other Oroqens all settled down after the government built them permanent housing. But not him. He still rides

his horse up into the mountains and lives in a teepee. Even the Oroqens are afraid of him."

Chen Kui said, "But he's scared your periods away for half a
year now. What if they never come back? Am I supposed to live
with a dry, barren old woman?"

Barren, old woman? Hurt and insulted, Xuezhen sneered back,
"If I'm a barren old woman, you're shriveled old eggplant."

That hit Chen Kui where it hurt, he being all too well aware
that the past few years had seen a sharp decline in his virility. His
libido was non-existent, and he barely muddled through their occasional couplings. He screamed at the top of his voice, "Fine! Go
out and find yourself an iron eggplant to fill you up!" He grabbed
the teapot off the table, smashed it down on the floor and dashed
out of the house.

Xuezhen didn't move. She stared at the floor and what was left
of the white teapot – broken pieces in grotesque shapes – and began
to fantasize that the teapot had not broken but just opened itself
up as a beautiful white lotus flower for her to admire. She allowed
herself to linger in that happy thought for a while longer and then
picked up a dustpan and broom to clean up the debris. As the shards
of porcelain clinked against each other the sound made her think of
the birds on her birch bark lamp at the clinic. If those birds could
ever make a sound, she hoped they would sound just like this.

Xuezhen was worried about Chen Kui. What if he got so
mad he went to find Meng? What if they got into a fight? Meng
could kill him! Nothing could come of this but embarrassment
and humiliation.

She raced over to Meng's house. But it suddenly dawned on her
that Meng almost never stayed home, so her husband's chances of
finding him were very slim and this realization brought some relief.

The town of Luoliqi had an unspoken but unmistakable divide: on the east side, all houses were red brick houses and were inhabited by Han people; the Oroqens occupied the west side and lived in housing known as *Mukelen. Mukelen* were like log cabins, made out of whole pine tree trunks, stacked one on top of another, and then protected by a thick layer of yellow mud on the outside. They provided good insulation during the long winters, and they looked good too.

When Xuezhen arrived at Meng's place, she didn't knock immediately, but listened intently against their front door. All she could hear were the sounds of a woman and children – Chen wasn't there after all. Between themselves the Oroqens still spoke their own language so she couldn't understand a word of what was being said; they might just as well be singing Italian opera. She marveled at how long this language had survived – being strictly a spoken language with no written script to preserve it. Speaking was the only vehicle by which it had been handed down from generation to generation.

Xuezhen knew Meng's wife. Her name was Wunaji. In winter she wore a blue dress in Oroqen style and in winter a buckskin coat. But whatever the season she always wore buckskin boots, the only seasonal concession being single thickness boots in summer; her winter boots had a rabbit fur lining. In summer, she liked to wear a necklace of fish bone beads strung on deer tendons, and her blue dress would be tied at the waist with a green silk band. Her Mandarin was poor and when she went grocery shopping she often had to resort to hand gestures. She and Meng had three kids, all boys and two of them already in school. Chen Kui had once told her that if any window was broken at school, any basketball hoop trashed, or a dead frog found in a chalk box in a classroom, everyone knew that Meng's two boys were the culprits. It was a well-known fact in Luoliqi that even though Meng was a little odd, he was very faithful to Wunaji and loved her. Granted, he might often wander in the mountains and stay out overnight, but he never neglected his wife. As for Wunaji, she was prettier than the other Oroqen women: she was taller, her frame slimmer. Even after bearing three children, her waistline was as fine as ever; she hadn't got flabby around the midriff and backside like other women of her age. Her eyes were characteristically narrow, but they were bright and spirited. She didn't say much and usually kept herself to herself. In summer and fall, she could be seen alone in the mountains with a birch bark basket on her back, picking wild berries, mushrooms and tree fungus. Being the strong and healthy woman she was, she almost never came to the clinic. She had come just once, timidly, and not for herself. She said hesitantly to Dr. Zhang that a snake had bitten Meng and that he had subsequently developed a big lump on his leg. She wanted to know if she should use a knife to cut out the lump or leave it alone. Dr. Zhang said it depended and that Meng should come to the clinic so he could take a look at it. Wunaji looked embarrassed and explained that Meng wasn't a bit worried about the lump, but he was afraid of bleeding. No, animal bleeding didn't bother him at all; it was human bleeding that always scared him. So there was no way she could make him come to the clinic if he didn't see any blood on his leg. Before she left, Wunaji asked Dr. Zhang if was better to use a pointed boning knife or a skinning knife made out of fish bone to cut the lump off Meng's leg. Everyone in the room burst out laughing.

In the end, how Meng got rid of his lump was a mystery to all. All anyone knew was that he rode in and out of the woods as often as ever, full of life.

Things seemed to fall together now. Wunaji was right about her husband being afraid of human blood. If it weren't for the blood on his forehead, Meng wouldn't have come in to the clinic that night. But what still didn't make sense to Xuezhen was how staunching the blood from Meng's wound should mysteriously coincide with a stop in her own bleeding.

Xuezhen arrived home disappointed and disoriented. Chen Kui still wasn't home and it was already time to go to work. No time to get lunch. She locked up the house and went straight to the clinic.

Once there, she immediately felt a weird atmosphere: Dr. Zhang was looking at her strangely; assistant nurse Wang Ling as well seemed to be sizing her up as some kind of freak. She'd barely changed into her uniform in the locker room before Director Wang came to invite her for a chat. Xuezhen nervously followed him to his office, her mind racing. So far as she knew, there hadn't been problems with her work so why the sudden meeting?

Director Wang indicated she should sit on the red folding chair across from his desk, and then made her a cup of tea. This departure from his usual casual and jokey style made Xuezhen even more anxious.

He first took a long and piercing look at Xuezhen, and then said slowly, "Chen Kui has told me everything. I've already given Dr. Zhang a talking to. He is a man, how irresponsible of him to sleep on his night duty!"

Everything came clear immediately. Flustered and embarrassed, she blurted out, "This has nothing to do with Dr. Zhang. I asked him to go rest. Besides, treating external injuries is my responsibility, not his."

Director Wang dithered a bit, then said, "What Chen Kui meant was…."

Xuezhen cut in, "He shouldn't have brought you into this. It's my business."

"But it did happen on your shift and one could argue that the clinic has a responsibility. Meeting Chen Kui's demands might be difficult, but I'll try. Let me write a report to the mayor first."

"What demands are you talking about?"

"He wanted to file an industrial accident claim on your behalf. He wants financial compensation. But you know, worker's comp is never easy and there's probably no precedent for a case like yours. How could one verify and make a decision? Suppose someone said you'd already hit the menopause and were just using the incident with Meng to extort money from the clinic? How would you refute such an allegation? Another thing. Nowadays, women's bodies tend to go downhill quicker than before. It's not unheard of for a woman of your age to have started 'the Change.' To be honest with you, I don't really know how to write the report."

At this, Xuezhen stood up, her face burning, her breathing short, her voice shaky. "Look, it *was* during that night, and after Meng Hezhe came that my period dried up. But I'm not about to extort money from anyone over something like this! As for worker's comp, the clinic can relax on that score."

The director's face softened. Relieved, he said, "Let me see if I can compensate you somehow from the clinic's budget. Maybe a little extra on the year-end bonus. You know you won't get anything from Meng. Legally you can't hold him accountable. Besides, it's not six months since your last period. Take some traditional Chinese medicine and it might just come back."

Xuezhen left the Director's office, embarrassed and humiliated, as if she'd just been stripped naked in front of a large crowd. It wasn't until she reached the locker room that she burst into tears.

Assistant nurse Wang Ling came to comfort her, "Sister, don't get so upset. It comes to all us women in the end."

She spent the whole afternoon disconsolate and depressed. Her colleagues suggested she should go home and rest. But she was determined not to and saw out her full shift.

After dinner with her son Yang, aware that there was a nasty fight brewing up between her and her husband, she sent Yang to play at a neighbor's home until she came to fetch him. He happily agreed. He would never pass up the chance of playing hide and seek or making paper boats with his friends.

Chen Kui didn't come home until nearly ten, completely hammered. Looking at her sloppy, weak, swaying drunk of a husband, her feelings were a mix of exasperation and sorrow.

"Why did you go to the clinic and broadcast my personal business?"

"What do you mean *why*? Did I do anything wrong? Something happened to my wife on the nightshift and she lost her youthful fertility. Why shouldn't I put in a claim for the loss?" he forcefully replied.

"Even if I did lose it, that's *my* business. Whatever I want or don't want to do is up to me. Me! It's not for you to get upset about it!" Xuezhen was getting more and more worked up. "Besides, you don't deserve a young and lusty wife. If I have lost my youth and fertility, maybe that's just what you had coming!"

Chen Kui was beside himself now. He bellowed, "You dirty whore!"

To which Xuezhen calmly replied, "OK. If I'm a whore, you're my only punter. All these years, I only picked up one man. You. Isn't it about time you paid me?"

Chen Kui spat on the floor, "Don't push my buttons! O.K. I've got no money and no power. I admit it. Happy? Or perhaps you're wishing you hadn't married me. Right? I'm just a elementary school teacher in a poor hick town. An ugly old woman is all I deserve, right? Goddamn me for snatching a pretty young lady like you! You should have held out for a much better deal. But now you're stuck with me and wasting away! How tough for you!"

Chen Kui's taunts went way beyond what Xuezhen would stand for. She slapped him hard across the face. The slap seemed to sober him up instantly: he suddenly stopped his nonsense, calmed down momentarily and then burst out wailing like a baby. The two had never fought like this before, and it was the first time Xuezhen had ever seen her husband cry. Her heart softened. She wanted to say something to console him. She walked over, put her hand on his head and started gently stroking his hair. He pushed her away roughly and she retreated a few steps. Gazing dumbstruck at her husband, he seemed to Xuezhen like a leaky, battered old boat with just one oar, but he had just thrown that oar overboard, determined, it seems, to drift off alone on a wind-blown, rain-lashed sea. As for her, she was the cast-off oar, unwanted by even such a wreck, quickly sinking to the bottom.

Spring had now arrived in force. The black and white monochrome dominating the long winter days was finally overturned by an onrush of spring color; trees were turning green; the multitudinous variety of mountain vegetation was coming back to life; joyous birdsong was waking up the woods. Where had all the blanketing snow gone? Oh, here and there you could catch the occasional patch of white among the trees, but that was the bark of the white birch revealing its unmistakable face from behind the new green leaves. The deciduous larches that once had been the dark contrast to the white winter landscape were now the newborn green backdrop for the early pink azaleas, blue bellflowers, and the other multitudes of beautiful wildflowers.

Xuezhen was still feeling low. She hadn't expected the

grapevine to spread her private misfortune quite so fast. It seemed that half of Luoliqi knew about it and every time she thought of all those gossiping tongues busy wagging about her, her resentment toward Chen Kui grew stronger. He was no help. Since their fight, he had become even more distant. Even though they still slept in the same bed and ate at the same table, they didn't talk to or even look at each other. Touching was entirely out of the question. None of this escaped the eyes of their innocent child, who, in his own way, became a stranger too. Besides going to school, once he'd eaten dinner and done his homework at home, he spent all his free time at their neighbors' house, playing with his friends until very late.

Xuezhen rarely went out shopping any more. Most of the shopkeepers were women and they never missed a chance to ask her, with an air of mystery, "Has your *visitor* really never come back again?" Xuezhen had nothing to say. So one day, she went out and bought extra supplies of everything: salt, sugar, soy sauce, vinegar, rice, noodles, toothpaste, soap and so on, stocking up and swearing she'd never go back to those shops again. Chen Kui, for his part, was getting sick of his so-called friends' endless prying into his wife's condition. One day after his usual drinking session, he came home exasperated and remorseful. "I shouldn't have claimed worker's comp at the clinic the other day. Now everybody in town thinks I'm useless and incompetent."

Xuezhen replied bitterly, "It's a bit late for regrets. Get over it!"

At the clinic, Xuezhen became very quiet. Only on her night-shift, when she was alone with her pretty birch bark lamp would her heart stir again. How she wished she could be one of the birds on the shade. Very late one night, she was sitting alone in reception when she heard steps coming down the hallway. They were heavy, so it couldn't be Dr. Zhang, who walked with a very light tread, so probably it was someone coming for emergency treatment. Just as she was getting ready to receive whoever it might be, the door was pushed open and Meng Hezhe materialized, like a brown bear strayed in from the woods. He was wearing blue trousers, an unlined buckskin jacket open at the chest, and a strange expression on his face as he stood there, silently, staring at her.

Xuezhen took a moment to steady herself and asked, "Are you unwell?"

He shook his head and asked awkwardly, "The gossip that's been going around, is it true?"

She nodded.

"You Han women are fussy and weak! Our women can hunt deer in the mountains and snatch fish right out of the river. That women's thing, they still have it even into their sixties."

Xuezhen fired back, "Did you come here just to humiliate me? Go!" She was about to say something much more vulgar, but bit her tongue.

"I came to cure you." He gestured her toward him. "Follow me. I have just the right medicine for you."

Xuezhen had heard that Oroqens would treat ailments with herbs and plants they picked in the mountains, and that this form of treatment seemed to work very well. For example, ground pine for rheumatism, fox tongues for diarrhea, horsetails for eye problems, puffballs for a sore throat, and so on. It wouldn't be too much of a stretch of the imagination that they should have some special medicine for women's disorders too. It was worth a try. It didn't look as if Meng was trying to trick her, so without bothering to say anything to the slumbering Dr. Zhang she left the clinic with Meng.

It was a clear spring night. Countless stars surrounded the round full moon, like bees swarming and buzzing around a swollen sunflower head. Immediately outside the clinic was the eastern slope of the mountain. Meng led Xuezhen straight in that direction. From a distance, Xuezhen could see the shadow of a horse standing on the slope and assumed that the medicine must be on its saddle. So her guard was down. But before they reached the horse, Meng suddenly took her in a tight embrace and started kissing her wildly. The stink of alcohol on his breath made her gag. She struggled to get out of his grip and managed to gasp out, "Let me go. I'll report you to the police!" To which Meng was completely deaf. He firmly laid her down on the ground, pulled her pants off and then, like a maddened bull, started recklessly charging at her. Initially she put up some resistance, but soon realized the futility of struggling against a man of such inexhaustible strength and with just one thing on his mind. She relaxed and let things take their course. Meng was right on top of her, his head rising and falling, now visible, now not, like a wild stallion galloping on the horizon. He finally reached his climax with a howl that reverberated in the night sky; the horse gave echo with a long, excited neigh! Xuezhen was consumed and exhausted; within she smarted with pleasure, drenched and lashed by this squall; on her skin she felt the tender caress of the cool air. A gentle breeze carried the sound of the shrubs and trees of the woods into her ears; her eyes looked up to a night sky brocaded with millions of stars for as far as vision could reach.

Meng clambered off her and said, just like a doctor prescribing treatment to a patient, "Right here, once a week, same time. I'll wait for you. I can put you right." Before she could even get up, he'd mounted his horse and left. Listening to the rhythmic clip-clopping recede into the distance, she cried in the nighttime breeze. She was glad to let the soft breeze be her handkerchief, gently drying away her tears.

Seven days later, Xuezhen didn't have night duty. After dinner, Yang went over to the neighbors and Chen Kui went to play cards with his friends – anything to avoid staying at home alone with his wife.

Xuezhen had no intention of keeping her "appointment" with Meng. She sat alone under the light, checking Yang's homework. But the words wouldn't stay still. She kept on looking up through the window, observing the intensifying darkness outside, her mind traveling to the quiet little clearing in the woods, to the moon above and the horse standing by, to that vigorous roar and to that delicate breeze…. Her heart was pounding. No way could she stay sitting there. She got out of the house. The sky was as clear as the week before but the moon was not quite as full, which somehow made it more subtle and attractive. She took a few steps then stopped, asking herself. "What on earth am I doing?" She went back inside, but couldn't sit still. To distract herself she got up and started dusting the furniture, but after a couple of passes with the rag she'd had enough. Next she tried folding their son's clothes still lying there on the bed, but before finishing a single garment she lost interest and returned to the window. Never had the dark night seemed so perfectly seductive, so overwhelming! "To hell with it. I'm going." She was resolved. Fearing that their son might worry, she left the door unlocked: there was nothing worth stealing anyway. In Luoliqi people were in the habit of calling on each other after dinner, so of course she passed a number of acquaintances on the street, but they simply assumed she was on her way to the clinic. Calm and unhurried, she made her way to the eastern slope, and caught sight of the shadow of a horse.

Meng was sitting among the bushes. As soon as he saw Xuezhen, he stood up, pulled her into an embrace, his big rough hands gently stroking her hair, kissing her, smothering her in love. Xuezhen caught a whiff fresh grass on his breath, and she tried to drink it all in. Her face was burning and down below she was on fire too. Meng had reignited the dying embers of youth inside her and made them blaze with new life. They slowly lay down on the ground together. This time, Meng opened her top, kissing her breasts and her belly, taking his time, before finally he entered her again. Xuezhen had never experienced such wonderful sex. It was like being half drunk, floating and flying like a god, like joining in love in the starry Milky Way. She pictured Meng as a strong and healthy tree undaunted by the harsh cold land her body offered, remaining proud and stubbornly erect, expanding and growing for what felt like for ever. It was like making music: Meng's irrepressible life force was the heroic melody, but the constant gentle breeze in the woods insinuated itself into the chorus too. And when Meng yelled out his climax, Xuezhen screamed in unison, feeling, in that instant, about to faint with happiness and joy. This time Meng's horse went on neighing a while longer, keeping pace with Xuezhen until her moans finally subsided.

Like the first time, Meng left before her. But before he walked off, Xuezhen asked, "How did you get that fresh grass scent in your mouth? It smelled so good."

"Oh that. I thought people from the health clinic must all be clean creatures. I don't brush my teeth. So I chewed on a handful of grass."

Xuezhen's heart warmed at the revelation. "Didn't you just turn yourself into an ox then?"

He ignored her teasing and simply replied in serious tone, "You must come back next week. It's going to work. If you don't come, I'll assume you're fine again."

"What if it's raining?"

"Even better. Rain is medicine too."

"And if it's a howling gale?"

"Wind is medicine too. Be there." This was Meng's succinct and firm order.

Meng left with his horse. Nobody in Luoliqi would be surprised to see him anywhere at anytime; to one and all he was such a wandering ghost.

The color gradually returned to Xuezhen's cheeks. The smile on her face came back, radiant and fresh as before, glinting like sunlight on a river. The dramatic change wasn't lost on Chen Kui, who sneered, "Hey, maybe your *visitor* never did stop coming. It was all just lies so you wouldn't have to do your duty by me."

"Oh, but I want to," Xuezhen countered, a smile playing on her lips, "Come on. What are you waiting for?" as she started unbuttoning her shirt.

Chen Kui's face turned ashen, scared and trembling like a mouse in the grip of a cat. Through clenched teeth he hissed at her, "Slag!"

For two months, as spring turned into summer, come rain or shine, Xuezhen never missed a single appointment for treatment from "Doctor" Meng. The weather smiled on them: during all their rendezvous, only one night did it rain – and that was drizzle. They made love in the gentle, whispering rain, their bodies drenched, their coupling wilder even than the pounding ocean surf. Meng's bellowing and Xuezhen's moans must have been even more passionate than usual; that night there was no sound of the horse neighing. He knew better than to compete with the two of them! Xuezhen felt as if she and Meng were two trees in the forest that had twisted around each other as they grew, a single living thing that could not be forced apart. Only together could they both grow and thrive.

At first, Meng didn't talk much with Xuezhen. Every time, mission accomplished, he'd rush straight off like a busy doctor having attended to a patient. By and by though, he stayed on a little longer to chat with her. One night with the breeze around them, Xuezhen accidentally touched a very noticeable scar on his right calf. She asked if it was the scar he'd got when the lump from the venomous snake bite was cut out.

"No," he said, all the while fondling her hair. He'd had this scar since he was six. He said he'd got it during the event to mark the third anniversary of his grandfather's death, an important occasion in Oroqen tradition. The master of the rite had led all the clansmen and the deceased's relatives to the hilltop where the tomb was located and where he started proceedings with a brief speech. "Today we are gathered here to bid our last farewells to you. Don't look back. Your children will carry on what you have left behind. That your journey be free of hardship is their only wish." He then selected one of the children of the deceased to draw and shoot two arrows to the west, to make way for his safe journey, and then one arrow to the east, a symbol of blessing from the departed to his descendants. People in the crowd then raced to catch the arrow of blessing. It was said that whoever caught the arrow would be blessed with a happy life thereafter. Meng was only six then, but was sharp-eyed and quick off the mark even so. He parted the crowd and ran as fast as he could to catch that arrow. And catch it he did, but the good fortune came at a price. Just as he seized the arrow, he tripped and crashed face down. A dead tree root, half a foot long and very sharp, lodged itself in his calf; blood gushed out immediately, leaving him with a scar that would forever remind him of the price of happiness.

Another time, Xuezhen asked Meng why he liked to wander alone in and out of the woods and stay there overnight. He told her because that was where his ancestors lived. He liked to smell the fresh scent of the trees and listen to the calls of the wild animals in the woods. When he looked down from the mountaintop, the houses lined up below seemed to him like tombstones in a graveyard and just as suffocating. They were stuck in one place, like domesticated animals, dull, soulless and boring – in a word, oppressive. That was why he was constantly on the move between the woods and his village home.

Then, what Xuezhen both longed for and most dreaded finally arrived.

One midsummer day, at dusk, she was busy fixing dinner when she felt a sudden moist warmth down below gushing out into her pants. She immediately put down what she was doing, closed the door to the bedroom, and checked her pants. There it was right in front of her eyes: finally, the beautiful red of her long awaited friend! Were her eyes telling the truth? How could it come just like that? She moved slowly toward the window, gazing up at the drifting clouds, emotions at odds, and crying. Should she tell him the truth? Suppose he was as true as his word and left her? She had a revelation: only now did she realize that she really was a patient, forever attached to a doctor who could bring her both healing and pleasure.

The next day was appointment day. If she didn't show up, Meng would know she'd stopped coming. But if she did, her body would reveal her secret and Meng would never come again. The eastern slope would be doomed to remain a secret sanctuary in her heart. She tossed the thought this way and that. And decided to go.

Reckoning that this would be their last time together, she took extra special care in getting herself dolled up. She put on a figure-hugging *qipao* in a silvery-gray soft silk. The combination of color and fabric would create the impression of a white candle glowing softly in the moonlight. She plaited her hair into a single braid that hung at the back of her head, and applied a light finishing touch of makeup – simple, youthful, and classic. As she was getting ready to step out, Chen Kui remarked cynically, "It's not your shift. Who's all the effort for?"

"The moon," she replied simply. "Don't take the moon for granted," came the acid response.

"He's an old hand at love affairs. He's had his pick of every beauty of every dynasty; there was Diaochan, Zhaojung, Xishi…. What makes you think he'd look at the likes of you? Who do you think you are?"

Ignoring Chen Kui's taunts, Xuezhen left the house and headed straight to their rendezvous. It was a half-moon tonight, for all the world like a white cat curled up in a ball. The stars were like golden honey candies scattered across the night sky, waiting for someone to come savor them. Xuezhen's dress moved in the soft breeze like ripples on a river; its silvery silk seemed to have absorbed the twinkling light of the stars and was giving off a faint glow of its own.

In the distance, she saw the shadow of a horse by the eastern slope. She was already excited. Tonight, the woods took on the appearance of a fine horizontal scroll painting, slowly unrolling and revealing itself to Xuezhen the closer she approached. On the left side of the scroll, the mountains were in dark, full-bodied ink. The peaks were not particularly high, but shapely, like arches, whereas most of the other mountains around there tended to be rounded and bun-shaped. Below the peaks stretched a belt of trees, and below that another, and then another – some high, some low, a beautiful composition laid out by nature itself. Where the trees were tall and dense, the black ink was thicker, more heavily applied; but in the airy clearings it was all shrubs and tall grasses depicted in light gray brush strokes. To the right stood a line of three summits, each one rounded in shape and a little smaller than its neighbor. They looked as if three hats, identical in every respect but their size, had been dropped from the sky to earth. A little below, there was an area that gleamed white light – the white birch woods. Immediately beyond that were the larch woods. And there was Meng's horse!

Like a man lost in the desert dying of thirst who suddenly catches sight of a stream, the second he saw Xuezhen Meng wrapped her tight in his arms. He kissed and licked her all over, his fresh grass breath kicking alive all of Xuezhen's senses. She let the intimacy continue just a while before saying, "I want to go to the birch woods tonight."

Meng took her hand and walked her toward the birch woods, leaving the horse where it stood. In the moonlight the birches looked like goose feather writing brushes, the flickering leaves at their crowns like a shower of stars sprinkled down from heaven. They found a small meadow full of wild white daisies. The dainty flowers were extraordinarily bright tonight. There was a faintly medicinal fragrance to them. The moon must have turned its other half into these lovely little flowers just for us, thought Xuezhen.

She lay down on the flowers and wistfully told Meng she wanted to see how he looked naked. Standing right in front of her, he obliged: coarse cloth top first, big black pants second and last. No underwear. Just like that, one, two, and there he was, stark naked. Xuezhen imagined that strong and sturdy naked body as an ancient pine that had withstood the battering of centuries but still grew firm and vigorous. How she wished the moonlight could become a rope to yoke her to this remarkable tree. Tears were running down her face. At the same time, down below she sensed the blood seeping from her like a gushing mountain spring. It soaked through her *qipao*, onto the white daisies, onto the wild grasses. Meng gestured to her to join him in his nakedness. She was still debating what to do when Meng put out his rugged hand and pulled her up. He then sat down where she herself had just been lying. But before Xuzhen could do a thing, she heard him suddenly yell out in surprise. He saw the stain on the daisies, wrenched them up and smelled the blood on them. "So you're cured?" he asked loudly.

Xuezhen had been hoping that nighttime would hide her condition for a while, but it was obvious now that nothing could escape Meng's acute senses. Her heart sank. How she had wished to drown him just one last time in the wellspring of her life! True to his hemophobia reputation, in a flash Meng dropped the blood-stained flower, put a safe distance between himself and the bloody spot, and stood shaking for a while before finally getting dressed.

"You're leaving?"

"You're OK now!"

"Don't you love me?" she asked, her voice quavering.

Meng was silent for what seemed like an eternity. Then, "I have Wunaji. We Oroqen take one wife for life. Just one. That will never change."

"So, what about me?" Xuezhen didn't relent.

"I made you sick. Now I've cured you."

Xuezhen shivered. There was so much she wanted to tell him, but the words stuck in her throat. Just then, there was a sudden neighing, or rather, an acute cry of pain coming from among the larches. Meng dashed out of the birch woods.

Xuezhen followed hard on his heels and found him on his knees, holding his beloved horse by the head. He said someone had taken an ax to its head, tried to chop it off. Thank goodness it hadn't been fatal. Even so, there was an open wound above its right eye and blood was streaming out.

"Do you think Wunaji did this?" she suggested cautiously.

"Our women would never do such a thing." He shouted back. "Just go. You don't need me anymore!"

Xuezhen staggered home, to be faced with a Chen Kui sitting on the bed, head bathed in sweat, an ax next to the bed, and blood all over the ax.

She looked at him and the ax for a moment, then walked over to the window, her back toward her husband. This is his chance, she thought. Any moment now he's going to take my head off. She was hoping her last view of this world would be this beautiful clear night. But the ax did not come. Instead, from behind her came gusts of cynical laughter, icier and more piercing than the lacerating wind of a winter night. Finally, she heard him say, "Fang Xuezhen, what an bloody liar you are! Look at the blood on your *qipao*. Who the hell were you trying to bullshit?" Then, came the wailing, like that of an aggrieved child. This was the second time she had heard her husband cry.

Summer was almost over. Every day, Xuezhen went to work at the clinic as usual. Life seemed to get back into its normal routine, its suffocating banality. Chen Kui continued to give her a wide berth; if he wasn't out drinking, he was out playing cards. Since their last farewell at the eastern slope, Xuezhen had not set eyes on Meng. Only once had she heard via assistant nurse Wang that Meng had trapped a deer. Wunaji wanted him to release it because of the fall in deer numbers in the woods. Meng had listened to her and let the animal go. The day he released it, many kids in Luoliqi went to watch.

This happened to be the day Xuezhen was working the night-shift. As usual, Dr. Zhang went to sleep after his routine rounds of the clinic. Xuezhen sat alone at the reception room for while, and then moved her chair to beneath the birch bark lamp and stepped up to remove the dust that had gathered on it. Gazing at the "heavenly birds," the birds she had painted with her own hands, how much she yearned to become one of them. What if, she thought, what if she were to take out the bulb and stretch out her hand into the fitting…, the current would run right through her in an instant and she'd have her dream come true. Gripping the scorching light bulb with the duster, she was about to take it out, when the birch bark shade fell without warning, and landed squarely on her head like a crown. Before realizing what had happened, she had fallen to the floor. As she discovered later, one of the pinewood sections making up the framework had come loose, causing the shade to come apart completely.

The fall cost Xuezhen a broken fibula, for which she had to have her right leg in a cast. During her convalescence at home, Chen Kui poured his heart and soul into caring for her. The bars and card games stopped immediately. In the evenings, even though he still couldn't talk to his wife, he would sit by her bed reading. Xuezhen felt terrible that she'd wronged him and wished she could say sorry. But memories of those tender nights at the eastern slope still filled her mind. The woodland breezes no longer played around her ears. But deep down, deep within her being, they were quietly whispering, blowing up stronger every now and then, and rippling the seemingly placid waters.

(*Translated by Zhang Xiaorong*)

Golden Ranges

Sana (Daur)

Sana was born to a Daur family of the Aola clan in Yakeshi City, north of the Greater Hinggan Mountains in Inner Mongolia. She taught for years before starting her writing career in 1993. Living in the remote Morin Dawa Daur Autonomous Banner in Hulun Buir, Inner Mongolia, Sana has long had a particular interest in the ethnic cultures of the Daur, Ewenki, Oroqen and Mongolian peoples. Her works have been widely published in literary periodicals such as *Harvest*, *Zhong Shan*, *Flower City*, *Writer*, *Master*, *October*, *Dangdai*, *Chinese Writers* and *People's Literature*. Her works have been included in *Selected Stories*, *Fiction Monthly* and *Novella Monthly* as well as in annual selections of Chinese fiction and on the top novel lists proposed by various organizations. Sana also writes prose and essays, some of which have been published in *Writer*, *Frontiers* and *Mountain Flowers*. A member of the Chinese Writers' Association, she is also a council member of the China Ethnic Minority Writers' Society and vice-chair of the Inner Mongolia Writers' Association. She participated in the Lu Xun College of Liberal Arts' First Advanced Seminar for Young Writers. Sana's fiction collection *A Sword on Your Face* won the Eighth Stallion Award for China's ethnic minority literature. Her latest novel is *The Duobukur River*, a novel featuring the history and culture of the Oroqen people.

Golden Ranges

At mealtimes, mom would often talk about my maternal uncle. My maternal grandmother had given birth to nine children, but only mom and my eldest uncle were still living. Of the other seven, most had died of natural causes, the only exception being one who committed suicide, unable to put up with the malicious gossip about him – a horrible way to go. Mom was the ninth child, with almost 20 years between her and my uncle. As I remember it, she looked on uncle as a father figure rather than as an older brother. His family was her only kin.

When I was little, mom and I would always go visit uncle's family. As soon as I started summer holidays, she would get fidgety, always bringing up the subject of the grassland and of uncle. She didn't do it on purpose, she's just straightforward like that. She could never hold in her thoughts and dad saw through her right away. He told mom she should go visit them for a while, taking Mina (that's me) along too so as not to feel anxious about getting back in a rush.

Whenever mom visited uncle's place, she wanted to take me along too. I got sick very often when I was little, and if I wasn't with her she felt uneasy, worrying constantly that if I got sick at home, dad wouldn't have a clue what to do. If she had the slightest bad dream, the very next morning, she'd pack up, leave and rush back home. If I really did happen to be sick, she'd be vindicated and gloat "See, I told you. I really could sense that Mina was sick." Then she would take out some medicine from our medicine cabinet and give me shots in my bottom. Mom was a doctor so she knew what medicine would cure me fast. She also believed in Shamanism, like many people in our clan. She believed that if I was sick I could send her a sort of dream SOS message, prompting her to return. If on her return she found me fit and healthy and playing with the other kids, the fault was down to me for intruding on her dreams and bothering her with false thoughts.

It's a funny thing, and I still don't understand why, but I rarely got sick at my uncle's place. Even when I did, it was self-inflicted, either from drinking too much yogurt or from stuffing down unwashed berries found among the grasses. If I had an upset stomach, I wouldn't go to my mother – I was scared of her syringe; I would go to aunty instead. She used needles too; but sewing needles. She would put a needle into a flame to sterilize it and prick it into my thickest vein, at which bluish black blood would flow out.

Aunty said that there's a river inside your body, and when you get sick the river gets blocked. She always said that you had to clear a path to release the flow, and the sickness would be cured. She didn't hold with medicine or jabs, saying that such things would make me weaker. She compared me to a little sapling that would, soon enough, grow up like a tree; the only thing I needed was more sunshine.

After dad's decision, mom started packing in great high spirits. Seeing her thriftily filling a huge pack of clothes for uncle's family, he sighed and handed over his latest salary, saying, "Don't take those old rags, just give them some money instead."

Mom blushed. My uncle's family was extremely poor and dad had helped them out a lot. Mom, a very strong personality, often felt indebted to my father. She rushed about cooking dinner and when she sat down to her first mouthful of cornbread, she bit the inside of her cheek. She told us with absolute certainty that uncle had moved on to new pastures, to the west of Baiyintala, a plateau grassland beyond the reach of the summer floods.

I believed her. She and her clan had an invisible gut-level connection, and if there was something happening, mom could sense it.

My uncle's family moved around a lot with their flock of sheep. A flock is like a living river, and my uncle's family like a boat afloat on this vast river. They didn't see anything wrong with this cyclical, nomadic lifestyle because in the eyes of grassland people, life is a kind of drifting, and death merely another kind of drifting.

Mom took me back to the Baiyintala grasslands. From the little town of Yakeshi in the Great Hingan Mountains, we took the train to the city of Hailar, where we hopped on a cargo truck to the Baiyintala. As for reaching my uncle's pastures deep in the grassland, we had to find a nomad ox-cart to take us. Mom, who's a doctor, used to treat people around here, so she knew people here, and we quickly found Mr. Basen to take us.

That summer in Baiyintala still lingers in my memory as full of blue skies, billowing grasses, and silvery rivers.

I sat in the high cart with wooden wheels and found it great fun at first. The cart moved slowly, as did the clouds, the sheep and the cows. There was a beautiful, seductive indulgence to the plateau sunshine, as if I were in a golden, gently rocking cradle, floating to the sky. Before long I got tired and my vision was filled with grass, and more grass, pouring towards me, making my head dizzy. Mom told me to go to sleep and when I next opened my eyes, we would be there. So I clambered under the canopy and fell asleep. The sounds of the wheels turning seemed a long way away, but I could hear the birds and crickets quite clearly. I slept and it was only when my face got bright red that I was woken up by the rocking movement of the cart. I opened my eyes only to find we were still ambling through grassland. I jerked up and screamed. Mom and Mr. Basen both smiled. Mr. Basen said it was normal I was scared, because the Baiyintala grassland was so vast even an eagle couldn't find its way out.

I heard the cart coming to a stop. Mom called out my cousin's name and I crawled out from under the canopy. My eyes were overpowered by the sunshine; even so, I could see my cousin Bilige.

He was on his horse in front of our cart, smiling.

He looked like the son of the sun, emitting radiance and warmth. Many years later, when I tried to recall what he looked like back then, I was surprised because my imagination was totally accurate. My cousin was tall, broad, sun-tanned, bold-browed and round-eyed. He looked like a warrior from classical tragedy, a figure from a painting.

Mom always used to boast to me that all my cousins were good-looking and nice-natured, unlike her own two kids, who had grown up pug-ugly.... Those things were intended for dad's ears. My paternal aunt had said my mother was too thin and too short, and that it would affect the offspring. Mom's most telling evidence was the offspring. As a doctor, she always pointed out that it was dad's genes that were responsible for any frailty in her two kids.

My cousin hopped off his horse and strode over. He bowed politely to my mother, who took hold of his head, kissed him on the forehead, and said, "Bilige, you've really grown up. You look like a '*bater*'."

I knew that *bater* meant hero, and I too thought my cousin handsome and dashing. For a short while he seemed like a stranger, a completely different person. I greeted him shyly. He came over, lifted me up in his arms and said, "Mina, you've got freckles now!" He smiled at me, his pearly white teeth gleaming in the sun.

I looked into his smiling eyes and immediately turned shy. Why did I have to get annoying freckles, and why did he have to notice them? I wanted to cry and turned my face away. Seeing I was upset, mom asked Bilige to let me ride the horse, since I'd been whining all the way about learning to ride.

My cousin helped me mount, and once I was steady on its back, my confidence returned. His horse was a strong, fine steed with a long mane that flew in the wind; it was beautiful. It was like a spirit, a spirit that could take to the air at any moment and fly me to a mystic place. Lovingly I stroked its chest and imagined I had a horse just like this one.

"Mina, you like horses so much, you should be a boy," said my cousin wistfully.

Imitating my cousin's posture, sitting erect and facing forward, eyes on the horizon, I called out to mom that I could see the Amur River. This made them all laugh. The Amur River is also called Heilongjiang. I've known this fact since I was very small. In her reminiscences, mom used to tell me over and over again that our ancestors used to live on the left bank of the Amur River. They built a fortified town with wood for the whole clan to live in. But the Russian army had invaded our reserve and killed men, elders, women, and children, forcing our surviving ancestors to move to the right bank of the river. In my mom's stories the Amur was like a golden river, glistening in my memory. From then on, I believed every river was a branch of the Amur, and every river was called the Amur River. As I took a nameless little stream on the Baiyintala as the Amur River, of course everyone laughed.

We started walking towards my uncle's home. I saw my uncle's felt yurt, pitched by the river all on its own, and then the whole family emerged to greet us. Shielding her eyes with her hand from the sun's glare, my aunty peered in our direction.

A brown dog came dashing towards us, recognizable at once as Lukele. When I had seen him last summer, he was only two months old and now he was fully grown. He romped around the horse in high delight, his tail wagging from side to side like an ear of wheat in the wind. My cousin said the dog recognized me.

When we had almost reached the yurt, mom and I dismounted as courtesy demands and walked over the rest of the way. Aunty came out to welcome us, wiping her hands on her clothes as she walked. She smothered me with smacking big kisses; my ears were nearly deafened by the sound. Then, my uncle and my girl cousin started kissing me too, making me wail that I couldn't hear or see a thing with all this kissing. They laughed. And then they kissed me some more. My forehead bore a row of red lips, and mom said these were my trophies.

Uncle was all smiles initially but when he came face to face with mom, he started crying. With shaky hands, he put on his rock crystal sunglasses, probably trying to hide his own emotions. After mom greeted him in the proper manner, tears started coursing down her face too. Then, aunty took hold of mom as she wiped away her own tears. I didn't understand; they cried when they were happy, they cried when they were sad. It was only a year since they had seen each other last.

Mom went into the yurt, where right in the middle facing the entrance, hung the pouch of Malu totems. Here she kneeled and said she had come back. Then, she made me kneel too and kowtow three times. Luckily my aunt had put all of the deity figures into a sheepskin pouch and put it on the same pedestal, otherwise I'd have been there bowing all day.

When I was little, I always thought that the Malu spirits were aunty's invention. She used sheepskin to cut out the shape of a bird with outstretched wings and told me it was "Wumai," the spirit who protects the lives of little children. From a piece of wood, she carved a simple pair of figures, a man and a women, dressed them in sheepskin coats and told me they were our ancestors – "Shewoke" deities. But my favorite was the silver snake, which aunty cut out from a sheet of iron. She told me its name was "Sheli" and it was the most powerful of all the gods. Under the protection of "Sheli," a man would become an invincible hero. The gods that aunty believed in could form a legion; the mountain had mountain gods, water had water gods, even trees and rocks had souls, all invisible to us humans. She put twenty different effigies into a single Malu pouch. Whenever difficulties arose she would pray to them.

Aunty told me "Everything has a soul. Everything on earth can see, and their eyes are watching you. Humans shouldn't hurt innocent creatures, or the gods will turn their back on you."

That day, my cousin killed a sheep, and during dinner everyone drank alcohol. First, we drank kumiss (fermented mare's milk), and then we opened the bottle of *Yakeshi* liquor that mom had brought with her. Uncle got drunk and kept on calling out "Mina." I would rush over to him but when I got there, all he had to say was how tall I'd grown. When he called me a third time, I answered but didn't move. I figured he just wanted me to sit with him all the time.

Because I was visiting, Lukele got the special privilege of being allowed inside the yurt and sitting by my side. While the grown-ups weren't looking, I snuck him some mutton, but he just stared at it and didn't move Then, Bilige patted him on the head and told him it was from me. At this, Lukele carried the meat outside the tent and gobbled it down.

I followed Lukele outside and fed him some cookies out of my pocket. "Eat," I said. "Everyone in the family is happy, so you should be happy too." Lukele stared up at me with his intelligent black eyes; they were spotless and clear, crystal clear.

When aunty came out to look for me, she found the two of us sleeping together on a pile of hay, completely exhausted from our games. She wrapped me up in her blue robe and carried me inside the tent.

Aunty would take pity on anyone, as if she had been brought into this world to pity everybody and everything. She would always take under her wing any suffering animal she came across in the grasslands. An injured wild goose, a dying wild dog, an orphaned lamb – all had been brought home and looked after like little children. Once, she had even brough home a wolf pup inside her cow manure bag. Everyone in the family urged her to send it back, but aunty stoutly refused lest it starve to death. Uncle finally decided it would be OK to keep the wolf pup until its mother came to claim it. Of course, its mother never appeared, and aunty adopted this orphan.

However, the wolf pup did cause a lot of trouble. When it was just two months old, it started rummaging through things. Even if there were people in the yurt, it was oblivious to them, using its claws to force open the cupboard, ravishing whatever food it found inside, then going outside to bask in the sun and sleep it off.

Everyone chastised it, but to no effect. Uncle also had a six-month -old sheepdog named Ba'erhu, and they would always fight when Ba'erhu saw it rummage in the cupboard. Aunty always tried to restore peace by dividing the food equally between them. She always said it would come to its senses once it had grown up. Oh my god, did Aunty actually expect the wolf to take care of her in her old age – like a filial son? It was ridiculous.

When the wolf pup was five months old it went missing. Uncle said he had probably returned to the pack. It returned a few times, observing the yurt from a good distance, like someone deep in thought. My oldest cousin saw it once when he was out grazing the horses; it had grown up to be a handsome creature, a fully fledged adult wolf. Then one day, Ba'erhu gave birth to three puppies, and everyone realized who their father was. Two of them were too savage to tame and ran off far into the grasslands to be with their father. Lukele was the exception; he was like a girl, with a girl's attatchment to family, and as loyal as his mother Ba'erhu. He was my oldest cousin's sheepdog – an exceptional sheepdog too – and not one bit afraid of wolves.

When my oldest cousin got married and left home, he had taken Ba'erhu with him to herd his cows. He had wanted to take Lukele too, but my uncle humphed and he realized how selfish he was being.

The next morning, I was woken by a sound. I lay still on the bed, listening intently. It seemed to be coming from the ground, like a giant ripple pulsating through the whole grassland. I had been sleeping on my stomach, so I heard it.

I assumed it was a flood; I sat up in a big hurry and looked round. I remembered another a summer morning. At the time, we were camped on a relatively low-lying terrain when it rained and floodwater completely swamped our yurt. I had been five years old the year of the great grassland floods. But the memory of those silvery waters were as sharp as ever.

I sat on the bed for a while longer. I was the only one in the yurt, the rest of the family had gone out. I saw flames in the fireplace and a pot full of boiling water, bubbling to the brim. Lined up by the stove were a wicker basket for the cow pats and iron water buckets. The entrance to our tent was open, and a beam of bright red sunshine was shining through the opening. I'd never before seen sunshine so ethereal, spreading softly into the tent like water, caressing the ground like moist balm. The sound I heard must have been the sunshine penetrating the earth.

I jumped up and ran out barefoot. The sun was rising above the river, so red, so big, so close – I could almost touch it. But I didn't want to reach out to it, in case it was just a beautiful dream and if I stretched out my hand the dream would vanish.

I'd never seen a sun so red, so big.

Everyone was busy outside; they were bathed in the bright red glow but they didn't notice, too preoccupied with what they were doing. I was fit to burst with excitement, but no one else was. I went round all of them, eager to share with one and all the miracle I had just seen, but they didn't even look up. The most response they gave was to ask whether I was hungry, and that breakfast would be ready soon. Mom brought me a bowl of milk fresh from the cow and urged me to drink it. The calf tethered to a stake nearby mooed at me, as if he was mad at me for drinking his mother's milk. I took the bowl over and offered it to him. There was no standing on ceremony; he stuck his muzzle right into the bowl and emptied it in two mouthfuls.

Aunty, who was sat milking the cow, noticed mom was

irritated at this; she got up and went to the calf, taking with her a small iron bucket. She untied the calf so it could suckle at its mother's teats. She told me — or perhaps her words were really directed at mom — I had grown up, and that kids on the grassland should be kind-hearted.

During breakfast, Lukele started barking in excitement, as if some happy event had occurred. Uncle gulped down his milk tea and said it was probably another family moving in.

My girl cousin went outside to look and shouted back, "It is. A new family's arriving!"

We all ran out. Far in the distance we could make out a flock of pure white sheep, and seven or eight oxen pulling a high jigger cart in our direction. Aunty crossed her arms in a happy gesture, a big smile creasing her face, "I've always wanted company round here. The Malu gods have blessed us with neighbors, and good neighbors will bring joy."

The other family came to a halt on high ground not far from my uncle's. Uncle untied his sash from around his waist and waved it in the air as he hollered across to them. The head of the new family started waving back. Uncle couldn't wait a moment longer and told my cousin to watch the sheep while he went across to give the neighbors a hand. At the last minute he decided to take mom along as well.

The long morning dragged on and I felt totally dejected. Aunty told me not to go too far. I was just about to sneak off to find my cousin looking after the sheep, but she saw me and stopped me — did she have eyes in the back of her head? So I plonked myself down on a sheepskin and watched my cousins and the sheep from there. The sheep were surrounded by tall grass, and they wandered aimlessly like clouds. I sighed, worrying for them like adults do.

Right now they were lucky; they could feed to their heart's content, simply by opening their mouths. But once winter came, and the Siberian cold current hit the Hulun Buir Grassland, it would be a sad prospect for these docile creatures. Aunty would cry then and pray for the souls of the sheep that had died of cold, praying there'd be a nice warm place for them in heaven.

By the time the sun was high in the sky, a yurt with a blue top was up. Aunty looked out in that direction and decided to make some pancakes to take over, assuming that the other family would not have had time to cook.

Aunty opened the cupboard, took out some wheat flour that was very precious to them and started making the dough. Pulling up the front of her loose gown, she then went out to light the stove. I trailed behind her, wishing to help, but I kept getting in her way. She stroked my hair and told me kindly, "Mina, Wait till you grow up. You'll have more than enough work to do then." I tilted my head up to her and said "But I'm grown up already." She knew she had to give me a chore to get rid of me, so she sent me to collect cow pats for fuel.

Keen to win aunty's approval, I rushed off with the wicker basket to collect dried cow dung. This time, I had experience. First you had to use a wooden fork to lift the cow pat to check whether it was completely dry. During my visit the previous year, I had gone out to the pastures to collect manure and I kicked some around on the grass and by the time I got back to the yurt my feet had swollen up. Mom told me that the underside of wet manure had a lot of toxins in it, and if they made contact with the skin they caused it to swell up. This was common knowledge among the herders, so they first used forks to lift up the manure and improve air circulation, only collecting it once it had dried. Mom told me all this whilst she was brewing up some medicinal herbs she had picked for me to take. It took many cups of that bitter and astringent stuff to get rid of the swelling.

I collected half a basket of cow pats, put it down beside aunty and waited for her to praise me. But she was too busy to talk and just told me to leave it there. I picked up some of the pats and stacked them near the stove; that got my aunt's attention. Brushing the grass off of my pants she told me there was enough there already. She still hadn't praised me. I stacked some more into the stove, and wheedled. "Aunty, I don't want to go home. I want to stay here. Can you talk to my mom about it?"

Aunty stroked my hair again and muttered to herself, "Neither the mother and dauther wants to go home. Isn't that sad."

I tugged at aunty's sleeve. "Mom listens to you. If you say you want to keep me here, she'll say yes."

"I know you love the horses," she said. "I've never seen a girl as keen on horses as you are."

At the mention of horses, I perked up again. I jumped up, "Horses are so magical, they're like fairies. When they gallop, the whole world runs with them. They take the world along with them, galloping and galloping to someplace I can't see."

Aunty laughed until tears ran down her cheeks. She fed me a soft, warm pancake, and seeing how much I enjoyed it, said with great satisfaction, "Horses are the sons of the sun. The god of the sun saw the grassland people praying to him faithfully, year in year out, so he sent his sons down to earth to fulfill their wishes. If they wanted to travel far, the horses were there to take them. When the horses died and returned to the sky, it's because they got homesick. They sang as they went, and the songs turned into clouds, and that's how we got the changing seasons down below."

A herd of horses really did drift down from the clouds, settling lightly onto the green grass and making their unhurried way towards our yurt. It was cousin Bilige! He had ridden out into the grassland with the horses yesterday, and now here he was back with them!

Delighted, I pelted toward him, my view filled with the sight of horses trotting towards me like a stream of water. From behind, aunty was calling out my name. Fortunately it was daytime; had it been nighttime, some would probably think my soul had got lost and that aunty was calling for it to come back. I ran towards the horses as if my life depended on it and they galloped towards me. Their thundering hooves seemed to make the earth's heart pound. Lukele was running after me, barking, leaping up in front of me, pulling at my shirt to hold me back. He had heard aunty calling me, so he'd come to bring me back. I took a piece of cheese out of my pocket and told him, "Let me go, there's a good dog. I like cheese, you like cheese too. If I gave you my cheese, I wouldn't have any left." Lukele let go of me and backed up a few steps, his ears pricked, not taking his eyes off me and refusing to give in. I put the cheese back in my pocket. He wouldn't take anything from me. He was Lukele, the incorruptible.

I stopped and waited for the horses right there. Lukele sat on his hind legs and waited with me. The herd finally appeared ahead and cousin Bilige gave a few shouts. They slowed down and began grazing. He dismounted, strode over and gave me a pat on the head. "Mina, what did my mom make for lunch today?" I took that piece of cheese out of my pocket again and handed it to him. "This is my last piece. Aunty said I shouldn't eat as many snacks. She's made lots of bread and we're going over to the new neighbors' for lunch."

Bilige chewed the cheese. His teeth were gleaming white, like the moonlight. I'd lost two teeth because of calcium deficiency, and the third was getting wobbly. I asked my cousin, "Could my teeth get to be as good as yours?" He got serious and examined my mouth under the sunlight. He sighed, "If you didn't have to go to school, you could stay out here. Drink milk, eat mutton, and in two years, you'd have beautiful teeth – teeth strong enough to chew through iron."

His words made me gloomy. Mom and I were due to leave before long. My eyes welled up with tears. Bilige was at a loss, confused as to why I was happy one minute and sad the next. "OK, Mina. How about a piggy-back ride home?" He coaxed me up onto his back and I was happy again. When I was little, my cousin had always given me piggy-back rides. He was so tall and perched up there on his back, I would feel taller than the sky itself. But this time, I didn't feel as tall anymore. "Cousin, how come you've got shorter?" "It's you that's grown taller, Mina." I suddenly understood and grabbed his neck with both hands, terrified of slipping off. Bilige walked so fast, and his neck was so hot. I let go and said his neck was scorching hot. But as soon as I let go my hands I started slipping, so I tried hold him round the chest instead. But his chest was too broad for me to hold, so I held on to his neck again. After a while, I couldn't take any more. His broiling back was hotter than the sun, making me feel dizzy. I told him I wanted to get off and walk by myself. He put me down, stuck out a finger and said, "This won't burn. It's not a red-hot poker." So I held on to his finger and we walked home that way.

Not far away, a girl suddenly appeared. My eyes were sharp and I said to Bilige, "The new neighbors have a daughter – that might be her." He looked up and stared at the girl walking towards us. Of course it was a girl; her raven-black hair was braided into two plaits and she had a side parting, unlike married women whose husbands parted their hair for them straight down the middle to signify their married state.

Cousin dropped my hand and dashed towards her. A long time later, I heard him cry out with delight, "Yalan!"

I didn't run after him, and Lukele didn't follow either. Bilige was standing in front of Yalan. They were standing close enough to hear each other's breath.

Something important must've happened. It must have. All seemed nomal: the grass was still growing under the sun; the glistening small river continued to flow at its own measured pace; the clouds went on moving complacently across the sky; the herds of horses and sheep kept on grazing. But something had happened. I could feel it. I could feel the earth gently rocking like water. Toing and froing uneasily among the grass, Bilige's chestnut horse raised its wise head, watching the two of them.

My tall cousin was standing right beside pretty little Yalan, but he didn't utter a word. And all the blushing Yalan said was, "Our family has moved to this grassland," before looking down and fiddling with her braids. Clearly they knew each other from way back, and she knew his name. But why weren't they talking? Especially my cousin. He looked as if he had just been drinking, his face was so red. He just stood there, awkward, not knowing what to do with his hands.

I had to help him out. I ran over, wedged myself between them and said, "Cousin, say something. Where's your manners? Ask her if her parents are well, if their livestock are well, how's their grazing land, and what about their yurt." I reeled off all the niceties that uncle came out with when he went visting.

Bilige relaxed and smiled. "My little cousin knows the form. She's done all the greeting for me."

Yalan looked astonished, "How old are you?" "Ten," I replied. She knelt down and hugged me and said something I still remember like it was yesterday "Bilige, your little cousin is like a little mother to you."

It was only once I'd grown up that I understood what Yalan meant. It's something non-grassland people would never really understand. Grassland women are born mothers, they're as magnamimous and understanding as the earth itself.

Yalan hugged me and I could see my cousin's eyes. His eyes were full of stars, so bright. He looked at Yalan, and she blushed, two red moons appearing on her cheeks. Aunty said that people with bright, flashing eyes had magical powers and as far as Bilige was concerned, his heart definitely held many a starry secret.

I helped Yalan pick white mushrooms from among the grass. She wanted to make soup for uncle and mom, and so had come out picking mushrooms. She told Bilige that her family had already slaughtered two sheep and was preparing to invite our family over for lunch. Between us, we quickly gathered half a basket of mushrooms. Yalan noticed her dad riding over to uncle's place so she quickly urged Bilige, "My dad's gone over to invite your mom. You have to come for lunch too." I quickly chipped in, "What about me? Why did you invite him and not me?" Yalan picked me up again, kissed my cheek, "How could I forget Mina? You're the first one on my list!"

She put me down and went to go back with the basket. My cousin whistled and his horse trotted over. Putting the reins into Yalan's hands, he told her to ride the horse home, and it would find its own way back. Yalan smiled and mounted the horse lithely. She was going to say something, but on account of me staring at her intently, she held it back and rode off.

Aunty, Bilige and myself went over to Yalan's together. Aunty put her bread and other food items into a huge sheepskin bag and loaded it onto the horse. Bilige drove the herd of horses to graze not far from where Yalan's family had pitched their yurt. But my girl cousin was afraid the two flocks of sheep might get mixed up, so she didn't come. Lukele stayed behind with her to look after the sheep, but I kept seeing his head poking out through the grass.

When we entered the yurt, Mr. Bieli and uncle were already well into the drink. Mr. Bieli greeted us with a beaming face, bowing formally to my aunt, and picking me up to kiss. Turning to Bilige, he bellowed out praise for my cousin, almost deafening us: "What a strapping young fellow! So valiant, so clever, so well-tempered. What a fine son you have raised, the whole grassland will envy you!"

Aunty was thrilled. She loved it when people praised Bilige, as if she had given birth to a rare jewel, but wasn't sure that others realized it. She stood smiling but silent beside Yalan's mom, not knowing the polite thing to say. Uncle saw she was stuck for words, and prompted her with a mention of their hosts' fine children. Aunty's doting gaze gave Yalan and her brother the once over: she nodded in agreement saying, "Whoever has the honor of marrying your daughter should really thank the Malu gods." Aunty's words were simple, but the women understood each other so Yalan's mother was happy too. She stretched out her plump hands, taking aunty's hands in hers, pulling her towards her so they could sit and have an intimate chat.

Bilige picked up a wooden water bucket and took it outside. Yalan followed hard on his heels, as nimble as his own shadow. I whispered to mom, "Cousin and Yalan are good friends. They're out together right now, talking about things that they don't want others to know." She jerked up her head, gave me a piercing look and whispered back, "Mina, you're too young to understand. There are some things adults can say, but it's not OK for kids to say." I made as if I understood but I was confused. She was being weird, always complaining back home that I didn't talk enough, but now, here, she was shutting me up. Bilige and Yalan came back from fetching water. Bilige put in a lot of effort. He brought in the cupboards and the milk jars from outside the tent and arranged them in the same order they were used to at uncle's home. Forgetting what mom had just told me I blabbed, "Cousin, you did it wrong! You just made their home look like ours!"

Everyone burst out laughing. Adults are strange creatures, they can laugh over nothing. But they all seemed to be enjoying the joke, so I joined in with the merriment.

Mr. Bieli held my little hands in his massive paws and said, "My daughter is starting college in the city this September and it's too late for her mother to give me another daughter. Why don't you be my daughter?"

"Wow!"someone exclaimed. It was as if we just seen a red carp leaping out of the Xini River, a portent of great success in life, and every eye was on Yalan. Mr. Bieli was really proud. He struggled with his broken Mandarin to explain about Yalan's college and everyone got confused. Finally, when Yalan corrected her father's pronunciation, we figured out that she had been accepted to study art at a teachers university in the city. Mr. Bieli wasn't finished; he claimed he was selling 20 sheep and two cows to send his daughter to college in style. The semi-drunk but extremely happy Mr. Bieli looked like a proud prince.

At the banquet, only Bilige had nothing to say. Yalan brought out the steaming lamb, set it in the center of the table, squeezed in next to him and surreptiously held his hand. My cousin wavered, but withdrew the hand that had so much it wanted to say. He sat straight and erect. He knew how to control himself, particularly on an occasion like this. He certainly didn't want the embarrassment of the adults seeing them touching.

But Yalan's eagle-eyed mom had seen her daughter's action. She deftly carved the mutton in the silver alunimium plate, gave Bilige a huge helping and urged him to tuck in. Then, she said to aunty, "Our children are the best gifts bestowed on us, a consolation for our life of hardship. Bilige is of the marrying age, and the girl who marries him will be happy forever."

Now it was uncle's turn to speak. He had just been talking with Mr. Bieli about two families in a dispute over a piece of grassland. Hearing Yalan's mother bring up the subject of Bilige and marriage, he did what every responsible father would do and proudly told one and all that he had already betrothed Bilige to someone and that the wedding was to take place at the coming New Year. In the autumn, the family would sell 20 sheep at the market in Hailar to fund a grand wedding party to which everyone on the Baiyintala would be invited.

My uncle had probably felt challenged. The family owned only 40 sheep in total and if he sold half to pay for Bilige's wedding, what were they supposed to live on afterwards? He was in no position to compete with their family; nor was it the right time. Even I felt for him. Uncle seemed not at all embarrassed, however, carrying on as normal and making everyone think he was quite a character.

My cousin kept silent, and his silence became a sign of maturity in Mr. Bieli's eyes, so he praised my cousin generously. But as soon as no one was looking Bilige got up and left. He must have been in very deep pain to leave without saying a formal goodbye and risk being chastised for such a breach of good manners. The bright sunlight shone through the tent, illuminating everyone's faces and the fragrance of milk tea wafted everywhere. Everyone was tipsy and merry and no one noticed Bilige had left. Not even Yalan.

But aunty sat sad and morose between us. The Malu gods were right about the connection between a son and his mother. Even though she knew nothing, her mother's intuition told her something was wrong. Bilige left, but the sound of him moving carried very far, and then came back to her, traveling just as long and difficult a distance. I knew she was worried for her son, that she'd pray for him once we got home.

Night was falling and she lit a fire outside the yurt, sitting there all alone. Uncle was drunk, snoring as loud as the piercing autumn winds; first a loud snore then a soft one, blowing around the wooden tent wall, the copper lamp, the old-fashioned chiming clock, and the iron stove. Mom and Bilige's sister couldn't sleep either, so they went out to keep aunty company by the fire.

On the way home from Yalan's, uncle and aunty had got into a fight, he blaming Bilige for disgracing him by leaving without a proper farewell, she complaining about uncle's crowing over a ridiculous marriage that she hadn't even agreed to. My uncle's friend Tuoke had suddenly arrived from the faraway Yileteli grasslands, bringing with him six bottles of *Hailar* wine and two boxes of fancy pastries from Beijing. He had come in person to suggest a marriage between his daughter and my cousin. Right from the off, aunty had mistrusted this way of going about things: according to Bayintala customs, the boy's family usually asked a go-between to ask for the girl's hand in marriage and should have done tons of research on the girl before daring to go forward with a proposal. The go-between had to bring gifts three times to the girl's family before her parents could agree for the two young people to meet. But uncle was too proud and, after drinking the wine and listening to all the flattery, he had agreed to the marriage without even asking about the girl. Later on, aunty had asked a trusted relative to check out what sort of a girl she was and it turned out that she was pretty, but lazy and gluttonous so no one wanted to marry her. Aunty blamed my uncle for doing wrong by their son. Uncle did regret it, but would he admit it? Summoning up all of his grassland machismo he told his wife that the matter had been decided, and that it was her job as the mother-in-law to discipline the new bride.

My uncle's snoring woke me up too. I tried stuffing his nostrils with wool from the bed covers and this only quieted him for a short while before he started up again. I yawned. Lukele popped his head in from outside, stared at me and I got up out of the stuffy yurt. Aunty and the others were sitting by the fire. There must have been something wrong with my eyes — all I could see was three very morose-looking rocks — their heads were slightly lowered, as if they had been drawn there by the rhythm of the dancing flames but their bodies had petrified into indistinct, static rocks. Then, the fire seemed to solidify into a golden bowl. Afraid, I called out "Mom! Mom!" She turned around toward me and I came to again. I didn't tell her what I'd seen; I didn't want to worry her. She always took things so seriously. Mom always held that my nervous system was to blame for all my strange dreams and worries that a child of my age should not be troubled by. She said I was a hard-to-raise child, a worrisome child, and what would become of me she just couldn't see.

I trudged over to aunty and asked for a story. Listlessly, she refused, saying she was tired and the story would sound boring. I touched her lined face and told her, "If you tell me a story, perhaps the spirits in the wind will be glad to hear it too, then tomorrow they'll remember your prayers and help you out."

Aunty brightened up. Maybe she really believed that there were spirits in the warm night wind listening to us mortals. She asked me to go fetch her tobacco pipe. Once she had drawn on the pipe a few times, she perked up and started her story telling.

All of aunty's tales came from her grandmother. The tales her grandmother knew, all nomads knew. These tales were like a meandering river, their beginnings flowed into their ends, constantly renewing in a never-ending flow.

This time, aunty forgot which stories she had already told me. She started with the Rock Maiden legend, and I'd heard it a million times before. She always started like this: "A beautiful girl in the sky was being eyed up by a devil. She wouldn't go with him so he imprisoned her under a rock. Ever after that, she could see everything on the grasslands, but no one could see her...." With every single telling aunty would stop at this point. Of course I knew what she was going to ask next: "And can you guess who it was that released her from the rock?"

Just as the handsome rider rescued the Rock Maiden, Bilige rescued Yalan.

When Yalan had first met Bilige, she was wandering around the grassland trying to find things to paint.

Yalan had loved painting ever since she was a child. Her mom used to boil up different flowers and grasses to make fabric dyes in every color of the rainbow, but Yalan often pinched them for her painting. She painted anywhere and everywhere: spirit eyes on rocks, white lambs on the yurt, with ears like palms of hands. These palms could hear trees rocking in the wind, the song of water in the wind, and the rising of the moon over the crest of the mountains.

In high school, a picture Yalan handed in for her art homework staggered her art teacher, who frequently complained that he was not born in the right era. He announced to the class that he had discovered a genius. She had painted some Buryat Mongolian girls, who were all as fat and round as their food tents, their hair in treetrunk-thick braids filled with bird nests. The teacher held the watercolor aloft and informed Yalan that her sole purpose in life would be to paint.

Yalan was sitting on a meadow, frowning. She needed to assemble a portfolio to get into art college, but she'd been wandering around for days now and still didn't know what to paint that would make her stand out.

Just as she was beginning to despair, Bilige had come flying into view. From out of the depths of the grassland came the thundering hooves of galloping horses. They raced towards her, and she was awestruck by how handsome they were, how elegantly they held themselves. Ever since she was little, she had heard from her dad that the famous Sanhe (Three Rivers) Horse from the grasslands was the best breed in China; the Mongolians called it "the prince of horses." It was such horses that the army of Genghis Khan had ridden to conquer the world.

Yalan saw several hundred of these thoroughbreds race past her; behind them rode a copper-skinned rider, coming straight for her. She waved at him and called out, "Hey there. Stop! Slow down!"

But Bilige couldn't stop. His chestnut horse galloped along with the rest of the herd across the surging grassland. Their manes streamed in the wind, just like clouds rolling around the sky, and their glossy bodies glinted with the sun's magical light. They dashed with the speed of a comet, their hooves thundering.

She watched Bilige dash off deep into the grasslands with those horses from the realm of gods.

Yalan painted Bilige from memory, making him the subject of her painting *Rock Maiden*. He was racing, the earth was racing, even the sun was racing. But they were all outpaced by the horses – those flying comets. She painted Bilige as a hero in hot pursuit of those heavenly animals.

Her art teacher was astonished that a girl like her could paint something so powerful. Yalan just smiled; no way could she tell him about that one special person in her heart, about the passion and strength coursing through her. As soon as she clapped eyes on Bilige, she had realized: "This is where it all starts."

That night, aunty told me story after story and I slowly fell asleep. Her langorous voice, her tobacco-smoke breath became increasingly fainter, seeming to drift away on the chill night wind, until I couldn't hear anything at all and fell into dreamland. Elsewhere that night, another fire was burning, illuminating the faces of two young people; their eyes burned more fiercely than the fire.

Yalan stared at the sky and asked sadly, "Bilige, are you really getting married? What will I do?"

Bilige pulled out some straw from under him. "My dad's crazy. He didn't even ask me. Just went ahead and agreed on this marriage. I never agreed to it!"

Yalan hit his chest flirtatiously. "You're not allowed to meet her. I'm the only one you can see! I've made up my mind. We'll get married as soon as I graduate. Will you wait for me?"

Bilige gazed at her lovingly, causing her to blush and bury her head in his chest. Stroking her long, long hair Bilige promised, "I'd wait for you forever. When our wedding day comes, I'll brush and part your hair to make you my bride. You'll be so beautiful, more beautiful than the moon itself."

Yalan giggled, teasing him, "What if I don't come back?"

Bilige was shocked. He turned the idea over for ages before confessing, "I never thought about us splitting up. I'd die if that happened."

Yalan's eyes moistened at this painful thought. As if making a vow, she swore, "I'll never let anyone split us up. I'll never leave you. You're the best man ever, how could I ever break up with you? I want to have ten sons with you, and build up ten huge ranges. We'll have flocks of sheep and cows, and thousands of horses. That's the life I want."

Bilige was carried along by the fantasy, believing they could actually live this dream. He could almost see his ten sons, all handsome and strong like the sun and the moon, as splendid and glorious as the great Genghis Khan.

Next morning, uncle woke up in a fit of coughing. He went outside to the sheep pen and counted out half their number. A shadow crossed his face. "Mina, I'm getting old." Taking my hand, we slowly did the round of the sheep fold. "Your aunty blamed me for bragging, and she was right. I was so drunk last night my mouth ran away with me. What a fool I made of myself."

I did feel sorry for uncle. He was indeed getting old. His ruddy face had been scoured to the texture of tree bark, through years of exposure to the grassland winds, and his wrinkled face put me in mind of water ruffled by an autumn wind. It's tough getting old; luckily for uncle, he had sons, so he wouldn't feel lonely and helpless. His strength and hopes would carry on in his sons.

Of course uncle couldn't see he was already going downhill fast. He said, "The only thing Bilige is interested in is horses. Nothing but horses. At his age, I shouldn't have to worry about who he'll marry!"

"But he loves Yalan! How can you say he's only got eyes for

horses?" I grabbed my chance to put in a few words for Bilige. Had it been anyone else uncle was attacking, I'd have kept my mouth shut. But this was Bilige. There's no way I wouldn't defend him.

My words stopped uncle in his tracks. His eyes goggled, staring at me in a way that almost made me giggle. Once, aunty had carved a "Shewoke" deity with staring eyes just like uncle looked then. He told me firmly. "Don't make up wild stories! If you don't stop the crows will come and get your tongue!"

I was furious. "There aren't any crows around, so you can't scare me! And stop fighting with aunty all the time! My mom and dad never row like you two!"

Not knowing how to deal with me, uncle made to go back inside. Thinking he was about to pick a fight with aunty, I rushed to get there first.

Aunty was sitting on the bed scraping a sheepskin. I ran inside and stood beside her, but she told me not to block the light. I didn't budge, as if the sound of her scraper scraping off the flesh was more beautiful than our grassland music. She looked up at me quizzically, put down the scraper and pulled me into a hug. "Poor little girl. Who's been mean to you?"

Uncle pushed in beside her, and saw I was about to start crying. He cleared his throat, "Mina never tells fibs. Tell me, my dear, what did Bilige say to you last night?"

Uncle had guessed right. The night before, uncle had been dead to the world, and everyone else except aunty had gone to sleep. But she waited up for Bilige, a coat over her shoulders. I don't know when he came back, but at some point I did smell a rush of fresh grass and woke up sneezing. Bilige had told aunty about him and Yalan. She listened without saying a word, only that he should get some sleep. Then she blew out the lamp and snuggled under the quilt.

From the hard look uncle was giving aunty, I could sense that that there was trouble brewing so I went out to fetch mom. She and Bilige were turning over to dry the cow pats that had got soaked in the rain a few days before. Almost breathless with indignation, I told them what had happened and they dropped their tools and rushed back, Bilige a little way behind mom and me.

I ran inside first, only seeing uncle rummaging around the bed for his pipe, too blind with anger to realize that he was already holding it. Aunty was too busy even to acknowledge his presence. She had to scrape off every bit of flesh from the hide and then soak the hide in fermented sheep brains or yogurt to soften it. Then, she had to remove any remaining meat in order to make nice clothes out of the skin. She was planning to sew a sheepskin coat for me to wear to school during the winter. In her opinion, our little town Yakeshi is a huge wind tunnel, where the Siberian winds pass through every winter. She was worried that on my way to school, I would be blown away like a little lamb.

Seeing us enter the yurt, uncle's mood changed back to its former confidence. Stuffing his pipe bowl with tobacco he shouted to me to get a light. I poked a dry willow twig into the stove to where a low fire of cow pats was burning. The twig caught light and I handed it to him. He lit up, very carefully and deliberately; only when he took his first puff did he seem suddenly to remember us. "I don't think we're good enough for Yalan. She's going off to study in the provincial capital, and maybe she'll stay on there. She won't come back to take care of this family. I can't count on our eldest son; he and his wife have left these parts. Second son is studying to be a vet, which will probably become a government job anyway. Bilige, you can't forget that you have parents too. We can't afford her as a daughter-in-law."

Aunty stopped what she was doing and tried to talk him round. "Even so, the two of them are in love. We can't force them to break up. If we do that, the kind gods will be displeased."

Uncle held back his anger and asked Bilige, "Son. You've given us a surprise. I just hope we're not just dreaming along with you. Your mom just told me that last night you and Yalan decided for yourselves to get married. I'm old and deaf, but not completely gaga. What I want to know is, have you taken leave of your senses?"

"Father, we're completely serious. We just can't split up. We just beg both sets of parents to grant us holy matrimony." Bilige said respectfully.

With a scornful expression, uncle made as if he were adressing some deities hovering overhead. "Look, he even knows that marriage is a sacred thing."

Mom could no longer stop herself: she went over to him. "Brother, you would like Yalan to be your daughter-in-law, wouldn't you? But you're afraid her parents won't consent to it and that Bilige will have loved in vain. Maybe it calls for a bit more effort. We should be humble and go over there and request the match. I'll go over there myself."

Uncle's head slumped, something that only happened when he was sad. No one said anything, but we were all moved by his expression - humiliated but dutiful. Aunty sighed, and the sound flowed out through the opening in the rooftop. My uncle said to mom, "Even if Bilige hasn't thought of it, surely you have? They're not a good match. Yalan will never come back here. She's like a lark, once she leaves the grasslands, she'll never come back and Bilige would be so hurt. The lad's so single minded, he'll go crazy over it. He'll carry the scars for life, then we'll have a serious case on our hands."

Bilige vowed, "Father, we'll never break up. You don't know

Yalan, she's not like that. She's a girl of the grasslands. Please back out of the other marriage. I never agreed to it in the first place."

Uncle jumped at this suggestion, bellowing, "What are you talking about? Bail out of the other marriage? How embarrassing would that be? How could I ever live that down? The whole of the Baiyintala would be saying behind my back that my word is not to be trusted. No one would ever drink with me again."

Bilige took a step forward. He wasn't finished pleading. "Please back out of it. It's Yalan I want to marry. She's a girl in a million. I want her. No one else."

Uncle lifted his tobacco pipe and hit Bilige on the head with it. "You've disgraced me!" He jumped off the bed, yelling at his wife, "A fine son you've raised, acting like an idiot over a girl. You'll live to regret it."

My uncle kept on cursing and gave my cousin a bruise on the temple. Aunty suddenly screamed in pain: her left hand had got jabbed by the skin scraper, and she was bleeding profusely. Mom rushed for bandages, shedding tears as she dressed the wound. Mom was crying but uncle calmed down. He stood stock still for a while, cleared his throat and went out. Hearing his footsteps retreating into the distance, mom dried off her tears and told Bilige not to hate his father, because it wasn't his fault.

Bilige croaked, "It's not my fault either. I just want Yalan."

Aunty, holding her injured hand with the other, nodded, "Bilige, you're my son and I know you have a heart of gold. Do what you need to do. You're not a calculating person. If you have to face something, then face it head on."

Yalan's mother came to call on us. She came on a piebald horse and dismounted at a distance from our yurt, as a mark of respect to the hosts. She brought over half a sack of white rice, a rare commodity back then. Aunty accepted the precious gift with gracious equanimity. Yalan's mother was greeted with great ceremony; uncle in particular was overly polite, bobbing his head up and down in gratitude. Lukele and I observed, listening with ears pricked; the dog wagged his tail and I whispered to him to come closer. His head nuzzled against my hand. "Lukele, aunty is not happy," I said as I stroked his head. "Her smile's not for real. She's being too polite to Yalan's mother, this can't be good. Their children are so close, their mothers should be close too – like sisters."

Lukele understood. He listened by the door, all attention, worrying just like a human about what was going on inside. Mom used to tell me that when adults were talking, kids should stay away. According to her instructions, I should stay outside; but I really wanted to know why Yalan's mother had come. Mom was out with my girl cousin, gathering medicinal herbs to treat aunty's stomach complaint. I summoned up my courage, walked in and sat on aunty's lap.

Yalan's mom sat sipping tea and took out a big paper package, saying it was food from the sacrificial offerings and everyone should share it.

I was enticed by the delicious-smelling food. Every time nomadic herders choose a piece of grassland to live on, they are sure to offer sacrifices to the kitchen god first and then share the sacrificial foods with their neighbors. Yalan's mom was plump, and I wished to press a finger into the cute little dimples in her arms and neck. The food she made was just as cute as she was, round and chubby. But aunty wouldn't let me touch the cheese, the rice cakes, or the buns. She thanked Yalan's mom and made small talk about their animals. Yalan's family was rich; their yurt was surrounded by their flocks of sheep and herds of cattle, countless of them grazing on huge swathes of grassland.... If aunty was going to ask after every one of them we'd be there until the stars came out.

Yalan's mom finally voiced what she was trying to say. "God has blessed us with wonderful neighbors and fertile land. We're content. But we're concerned about Yalan. She likes Bilige, and she's been very stubborn ever since she was little. Her dad and I have spoiled her. Originally we were planning to stay here for a while, but for the last few days Yalan has been fighting with us. She wants to get engaged to Bilige before going off to college. Her dad and I have decided to move on to new pastures in a few days so as not to cause you any trouble. We're really sad to be leaving you all."

Uncle was displeased. He knew what message her words really carried. His favorite son was being belittled and it was insupportable. Uncle pronounced seriously, "This is not a problem at all. After all, Bilige is getting married soon. I'm off to Hailar pretty soon. There's a famous silversmith there I'm going to commission to make jewelry for his bride-to-be. Jade and amber, that's what it'll be made of. Bilige will be so proud. Marriage is such an important matter, of course both sets of parents have to agree."

This time it was Yalan's mom's turn to be embarrassed. Her carefully planned visit wasn't turning out right at all. The stubborn old man opposite her was actually lecturing her on what proper parents should do, deliberately embarrassing her. At this she abandoned her high and mighty attitude and said, "Bilige is a wonderful young man, whoever marries him will be happy."

My aunt became happy too, as she loved it when people praised her son. In a gesture of thanks, she took Yalan mom's hand and said, "We mothers all want our children to be happy. When my son gets married, please do come to the wedding with all the family."

Listlessly, Lukele followed me around. The sun was shining, the light flashing and dancing. Just then, I felt as if I'd fallen down a bottomless golden hole and couldn't climb out of all this golden light. The grown-ups were all concerned with their own business; no one paid any attention to me....

"Mina, run off and play. I'm busy right now." I ran around the hay stacks with Lukele but even he got tired of that after a while. The green grass was beckoning to me and the silvery river was shining. I scurried down the hill while no one was watching. No one called out after me and Lukele happily followed as well. I guess he was bored too.

I pulled at the tall grasses as I walked, hoping a fairy would jump out and play with me. In aunty's stories, the Baiyintala is full of fairies. They sleep in the grass during the day and roam around at night. How I envied the freedom and romance of their wondering lifestyle.

Lukele suddenly stopped, staring at the movement in a patch of grass ahead of us and growled. Like a wise old man, the dog was giving me a warning. I saw Bilige's chestnut horse standing motionless amid the tall grass, as if daydreaming. But the grass was shuddering in the sun, as if being whipped by some strange force.

I wanted to call out to Bilige but I couldn't. I bowed my head and felt my own loneliness.

Lukele's eyes kept returning to the patch of moving grass, and then back at me, as if he knew something. Aunty's anxious voice was calling out to me, so I took the dog back home. He followed me for a while and then ran off ahead, waiting for me quite some way away. Then I realized why he'd been running so fast. The grassland climate was so volatile and the weather was constantly changing. It had been sunny when we came out, but now black storm clouds were right behind us.

Lukele and I dashed back, and we could hear raindrops at

our back. The rain was weird; it fell only on that patch of moving grass; not a drop fell anywhere around our yurt. I ran up the hill and looked at the grass patch from there. The warm and passionate rain, like a white veil drawn across the sky, hid everything that was happening in there.

I held aunty's hand and pointed at the rain. "Why is it raining over there and not here?" She just patted my cheek and told me to go ask uncle because she was going to sew something for me. I grabbed hold of him, "Why doesn't the rain come here?" He donned his sunglasses, looked at the sky and concocted a story: "The rain god had too much to eat today and he was puffing and panting; he was so tired of coming and going, he just let go of his load in one spot. That's the explanation." My uncle always had a fantastic explanation for anything.

Bilige appeared on the grasslands. He was carried away by the passion of the pouring, pelting rain, leaving his horse to make its own way home. He didn't know what trouble was waiting for him.

I saw him at last and whooped as I came out of the yurt. I'd waited so long for him I'd given up hope. Now, there he was, making for home. His walk looked different today. He was proud and happy, as if just returning from a celebration banquet. I wanted to cry but didn't know why. This summer, I'd become pretty emotional; it didn't take much to get me crying. I didn't want my cousin to call me a crybaby so I held back my tears in case everyone laughed at me.

Bilige called out, "Mina, I'm home." I ran over to him, and looked up at him without a word. Usually, when he came back, I would stand with him chattering nonstop, so my silence this time startled him. "Mina, what's up? Who's upset you?" He'd have been better not asking, but when he did, I whinged "I saw you with

Yalan. Right through that huge rainstorm. You've been with her all the time." I sobbed uncontrollably.

He froze, motionless and mute. Then, he bent down and wiped away my tears. "Mina, if you're like this when you're so young, what will become of you I don't know." Without any warning, he hoisted me up onto the back of his horse and stood me there. I was so scared I forgot what had just happened. "I'm frightened. Let me down."

But Bilige encouraged me "Grasslands kids can ride when they're seven or eight. You're ten already, Mina. How can you learn to ride if you can't even stand up on horseback?"

I was really unsteady up there, about to fall off. He lowered his voice. "There's a brave girl, stand still." The chestnut horse was my friend. Any of my snacks that Lukele didn't get, I fed to him. The horse encouraged me too by standing still as a stone. I stood up on the saddle. Cousin was right, if I was brave enough, I could stand on horseback just like an acrobat. I gazed into the distance. The Yimin River was like a pregnant woman, curvaceous and indolent, flowing in the sun. I saw a girl by the riverside washing her long hair. "I can see Sister Yalan!" I shouted. "It must be her! Her hair is so long. I'm gonna grow my hair long like that someday."

Looking up at me, he joked that with my wispy hair, I'd be lucky to get that much hair in five years.

My cousin had really bad timing and I got mad. I hit back. "It'll be you crying before long. Yalan's mom came over earlier and told us they're moving on soon. You'll never see Yalan again!"

My words were like cold water to extinguish my cousin's happiness. He lifted me down and covered his face with his large hands.

I tugged at his sleeve and he brought his hands down. With a bitter smile he said, "Birds will always fly free. Mina, someday you'll become a bird and fly away too. But I belong here." Sadly, he looked over to Yalan's yurt; we could see the smoke curling up and drifting off into the distance.

Uncle was sitting on the ground fixing the wooden wheels on the cart. He was giving one of the joints a good hammering and asked aunty to find the soybean oil to lube the axles. Last night, after everyone had gone to bed, uncle had announced his intention to cut the reeds growing by the river and take them to the Hailar Paper Mill, saying he was told that a cartload of reeds could fetch a good price. He said he'd had it in mind for some time. Before anyone could respond, his snoring told us he'd fallen asleep. Mom complained, "He's so impulsive. He's always been stubborn. Take no notice of him and let him go his own sweet way."

The reeds by the river were not yet tall enough in summer, but uncle was too impatient to wait until autumn when they would be taller. He was spontaneous like that: if an idea came into his head he would act on it immediately. After fixing the cart he drained a cup of milk tea and patted aunty's backside in a conciliatory gesture, "My dear, whoever the bride is, I should be preparing for Bilige's wedding. Bloody autumn moves too slow – it's like an arthritic old dodderer."

In high spirits, uncle went off to cut the reeds. He was really strong and had the stamina of a young man. On the third morning, uncle loaded up the cart with cut reeds and set off on the small road leading to the nearest little township. The Hailar Paper Mill had a collection depot there.

After uncle left, aunty spent the whole day fretting, unable to get interested in anything and constantly looking in the direction uncle would be returning from. Mom was right, they're inseparable;

you can't have one without the other. Their constant arguing was just their way of showing affection. Mom said, "It's your uncle's nature to be very direct; he's always got to shout to get his point across. He's totally transparent. Everyone can see right into him."

I went to pick herbs with mom. She was figuring to treat aunty's stomach problem first and then treat uncle's bronchitis. I didn't think uncle would be as amenable as aunty in taking doctor's orders and drinking the bitter medicine without kicking up a fuss.

Mom kept telling me off for picking the wrong herbs, so I threw away all the herbs I had and ran off to pick flowers. It was as I was messing around that I saw Bilige. He was riding with two other people, following a great mass of horses off into the grasslands. I thought about my uncle riding off on an ox-cart that morning and asked mom, "Bilige herds horses everyday, so why doesn't uncle's family own any horses?"

Mom told me, "The horses Bilige grazes are army horses; you could buy half a yurt for the price of an army horse. There's no way uncle could afford a horse like that."

I was disheartened. My uncle didn't have a horse with the speed of a comet. To pay for Bilige's wedding, he would have to sell so many reeds and make so many trips. I stared at the horses until they were completely out of sight. I sighed, thinking that if we had a fine horse like one of those, then maybe life would be better for uncle's family.

Mom went to pick herbs in another spot, leaving me to my own devices. I picked a bunch of flowers and went running towards her. A toad crouched in my path and I jumped over it for fear of treading on the little creature. Then I heard the sound of the wind and the shivering of the reeds by the river. I saw the wind bending them in one direction and then the other. Then I smelled wetness heading straight in our direction. Mom always said I had a dog's sense of smell. I warned her, "Mom! I can smell rain coming!"

Mom came dashing towards me, grabbed my hand and we ran back together. "Your uncle's on his way back," she panted. "Where would he go to get out of the rain? With a physique like his, if he gets drenched he's bound to get sick." She sobbed and cried, her face coursing with tears and with rain from the downpour.

It kept on raining for a very long time, enveloping the whole of the Baiyintala grassland. The rain and fog were as scary as a winter blizzard. My girl cousin rounded up the sheep back into the pen and I stood watching them. They stood there in that never-ending rain; static, stoic and silent, like a group of white rocks. A few of the weaker lambs started whimpering and those whimpers became loud, distressed bleating, calling out for help. Aunty and mom were frantically busy moving things in the tent to where they wouldn't get wet – the rain was rushing in through the smoke outlet in the roof.

I ran outside, squeezed my way into the sheep pen, grabbed the three smallest lambs and rushed back with them toward the yurt. Aunty came out from inside, wrapped a cloak around me and scolded me for running out like that. Inside, the three little lambs cuddled up beside me; my cousin fetched some dry clothes to put over them and moved them closer to the fire.

I warmed up too. Aunty gave me a winter jacket that wrapped me up like a bun, and made me drink two bowls of hot milk tea. Mom wouldn't let me sleep; instead she told me to walk around and get rid of the coldness inside. The rain subsided into a drizzle. The rain coming in gradually subsided to a drizzle, eventually tailing off into a drip, drip, drip, into the milk buckets. Aunty told me to go outside because there should be a rainbow.

I came out of the yurt and looked towards the sky. The three little lambs had followed me and were frolicking in the wet grass. Aunty had promised a rainbow and there was one. Actually, there were two rainbows, like a lucky double arch bridge linking earth and heaven. "Uncle's back!" I shouted. Everyone came out of the yurt to see. Could it have been a mirage? But no, there he was sitting on his ox-cart emerging from the rainbow; that spectacular heavenly bridge seemed to be escorting him home in a blaze of color!

If Mr. Tuoke had insisted on uncle acknowledging the marriage agreement, it probably would have gone ahead. The men of the grassland were true to their word. Even if they make a mistake, they own up to it. Mr. Tuoke did not smash wine glasses or force my uncle. He just drank himself into a stupor. Uncle couldn't drink as much and he fell asleep. It was the perfect timing to avoid embarrassment and humiliation. Mr. Tuoke rose to his feet like a hero, got dressed for outside and said to uncle. "I know you did this for a reason. Let's let the winter snow decide. If you haven't come over by then, I'll marry my daughter to someone else. If you do come, we can still be in-laws. I'd hate to see Bilige go, he's quite a catch."

Mr. Tuoke did not stay over despite our inviting him to. He left calmly without any rudeness or trace of drunkenness, and his words of farewell were so fine and dignified that even mom and I felt embarrassed. Aunty brought out all of our decent-looking food, packed it up and presented it to him. He swung onto his horse and rode away into the sunset.

We watched Mr. Tuoke disappear into the reddening grassland. A crimson sun seemed to fill the entire sky and Mr. Tuoke was racing into the sun. He suddenly stood up in the stirrups and waved his hands. Instantly, the grassland echoed with his uninhibited shouts.

Every morning my uncle would stand outside the yurt, looking toward the river, where the soft reeds were growing, standing in the wind just like him. The staff in the depot had said that the autumn reeds would fetch the best price; once they'd changed color they were stronger and could make the best quality paper.

After uncle's sixth trip to the depot he finally heeded the advice of insiders to wait until mid-autumn before harvesting the reeds. He'd never been like this before, blindly pinning his hopes on reeds that would bring him golden days. In his mind, he couldn't stop mentally converting the reeds into the finest wedding imaginable, into endless praise from all the relatives and respect for him as an elder of the bridegroom.

He kept his secret strictly to himself. Even though he was bursting to tell someone, he didn't want others to know his seemingly ridiculous ideas. He was always calling me out of the blue, for no good reason. "Mina…," he would cry, but when I ran over to him, he'd stare at me all puzzled, like I'd misheard. I'd tug at his hand but to no response. I'd dig my fingers into his tightly clenched fist. Finally he asked…,"Mina.This thing with Bilige. Do you think they could last? Or are they just playing around? I'd like to see him married before I get much older."

I spoke up for Bilige. "He's not joking around. He really loves Yalan. They should spend the rest of their lives together, like my mom and dad."

"Maybe only kids can see the truth. Grown-ups have experienced too much to see clearly," said uncle after a while.

Yalan would be off to college soon so she asked Bilige to keep her company when she went painting in the grassland and Bilige took a few days off from herding the army horses. They had limited time left together; the uncertain future and sense of foreboding made Bilige uneasy about Yalan's imminent departure. One night, he woke us all up with his shouting, "I don't want to close my eyes. I've not spent enough time with you."

But his eyes were shut tight.

That afternoon, I sat outside the yurt waiting for Bilige to fetch me. He was going painting with Yalan by the river and I wanted to go too. Bilige hadn't wanted to take me at all but uncle had scowled and banged his pipe on the table, so he'd had to agree in the end. Otherwise uncle might have made him stay home and keep my mom company. Uncle really didn't want us to go, so he'd been unbelievably cranky over the last few says. While busying herself in making a lambskin for me, Aunty whispered in mom's ear, "When are you both coming again? I wish Mina could stay on out here, but there aren't any schools for her. But if Mina goes, I'll miss her too much."

"We'll come back in the winter. Maybe Bilige's marriage will be settled by then," said mom sadly.

I sat waiting for Bilige outside the yurt, so I could see him no matter which direction he was coming from. But I couldn't tell. Even ever-so-smart Lukele couldn't tell. He just put out his long tongue and panted. The heat was searing, but I liked it hot, preferring to stay outside rather than going inside to escape the heat. Everything was so silent. I could hear the sunlight touching the tips of the grass. I felt overcome with sadness, a grown-up kind of sadness. In a few days, I would have to go back to my horrible little town. It's so damp there whatever time of year, and our house was like a little black box. In all my born days I'd never seen warm sunlight come in. In that room, everyone seemed like a shadow, insubstantial and unreal. But I missed my dad. Just then a big dog came out of the grass towards us. Meekly, with head down and tail between his legs he came over to us. I was sure it was the sheepdog of Yalan's family coming to find

Lukele. I looked over towards Yalan's place where her family's sheep and our own flock were about to mix up and wander about together, like fat white clouds fallen to the earth.

"Lukele, your friend's here." Lukele first looked up lazily at me. Then he jumped to his feet, and made a strange noise in his throat, like rumbling thunder; his hackles rose hard, sharp and hostile.

The other dog froze, staring at Lukele. Lukele bared his teeth, and viciously barked at the newcomer. He studied Lukele for a while and then made off, heading back in the same direction he had come from. Lukele's loud barking followed the dog's measured retreat through the grass; he stopped, turned to take another look at Lukele, and then was gone.

Aunty dashed out and stood in front of me, amazed and excited "Oh heavens, he's come back to see his child!" She patted Lukele, trying to calm him down, but it was my hands he licked. Mom came out too but she had no idea what had just happened. Aunty, afraid of scaring her, chose her words carefully, "The wolf came back. I'm sure it was because he wanted to see Lukele but Mina thought he was a dog. Lukele was afraid it might hurt Mina. That's why he was barking like that. Poor thing, he's never barked like that before."

Mom's face blanched. She paced around the tent, her hands to her head, muttering. "If your dad knew about this, he'll never let you come again."

"He didn't even notice me. He only looked at Lukele. He was sad when he went off." I blurted out.

Aunty bowed her head, put her hands together against her chest and prayed: "Almighty gods, Mina has been like this ever since she was little. She could take stone for treasure and gold for manure. Please protect and take care of her."

I saw another Bilige. He was smiling to us out from the

painting. He looked heroic and handsome, just like Genghis Khan on horseback.

I saw uncle's family too, all of them smiling and content. Yalan depicted their bodies as a huge, flourishing tree, a tree whose roots extended deep throughout the grassland. Their herds, their sheep, their cows, their wooden cart and their yurt were dotted around beneath its roots – a fantastical and wondrous scene.

I begged Yalan to give me the picture but Yalan looked at my cousin. "How about we give it to Bilige to hang in the yurt so he can see it every day?"

I wasn't ready to give up; I kept pestering Yalan to give me another picture or I wouldn't leave them alone together. That worked. She sat herself on the grass, took out her sketch pad and told me to sit still and shut up while she did a picture of me.

I couldn't sit still; I stuck my leg out and then brought it back again; I plucked out the grass beside me to make a straw hat for Lukele. Lukele sat beside Yalan and watched her every stroke, intrigued to see me slowly taking shape on the thick white paper but not connecting the image with the real me. From his astounded look I could see he had no idea who I was.

At last Yalan called me over to look. She named the picture *Shepherd Girl*.

"Mina the Sepherd Girl" had waving, bending rivers flowing from the crown of her head; her hair grew from distant places and changed into rivers and streams. She had stars on her face, shining and glowing, a faint dusting of freckles like the stars of the Milky Way. Mina's mouth was extraordinary – like a erupting volcano spewing out beans, wheat, barley, and big round potatoes.

I complained that there was not enough stuff coming out and made Yalan add in tigers, lions, bears and snakes. After she'd done that, I took the messy picture and boasted that I'd show it off to all my friends back home. They would totally believe I'd just come back from Russia. If they'd heard me once they'd heard me a thousand times telling them that my ancestors came from Russia, from a place called Yaksa, where the water was sweeter than candy, the animals more abundant than stars, where the trees grew so thickly that not even wasps could fly between them.

Yalan got excited as well and said it was her biggest ambition to go to Russia and France to study with famous masters in order to become a successful artist herself.

For me, Yalan's dream was established fact! "I want to go with you!" I shouted. "Then I can become an architect like my dad and we can build a castle in Yaksa and all live in it. My dad told me Yaksa castle was our clan's home, but it was taken over by the Tsar. When I get it back, I'll build lots of houses and give them to the poor."

Bilige laughed and hoisted me up in the air to show he was proud of me. Yalan had been smiling but soon she started feeling sad. Before long, she would have to leave Bilige and pursue her dream in the city. Deep down she felt unsure about her future. As she watched my cousin lift me to the sky, the two of us so happy, her eyes filled with tears. She was reluctant to leave the grasslands; still less did she want to leave Bilige behind. She looked at Bilige who turned towards her smiling, and said, "Bilige, when will we be able to lift our own kids up to the sky?"

It was only afterwards that I learned that for women of the grasslands their dearest wish was to see their husbands lift their newborns into the air. At that moment, the child is an oath for life. The woman commits herself for life to the man and he to her, sticking together throughout all of life's hardships. The gesture is a sacred promise witnessed by the gods.

Bilige understood. Yalan was telling him that all her love and life belonged to him alone. He embraced her tight and promised, "I'll lift up our child one day. My heart will always be yours."

"I will come back. With god as my witness, I want to be with Bilige. I never want to leave him," Yalan smiled again.

Before mom and I left the grasslands, Yalan's family invited us all over. Our families sat together and our flocks were grazing together too; we got the occasional glimpse of Lukele, romping around happily in the dense grass along with the neighbors' sheepdogs.

Yalan's father gave us a huge surprise: he agreed to Yalan and Bilige's marriage. He raised a toast to the heaven and earth, and then to my uncle. "We're going to be in-laws now. Bilige is a good lad, my daughter has insight. Our grassland women are different from other women. Since the beginning of time they have loved eagles in the sky, horses in the grass, and brave heroes. Let us old folk give them our blessing, may they hold to their vows and spend the rest of their lives together."

Uncle's face was bright red; he was dead excited. He knocked back all the wine in the bowl in one swallow and then took out a silk-wrapped package from his pocket. Aunty, who was sitting beside him, gasped. It was a dagger, our clan's heirloom dagger. Uncle usually kept it hidden away, but today he brought it out and, in front of everyone there, presented it to Mr. Bieli.

Mr. Bieli respectfully took the dagger in both hands and removed it from its sheath. We could all hear the dagger sliding from the sheath, like icy-cold water running from a distant underground pool. When the blade itself appeared, it was like an ancient person emerging from history itself, carrying all our unknown secrets, standing in the shadow of time.

Taking the greatest of care, Mr. Bieli replaced the dagger in the sheath and held it to his chest. "My dear brother, this is your heirloom. How can I accept it? Tell you what…on our children's wedding day I'll present Yulan as a bride to Bilige and the dagger too. That way it will become our joint family heirloom."

That day was the happiest day of uncle's life. He got drunk again. He wasn't the only one; everyone there got tipsy, drinking and singing old songs I'd never heard before. I didn't drink a drop but my eyes felt tipsy. I could see the Malu gods quite clearly, coming out of their pouch, drinking with the rest of the party, crawling up out the roof opening then dispersing to wander the earth.

When I got back home with mom, dad said I'd got taller and plumper. Mom said, "What a shame Mina can't stay out there on the grasslands. She doesn't get so much as a sneeze out there."

She also said she'd get someone to buy some Hangzhou silk to give to the couple as a wedding gift. She was convinced they'd love it.

But once dad saw Yalan's picture of me, he started to look dubious. "This is no ordinary girl. Who knows how things will turn out,"he warned.

The way things did turn out reminded me of what Mr. Tuoke had said when he suggested to uncle they should let the winter snow decide matters.

At Spring Festival of the following year, Bilige married Mr. Tuoke's daughter. Mom went to the wedding without me and she was back in no time. We'd thought she'd stay for at least a week but, that morning, she showed up back home covered in snow. Far from looking festive, she seemed worn out and withdrawn, quite downhearted. She told dad that Mr. Tuoke had given his daughter a huge dowry, that the wedding had been a very grand affair and that even faraway relatives had ridden over to attend.

I yelled. "Mom, why didn't Yalan keep her promise? She swore she'd stay with Bilige for ever and ever."

Mom's expression was impassive; she didn't want the subject ever brought up again but to cut a long story short, she told dad that Yalan had got a new boyfriend, a prominent artist in the provincial capital. Just as the lush green grassland was turning gold and the autumn winds from the distant Mongolian Plateau were starting to sweep the Bayin…that was the time that Bilige learned the heartbreaking truth. Yalan's dad had ridden over to uncle's to return the betrothal dagger; in tears, he had sworn that he no longer recognized Yalan as his daughter.

Actually, Bilige had had a foreboding this was going to happen, but he hadn't thought it would be this soon. That summer of passion, that all-consuming love still lingered in his heart, and would keep on lingering. The golden sunlight still flickered over the boundless grassland; time and time again he rode to the post office in town; but he stopped getting letters from Yalan. Deep down he sensed that he was losing Yalan, she had flown away to another world, a world very distant from him, more distant even than heaven.

After Yalan's father had left, uncle called Bilige over and told him solemnly, "Son, the men of the grassland have hearts big enough to hold the sea and the sky. Bilige, try to forget Yalan and forgive her. Don't think about what you've lost. Start counting your blessings instead. Are you so blind you can't see the precious blessings heaven has given you – your health, your peaceful life…?"

But Bilige didn't quite see things uncle's way. He couldn't take this blow. He wandered aimlessly over the grassland, deep in his grief. Everywhere he turned, there would be something to remind him of Yalan: every river was their love song and every cloud was witness to their love. The bright sun was his faithfulness to Yalan and the moon was his pure heart. In his overwrought state he imagined he could see Yalan right there, patiently waiting for him; he set out toward the mirage, a dreamy smile on his face.

Aunty stopped everything; every day she would follow Bilige around. She knew within her bones something bad was about to happen to her son, something really bad. She had to save him. She followed every step of Bilige's erratic wonderings, kneeling in prayer every few paces and imploring the gods to protect him and let her take his pain. The Malu gods responded. They made Bilige stop his running and realize that what he saw behind him, that motionless black shadow, wasn't Yalan but his mother. She moved towards him, panting, her knees caked in dirt and grass, holding a scarf over her head. How many paths she had taken, how many rivers crossed mattered not one bit. If he'd gone to the end of the earth, she would still have followed him.

Bilige finally came to his senses. Weeping, he clung to her. "Mom, I'm sorry. So, so sorry!" Aunty brushed the grass off his clothes, arranged his messy hair and gently led him home by the hand just like a little child. "Son, it's not your fault. Your dad's right, you need to take care of yourself. We'll see that to it that when the tree falls the root will still be there, and when the stream runs dry there will still be a source."

Bilige understood.

Then aunty fell ill. She'd be fast asleep all day but when she did wake up her eyes would search around for Bilige. Bilige had never left her side, wanting to be the first thing she saw once she opened her eyes. Then came the day that she smiled and said, "My son, the light in your eyes has returned. Thanks be to the allmighty gods. Your soul is beginning to find peace."

He danced with excitement, "Mom's better! Mom, you've just

taught me the meaning of happiness."

More than any other people, the men of the grasslands love their mothers. Bilige was a good, considerate son. So, having first got the go-ahead from his parents, he went in person to Mr. Tuoke's place to propose marriage to his daughter.

When snowflakes still floated in the sky and a thick white blanket still covered the vast expanses of the grassland, Bilige had the wedding that fate had arranged for him at long last.

Many years later, I went to an art exhibition in the provincial capital. It was humid that day, with just a few people in the hall. It was dark in there but the lighting was good and it was very quiet, allowing me to take my time and give my full attention to every painting. I stopped in front of one of them.

There was Bilige.

From within the gold frame, Bilige's face smiled out to the world. Many years had gone by but he still looked dashing and brave. Time had not aged him, how could it? He was born to a life in the saddle. In the background stretched the vast grassland and the dense, luxuriant grasses, colored gold by the ancient but undimmed sunlight, grasses that swayed in the autumn wind like the long tresses of a young girl dancing.

My gaze moved to the painting on the right. It was uncle's family – a tight little group, arms around each other, smiling out to the distant world. Their bodies were growing out of the grass itself, before becoming great sturdy trees. Their leaves covered the entire picture. Under this family tree, there were cows, sheep and horses. Yurts too, looking like white field mushrooms. Like a soundless song of the grasslands, it drifted, unhurried, carried along on a timeless silvery river.

I found the signature in the top left corner of the oil painting. Yes, it was Yalan. Only she can paint pictures that reduce me to tears like a child.

(Translated by Lian Wangshu)

The Mud Boot Wedding

Long Renqing

Long Renqing was born to a Tibetan family in Tiebojia, a grassland area by Qinghai Lake, in March, 1967. He graduated from the Tibetan Language and Literature Department of Qinghai Province's Hainan Ethnic Minority Teachers Training School in July 1986. He committed himself to public communications and has been a journalist, editor, director and producer over the years. He now works for Qinghai TV. In 1992, Long began writing and has been widely published in literary periodicals such as *People's Literature*, *Chinese Writers*, *Fang Cao* and *Shanghai Literature*. His major published works include the fiction collection *Guozhuang* (Tibetan folk dance), the documentaries *The Spring and Autumn of Tibetan-Inhabited Areas* (with a coauthor) and *The Secret History of Tsangyang Gyatso*. Long is winner of many literary awards, including the First and Third Qinghai Youth Literature Prize, as well as the Chinese Language Literature Award from a Female Jury – Best Narrative Prize. His works have been included in numerous annual selections and top lists, including *Chinese Short Stories Yearbook 2006*, *Chinese Short Story Classics 2006*, *21st Century Chinese Literature Series – Short Stories 2006*, and *Selected Short Stories of the New Times*. His works *Guozhuang*, *The Love Song*, and *Overlooking Solitude* were included in *Selected Stories*, *Selected Chinese Literature* and other literary periodicals. Long is a member of the Chinese Writers' Association, presidium and council member of the Qinghai Writers' Association, executive council member of the Qinghai Poetry Academy and council member of the Qinghai Film and TV Producers' Association.

The Mud Boot Wedding

1

Tselob is seven years old now and hasn't a care in the world. Every day he roams about along the bank of the Chamed River. Every pebble on the shore has got to know him. And the twinkling little pink primroses know him even better. Each time they see those corduroy shoes, one of them with a big hole in it and a big toe sticking out, coming towards them along the grassy bank, the primroses start trembling – if they could grow feet and if they could walk, one sight of these cloth shoes and they would make a run for it. Tselob always comes striding along, never even noticing what is underfoot and lots of the primroses have been trampled by those feet. Their tender, newly opened petals bear the scars left by Tselob's careless passage. Some of the flowers have had their stems and stalks broken and they wilt, ending up as a little bit of sludge on the grassy strip.

The primroses along the bank cherish a bitter hatred of Tselob, but of this Tselob is totally unaware. He doesn't know he has made himself so many enemies, nor that all those flowers are like little pink eyes, glaring at him with loathing.

This morning Tselob drives his family's cattle and sheep to the grassy riverside and arrives at the bank of the Chamed River again. He walks across the grassy strip and, as usual, takes no notice whatsoever of the primroses. He is totally oblivious to the angry stares directed at him. But the sudden surging of a wave in the river does catch his attention and he immediately concludes that it must be a fish.

The Chamed is a small river that drains into Qinghai Lake. Qinghai Lake has an abundance of naked carp and at the time of year when the primroses come out, the carp swim up the rivers feeding the lake in order to spawn. The fish that Tselob has spotted is one of the advance party, on a scouting mission to explore the Chamed River before they come to spawn in large numbers.

Tselob looks in the direction of the sudden surging and indeed he does see a small fish. Then he sees more of them. Without exception, every fish is trying its hardest to swim upstream against the current. The fish are sending up ripples, one after another. Excited, Tselob runs along the bank keeping pace with them. But now the fish have noticed they are being followed; in their panic they swim upstream at lightening speed, their yellow fins working even harder and thrashing up behind them a pretty, rippling train of wave spray.

"Flowers in the water!" cries Tselob in delight, running along the bank after the fish, completely absorbed in the wave spray and trampling yet more of the primroses.

The Chamed River makes a turn at the foot of the hill, creating a huge eddy. When the fish reach the bend in the river they dart into the eddy one after the other, and are lost to view. Tselob stops, almost mesmerized watching them. After a while he feels a bit dizzy and only then does he look back up on the bank.

It's a fair-sized strip of sandy beach, formed by repeated

encroachments over the land of the little Chamed's seemingly gentle waters. There are no primroses here; they have given way to a stretch of bushy plants. They grow about a foot tall and every one of the stems carries a mass of bright yellow flowers, dazzling the eyes.This is the potentilla, or golden-dew plum, so called because of its color. Plucking off a small, flower-smothered sprig, he charges off into the bushes. Every one of golden-dew plums can hear the agonized scream of the plant with the torn-off sprig, but Tselob remains deaf to such cries. He is like an agile little rabbit dashing hither and thither in the bush. Before long he comes to an open stretch of land.

Tselob has gone into the bush, not just because of all the golden flowers, but also to find a place to piddle. Tibetan people have a taboo against urinating into a river or close by a river bank. This is something Tselob has known since a very, very young age. Pa told him that if a boy pees into or close to a river, the dragon god in the river will get furious and bite off the boy's little cock. Tselob would never think of doing it by the river, never ever. Even if he's bursting to go he'll find a spot far away from the river. He runs off to some open ground.But before he's even untied the belt of his sheepskin overcoat, he sees there are two people there already.

And they are locked in a tight embrace.

Tselob stares in shock and surprise. The flower sprig falls from his little hand. Now he recognizes them. One is Xaichu, the eldest daughter of his neighbor, Uncle Nanji, whose tent is in the same circle as his parents. The other is Awu Dabei, a well-known singer of folk love songs, who lives in another tent group. Tselob remembers these two names coming up once when his parents were chatting at their fireside. Ma had said that these two were a couple made in heaven and Tselob had asked, "What does it mean, a couple made in heaven?"

They had exchanged a glance, and Pa said with a smile, "Just the way your Ma and Pa are a couple."

"So will they get a little kid just like me too?"

This sent them into gales of laughter.

"I want them to have a little girl," said Tselob, before they'd even finished laughing.

They stopped laughing, looked at each other once more and asked with one voice, "Why a girl?"

Tselob thought for a bit, then, selecting his words carefully, responded, "If they have a little girl, when she grows up, I'd like the two of us to be a couple made in heaven too."

This set off his Ma and Pa into another fit of laughter.

The two people quickly become aware of Tselob's sudden appearance out of nowhere, and hurriedly let go of each other. Xaichu, whom Tselob calls Big Sister, looks a little dishevelled, her hair is messy and her eyes lack spirit. She plays with the pleats on her sheepskin robe. There are tearstains on her face.

Dabei, the singer of love songs, has red eyes too. He gets up and walks across, "Tselob, what are you doing here?"

Tselob seems not to have heard him. He looks at Dabei, and then at Xaichu behind him. Puzzle and bewilderment are written all over his face.

"Have you both been crying?" he asks, ignoring the question.

Dabei instinctively turns to look at Xaichu. He grabs Tselob's hand, not knowing what to say.

"My Ma says you two are a couple made in heaven," Tselob blurts out.

Dabei is in a complete state of shock. He looks at Tselob, then turns back again to look at Xaichu. She breaks into a little sob, comes over and takes Tselob's other hand.

"Are you going to have a baby?" he blurts out again.

Taken aback, Dabei and Xaichu exchange the same look that had passed between Tselob's parents and Dabei asks, "Uh? Why ask that?"

"A baby girl would be best." Tselob totally ignores their question and just comes out with what's on his mind.

"Why?" Even more taken aback, Dabei and Xaichu's sad expressions give way to stunned bewilderment.

Tselob does a bit of thinking to come up with the right words, "Well, if you have a baby girl now, when she's grown up, the two of us will be a couple made in heaven as well."

What could the two do but laugh. Tears well up in Xaichu's eyes all over again.

2

Although it is summer, the early morning still feels a bit chilly. Inside the tent Tselob stirs beneath the heavy sheepskin coat that is his cover, and opens his eyes. Ma and Pa are already up. Pa is sitting cross-legged by the hearth; between his hands he has a sheepskin that he's rubbing ever so gently and carefully. The skin has been processed; the rubbing process will give it a softer, finer texture, almost like silk. Pa is planning to make Tselob a sheepskin *cari* robe (robe made of lambskin for children in Tibetan-inhabited areas — *ed.*) so that when Tselob turns nine he can wear it to school. Only two more skins are now needed.

Ma is on the other side of the hearth, scrubbing out a milk bucket in readiness for milking the cows. The kettle sitting on the cow dung fire looks as if it's seen a few years. It sits there comfortably, spouting steam, singing a long and sentimental melody as though rapt in memory of things past, memories that sadden yet keep drawing you back. A pot of brick tea is about to be served. It's what Ma makes for the family's breakfast; tea made by steeping a tea brick, and with that *tsampa* roasted barley flour. Virtually every tent family eats this breakfast, without fail and without variation.

"Nanjie's oldest daughter, Xaichu, is getting married. The wedding send-off is on the tenth of this month, on the Tibetan calendar. Nanjie asked me to go and help." Pa says this just as Ma is about to leave with the cleaned milk bucket. Ma, already in the doorway, turns back towards the hearth, about to say something in reply; but before she can open her mouth, Tselob gets in first, "Is she marrying Awu Dabei?"

As one, they turn towards Tselob, staring at him in surprise. The tent has fallen silent: just then, the singing of the kettle all of a sudden gets louder. It's poignant, even longer and more plaintive than before and the tent suddenly seems a melancholy kind of place.

"Where did you get the idea she's marrying Awu Dabei?" Pa quizzes him.

Tselob wants to tell them both about what he'd seen that day among the golden-dew plum bushes. But Ma and Pa are looking very surprised, so he asks, all curious. "Is something wrong?"

Ma and Pa exchange looks. Then Pa says with a smile, "Come on. Get up and eat your breakfast, baby. You have to herd the sheep once Ma has finished the milking." Then he puts his big hand under the sheepskin coat and gives Tselob a light tap on the bum.

Obediently, Tselob gets out from under the sheep skin and puts on his own small sheepskin coat. As he is tying the belt he asks, "So, is Sister Xaichu not marrying Awu Dabei then?"

Pa looks across the hearth to Ma and answers, "Xaichu is being married off into a farming district a long way away from here."

Just then, the lid on the boiling kettle starts jumping about. Some of the tea seeps out from the side, falling onto the burning cow dung with a fizzle. Smoke suddenly belches up from the clay hearth — as if the kettle is getting angry and throwing a tantrum for no reason at all. Ma quickly puts down the milk bucket and takes the kettle off the fire and put in to the side while she puts some more cow dung on the fire. As she does so, she seems suddenly to get red around the eyes, and her eyes fill with tears. Perhaps from the smoke, perhaps for some other reason.

The fire in the hearth blazes with new life. Ma carries the milk bucket out of the tent, leaving Pa and Tselob to their breakfast. She won't eat until she is done with the milking. Pa puts down the sheepskin and gets up to pick up the kettle. He then takes two bowls from the cupboard above the hearth. He pours a little tea into each bowl, and then from a wooden chest he takes out a small amount of butter, dividing it out between the bowls. From the same container he adds some *tsampa* and yak cheese. He says to Tselob, who has just finished washing his face, "Son, let's eat breakfast."

But Tselob seems preoccupied and heavy hearted. He does not even hear his Pa.

3

Xaichu's wedding is imminent. Pa is busy helping with her sending-off ceremony: he has groomed his chestnut horse with extra care; every inch of its body has been washed and not a single hair is out of place. Its mane has been trimmed to perfection, so the horse looks clean-cut, soldierly, and confident. The tail hair has been braided and decorated with ribbons of many colors. It is a fine-looking horse indeed.

The horse's new makeover fills Tselob with delight; but even more thrilling is the fact that Ma and Pa have decided to bring him along too on the sending-off day. Their son is seven years old now and has never been to a farming district. He has never seen grain fields. Nor has he ever seen chickens, ducks, or geese, or pigs, that are raised on the farms. More important still, he has never eaten green vegetables, which are a rare commodity in pastoral areas, so the wedding banquet will be a good chance for him to taste farm-grown vegetables. Tselob is so excited at the prospect he's not slept soundly for a few nights now. But there's an immediate problem, one that almost prevents him going; namely, the gaping hole in one of his cloth shoes. He has no new ones and these are too shabby to wear on such a festive occasion; it would be an embarrassment for his parents. Just as Tselob, after a few days on top of the world, is plunged into gloom worrying about his shoes, Ma suddenly remembers that Uncle Nanjie's family has a pair of mud boots for rainy days and they are usually just lying about idle. Maybe they can borrow the mud boots for Tselob so he can go to the wedding. Since it could rain any day now, wearing mud boots wouldn't look too odd. So Ma gets on at Pa to ask whether they might borrow them.

Pa looks doubtful. "First we want to bring the boy along to the wedding, and on top of that we ask to borrow their boots... It doesn't look too good."

"What's wrong with taking the boy? You won't be the only one doing that. We do it all the time around here."

Pa is still unconvinced. Tselob speaks up, "But I want to go to Sister Xaichu's wedding."

"Go and ask them," Ma urges Pa again. "It'll reflect well on them if the boy is well dressed."

Seeing the pleading look in Tselob's eyes, Papa gives in to his wife and gets up to go. "Looks like it's the only way," he sighs.

In no time at all Pa comes back with the boots. "I worry too much," he says. "They didn't even wait for me to finish asking before giving me the boots. And as for taking kids to the wedding, they said the more the merrier."

"What did I tell you?" says Ma, happy at being proved right.

The boots, long in the leg and of black rubber, are made for rainy day wear. Local people also wear this type of boot when mixing water and mud, so they also call them mud boots. Now that the loan of the boots has been sorted, Tselob can definitely go to the wedding with Pa. These last few days Tselob has been so happy he can hardly stop smiling all day. The family tent seems happy for him too. Whenever a wind blows up, the many-colored prayer flags strung from the top of the tent start dancing along with the wind, flapping in loud gales of laughter. Tselob can actually hear the happiness and blessing in that laughter; and of course a tinge of envy too. Moreover, every day a bird comes to perch on the anchor rope of Tselob's tent, a grassland bird with a black back and red underside, the type that locals call a "flame swallow." It bobs its head and shakes its tail, and sings a very joyous tune, wishing for Tselob to eat good food, have great fun, and learn lots of new things on his trip.

To go with Pa on the bridal send-off on the very first day of the wedding, Tselob has already put on the boots. He walks back and forth in front of the tent, tilting his head one way to look at his left foot, and the other way to look at his right foot. He takes few steps forward and then a few steps backward, completely immersed in his joyous mood. A two-year old calf, curious as to what his young master is up to pacing back and forth, comes over, a little dubiously, and moos at Tselob. But this irritates the boy: he immediately gets ratty, picks up a stone and chucks it at the calf, scolding it, "Get lost. Go away. You'll make my boots dirty." This scares off the calf. It doesn't know what's got into his young master today. It stands off at a safe distance, but continues to keep a suspicious eye on the boy.

"I'm going to Sister Xaichu's wedding!" Tselob yells out towards the Chamed River. As a result, the river, the primroses along its bank, and every flower in the golden-dew plum bushes a little further on, all receive the good news.

Every now and then, Tselob vaguely remembers that the wedding he's off to is not between Sister Xaichu and Awu Dabei, but between Xaichu and some other person Tselob knows nothing about. Every time this thought occurs to him he feels saddened; but, compared to the exciting prospect of a totally new world that he has never experienced, this sadness is just a fleeting and transitory feeling. Tselob longs for the wedding day to hurry up and come. In his urgent longing that little sadness sometimes feels lighter, and sometimes weighs on him more heavily.

4

Inside Uncle Nanjie's tent, Xaichu is flanked by two older women just starting the job of braiding her two braids into lots of small ones. Xaichu herself is covering her own face with her big sleeves, sobbing and sobbing. Xaichu does not have an older brother so Tselob's Pa has been asked to play the role of the bride's big brother in the hair-combing ceremony. He stands behind Xaichu, and begins to sing the hair-combing song:

> Little sister is getting married,
> On the road to the wedding
> Please walk slowly....

Tselob has come with Pa. The excitement of going to a strange new world had got in the way of a good night's sleep the night before. That slight sadness has been completely forgotten. He sits on his family's chestnut horse, among the bridal escort, waiting excitedly for the hair-combing ceremony to finish so he can get on the road to the wedding with Pa. Then he hears Pa's singing coming from the tent, a melodic and poignant air and the sadness that had been forgotten takes hold of him again. He bites his lips a bit. That nagging question he cannot understand keeps going round inside him: "Why isn't Sister Xaichu marrying Awu Dabei?"

Before Tselob can do any more thinking, the people who have come to the send-off ceremony have lit a ceremonial bonfire on the altar behind the tent. The smoke curls way into the air and the banners dance with it. The chief bridesmaid leads the recitation of the "Bonfire Burning Verses," paying respects to the spirits and gods of the sky and the earth, praying for peace for the world:

Qiao weng maniu –
On a blessed day like today,
I call on the gods from all directions,
I pray to the dragon's ancestor, and its offspring as well,
I pray they obey my wishes
Just as my own limbs act on my desires.
I pray they follow my instructions,
Just as the way my shadow
Stays close by my side.
Let me call on
Longbaoxai (Qinghai) Mountain,
This mountain of the spirits,
Like a parent to us all.

May you, when my eyes fail to see,

Point the path for me.

May you, when my mind cannot understand,

Teach me the way.

I pray to you,

Chishou Jiawu (Qinghai Lake).

This lake who nourishes us like our parents,

That you take care of our old folks,

Give them good health and long lives.

That you take care of our young ones,

Give them strong bodies and mighty strength for ever....

Amid the singing and chanting, the freshly made-up bride emerges from the tent on the arms of the two older women, and is helped onto the horse by the bridesmaids. The bridesmaids are getting ready to escort the bride off. They are now mounted on their horses and in position around the her horse. Together with the bride they circle the tent in a clockwise direction three times. At this moment Xaichu's mother seems to suddenly remember all the work she put in and all the worries that consumed her in raising this child of hers, who is now leaving home. She shouts from inside the tent, "Xaichu, please take from here good fortune and happiness with you. Please leave peace and well-being with your Mama." To the mother's pleadings, the bridesmaids, leaving with the bride, wail back on her behalf " Ao. La-su!"

The bridal escort party is met and welcomed by the groom's reception party which clusters around them for the rest of the way, and by sunset they reach the groom's village. For Tselob it is indeed a different world. It is like everything is magnified: the trees here are so tall he can't see their tops even if he cranes his neck to try. These trees are many, many times taller than the golden-dew plum bushes and the gritty willows that are the tallest trees in the grassland. And the grain crops in the fields that stretch between these towering trees grow higher, greener, and more lush even than the enclosed areas of grassland fenced off from cattle and sheep. And the close-built clusters of houses give an impression of bustle and vibrancy compared to life on the grassland where the next tent might be five miles away.

The groom's family lives in one of those groups of houses – a small yellow-mud house with a flat roof and surrounded by a thick mud wall. In the middle of the courtyard are some ordinary-looking flowering plants, blooming with red and purple flowers. The wedding banquet is arranged around this flower garden. There are huge platters of mutton and fried buns set out on rows of low square tables. The guests of the bride's family and those of the groom's line themselves up in two rows and sit themselves at opposite sides of the tables. The wedding has begun. But Tselob is paying no heed to the complex ceremonial. His attention has been grabbed by a long wooden ladder leaning against the side of the house – two very long poles the thickness of a grown-up's arm with wooden cross bars set in at regular intervals. You can just hold on to the poles, step up the horizontal bars one by one, and clamber up onto the roof of the house. Tselob has never seen anything like it. Even more tempting…once he's got onto the roof, he can see the whole village from the top of the house. In the setting sun, he can see that in front of each of the houses there are huge stacks of hay, just like the big piles of cow dung in front of each tent on the grasslands. He can see a lot of women stooping in the fields beyond the village. For ages they remain motionless and Tselob has no idea what they are doing. He sees a lot of chickens – he is guessing they are chickens, from what he knows about the wild fowl he knows so well in the grassland, which, although they have wings, seem unable to fly. They waddle around on two legs, walking on the paths just like people.

Just as Tselob is straining to look as far as possible, all of a sudden he hears the sound of a drinking song from the court yard. The voice is very familiar and Tselob recognizes it instantly as Awu Dabei's. He immediately rushes to the ladder, about to climb down so he can see. But he sees a pig at the bottom. This pig is sniffing around the ladder, raising its head every now and then to look up at the top. Tselob has never seen a pig before; he has no idea what this ugly, mean-looking creature is. He's a bit scared. So he yells, "Someone come and stop it!" – as you do in the grasslands, when you pass in front of a tent, you call out to the owner so he will mind his dog, so that it doesn't come and bite you. People hear the shouting, and look up to see Tselob. Awu Dabei stops singing the drinking song. He sees Tselob on the roof. Tselob notices that Awu Dabei's eyes are a little red and that he's not standing up straight. Obviously he's drunk. Who knows how long he has been here already.

"What did you say?" someone asks Tselob.

"Come and stop it," says Tselob, not taking his eyes off the pig.

Now that they understand what Tselob wants, they break out laughing. Someone comes over to shoo the pig away and tells Tselob, "This isn't a dog. This is a pig. Pigs don't bite." Tselob says to him, "But it looks meaner than a dog."

Everyone laughs out loud again.

While people are still laughing, Tselob comes down the ladder, but on the way down one of his boots is slashed open by a nail sticking out of the ladder. Pa is sitting with the other guests, and he can see Tselob seem to trip a little on the ladder. He lets out an involuntary gasp, sensing something has gone wrong with the borrowed mud boots.

Then something happens at the wedding and the mood suddenly gets lively. Tselob and his Pa can't seem to get happy, though. When Tselob timidly goes up to his Pa, he can see that Tselob's left boot has a gaping hole in the leg. It's like an open mouth, laughing at them sadistically.

Although Pa is upset, he cannot let it show, so he gets Tselob to sit next to him and stay there. Right then, Awu Dabei starts up again. He's so drunk he is a little out of control. This time the song is not a drinking song, but a lament!

> Oh, the beautiful primroses!
> They want to bloom by the Chamed River.
> But the cold hearted frost!
> It destroys their beautiful blooms.
>
> Our romantic singer, our love-smitten Dabei!
> He was all set to marry his precious sweetheart.
> But the cold-hearted parents!
> They marry her off in a faraway place!

All is suddenly silent, totally silent, but for the sound of uncontrolled sobbing coming out of the bride's quarters. Then comes the sound of angry cursing rising from the crowd: "Throw the shameless fool out!" At the same time several young men rush at Awu Dabei. One of them has a riding whip, and he lashes out wildly at Awu Dabei. A bloody welt appears on Dabei's face. It looks like an earthworm wriggling on his cheek. The young men manhandle the singer off the premises. In shock, Tselob's eyes follow Dabei's forced exit. Then he looks at Pa sitting next to him. Pa's face is totally without expression.

The sky is slowly getting dark.

Next day, the bridal escort returns to the grasslands. Pa does nothing after returning home; he needs to figure out how to pay for the mud boots Tselob damaged. What happened at the wedding dwells with a vague kind of presence in Tselob's mind, like an unsolved puzzle. He doesn't dare ask Pa about it and nor does Pa seem to want to talk to him at all. After some discussion, Ma and Pa have come to a decision about the mud boots: they will sell the two   lambskins and use the proceeds to repay Uncle Nanjie for the mud boots. The original pair, the ones Tselob damaged, can now go to Tselob, but it will mean having to delay the plan for Tselob's *cari* robe.

Ma carefully sews up the hole in the damaged boot with woollen thread. The stitched-up hole now looks like an earthworm crawling on the boot. From now on Tselob has these boots all for himself.

Every early morning, he keeps going along the bank of the Chamed River. The primroses on the bank notice something different about his feet: Tselob's corduroy shoes have gone; there's no big toe sticking out either. In their place are these mud boots, with a stitched-up hole like an ugly, mean-looking knife wound on the left one of the pair. The flowers also discover that Tselob has not been his old self since the wedding. At first, they thought Tselob would tell them what he had seen and heard at the wedding. Even if he didn't tell them, and even if he continued to treat them as invisible just like before, he would at least go and tell everything to the sheep, so the flowers could eavesdrop. But Tselob has said nothing to anyone. He does not say a single word all day. He looks a little down. Often they just see him sitting on the grass by the shore staring into nowhere. The primroses are bemused.

Actually the flowers have given up the idea of punishing Tselob. They have come to a common consensus that the boy has something on his mind, and they want to find out what about it is. But these days Tselob doesn't come to the riverbank very often. He used to come several times a day at least. Now, even though this is the spawning season for Qinghai Lake naked carp, he may only come once or twice, or not at all. The last two days or so, carp have come in great numbers to spawn in the river and it is packed with fish. In previous spawning seasons, the moment he got here, Tselob would hurry his cattle and sheep to the grassy shore. He would then rush to the river himself to play with the fish: playing hide-and-seek, chasing the fish, teasing them, stirring up waves in the water, shouting and laughing. Day after day he would come to the river and play his heart out. But now, he doesn't play with the fish at all; he totally ignores them. His unusual behavior causes them some surprise; and concern for him as well.

Today, Tselob comes walking towards the river, but it seems his intention is not at all to visit the stretch of grassy land with the primroses; instead, he heads directly for the golden-dew plum bushes. The flowers watch him disappear into the bushes, and feel a little lost and disappointed. They can only put their hope on the bushes now; maybe they will be able to tell them something about what is going on with the boy.

Tselob goes into the bushes and stands once again at the spot on the sandy beach where he had come across Sister Xaichu and Awu Dabei. He sits down on the sand and stares at his mud boots. All the golden-dew flowers are now holding their breath, quietly watching Tselob. The primroses on the grassy land on the other side of the bush have no view of Tselob and are getting even more agitated. They crane their necks in the direction of the bushes in anxious anticipation.

Tselob takes off his mud boots and lines them up side by side.

The two boots lean closely on each other. They have a serene and obliging air about them.

"You two are a couple made in heaven!" Tselob says to the boots.

"Oh, the cut on your face hasn't healed yet?" He enquires of the boot with the cut.

The golden-dew plum flowers stare at Tselob in surprise. They see tears streaming down his face. But the primroses still have not a clue about what is going on. Nervy and agitated they wait on tenter-hooks for Tselob to come out of the bushes.

(Translated by Yuvonne Yee)

The Land of Green

Liao Yirong

Liao Yirong was born in 1976 to a Dongxiang family in Shagou Village, Xiji County, Ningxia. Now a member of the Chinese Writers' Association, Liao has been a herdsman on the grasslands of the Tianshan Mountains, a gold miner in the Bayan Kara Mountains and an ardent traveler over the vast lands of China's west. Liao attended the third advanced course for young writers at the Lu Xun College of Liberal Arts, and began to produce works in the early 1990s. A substantial body of his work has appeared in such literary periodicals as *Selected Stories*, *Selected Fictions*, *Fiction Monthly*, *Beijing Literature Novella Monthly* and *Selected Chinese Literature*, annual literary selections, and various types of literary collections. Some of his works have been translated for overseas publication. In 2001, Liao was the youngest writer to attend the National Young Creative Writers' Symposium. In 2005, his short story and novella collection *The Copper Soup Pot Dangling in the Moonlight* (published by the Writers' Publishing House) was selected for the *21st Century Literary Star Series*. His other publications include the short story and novella collection *On the Road to Galeng* (People's Literature Publishing House), the documentary *The Iron Lance Cries* (The Writers Publishing House), and the short story and novella collection *In My Arms Till Dawn* (jointly published by Jiangsu Literature and Art Press and Ningxia People's Publishing House). Liao is a multiple winner of the Ningxia Literature and Art Prize, and winner of the Chinese Contemporary Ethnic Minority Literature and Art Research and Creation Award – New Writers Prize, and the Fei Tian Literature Prize. In 2004, Liao won the Third Spring Literary Prize and, in 2008, his work, *The Copper Soup Pot Dangling in the Moonlight* won the Stallion Award for Ethnic Minority Literature.

The Land of Green

1

The land grows so verdant and bright you can see your reflection in the green.

"Jiayina, come quick! I've got a really long sash to give you," Yishiha calls.

The water from the Tianshan Mountains descends as shimmering silver, a gurgling knife carving a gully in the belly of the grassland. The grassland seems to moan like a mother in labor. The stream shivers, and seems to waver slightly. From far away it looks still, but once you come close you see how it pulsates with life.

Jiayina laughs heartily, turning her stallion to gallop back, a stallion as white as snow.

Her black robe flutters as she rides her mount in the windless summer day, and her long, white waist sash trails behind. Several butterflies follow close behind tracking the hint of a scent from the horse's hooves.

"Women are the poetry of the grassland!" The young man, eyes fixed on Jiayina galloping towards him, is suddenly hit with this idea.

And Jiayina is the quintessence of Tianshan grassland poetry. She is also a fine horsewoman. Every young gallant wants to conquer her. But she is, like a wild doe whose desires run under the surface, free and untamable. She is like a wild flower blooming on an inaccessible cliff, beautiful and alone.

The boys often call out to her, in sweet, ingratiating tones, "Sister Jiayina!"

"Yo! Lad! Ha-ha…." She yells back. Then comes a wave of laughter, a cascade of laughter, like green beads falling from a jade platter onto the grassland, coloring it even more intensely green.

Her laughter makes the men of the grassland swoon. And not just them: earthworms, butterflies and bees follow her, dancing just for her; snow lotus, roses, grass lilies, and all the other plants and flowers are moved to nod and bow to her; animals hiding in the woods pay attention from afar, their hearts fluttering; the hooves of the galloping horses drum out a passionate fantasia.

Yet there is, by common agreement, a man of the grassland good enough to be Jiayina's match. He is Bawunihan, and they call him the hero of the grassland. The problem is he seems to have no interest in women.

"Hey! Jiayina, It's me, Yishiha, who's the grassland's hero. Come with me to my hideaway deep in the grassland and I will give you the sun, the moon, the mountains, rivers and streams as my wedding presents to you. I will give you everything in the grasslands if you marry me. On our wedding day I will command a reception party of deer, bees and butterflies to your tent to bring you to me as my bride." Thus the young man greets her happily.

"Stop blowing your own trumpet. Bawunihan's the real hero of the grassland. He's a real man – so strong and able."

"Bawunihan – you can forget about him! He's a loner. He's not one for the girls. He only likes good horses and the best liquor." The young man is obviously full of respect for Bawunihan, because a solitary nature has a certain beauty about it. But the young man also feels a little sorry for Bawunihan not knowing a thing about women. Without them there would be no grassland, and the world would cease to exist.

"Would you dare take him on in a wrestling match? If you beat Bawunihan, then the sun will rise in the west, and I'll go off into the tall grass with you. Ha, ha, ha...."

Her laughter skips over the tip of each blade of grass, ringing as clear as the waters coming down from the mountains. It draws out onto the grassland things that are hidden in the deepest recesses of the soul.

Yishiha is uneasy at the suggestion. He knows he is no match for Bawunihan: the guy's got muscles the size of mountains; if he gives a holler he can be heard from the grassland all the way to the highest peak of the Tianshan. Bawunihan is indeed a hero in Yishiha's mind, being so strong and so powerful. But this hero knows zero about how to nurture and irrigate the women of the grassland. Yishiha had once tried talking to him: "Don't neglect Jiayina – she's the purest and most beautiful woman on the grassland, and every man wants to court her. If the women of the grassland do not get the nourishing of heroes, the grassland will gradually dry up, and life will slowly fade away. Then will this grassland still be so green it shimmers? Will it still be so fertile? And will there still be horses galloping all over the hills? We herdsmen will have nowhere to call home."

"Jiayina, I'm going to take my horses to graze now." He raises his horsewhip to goad his horse; his legs tighten around its body and his expert heels hit its underbelly. The black stallion neighs, kicks up its heels, drawing a sharp arc in the air, and takes off like a flash of lightning to a far place.

This horse of Yishiha's is the finest on Xinjiang's Tianshan grassland. There was something different about it right from birth. The grasslanders feel there's something different and mysterious about this horse. Since growing to full size, no one other than its own master Yishiha has been able to come close to it. The horse seems to understand human feelings, seems to have a sense of honor and shame, and to know reason and sentiments. Because it is an astonishingly big horse, way bigger than any of the other horses, the grasslanders affectionately call it "Super-Size." When Super-Size neighs from far off, all the other horses immediately quiet down. This is the demeanor of a real king of horses. It gallops at the front, head held high, its mane streaming at its back like a black banner. All the horses follow it, as if they are following a leader of the grassland, as if they are following behind their king.

"There's one set of rules for everything in the universe. It's the same for horses as it is for people." Yishina's father tells the grasslanders, not without a sense of pride.

Riding a horse such as this could, without a doubt, make a man the focus of attention on the grassland, and splendid enough to make others jealous.

Super-Size neighs long and loud. Suddenly all the other horses gallop towards it from every direction. Several of the naturally more playful foals, ears pricked up and tall, start running about like kids, their heads bent, neighing with delight. They seem to cling to the grass. When they run over low spots in the terrain, they rise like swallows gliding over water and elegantly soaring into the air. It's a scene to make the heart quiver with its beauty.

Summoned by their leader, the horses assemble in an instant, their galloping hoofs filling the air with thunder.

Yishiha cracks his whip loudly, sweeping it through the glinting grassland air. "Ooh ooh ooh, d'r cong – " he whoops, and the horses begin to run. They run faster and faster. The sound of their hooves is disparate at first, confused, but gradually starts to come together in one concerted pounding, that of a raging torrent rushing through the grassland, as if about to echo over all of Central Asia. Even the deep underground seems to reverberate with a low weeping sound.

This is a very familiar feeling for Yishiha. For many years now, whenever he drives his horses he re-experiences the same emotion at the sight of the jade-green grassland, that gently rolling terrain and the embrace of the distant mountains, stretching out ahead of him, rippling like a sea.

"We'll see. Jiayina – you belong to the grasslands. And you are mine!" He says to himself, stirred with emotion.

Previously he had been a sheep herder on the South Mountain. He remembers a river back there; it was fed by melt-water from the snows up on the mountain and empties directly into the Urla Reservoir. In spring, when it got warm and the flowers came out, people came to pan for gold in the mountain rivers. They worked very hard. Later, he had left the South Mountain and moved to the Tianshan grassland. The reason behind this was the South Mountain's becoming the "White Poplar River Tourist Region." Yes, that all-embracing, welcoming land had begun to feel kind of nameless tension and constraint. It is in Man's nature always to try to alter nature. He began to not like South Mountain. Strangers came in their automobiles and stayed. They brought with them the unfamiliar industrial smells and the odor of burning fuel that belongs to cities. When he decided to leave, indeed he could hardly bear to leave behind the mountain pine trees and the thick scent of pine needles. But he knew, as a man of the grassland, that place could not nourish him enough. Men keep pressing forward and Nature is in retreat.

He looks at the waist-high grass with a dejected gaze – this is a land of fertile black soil, a land so vast it stretches from where the sun rises in the east to where the sun sets in the west, black and oozing with fertility. It stretches on to the cultivated fields where people turn the soil to cultivate wheat, cotton and potatoes. The grassland has always kept every herdsman's heart vibrant and young. This is the herders' paradise.

When he was young this was such a happy land. Early one evening his father had taken him by the hand and gone with him into the grassland. There was no sign of human activity for miles around; only a vast sea of grass, just like in a photograph, stirred by a gentle wind, and whispering like moving water. Then they had met a pack of wolves. Stalling for time so Yishiha could escape, his father had sacrificed his body to the wolves. They had consumed him entirely, leaving not so much as a hair of him. It sounds like a story, but this was exactly how things had been back then. For Yishiha the grassland is a knot of emotions he cannot express.

The galloping herd slows down and comes to a halt. The horses lower their heads to munch the grass, relishing their good fortune. They eat away noisily, making a noise like a scythe cutting through the grass.

The grass is eaten but it will grow back!

Astride his horse, Yishiha is imagining a lass and her young man walking through the grass, and then making their way into the woods. They go into a white felt tent, and make wild and moody "music."

The grass is growing at phenomenal speed. Just now it was brushing at your feet and all at once it's around your legs. Pine trees, snow lotus, forget-me-nots, all the flowers and plants, seem to be whispering about something. Who knows what they are talking about. It all seems so mysterious and profound.

Flowers in full bloom are like the chubby round faces of babies, pure and clean, unblemished by dirt or dust. To look at them is like looking at your own children.

He dismounts and sits on a grassy slope. He is thinking that tonight will be a sleepless night for sure. He will lie quietly in his bed in the tent, with eyes wide open and dream of beautiful things between Jiayina and himself. But what will he do when the he wakes from the dream?

Far, far away, where the dense verdant grass meets the horizon, there suddenly appears a man's head bobbing in and out of sight as if emerging from a mirage lake. The head seems to rise gradually from the morning light. And now a hazy body rises to the surface. It is a blurry figure, and he can't yet make out the facial features. But the sound of galloping is getting closer.

Yishiha keeps his eyes glued on the horse and its rider. Suddenly his heart leaps, every nerve ending agitated. He stands, waving his arms high in the air at the horse, shouting at the top of his voice, "Jiayina! Jiayina!"

"My lad, don't day dream. Jiayina doesn't fancy you. Her heart's long been set on my son, Bawunihan."

Not Jiayina after all, but Bawunihan's father. This old man has lived on the grassland for half his life. He is an excellent hunter. People are little nervous of that old gun he carries around. It just may go off if he gets offended. Life on the grassland has gotten more and more prosperous for the old man. Without any reason or encouragement he is prone to say, "This piece of grassland is mine now. You guys take off somewhere else!" Having enjoyed a few good turns of fortune he is now reckoned as a man of status in the grassland. As the saying goes, "When a horse gets fat, it feels nervy; when a man gets rich, he feels secure."

Previously, Yishiha has been very humble and respectful to the old man. But right now, he feels nothing but humiliation and injustice. By what right does he claim possession of the grassland? He even wants to claim ownership of a girl for his son. By what right? Maliciously, he says to the old man, "Uncle, a bull's gored your son's leg and cut a ligament. Go ask him if you don't believe me." Then he laughs.

The old man looks at him with suspicion; when he sees Yishiha laugh, his face swells and reddens like a horse's lung. Up in the saddle, his old man's body, not big but quite sturdy, is shaking with anger. "You son of an ass, don't mess with me. Make me mad enough and I'll put a bullet in your belly." His voice is full of venom and he even threatens Jishiha by making a gesture to fetch the gun; but he's not carrying his gun. Suddenly, at this loss of face, he feels foolish, and his voice starts trailing off.

Yishiha feels the old man is being totally out of order, thinking to himself, "Don't you think you have might and power to lean on. This is the grassland. On the grassland we go by reason and decency."

The old man stays there reining in the horse, like he has just been cleaned out in a gambling house and doesn't know whether to leave or to stay. His face keeps changing color.

"So, Uncle, where are you heading for?" Yishiha takes the initiative to give the old man a dignified exit.

"Have you seen my son? I'm looking for my son. God knows where the son of a bitch has got to. He runs around all day long and I've got to look for him all over the place." The old man puts on an annoyed look, and looks into the far distance. Then he pretends to have found his son, "D'r – cong!" He cracks his whip on the horse and takes off.

The way the horse is running looks a little on the daft side, its body looks a little sloppy and its head droops in a lackluster kind of way.

Yishiha shakes his head at the old man's retreating figure and grins. He feels that whatever it is that's flowing in his veins right now is flowing through the grassland too. He puts his back against a big tree trunk, and lets his body go sliding down, sliding down.

Super-Size lifts his head, and neighs in triumph, the sound reverberating in the sky like a thunderclap. The horse seems to be applauding him.

He knows that age-old feeling of being humiliated and wronged actually stems from his own feelings of regret and remorse about his life. This is the root of the problem and he must put it right. He turns to look at his beloved horse. The horse is looking at him, as if it can see right into every fiber of his body. He can feel the blood coursing quietly in his veins.

At some point, he falls asleep, prone on the thick carpet of grass beneath the tree. There could be no finer bed on this earth! The green grass is shimmering. Far away on the grassland, a filly, gently wafting its brown tail from side to side, turns towards Super-Size and calls invitingly, "hmm....hmm...." It sounds so courteous. The grassland is filled with tranquility and peaceful silence. There is the light humming of bees gathering nectar. The young filly keeps on calling to Super-Size, "Come over! Come over here! The grassland is so beautiful today."

So, Yishiha lies there quietly, not moving a muscle, his eyes shut tight, his breathing even, gentle, and calm. He hears the sounds of every thing and every creature in the grassland; it sounds like speech – speech, moreover, that he understands; from beneath the earth's surface he hears the sound of the earth's blood pumping through its veins and arteries; he hears what unquiet emotions keep them from sleep. Now he is thinking of Jiayina and wondering what she is doing right this moment, thinking about how uniquely beautiful she is, even when she weeps. Even dead grass would be come to life again if watered by her tears. But it seems she's in love with Bawunihan and Yishiha's heart fills with sorrow at the thought. Gradually the profound silence returns. The only sound is that of horses grazing.

Maybe in a while he might hear some other animal calling, making its way from a distant place far across the grassland, and then fading back into the distance in the shimmering light. He moves his foot a little, and then goes back to his original position. But something hits his foot. Before he can get his eyes open, some-one's hands part the long grass and take him by the shoulder.

He yawns.

"So sorry to wake you up." It is Limping Ma. He was an old soldier who'd served time in a cavalry unit in Xinjiang and had spent half his life on horseback. Later he had developed a tumor in his leg, which had to be amputated in order to save his life. Now he depended on a false leg. It was just so sad. Limping Ma's son had been a veterinarian for a while but had changed career. These days he and his wife journey deep into the mountains to collect and trade in medicinal herbs. He is doing very well, since the Tianshan Mountains are a treasure chest of medicinal plants.

Yishiha turns and sits up, a little bashful. "Oh, I was awake really, Grandad. What is it I can do for you?"

"I want to ask you a favor."

"Just say the word." The minute someone asks him for help, Yishiha assumes a look of wisdom and experience.

Limping Ma gives a sigh, "My boy's mother is ill. Very ill. The old woman is crying to see her son. I don't know what to do. So, I thought, maybe I could ask you to make the journey on your fast horse. But perhaps you don't have time."

Yishiha agrees right away, "Don't worry. It'll only take a few days. But you'll have to promise to take care of my horses." Whenever anyone says anything good about himself and his dear horse, Yishiha feels very pleased with himself and assumes the air of a champion rider. He swaggers a bit and gives a little snort of laughter.

They sit down and talk a while.

A mood of gentle kindness fills the grassland.

The horses wonder farther off.

2

The next day, Yishiha steps out of his tent and sees Bawunihan outside the entrance. Bawunihan is a big man. He has the same Khazak eyes as his father and curly hair. He sits coolly drinking his liquor. His expression is somber and his eyes have an icy look that nothing, it seems, could shake. He is so deep. Every little expression and gesture commands admiration. In short, he is the image of a grassland prince. Yishiha's resentment towards Bawunihan's father doesn't carry over to the son at all. Yishiha has only admiration and liking for Bawunihan.

When he walks towards Limping Ma's tent, right away he spots "Laughing Jiayina." Like a dream, the rising sun shines gently and moistly on her jade-smooth complexion. A gentle and mysterious radiance lights her skin. Her hand rests on her braids. Her wrist, ring finger and little finger combine to make a white butterfly about to take flight; she leans against the tent door, standing on her left foot, her right foot hooked around her left ankle – so linear, like flowing water; the undulations of her black robe indistinctly reveals her soft pink flesh underneath. The grassland is silent; no sound whatsoever. Sound has transcended time, and time has come to a standstill. And this kind of soundless silence is meant to release the spirit! Today, for some reason, Jiayina is not laughing.

They stand there – Bawunihan, Jiayina, and Yishiha – the three points of a triangle. Bawunihan's face is without expression; Jiayina looks lost and sad; Yishiha looks into her eyes and feels panicky. His heartbeat seems to drain away. A second seems like a year. There's nothing that can be hidden from a woman's intuition. He knows that.

Above, the clouds float slowly along, veiling everyone's mood. And the green grass stretches on so far, like a carpet rolling out to a remote and nameless place.

"Hey!" Yishiha greets Bawunihan lightly.

Bawunihan just frowns back at Yishiha, and keeps on downing the mare's milk fortified with rice liquor. Not even a hint of a dry smile.

"Jiayina! Jiayina!" Silently, Yishiha calls the name inside his heart.

Once his heart seems to have settled down, he turns his eyes away, gives himself a shake, straightens up and goes into Old Ma's tent.

From the bed a pair of sad eyes stares out from an ashen, lifeless face, as if poisoning had taken the life and luster from them. From between lips cracked with countless silk-fine lines comes rapid and weak wheezing. The old woman sees the young man come in and, struggling, turns so she can look up at him. He hurries to sit by her bed and supports her on his arm. Her sick, dark face quivers with the unvoiced question: "Will my son come and see me?"

Instinctively, he nods a couple of times. She stretches out a tough, coarse hand toward him, dry as a dead branch but still with a hint of life. Dirty bedclothes hang loosely from her body, draping into her lap in a chaotic pile.

This makes him want to bend down and kiss her hand in the deepest respect, a hand as light and insubstantial as an autumn leaf.

He does not know how to comfort this old woman, whose life now flickers like a candle in the wind. He can only say, "You hang on in. Your son will come and see you." He gets up to leave, but on his way out he turns and notices her eyes – one might even say her soul; they are lit with determination and profound thoughts. With the single-mindedness and innocence of a new born those eyes follow him out of the tent and out of sight.

The sky is as blue as the sea in the early morning.

Whilst man lives this life, he must have a hope. Who does not have something he hopes for?

Old Ma has already taken the horses out to graze the pastures without waking the young man – he wanted him to sleep a while longer.

Now people are just beginning to come out of their tents.

Bawunihan is still standing outside the tent, slowly sipping his fermented mare's milk.

Jiayina is still standing in the same spot.

From time to time one can hear talking inside a tent, but in most of the tents silence reigns.

Bawunihan's father comes out of his tent, coughs a couple of times and then walks straight past Yishiha, heading directly for the tent of Jiayina's family.

He sees Jiayina greeting Bawunihan's father warmly, but before entering the tent she suddenly turns back toward Yishiha with a look laden with a terrifying sadness. One side of her face is now in shadow but her skin still gives off a faint radiance. Something pulls at his heart, "Jiayina, wait for me!"

The grassland puts its hope in tomorrow's sun. Yishiha's hope is Jiayina.

Super-Size is completely kitted out, handsome and impatient to leave, quietly intimating that its young master should get a move on.

Yishiha hops on its back, and circle rounds a couple of times at a mad gallop.

"Have a safe journey. Mind how you go, my young lad." An old Khazak reminds him.

"OK. I will remember your words." Yishiha gives his horse a gentle squeeze with his legs, thrusts his body forward and is off into the wild, gradually leaving the tents behind. The sun is now high over the grassland, casting a million golden rays over the land, enhancing its beauty to a point beyond compare, He cannot see his horse's hoofs; but he can hear their steady beat, like oars rowing across the earth.

3

Despite the gentle wind on this summer day in this part of Central Asia, the sun is still scorching hot.

The hot wind sets in motion waves and ripples through great dense stretches of high grass, green as fields of unripe wheat.

The red sun bathes the thick grasses in its flaming heat. Against the blazing red horizon is a lone rider; he seems to be riding in pursuit of the sun. It appears almost within reach.

The rocks are like wild beasts, hiding amongst the dense tall grass, motionless, waiting for the first opportunity to pounce. Many times, Super-Size almost stumbles and leaps over the rocks like a blue flame.

Yishiha is reminded once more that a good horse, like the one he now rides, can make the difference between life and death on a long journey such as this.

He stops by a rock the size of a house and dismounts. He climbs up the rock and sits himself on the top, wiping the sweat from his head with his sleeves. Then he opens the bag of fried flour. He feels around inside his clothes and pulls out a piece of paper which he proceeds to shape into a little scoop and uses it to scoop out the flour from the bag. He lifts his head and down go the flour. Absolutely delicious!.

The aroma of fried flour fills the air.

He takes a pull at his metal canteen. It contains water from the Tianshan Mountains, pure and crystal clear, like manna from heaven.

Yet again he thinks of Jiayina.

Hunger satisfied and thirst quenched, he gets back in the saddle.

Wafted along on the breeze comes the pleasantly astringent fragrance of pollen from the artemesia flowers now blooming across the grassland.

Super-Size seems no less excited and enthusiastic than at the start of the journey.

He feels for his horse. He tries to rein the horse in a little.

The green grass is like an ocean of shining green which merges with the horizon. High in the sky a few black birds are flying this way from the direction of the Tianshan Mountains. Sometimes they circle, dotting the sky with their silhouettes.

Suddenly, he is enthralled by the fantastic scenery before him. All the colors of the rainbow and more are dancing gracefully all around him, as waiting their turn to come into to his field of vision. It is a dreamy kind of languid beauty. Every image is full of life and free of spirit, yet so loving and gentle. Just like the women of Tianshan, beautiful and unspoiled.

The horse really wants to stay a while, or maybe forget about the journey altogether. It makes gentle whinnying noises, turning this way and that, stomping its hoofs. What look like little shiny pearls seem about to fall from his eyes, as if in worship and adoration of the goddess of the grassland.

Now Yishiha, fed up with the horse being so dilatory, gives it a crack of his whip.

Super-Size gallops at speed for a stretch. Suddenly, it raises its head high, its neck at full stretch, rearing on its hind legs and screaming. Its tail is whipping around its hind quarters like black lightning. Abruptly, its body stiffens like a steel rod and then hammers back to the ground. almost throwing Yishiha in the process. He takes a huge breath, and presses strongly into the stirrups, his knees tight to the flanks, his body tightly hugging the horse's back. He grabs its mane, and screams, "What's the matter, you cursed animal!"

Super-Size screams again with a shrill call that seems to rend the Heavens. It will not obey its master.

From just where the warm wind is parting the tall grasses, comes a hissing sound, piercingly sharp and out of this world.

His every muscle freezes. Now he sees a long black snake, its girth the diameter of a bowl. It raises its head from the grass and rattles its tail in threat. This is the most poisonous snake in all of Central Asia. Its bite is fatal, in whatever part of the body. People in the grassland call it "stinking black." Its nature is that of an aggressor. Moreover, it likes to provoke.

The horse is showing a kind of human intelligence. It knows there's no time to get away and stands ready with its steely hoofs. Icy calm, it holds its ground in the face-off.

The snake keeps on hissing with its flickering forked tongue, like a little sizzling flame. In its triangle-shaped head, that tongue moves rapidly back and forth, side to side like a blue flame. Its cold, unfathomable eyes, fixed firm ahead, have deadly intent; it will not give way. Its glossy black tail flashes in the grass as it drums against the ground.

"It looks like a fish, all beautiful and sleek! They say that the snake was once the most beautiful angel in heaven but committed the unforgivable sin of greed and was expelled, banished to the world of men." He cries to himself, "Hey, you incarnation of the devil, get out of here!"

He pulls out his whip and takes aim.

But from its years in the wilderness the snake seems to have acquired precognition. Before the whip comes down, it leaps into the air in a flash of black. Like a flaming thong quivering in the air, it flies over the head of the horse, over the head of the man, drawing a perfect arc. From the high point of its trajectory it aims directly at the horse.

The horse is making nervous snorting noises. Its front legs rear high; its mouth yawns as wide as an open basket and from it issue heart-reading screaming sounds "Yi – ang, yi – ang!" It shows no fear whatsoever, readying its steely hoofs, now high in the air, to trample the evil snake to death.

The snake writhes in the air, menacing, ugly and eerily beautiful all at once, like a strike of black lightning, displaying all its might and beauty.

Yishiha aims his whip at the snake, and cracks it fast.

The whip makes a direct mid-air hit and from the snake comes a sound to chill the blood. There is no sound darker than this "sss – ." This is the sound of evil. The snake, stifling its pain, rushes at the horse's front leg with its sharp fangs and seems just to brush it for an instant, before sliding off into the grass. Like a whistling arrow, the snake parts the dense grass and disappears without a trace, like nothing had just happened.

But nothing escapes Yishiha's eagle eyes. He leaps off the horse. He can see his horse's front leg is in muscular convulsion and is swelling up. The horse snorts, rubbing his master with his muzzle, and looking into the dense grass with a baleful gaze, scraping the ground lightly with its hoof, eliciting compassion and love just like an injured child.

Yishiha quickly scans the surrounding pasture grasses and starts searching for something among them. In no time he yells: "Found it! Found it! The horse will be OK!" He plucks something out from the ocean of luxuriant grass, something tiny. This plant is called "1-shaped" wormwood because its shape is that of the number. It is about five inches tall, and grayish-white all over. The grasslanders say, "If you keep some 1-shaped wormwood in the house, you needn't be afraid even if you have three snakebites." He stuffs the reed into his water canister. He searches around for firewood but can't find any and is starting to get a little anxious. From the horse comes a low and pleading sound. Its front leg is shaking even more violently.

The horse lies down and turns to look sadly at where it has been bitten.

Yishiha sets fire to his clothes and boots and these kindle some the pasture grass he has collected. He puts the metal canteen containing the herb onto the fire and soon the water inside is making a noise like the buzzing of an insect. He pushes some grass into the canister and washes the horse's leg with the medicinal brew from inside.

His heart leaps with joy, "Jiayina, where are you? I have won victory over such great hardship!"

The swelling in the horse's leg has subsided. It rises to its feet, nuzzling its master most affectionately.

He does not know if Jiayina is thinking of him now. He looks at his bare feet, and his heart fills with a chilling sorrow.

He turns to embrace the horse's head, but just can't stop thinking about the beautiful Jiayina, playing out possible scenarios in his head. There's the happy ending version which makes everyone happy, and then there's the tragic drama which makes one and all feel desperately sad. So he's smiling one minute and weeping the next, making Super-Size completely baffled. So the horse sinks into silence and his own deep musings.

Once refreshed, they continue their journey.

They journey on into the afternoon without a break; man and horse are bathed in sweat.

A searing hot wind has blown up a mass of thick dark clouds that fill the sky. Even the horse feels a heaviness in its lungs. The sky looks heavy enough to fall in. Just then he feels the first few drops of rain and the wind whips up harder; now he's dealing with a real rainstorm, rain upon rain without any let-up. Yishiha cracks his whip to fire up his horse, his eyes scanning the horizon for the sight of a tent.

The sound of hoofs, the wind, the rain, the occasional shriek from the galloping stallion... how dreamlike, how soul-stirring! What a picture of speed, tragic heroism and beauty! The mad wind and torrential rain tear at the few clothes he is left with. Raindrops batter the ground, splattering chill muddy water onto the faces and bodies of horse and rider alike.

The horse starts galloping even faster. smarting from the pain of the cold rain striking its face.

He lies low against the horse's body, his head buried against its neck. The horse turns its own head around towards Yishiha, checking its forward direction from the corner of its eye. The sound of hoof beats grips the rider's heart.

The rain relents a little, then comes the muffled rolling of thunder on the horizon.

There's another flash of lightning, then a heart-stopping crash of thunder: "Ka-Cha – !"

His remaining clothes seem touched by the lightning. There is a big black hole burned into his clothes, and the ragged garment flaps about loudly.

His horse scrapes the ground, bringing up clods of mud and grass, "Ah – ang, Ah – ang." It is now circling round, his master on his back, perhaps in fear of its master falling off.

Not far away is an old tree with a big thick trunk scarred by a black cavity where the lightning has struck. After a little while the tree splits and falls.

He feels that what just happened is a warning from nature to mankind.

He rolls off the horse's back, crawls to a big growth of moss and breaks off a piece; He squeezes out some sap and drips it onto his wound. Its cooling effect is immediate and deep, penetrating right to the bone marrow.

The horse lies down alongside him. The grasses make a low weeping noise as the wind moves through them.

The thunder sounds farther away now, and the rain is easing. There's a sound of water way in the distance, perhaps a big river in flood.

He is completely drenched and bits of mud are falling off him. He shakes the muddied water off his fingers and struggles to remount. Too exhausted and drowsy to exert control he just lets his horse run on its own for a while.

The sky is dark now. The shade of night has fallen. He wonders, but does not know, whether they are lost. The events of the journey are now coming back to him in shadowy images.

The inside of his mouth is parched. He rolls down off the horse's back and kneels on the ground, gesturing the horse to lie down, which it does, gently and obediently. He retrieves his water canister and drinks from it. He gropes for the fried flour, now a mushy mass, and fills his stomach. After lying on the grass for a while he gets up and leads his horse to a safe hide of thick grass. He worms his way into the grass like a dog and puts out his arm as a sign to Super-Size not to go far. The horse puts out its nose to sniff out the grassy hollow, swinging its head from side to side. Yishiha says, perhaps to himself or maybe to the horse, "Looks like we're spending the night here!"

Night is falling right now. A full moon has risen from among the grasses to hang high in the sky, illuminating the great land of Tianshan that stretches out in the green night. With the deepening night, lying there in the dense grass, and deep in his own thoughts, he has the vague sense that the grassland feels uneasy, unquiet. He turns to listen. From far away comes the faint, high pitched cry of a horse; actually not just one, but many similar cries combining. After a while the cries seem nearer and ever louder. It's as if he has just come to understand this land of green, understand that those cries are sounds he heard in another world, locked within his memory. He listens with his whole being; it is indeed the sound of nature calling out to man. The crying now reverberates even more hauntingly.

Strange images flood into his head, images no language could describe. The stars come out. A falling star rips the sky apart, bathing the grassland in a red glow.

Through the fine grass blades he can make out the silhouette of his horse Super Size. It has fed well on the green grass, wet from the rain and dewfall, and is half-dozing, half awake. Every now and then it snorts.

Yishiha wonders, "What is Jiayina doing now? The grasslanders have no idea of my situation now, that's for sure. They have no idea how I long for the lovely warm fire that lights up the tents. Maybe Old Limping Ma and his sick wife are talking about me. About what might be happening to me."

A cold wind blows up. The cries of unknown creatures seem so close, there's no defense against fear setting in. This chilling sense of aloneness is something he has never felt before.

From time to time the horse snorts.

In this night so quiet, and yet so disturbing, he eventually falls into a deep sleep. His pale lips curve in a faint smile and, as if he is shy about something, his cheeks redden. He dreams that he and Jiayina are sitting shoulder to shoulder on a meadow by the river. She has turned her head to face him, her hair falling on her face and her neck, smiling at him. As he helps her stand up, his arm comes to rest on her breast.

Her breast seems to have a nose and a mouth. It rises and falls like it is breathing evenly yet uneasily. How wonderful and yet so scary!

The next day, he is up on his horse before morning has barely broken. The horse's mane once more dances in the air as it gallops. Yishiha seems to have emerged even more handsome and strong from all the chaos of the previous night. The earth has been washed clean and fresh. On the faraway peaks of the pure and elegant Tian-shan, the white snow glitters. With a few slaps of the whip he gallops straight into the mountains.

Along the way he keeps stopping to ask for Limping Ma's son.

Then he sees a mud house on the hill. An old Ugyur grandpa tells him that's where he can find Ma's son.

It's dusk, there's a red glow on the horizon, and the open grassland is quite cool and damp. His body feels feverish and cold at the same time.

His heart stirs with excitement. Whipping up more speed, he makes for the mud house....

4

Several days later, just as the golden sun is rising, the travel-weary Yishiha appears on the grassland, riding Super-Size, with Limping Ma's son following behind. He is bedraggled and dirty but the very picture of a hero. His face is radiant.

Jiayina comes out of Bawunihan's tent, probably because of the sound of horses. Oh no! He didn't expect this! Her braids are undone and she is combing out her damp, heavy hair. Her eye-lids look slightly dark, as if she has spent the whole night making whoopee. But her complexion is a dewy pink as she walks towards Yishiha. She has a languorous look to her as if she has just emerged from bed. To his eyes, her breasts have suddenly got fuller over these last days. From every part of her body pours the heat of her captivating beauty.

His heart is gripped with a sudden sorrow: "The last few days.... I'll have to think of them as a dream!"

She comes over and caresses the horse's head. The horse looks a little sad. After a long, long while, she says, "You're back. I, ... em. I have been with Bawunihan."

He takes a deep breath, but he's choking with emotion and wavers a bit before he finally manages to steady and straighten up in the saddle. Then he says in a stiff, measured voice, "Good.

That's good. Please convey my congratulations and best wishes to Bawunihan too."

Super-Size gallops away with him. His back fades into the blue distance. Jiayina weeps, tears flowing down her beautiful face.

Finally, he and his horse drown in the vast sea of grass, merging as one color with the land of green.

(Translated by Yuvonne Yee)

Lake Hanas

Hong Ke

Hong Ke (original name Yang Hongke) was born in 1962 in Qishan County, Shaanxi, and is a member of the Chinese Writers' Association. He began to publish works in 1983 whilst still a student, and became a faculty member at the university after graduation in 1985. In autumn of 1986, he volunteered to teach at Yili Prefecture Technical School in Xinjiang, and for the next decade travelled extensively across the vast regions of the Tianshan Mountains. At the end of 1995, Hong Ke returned to Shaanxi, where he taught at Baoji College of Arts and Sciences. In 2004, he moved to Xi'an and lectured at Shaanxi Normal University. His major works include the "Tianshan Mountains Series" which describes life in the desert and on the prairie, represented by eight works including *The Horseman to the West*, *The Grand River* and *Wuerhe, the Windy City;* and 12 short story and novella collections including *The Merinos*, *The Golden Altay*, *The Golden Prairie*, *Galloping in the Heavenly Mountains* and *The Sun Sprouts*. Hong Ke's many awards include the Lu Xun Literary Prize, Feng Mu Literary Prize, Zhuang Zhongwen Literary Prize, Pu Songling Literary Prize, in addition to awards sponsored by various literary periodicals such as *Zhong Shan*, *Fiction Writer* and *Shanghai Literature*. His novel *The Horseman to the West* won the First Fiction Prize of the Chinese Fiction Society and the First Shaanxi Literature and Art Prize. In *A Dou*, another novel, he employs absurd humor to good effect.

Lake Hanas

The Bell

They say that their ancestors reached Lake Zaysan and, awoken by the pleasant sound of a ringing bell, left the Ubashi Khan without formally taking their leave. Rather than making for Lake Balkhash or Yili, they headed due east, came to the Altay Mountains and to the shores of Lake Hanas, the navel of the Altay. With a great noise, that magical, monstrous red fish emerged from its depths, from 200 meters below, as if pulled up by a clanking iron chain. There they settled.

The bell they heard was extremely ancient, earlier even than the heroic age of Genghis Khan. When the Mongol army first set eyes on this blue body of water, the Xiongnu (Huns) had already named it Lake Zaysan, meaning "bell ringing on the sea." Only then realizing that they shared kinship with the Huns, the Mongols gathered on the shores of Lake Zaysan listening hard to the sound of their blood rushing through their veins. Simple and taciturn, the Mongols loved this kind of silent pleasure and their wide faces reddened like cherries. So as to preserve that sacred memory, they put bells of copper around the necks of their horses. The copper bells were hand-crafts made by the Uygurs who had brought them when they pledged allegiance to Genghis Khan. They had also brought ex-quisite hand basins from Kashgar. A turning leaf inside the basin kept the water clean by making it flow constantly, producing a delightful ding-dong sound as if the metal was singing. Thus the Uygurs introduced them to copper. Up to this point the Mongols had known only iron, and believed that iron was extracted from the sun to be cast into weapons to demonstrate courage and hero-ism. But the wise and humor-loving Uygurs had no interest in making weapons; they much preferred singing and dancing. Under the pounding of their wooden hammers, the same sun was turned into musical instruments of every type. Music filled their every-day life and the things they used. Their vision thus widened, the Mongols immediately fell in love with copper. It became a religion with them; they hung it on the tops of temples and raised it to the same status as gold. They loved the wailing sound of their lamas blowing the long horns – this was the sun talking. They loved to string copper bells around the necks of their horses – these were the souls of their handsome steeds.

By the time they saw Lake Zaysan again, that great sea had al-ready receded, leaving behind a vast, tranquil body of water. Along the length of the lake, swans were gracefully circling, its waters were silent, silent as stone. So too was its blue radiance. That ringing sound was a memory of the past. They narrowed their eyes; their broad faces were as red as before. What was it that had bewitched them? None could say.

When they left behind the Ubashi Khan, they also aban-doned life in the saddle. Their later livelihood demonstrated their allegiance to Genghis Khan, a loyalty intense enough for them to confidently step down from their mountain-high horse-backs, to cultivate crops and to build houses. The first sentence in the Grand Code of Genghis Khan read: "Mongols! You are doomed once you leave your horseback." But the ringing of the bell seemed to carry toward them the sound of the great sea breathing. Now the great sea had sustained a mortal blow and Lake Zaysan, alone and isolated on the steppe, had no song any-more. The ringing they heard was a kind of consolation for their souls. Hence they left the Ubashi Khan and headed straight into the Altay, on foot.

They left their horses to the Ubashi Khan since the khan's troops had to continue their expedition. They could not let their steeds drag ploughs in the Altay – this would be an unbearable in-sult to such heroic horses. So they walked out of their tents, carry-ing their possessions on their backs or in their hands. Lake Zaysan lapped at their heels lingeringly; they quickened the pace and the lake roared, pushing up huge waves. It had slept peacefully for thousands of years but now the mighty Lake Zaysan was trans-formed into a billowing sea. It burst the banks at one rush and the ground under their feet shattered like ice. Confused and disoriented they slipped and crawled, fell and floundered.

It was then that the "plant horses" emerged. First it was the slender grass sprouting from the ground. Grass was familiar to all Mongols, for whom it was a totem of the earth and who regarded it as a great crime to pull up young grass. The green grass speared up out of the ground and skywards. Handsome horses' heads appeared from among thick grass patches. Pairs of sparkling eyes, sharp erect ears, long manes flapping as gracefully as eagle wings … entire horses sprang up. One by one, a herd of fine steeds grew out from the depths of the earth.

"Plant horses!"

They gave that sacred name to those horses without reservation, and have cherished that fresh and tender memory ever since. The war campaigns that fired the blood of the Mongols were over. Together with their plant horses, they returned to the sun, moon, stars, wind, fire, soil and water – to the elements of nature. They put themselves beyond the check of heroes and khans, and directly under the care of Mongke Tengri the sky god.

They arrived at Lake Hanas at midnight and saw an arc of blue light gleaming across the darkness from the Altay Mountains. Mongols loved blue, believing it to be the color of Mongke Tengri. Since they thought this color should not be visible at night, they reasoned that it could not be night and so continued on. They, and their plant horses too, were enchanted by the blue sky but they failed to realize that the blue light was coming from Lake Hanas. Had it not been for the huge red fish lighting up the terrain for them, they and their plant horses would have fallen into the lake.

A great red fish rose majestically from the lake – they thought it was the sun coming up. Like a great boat, it swam from the depths of the lake, the blue light glimmering around it. The sky above slowly got lighter, though the surrounding mountains were still shrouded in darkness. When the "sun" appeared in their vision, they found it to be dripping with water, its body round and sturdy. Not only that; it had wings, a huge maw, large gills and a long body - it even had legs. Its skin was flaming red and its blood more crimson even than the rose.

"It's the fair beauties! It's the fair beauties waiting for us. It's the Red Fruits!"

The Mongols and their plant horses lay down on the pasture, and the grasses growing around the lake turned thick and lush immediately. These Mongols seemed to have sprung straight from the earth. The vegetation kept on growing, silently, through the night.

The Red Fruits

What they were calling "the Red Fruits" were indeed beauties. The name, a wonderful Turkic term, was first uttered by their ancestor Chaghatay Khan.

When opening up the western trail through the Tianshan Mountains, Chaghatay encountered the most beautiful women under heaven by the Sayram Lake. He called them "Red Fruits," and the valley carpeted with wild fruits through which his army passed he named the "Vale of Fruit." For three days and three nights, his army went by amidst beauties and fruits, intoxicated to the soul by that marvelous feeling. In the ensuing years, fighting and subjugating tribes and kingdoms around the world, they would often recall that unforgettable lake and its women as charming as red fruit. Those fair beauties were as high above them as the sun in the sky. All other women now seemed like dross. The great dream, the great yearning for the "red fruit beauties" passed down the generations – from Chaghatay to Batu, to Tamerlane, down to the Ubashi Khan. The marvelous dream had at last become clear; that vast lake had been summoning them toward it.

The great Ubashi Khan crossed the River Volga, the Caspian Sea and the Aral Sea. At Lake Zaysan he turned toward Lake Balkhash, followed the course of the Yili River in the direction of Lake Sayram. The great Ubashi Khan searched for that grand lake all his life but time after time he met disappointment, none of the lakes he found having such lovely "red fruit beauties."

There were no fruit trees up in the Altay either. The beauty as fair as red fruit hid deep in Lake Hanas for 500 years. The lake water was permeated with her blood so her whole body turned scarlet. Her legs evolved into wings, which carried her, leaping out of the lake when the Tuvans finally reached the Altay. Her glimmering scarlet radiance lit up their exhausted eyes.

Wooden Houses

Once they had carried the Tuvans to their new home, the plant horses returned to their original forms; one after the other, huge and handsome trees materialized; there were spruce, red leaf poplar, silver birch, red birch and oak trees – clearly intended for them to build their homes with.

The Altay winter felt like a huge icehouse but they believed that the warmth of mother earth would protect them, so they dug pits into the ground, three feet in depth. Once the earth began to send out a warm haze, they pulled round logs into the pits, setting them upright with the top halves protruding above ground. When they built they imagined their horses. Horses had big eyes so they set window openings in the roof for them to look up at the sky from inside. The sky seemed so close that it touched the blue-gray mountains, eroding and smoothing off the peaks so that both the slopes and the summits looked rounded and smooth. Heaven seemed to favor their mountain so it chose to cling to her devotedly. It was the doing of immortal heaven that they should settle here in these mountains, just as they had once lived on horseback.

Afterwards, when the Turkic leader Tamerlane was preparing to fight in the west he sent his envoy to mobilize them, to come down from their mountains and join his armies, they replied: "Is Tamerlane not a Mongol?" The messenger looked embarrassed and whispered back: "He is the son-in-law of Mongols." "We don't get involved with a son-in-law's affairs," they told him.

Even later, when the true Mongol Emperor Babur went to conquer India, he too sent his envoy to persuade them to join him. In response, they patted the spruces, alders and birch trees up and down the mountain and told him: "Ask these trees whether they are willing to go to India." Emperor Babur did not make it hard for them as the result of their refusal. After he conquered India, he leaped out of the saddle, as did all the Mongol troops on the Indian campaign. They started to fell trees and build houses on the banks of the River Ganges. The local people had never seen this strange, semi-subterranean type of house. These wooden dwellings were immune to the scorching heat of India. Emperor Babur sighed with emotion: "Our house fears not the chill winds of the Altay nor the burning sun of India. What a special god is it?"

All the Mongols that settled in India turned into trees. Nourished by the strong sunshine, they grew greener and taller. If one of their huge branches, like the trunk of an elephant, jabbed at the sky, the sky would redden and send down a storm.

When he grew old Emperor Babur became confused. He kept on mumbling, "Turuun. They're Turuuns. They must be Turuuns." He had thought it through: it was the Turuuns, the most ancient Mongol tribe, who had invented that kind of wooden house. They built the first batch at the foot of the Burkhan Mountains, the source from which three rivers flow – the Kherlen, the Onon and the Tuul. With the resounding battle cry: "Defend the joint cradle of the three great rivers,"Genghis Khan had roused the separate Mongol tribes from their sleep and unified the Mongol empire. With these words Emperor Babur breathed his last: "They rejoined the Turuun. We too have rejoined the Turuun."

Emperor Babur's tomb was built from white stone cut from the Himalayas. Those who built it carved it into the image of a wooden house and opened skylights in the roof so the vault of heaven could continue to circle like eagles in his dreams. The smile on his lips was a puzzle: people believed Emperor Babur would one day step out of his white tomb, jump onto his battle horse and gallop on earth once more.

The Mongols of India's Moghul Empire gradually lost their original skin color of noble gold, their complexions turning darker and darker. The toxic Indian sun blackened the skins of all those living there. They believed, not in the sun, but in the soul. A sacred and great longing burned in their hearts, so their appearance turned darker by the day.

By the time the British arrived there, their faces were as black as night. They understood no English, no local languages, not even Turkish.

"Why are they like this?" cried the British.

The locals said, "They are missing the Turuun."

"And what is the Turuun?"

There was no one left who could explain the meaning of soul-longing for Turuun. The British jumped to the conclusion that Turuun mean Turkic. Turkic meant iron, and iron could be cast into swords. Hence it signified cold weaponry. Iron could plough the earth to grow crops. To the eastern way of thinking, crops and human lives both grew from the soil, and this sounded like the word "Turuun." The British assumption drew on their own imagination and experience and, judging from what happened subsequently, perhaps they were not altogether wrong.

The Young Stallion

They lived in the remote Altay interior, unaware of the British or indeed any others in the world. Even if the British were circling the globe and could wrap the Union Jack around the sun, the Altay still stood proud, independent and aloof. Range after range, the mountains blocked out the outside world like a solid fortress.

Occasionally they would go to Bu'erjin county seat, a quiet small town walled in by mountains too. There they heard strange names mentioned - "British," for example. They thought the name laughable because it sounded to them like their own word for "eagles," which were a familiar sight in the sky over the mountains and grasslands. How come a country wanted to soar into the sky? Their tone was haughtier even than that of the British colonialists, recently arrived in India: "That strange country cannot stay long in the sky. They may try to block the sun for a while but who could ever succeed in that? The sun will surely drop their souls onto the earth."

Those noisy students would tell them, "The 'Empire on which the sun never sets' has already landed!"

The middle school kids thought no backwoodsmen out of the mountains could know more than they did, so they gave them the benefit of their knowledge: "The fastest thing in the world is not a horse. It's light. Light travels at 300,000 kilometers a second."

The backwoodsmen replied, "We abandoned horseback hundreds of years back."

"What's that you're riding if they're not horses?"

Their horses, all proud Yili steeds, were tethered in the woods. "Those are not horses. They are our mental strength and courage," they replied. "A man's mental strength and courage is faster even than lightning."

Their teacher was there too and told the students: "Even Einstein acknowledged the existence of a universal force greater than science."

The backwoodsmen from the mountains quaffed their liquor

with gusto. Having drunk the jugs dry, they checked them carefully against the sunlight and drained out the last drops. They got on their horses and left.

The teacher asked, "Were they Kazakhs or Mongols?"

The shop keeper replied, "They are the most ancient Mongols, the descendants of Ögedei. Ögedei drank himself to death, and his descendents are still drunk today."

"Don't they live by Lake Hanas?"

"That is not a lake, but a path in Mongols' dream."

"A dreamlike journey. How sublime!"

A recent graduate from university, the teacher had come to Bu'erjin just a short time before, so many things here came as a surprise to him, and the shopkeeper revealed a few more. For example, the Mongols living by Lake Hanas were known as Tuvans. It was a struggle for the man to pronounce the name; he had to twist his lips to do so. Away from the lake the pronunciation became "Turuun," and beyond the Altay in Beitun and Kelamayi they could not even pronounce the word "Turuun."

The teacher longed to see that mysterious, beautiful lake for himself and his mind often flew in that direction. Consequently he was always making mistakes in class. Taking the young teacher to task, the principal was surprised to perceive a upturning of the mouth in a faint smile, his black eyes sparkling. The principal was really annoyed but his attempt at a roasting had no affect on the young man, whose face continued looking dreamy. Other observers remarked that he must have fallen in love with a pretty girl. The girls in Bu'erjin were quite attractive even though it nestled in a remote corner of the world. The forests, grassland and green, warm rivers nurtured their women.

The soul of the young language teacher was bewitched by that flame with its blue light and he spent the rest of the semester in a total dream world. There was not much the principal could do about it, university graduates being very rare commodities in their area He put up with him, with difficulty, until the vacation came around and was planning to give the young teacher a good talking to. But his room was already empty: the bird had flown.

The young man walked up into the mountains. All the way he rolled the words "Turuun, Turuun" around his mouth. "Turuun, Turuun, Turuun Turuun....," he mumbled, repeating the name for two days and nights, until finally the enunciation became more and more precise. Suddenly the name sounded out clearly, as if his throat were an organ played by the mountain wind. The name "Tuvans" came out loud and clear, as he stood by the dark blue lake, as straight and erect as a tender sprout emerging from the earth.

Just like his geography books had stated, the breath-taking Lake Hanas lay in a long valley, extending over 30 kilometers. It was flanked by lush forests of deep green that glistened as if painted in oil-color, their foliage like metal. What the books failed to convey was the cool breath from the lake and mountain landscape. That metallic chill pressed into one's back; the lake curved its way between the mountains, writhing and turning like a huge green snake; the sky was slowly squirming too. The sky felt immeasurably deep, submerged below banks of steep white clouds. The lake and the sky seemed to flow into each other.

Evidently the name "Tuvans" had come to his lips via the beautiful landscape. He coughed and coughed again, feeling a slight pain in his lungs.

The locals told him: "The Lake likes you so it is washing out your lungs."

"But I am very fit. I was once an athlete."

"Your lungs are all black. It's the same with all you incomers."

The Tuvans pulled him down onto the grass and he quietened down as he lay there. They told him, "Fill your nose to the full. Fill your eyes to the full, and then your ears."

His nose began to sniff uncontrollably, throbbing like a pump; pure, clear air rushed into his lungs and he felt a warm stream go through him; all was as crystalline as if his viscera had been put in a bright glass bottle. His eyes were drawn like moths to the brilliant wild flowers. They shone like candles everywhere among the grass and bushes.

The Tuvans took him to their village to listen to the birdsong. On every tree, there were birds singing with all their heart and the leaves took up the singing. The trees all sounded out like a thousand instruments.

They left the forest and went to a wooden house to eat horse-meat. The meat was prepared alive. They picked out a small three-year-old stallion, but before slaughtering it they had the teacher ride it along the lakeshore. The stallion galloped along happily and its warm body returned all foam-flecked. The teacher was sweating all over. The host was happy to see this.

"Your sweat is mixed with the horse's. Now for your blood and flesh too."

The teacher was perplexed but he very soon understood. The horse was led into the forest and the host felled it with one strike of his knife. But its hooves kept on flying, galloping in the air for a long time. He heard its fine blood splashing into an iron bucket. He had heard about this grassland custom from a university friend but witnessing in person made him tremble and shiver. He feared he would not be able to swallow down the fresh flesh. But as soon as the hostess offered it up, his mouth and stomach immediately became alive and eager. He wolfed the meat down, to the immense gratification of his host, who kept piling more meat onto his plate and pouring liquor into his bowl. Never before had he experienced such happy enjoyment of food, never been so completely satiated.

After feasting on the meat, he went behind the house and saw large blood stains on the grass. The sunlight was as thick as honey, the horse's breath lingered among the trees. Softly, he walked over to it, sensing its presence, alive in his body. His body had grown conspicuously larger. He hit a tree with his hand, almost felling it with the blow. The strength of the horse had entered his body. He enquired of his host: "Do you eat horseflesh a lot?"

"Sometimes a lot, sometimes a little, it's hard to say."

"How could you bear it if all those horses entered your body?"

"Some of them came in, but some left later."

"Are you OK with that?"

Not understanding the question, he had to repeat it before his host got it.

"Who could just casually let go of a good horse? A good horse will find a good woman. Is your woman good?" the host asked. "Yeh, she's good," he replied.

"How come she's not here with you?"

"She's in Urumqi. That's too far from the Altay."

"What's the use if she can't stay with you?" The host lowered his voice: "Have you two tried it?"

"We've been lovers for a few years."

"Never!" The host pinched his shoulder, back, arms and legs before continuing: "How can this be a body that's enjoyed a woman? If it weren't for my horse inside you, you'd never remember a women." Then he turned serious. "My Han brother, get yourself a woman fast. Once you do, one horse won't be enough. You'll want to let your horse graze every day, and you will need a prairie. Once a man has his own prairie, you can release one horse after another and you could do it with good women no matter how many there are." Like a big brother, the host patiently tried to educate his Han brother, "My horse will surely bring you good luck."

Only just out of university, and like many guys of his age, the teacher had wet dreams. Wet dreams, seen by many as something shameful, were transformed by the Tuvans into something hugely poetic: when you find a good woman, your life river will flow into an oasis. Just like many rivers vanish in the desert, everyone has a bleak period in his youth. The Tuvan Big Brother took a big gulp of liquor and patted the teacher on the shoulder, "A river must flow into the sea. You must let liquor irrigate your thirsty heart." The liquor had been tumbling down his throat, like a river gurgling its way through high mountains, never stopping.

"Han brother, life has no end. Once you start with your love, don't ever stop. If you do, you'll run dry. And what sort of life is that if you run dry?"

The teacher was tongue tied. He tried to get out a response but the Tuvan Big Brother shook his head, "So you haven't done it with your woman yet? Well, you can't call her your woman then. If things worked like that I could call every woman in the world 'my own.' The way you Han people love, well, it's really like mistreating your woman." Earnestly, he urged the young man, "You've got my horse inside you now. It's a three year-old stallion, so don't you go wasting it."

Although Bu'erjin is in a remote neck of the woods, its girls are very pretty. The glow on their cheeks was painted by the forests, steppe and green warm rivers. The Altay sat right on top of precious gold and diamonds. So its women had no need for make-up; they had a natural glow all of their own.

The teacher had a young stallion throbbing in his body now. It was plain for all to see, kicking and galloping, not on the golden grassland, but in the broad chest of the young man.

Now a fine young girl, the best, was destined to become the sea to his river. He invited her to a secluded spot by the Bu'erjin River, a point where the waters flew at their swiftest. There the stallion plunged deep into the dashing waters and leapt, dripping, onto the steep riverbank. The sun soon dried their wet bodies. The stallion's energy was not spent: once more he charged in and the river could no longer contain his ardor. He loved to swim in its deepest places. Once you've made love with a good woman, once is not enough. Proud and confident, he urged her: "Marry me!"

Sexual Punctuation

He forgot his girlfriend in Urumqi quite easily. Were it not for the fact that she came to seek him out, his memory of her would have died like a river drying up in the desert. Quietly, across Xinjiang, many a river disappeared that way. For most people living in Urumqi, Bu'erqin was a remote, bleak place and the mention of it evoked only sympathy and unease in the listener. They had been fellow students for four years and fell in love on campus. After graduation, he was assigned to Bu'erjin and she remained in Urumqi. It was not long before she fell in love with another man and though she took up her pen several times, meaning to write to him about her change of heart she never got further than a few lines. Like the state leaders of the nuclear powers, none dared push the nuclear strike button no matter how angry they might become. Finally she decided to pay him a visit to tell him her decision face to face. When she boarded the long-distance bus from Urumqi to Altay it was like setting out on an aid mission for African refugees. At Beitun she transferred to a local bus that turned and twisted its way through steep mountains before finally arriving at Bu'erjin. There he was, but free of any sign of the depression she had anticipated – no despair, no sadness, no frustration. In fact, he could barely recognize her. The flashing of his eyes scorched her but, of course, she could not see the presence of that stallion in his body.

He took her to a small, quiet restaurant in the town. From their seats they could see a group of horses leisurely grazing on the gentle hillside. She mentioned the horses a few times but he just made perfunctory responses and the horse within him did not stir. They recalled the love they once had for each other and were happy and relieved that their reunion had turned out as contented as the horses on the hillside pastures. A meeting fraught with danger thus ended as a happy excursion.

He took her up into the mountains. The mountain range rose gradually; like the slow unrolling of an oil painting the land revealed itself – the gray-blue rocks, deep blue rivers, the moving waters of the lake and the sky; and, in between, large swathes of forest, golden-red and golden-yellow. In a valley below they saw a calm, mysterious blue luminescence.

"That's Lake Hanas."

"There's supposed to be a huge red fish in that lake. Can we see it?"

"If young people see the red fish, they have to tie the knot."

"Let's take a look anyhow."

"Cars can't get up there. There's only an eagle's trail."

"You don't want to take me there?"

"The eagle will duel with me."

"Let the big fish judge then."

"That seems fair enough."

They both laughed.

He said good-bye to her at the bus station.

"So I'm an OK guide, right?"

"Thank you!"

"Don't thank me. Thank the Altay."

As the bus started moving she took a last look at the Altay Mountains Afterwards, that remote, pure place often appeared in her dreams.

Her husband loved her and she loved him right back. How could she not? He was the first high achiever she encountered after leaving university. He was made director of studies at a key high school at a very young age and continued to be exceptional. His kind of masculine charm eclipsed all the young men of her student days. But though she led a very happy life, she desired even more happiness. She was greedy: after one careless encounter with a new man she would move on to the next. Every affair was followed by tremendous remorse and this regret and guilt made her love and depend on her husband ever more deeply.

The husband taught math. A very fine teacher he was too. He concluded that his wife's periodic sexual flings must be parabolas diverting from a coordinate axis. He kind of enjoyed the swings and curves in her behavior and her slender body displayed that kind of curve as well. With her every up and down, his wife's curves appeared fuller and more dynamic to his mathematician's eye. In the third year of their marriage, he could casually chalk coordinate axes on the blackboard and then draw extremely complex curves, circles and elipses from those axes all in free hand. This skill of his impressed students and colleagues no end and it became a bit of a party piece. Like a veteran cadre practicing calligraphy, cigarette in mouth, he would draw circles and parabolas on paper after dinner.

His wife was too much of a mystery to him, too incredible.

But she was equally baffled by his reaction.

She taught languages and was totally indifferent to graphs and parabolas, but she didn't actively take against his hobby. Sometimes she'd even dole out a word or two of praise and the curves would continue like sweeping waves. She even added a few strokes sometimes so the curves could go on for forever. Certainly her drawing was no match for his. He would keep on making amendments to his drawings, always in pursuit of perfection.

"Numbers must be precise, as precise as possible."

When the husband's parabola activity reached its climax, her new secret life began to peak too. She was beginning to feel fearful though. Punctuation marks began to appear on the pages of her diary. She had marked the success of her first love with a perfect small circle, and believed she could mark the conclusion of all her secret adventures with perfect circles too. All the men between those marks were out of her life: if she happened to encounter one or two of them outside they would just glance at each other, nod briefly and hurry off on their respective ways. That full and perfect circle had ended everything, cleaned up everything, leaving not a hint of scandal. At first, the minute details of these risky experiences all went into her diary, or rather diaries – several large volumes of them. These she locked in a small case and kept it at the office rather than at home. She was a woman with secrets but the details of those secrets were shrinking, getting ever simpler, at first a few sentences and, finally, just a round circle. In fact, she never stopped living that kind of life. She would look at those circles in her diary, visualizing them larger and larger, first to the size of beans, then coins, then eggs until they were perfect large circles. It did not dawn on her that her circles had anything to do with those her husband drew. She was a language teacher with a rich emotional life that had nothing to do with mathematics. She was addicted to the contents of the circles. Lining up all those circles created a deep, immeasurably deep, tunnel It had no end but it did have a beginning. It started with that first full circle.

The first circle marked the very first time.

She picked up the phone and called several student contemporaries until she found the phone number of her first "full circle." Its six digits seemed an astronomical number to her. She pressed the first round button on the handset, then the next, producing a different beep each time like a piano tuner testing the keys of a piano. The signal flew through space above the Zhunger Basin until it reached that small backwoods town of Bu'erjin in the remote belly of the Altay. The melody began:

"Is Lake Hanas like a circle?"

"Not at all; it's elongated. It lies the length of a valley."

"How long is it?"

"Over 30 kilometers. But if you include its river course it's hard to give an accurate figure."

"It has a river course?"

"It lies on the upper reaches of the River Erqis, which flows across the Chinese border and empties into the Arctic Ocean."

The Erqis was a serene, quiet river.

She went into the study and saw her husband taking his hand away from a new parabola he had just drawn. He told her calmly that he had followed her to the Altay when she gone there a few years back.

"I was worried about your safety. Who knows what might have happened."

"What did you see?"

"He was your university boyfriend!"

"That's right. So?"

"I was worried about your getting together."

"How could anything happen in that secluded place?"

"It was peaceful there, that's for sure."

"So you feel at ease?"

The husband smiled and his hands smiled too, "You are my good wife." He let his smiling hand draw circles and they made love, a perfect union.

"We'll stay perfect like this forever!"

"Yes, forever and forever!"

This was like making vows! She clenched her teeth and gripped her fists, silently repeating that unreachable circle in her mind. The circle was revolving like a huge wheel, making her head spin.

Another liaison started, crazier and more passionate than the last. After the affair was over, she fled to her husband in panic and urged him to hold her tight. Even when his grip was as tight as ropes, she was still not satisfied, "Tighter! Harder!" She got upset and ridiculed her husband but he refused to speak. When she finally calmed down, she gave him a guilty smile, "You should put me in cuffs."

"What's scared you? Some bad guy giving you a hard time?"

"All the world's bad guys are giving me a hard time."

"It's just your imagination. You need to calm down."

That faraway, pure place appeared in her life again. The telephone seemed like a musical instrument playing wonderful tunes to her. As she pressed the numbers, she experienced a kind of sacred feeling.

"How are you?"

"Just fine."

"How come you feel so fine?"

"Just live a peaceful life, no stress, I guess."

"How can you feel so peaceful?"

"Hard to be anything else when I live by such a big lake."

"Yes, it's so peaceful over there."

"The Tuvans are even more peaceful than me."

She tried to pronounce "Tuvans," but it just tied her tongue in knots. At the other end of the phone he laughed: "Don't try to say it. You can't."

"If you can, why can't I?"

"This is a pure name, and once away from Lake Hanas people get the pitch wrong. Bu'erjn is only just across the mountain, but that divide results in them being pronounced as Turuun. And once you are out of the Altay, even Turuun vanishes."

"How about in Urumqi?"

"Didn't you try saying it just now?"

"Why are they so lucky?"

"They conquered the world, but after several hundred years, they grew weary of that unsettled way of life, wondering from one place to the next. They wanted to go back to the Turuun River at the foot of the Burkhan Mountains, but the Altay became their home.

"That's a punctuation mark then."

"What do you mean - punctuation mark?"

"A language teacher, and you don't know what it means?"

"I've never thought of myself as a teacher."

"What are you then?"

"Out here, I'm just undergrowth."

"What does that make your wife and kid then?"

"They are trees. One's a silver birch, the other a red birch."

"The red birch?"

"That's my daughter. She's as tall as her mom now."

"Are they growing on your paddock?"

"To call it a paddock is way too small. Mine is a grassland for the two trees."

His broad voice filled the entire Jungar.

She put down the phone. The night was deep but she could sense a mighty blue tide billowing in the darkness. The turbulent tide did not subside until she was lying in bed. It would be easy for her to go to Lake Hanas but she preferred to listen to him over the phone. When he described the lake she felt its vastness and limitless depths, like a sea. Say "Hanas" - at least she could pronounce that pure name. Say it, "Hanas." She could get her tongue around that word but not that sacred name "Tuvans." She could only turn that name round in her head, and her head became an ocean. So long as they spoke about Tuvans, he could never cut her off. "I never left you." Her repeated rebellions had resulted in a tale of desperation – "Let me be reborn in language!" She believed the bottomless sapphire lake was another kind of flame, the red tongue of Hanas. "I'm down and degraded. But its waters can bring me back to life." Deep sobbing engulfed her like a sea. She buried her face in her pillow as if she were diving deep into the lake. Every sound now seemed pure. Why not say it? "Hanas." Say it. "Tuvans"…That's an end to all the circles. Never again… whether Lake Hanas or Zaysan, the blue river would surely flow on for ever? …

Talgan Flour

Where the snow had thawed, patches of earth like brown horsebacks showed through. Horse manes fluttered in the wind, causing crop ears to spring up. Those that looked like swallow tails were oats and those like girls' braids were barley. These were the earliest crops cultivated by the Tuvans and the favorite fodder of their horses. "We eat the same food our horses eat."

"That is the bounty bestowed by our horses."

The Tuvan Big Brother had the teacher eat some oats and barley.

"Our stallion is in your body so we must feed it with our grain."

"Give me some then. Feeding me is the same as feeding your horse."

"Take more then. You can't be stingy with our horse. And take some with you when you leave."

The Tuvan Big Brother called his wife for her to make some talgan flour for their Han brother. The teacher wanted to help but his host got angry: "It's a woman's job. Are you a woman?"

"I just wanted to look."

"What's to see? It's nothing special."

"How you and your wife live is like something out of myth for us Han people."

"What myth? Do you mean the *Jangar* epic?"

"*Jangar* is *Jangar.*"

The teacher was a university graduate. Big Brother trusted him and respected his learning. He went with him to look at the flour being made from the barley and oats.

"In the past, you'd have been the Great Lama on our prairie."

"Why is there no Lama temple around here?"

"Hanas doesn't need a Lama temple. The Altay is our golden throne. The blue lake is the glow of the Buddha."

They were seated on a jetty smoking tobacco grown by Big Brother. The teacher took just one a pull at the pipe and started coughing violently. With eyes watering, he choked out the words: "Smoke one of my my cigarettes."

The teacher took out his pack of *Red Snow Lotus* but Big Brother said cigarettes were too insipid.

"Give it a try. Just a try."

"I have tried cigarettes but the more I smoked them, the more tired I felt. In the end I couldn't even open my mouth."

"Was it really that bad?"

"Do you think smoking is for fun? Tobacco is to open one's mouth. A man must have a mouth as big as a bread oven so he can fire up a woman."

The cheeks of Big Brother's wife were on fire and, bashful to perform her chores in front of a male stranger, she went to a neighbor's house to get her friend over to keep her company. It was at least ten minutes walk to the neighbors as the houses in the village were scattered far apart, somewhat like a huge tree having branches with large empty spaces in between. All the timber houses were surrounded by low wooden fences. Spear and feather grasses grew vigorously and extended as far as the roofs. The front face presented as a neat log wall, inset with a door and windows. At the rear, the walls tailed into the ground, giving them the look of low earth mounds.

Their neighbor's wife came to help Big Brother's wife to make the flour. The oats and barley were newly harvested and had been aired in the courtyard. The two women grasped a handful of the grains and threw them up in the air. The clear sound showed that they were dry. Even so, they were still a little uneasy about the effect of sunlight, so they put popped some into their mouths to chew on. Reassured by hearing how crisp they were, they set about pounding the barley and oats. Two wooden mortars made from the roots of oak trees squatted in the center of the courtyard like two sturdy black bears. The bears jaws gaped wide and greedily to gobble up the grains. The birchwood pestles fell into the mortars and fell again, each loud bang sending up a cloud of fine white dust. The fragrant scent of freshly pounded grain filled their nostrils.

Big Brother said, "Our women love doing it. Whoever gets the grain soul falling on them will receive blessings."

"Why don't you do it yourself then?"

"How could I be called a man if I snatched a woman's luck? Once the government got us an electric grinder in the village and connected power for us. But our women wanted nothing to do with it. They are smart; they refused to hand the soul of the grain over to a machine."

"But you refused even to look at it," his wife added.

She was now getting used to working before a stranger; enjoying it even. Her neighbor became merrier too, "It's like being warmed by two suns and we have nowhere to hide." Big Brother remarked loudly, "I'll go and get your man here. He doesn't have to graze the sheep; he could be here shining on you."

"Sure. Let Big Sister-in-law grind the grain for me a while so my Melhan can shine on Big Sister-in-law."

"Melhan's taken the flock to the Kaba River."

"No matter how far away the sheep roam, the shepherd's eyes remain on his wooden house."

The thumps of the flour making got louder and louder. The barley and oat flour tumbled in the wooden mortars like rapid whitecaps turning in the Bu'erqin River. From the solid, ample bosoms of the two women came the words of the talgan song:

"Belgre – run, thump! Belgre – run, thump thump!

The sun spins yarn, thump! It spun the horse's mane, thump, thump!

A swallow flies from the horse's mane, thump! A pretty girl flies from the horse's mane, thump, thump!

The girl holds a log, thump! The log is from a silver birch tree, thump thump!

The log is from a red birch tree, thump thump!

The girl the log, the girl, the log, thump thump!

The log is from a silver birch tree, thump thump!

The log is from a red birch tree, thump thump!

Belger's bones, thump thump!

Belger's sweat drops, thump thump!

Belger – falls down, ah, thump!"

The women stopped thumping their wooden pestles into the mortars; their faces were as red as branding irons. The sunlight was distorted by the heat. They leant against their pestles to gasp for breath, but they didn't seem to be sweating.

"They're not sweating. Why were they singing about sweating?"

"That's how the song goes. Han brother, how come you don't understand songs?"

"But sweating as you labor is totally justified."

"Before they married both of them were good helpers at home and in the fields. A good fieldwork hand doesn't sweat. Men don't want to marry a girl who sweats over a small chore. A wet girl will go moldy." Big Brother clutched the teacher's ear as if to hold a leaf and whispered into it, "They'll sweat when they are in bed with men." The teacher's eyes opened as wide as his mouth, "Can they still sing?"

"But that is labor too, my Han brother. No field work, grazing sheep, herding horses, farming or catching fish can compare with that kind of labor!"

Big Brother stretched out his legs and a heroic song sped from his horse-wide chest:

"Belger – run, thump!

Belger – run, thump thump!
Good Belger is sweating, thump!
The sweat flows into a river, thump, thump!
There's fish in the river, thump!
That's the great red fish, thump thump!
The great red fish comes out of the water, thump thump!
The great red fish rises, thump thump!"

Big Brother pounded his fists on the ground to make the thumping sound. By the time he'd finished his fists had made a depression in the ground.

His wife crouched by the mortar, scooping out the ground flour and all the time shooting happy glances at her companion, who was smiling as broadly as herself. Like naughty kids, they pinched each other's faces, spreading the flour onto their blushing cheeks. The fresh flour sent out a delicious, grainy, aroma.

Soon they were able to taste the newly made talgan. Big Sister-in-law prepared the fresh flour, mixed it with milk tea and fetched them each a bowl of aromatic talgan.

The two women had a quick mouthful or two and went back to their grinding.

Grains of oat and barley poured into the wooden mortars in a shining golden stream that seemed to flow down from the sun in the blue sky above.

"I'm as full as a cow's udder! Women are really something. To combine a cow with grain like that."

"But how come I can't feel a thing?"

"Because the food you've been eating has no soul. Your tongue is a like a fish stranded out of water for a long time."

Big Brother's eyes were melancholy, "Han Brother, our hands are precious treasures given us by eternal heaven. We must use them wisely and well. Use your hands to find the woman you like, for food and clothing. Everything passing through your hands will take part of your soul with it."

The teacher's tongue stretched out of his mouth; it even turned cold.

Big Brother said, "Our fish should go to the lake."

His tongue shrank back but kept writhing in his mouth as if it had been injured. The teacher covered his mouth with his hand and headed back.

The wife said, "Will his tongue fall out?"

"Han people are too far away from water. It's not easy for them to recover."

"He is our honored guest. You should accompany him back."

"He wants to be alone. Lake Hanas is a god for both our people. For Tuvans and for Han."

"May the god of all creatures manifest its spirit!"

"It will."

The teacher walked out into the dark night. He stumbled over rocks several times, but kept his hand over his mouth, refusing to let go even when he fell, for fear that his tongue might fall out. Like a fish, a tongue should return to the water.

He stood up, knocking his head against tree branches, that sent golden stars shooting before his eyes. The stars flew off, not stopping until they reached the treetops and the sky. His stars shone down on him and now he could see the branches by their light. The trees were widely spaced: you could easily run a herd between them.

He stepped into a cow pat, triggering off a smell, harsh on the throat, a tobacco-like smell. He coughed. The closer he came to the lake, the more animal dung he saw. He trod into horse dung and cow dung. In the icy cold night it smelled just like beer.

The wind off the lake blew ever harder, his whole body seemed thinner and more streamlined. There was still some distance between him and the lakeshore, but he felt he had already entered the water. The brushing of the forage grass around him felt like water splashing. The light from the lake — much larger than the lake itself — welled up over his chest and over his neck. His breathing became a little strained; his tongue, however, came back to life. He let go his hand, allowing his tongue to move on its own. Rather than thrashing around as he had feared, it just licked his upper jaw and tooth line, gently, like the lake lapping away at an embankment. He crouched down and set his imagination to work. He thought about his tongue returning to the bottom of the lake, regaining its vitality from its clear and deep waters. Down the remaining years of his life, he would kiss his dear wife with the same gentleness; with the same tenderness, the vital life breath from his healthily cracking bones and his manly chest would enter her good earth.

His tongue had returned to water.

The teacher was as frank as his Tuvan Big Brother. When the limpid lake water welled up his throat, his hands rose like the red fish and he reached for the phone and called Urumqi. He told that constantly agitated woman: "Return to the water. As soon as you do you will find some peace."

"I know what you mean by water."

He heard her sobbing.

"I don't mean tears."

"I know you don't. But I just want to cry." Her tears kept coming. "Go on. Tell me more about that lake."

"It's not like a sea or a river. The lake sucks the earth gently like a tongue."

"It should be the earth that sucks the lake."

It was his turn to be startled. He held the handset to him and fell into the plight men often encounter.

That night by the lake, all the gods and spirits came out. The tips of the forage grass seeped out crystal dewdrops. Owls glided softly in the forests. The women of the grassland and mountains drifted to sleep under a cover of owl feathers, their cheeks blushing like red roses. Foxes begged the moon for a fine silver coat: a silver fox was a proud creature on earth.

The teacher was so close to them; when the grass licked his feet he did not feel it. He was too wrapped up in his fantasy.

Big Brother said his fantasy-loving nature was not a problem. In fact it was a most precious thing you could find in a human. If fantasies dried up, how could there be such a crystal clear lake?

Big Sister-in-law said the owl and the fox were following him all the time.

"Why's the fox following me?"

"You don't want your wife to charm you?"

The term "bewitched by a fox fairy" flashed into the mind of the language teacher.

Big Brother laughed, "Your wife is missing you. Even when she's dozing, a good woman will miss her husband."

"Do you want me to leave?"

"To have a visitor living in your home is like having the sun shining into your courtyard. To have a wife missing you is like having the moon light up your window. Let the moon cover your window in silver, and your wife will become prettier."

One night when the teacher went to the toilet in the village, he suddenly cried out: "Fox! fox!" Big Brother ran out with his hunting rifle. He sniffed the air but there was no tell-tale stink of fox.

"You've been bewitched."

"How could that be?"

"There are good women other than your wife. Don't be so stubborn. You've just fallen under the spell of a fox fairy. You have the smell of sulfur on you." The teacher kept protesting his innocence but his host told him just to go back to bed and not to catch a cold by staying outside.

"I...."

"You dream up fantasies. Maybe it's the fox in your imagination."

The night sky turned to a pure deep blue. "How come the night's not dark even though there's no moon or stars?"

"You should have dreams. It is like planting crops. You have to cover them with a thick bed of cow, horse and sheep dung."

"An imaginary fox can't do any harm, right?"

"No, it's a good thing."

"How can it be good?"

"Lake Hanas came from Lake Zaysan with our ancestors."

"Are foxes related to women?"

"It's a fine thing to dream of a woman. My Han brother, are you ill? How can you call your life a good one without a good woman?"

"But there are so many of them."

"You are a like a sea. Not a turbid puddle."

Thus the fox entered the teacher's imagination. The fox was highly vigilant while the teacher dreamed cautiously. He also dreamed that Big Brother was scolding him and stamping his feet, "Han brother, the fox has gone back to the water. Do you want it to change into to a shrimp or a frog? It's a red fox — a beautiful red fox!"

That red fox in the white birch forest on the Altay suddenly leapt up and plunged toward the lake like a hawk.

The great red fish! Tuvan Big Brother sat up with a start. The teacher remained sleeping.

The Great Red Fish

Tuvan Big Brother recalled that early morning when the great red fish had risen from the lake. The fox had been up on the roof all night, sitting there on its hind legs. Came the dawn, the fox jumped down to the courtyard, its fiery red tail flashing past the window; the courtyard seeming to catch fire. Then the fox ran across the firewood stack and fled into the white birch woods. It scurried up the grassy slope where a large spread of oats was growing. Startled by the intrusion, the oats gave off a loud rustling.

His old dad said, "Child, you've been bewitched by a fox. Quick. Get down to the lake."

His old mom said not a word, but silently watched his back as he left.

That morning, the cloudy eyes of his mom suddenly cleared, becoming as limpid as the blue lake. She saw a group of red fish rise from the bottom of the lake. Her eyes flashed. Her old man told her to get food ready but she said "You expect me to cook on a day like this?" The old man was puzzled. After cooking meals for decades, why was she refusing to do it today?

"What am I supposed to eat then?"

"On such a wonderful morning, stop thinking about food for a minute."

Seeing the clear lake in his wife's eyes, the old man fell silent and even snuffed out his pipe. On such a fine morning, the bluish mist spilling out of the valley was enough for him to enjoy. His lungs were a little golden yellow in color and rustled like leaves on a tree. All the trees by the lake started rustling too. A blue light flashed through the trees, and instantly turned white.

Tuvan Big Brother never found that fox. His dream still wafted and whirled around his head. He walked to the lakeside and the water reached out its tongue to lick his feet. He watched the lake listlessly, thinking that he must find how deep its water was. He had lived by the lake for over twenty years but he had never felt such a strong impulse as at that moment. People always said that Lake Hanas was beyond measurement. To them she was a goddess. Looking at the vast and sacred lake, how he wished he could see that goddess. The goddess was licking his feet with her icy tongue.

He walked up the hillside but the goddess' tongue followed him.

He reached the hilltop and stayed with the trees there, but the tongue still followed him. Behind him towered a big poplar tree whose leaves beckoned to him in the wind. He climbed the tree and the tongue continued to follow him.

Was the lake really immeasurably deep as the legend claimed?

From atop the blue poplar at the hilltop, he could see the lake continue on the other side of the ridge, just as if she were holding the mountain in her arms. That was how he had grown up. No matter where he stood on Altay, he was a mountain and his two outstretched arms formed a solid dike. He must find out the depth of Lake Hanas.

The red fish rose from the lake at precisely the spot his eyes were focused on.

There are many red fish in Lake Hanas but only one that could leap out of the water. It was as large as a boat and it stayed at the bottom of the lake all the time. In Tuvan legend, the great red fish was there to pull people together — a man with a woman.

The icy cold tongue of the goddess licked the feet of Tuvan Big Brother until he felt them getting warm. He jumped down from the tall blue poplar. Generally, anyone jumping from a thirty-foot high tree would get splattered but the goddess had licked him warm, so he floated to the ground as light as a swallow and ran off downhill.

A good girl living by the lake got up early and went out to fetch water. The goddess licked her hand, warmed it up and soon it was as red and glinting as a red fish. The good girl wondered what on earth that red fish was doing on her hand. Its flashes reached the bottomless lake and shone on the red fish as big as a small boat. As if a boatman had given it a hard shove, the great red fish turned into a whistling rush of wind. The lake waters rose higher and higher and the rocks on the shore cracked open with a great resounding noise. But, once the red fish leapt out the lake, the waters retreated. The great red fish climbed higher and higher like the sun, until it reached the top of the Altay and jumped over the summit like the arc of a rainbow. The lake water on the far side received the fish gently and it circled back down to the bottom of the lake.

A man and a woman stood watching that strange, mysterious rainbow, lost in wonder. After an age, they finally saw each other. The woman scooped up a ladle-full of water and handed it to the man. He gulped it down eagerly.

"I have drunk the water."

"Come here whenever you want to drink it. You couldn't drink the lake dry."

With that, she picked up her carrying pole and walked away, swaying with her burden.

Lake Hanas stretched along valley, its deepest places unseen beneath its sapphire waters. He married the girl and sure enough, she was a wonderful girl. When he was making love to her, he felt like that great red fish leaping across the Altay. No matter how fervent or wild his lovemaking, his good woman would always receive him as gently as the lake did with the fish and let him spin back down gradually and tenderly. So he kept on leaping, again and then again. The water did not run dry. He often heard horses neighing.

They were proud Yili horses.

After leaving their Mongol horses to the Ubashi Khan, his ancestors had been carried to Lake Hanas by the plant horses of Zaysan and they had taken up farming beside the lake.

Cultivating the soil was how the Han and Taranchi ("wheat grower" in Uygur) people earned their livelihood. On the oases scattered across Central Asia they dug irrigation ditches and deep wells to cultivate wheat, corn, paddy rice, indeed anything that would grow.

Of all the crops, oats had a special place in their heart, because they had flown from the manes of those horses to their side. They loved barley too. How could you call its ears small? One barley ear was a cow's tit, a goat! They grew oats and barley on the land but absolutely refused to dig wells or ditches. It was their belief that man must not alter the course of a river; in this they were unshakable. The Han and Taranchi people urged them to make better use of their precious land, telling them if they could bring water onto the land, it would grow much more food. But they replied, "Our land was bestowed on us by immortal heaven so all we need to do is to sow seeds in the earth." They kept on repeating this reply. The Han and the Taranchi people were the earliest farmers on earth and they planted crops wherever they could across Central Asia. No one had considered arable farming in the mountains; these were the winter retreats for the Mongol, Kazakh and Khalkha herdsmen, a paradise for their animals. Crops grown there would quickly be swallowed up by weeds. But, who could ever imagine such a treasure trove right in the navel of the Altay and where no well or ditch or even spring was needed?

The Tuvans claimed, "Spring water is for relieving thirst only."

The Tuvans planted crops on the hillsides facing the sun. Grain was the king of all the plants and the Tuvans overwhelmed the Han and Taranchi people simply by means of their green thumbs. It was the Taranchi ancestors who first taught the Mongols how to write. And it was Han forebears who sent countless books to the Mongols. Han and Taranchi people knew grain was the best, the best thing on the earth but they just failed to know how to give the thumbs up. Well, they knew how to give the thumbs up to heroes, saints and sages but they never thought of giving the thumbs up to crops in the field. The Tuvans would say in their drawling speech: "Wheat ears look like this. Every one of them good and sound. How can cattle or goats compete with that!"

The Tuvans transformed the hillsides facing the sun into golden forests of sturdy "upturned thumbs." Even having absorbed Han, Uygur and Arab cultures, the great world conqueror Genghis Khan still held to the simple old ways of the vast desert. He would not use a seal to sign imperial decrees and proclamations; rather, he would impress them with his thumb mark, leaving to posterity a series of fingerprints pulsing with the warmth of his blood.

"Their grains were 'brought out' by the hooves of horses." Thus the Han and Taranchi people consoled themselves when they failed to grow such sturdy crops.

And it was no less than the truth. Since their farm tools were short and crudely made, they had to exert a lot of strength. At the hands of the Tuvans, the Han people's iron harrow and the Taranchis' mattocks changed from their original form. They just loved their plain tools, and they had sound reasons for this, saying: "If you let your hands rest, your work rests too." They knew their fields better than the Han and Taranchi people. They opened up land on gentle slopes where the soil had the greatest vitality and where the grasses grew tall and thriving, moving like green flames. In late autumn when the forage grass turned golden and ripe, they would take their sickles to harvest the gold. It was a solemn ritual. Women were in the fields to dry the grass, tie it into bundles and store it for the pregnant livestock. Female livestock had a holy connection with the land. The menfolk turned over the virgin land at least three more times before the arrival of the first snows so that the earth could absorb and store enough sunlight. The land was as dry and soft as a felt carpet as the snow covering fell over it, ceaselessly, silently. The field remained dry within the tight embrace of the pure snow right through that winter. The next spring the sun burst out through the earth; in an instant the snow dropped into the earth Such was the pressure of the snow cover, how could the sun come surging up out from there? It was indeed the sun; it had been lying there hidden right through the winter, but now it came charging out from hiding like a herd of wild horses.

The Tuvans got the fertile land they had waited for…fertile calcium-rich black soil laden with nutrients from the mature forage grasses, the same nutrients to feed the grains of which they dreamed. Their bodies shone with a noble golden color, for all the world like golden figures bursting out of rocks. Under their expectant watch, the land quenched its thirst with snow water. New sprouts burst out. The land was chasing the sunlight.

"Their crops were carried on the backs of horses."

The Han and Taranchi people were green with envy.

Early that morning, Tuvan Big Brother heard the sound of horses neighing and rushed off to the fields right away. The crops were rolling like galloping wild horses but he had no idea where they were heading for.

When making talgan flour it must be pure and uncontaminated.

The waves of the crops pushed him up the hillside until he stood before a big oak tree. It was a young and vigorous tree. A good woman deserves a tree like that. It took him an entire day to cut it down and he used the root to make two new mortars. The old ones used by his elders were chopped into firewood already. His wife would start her own life in the wooden mortars made by her man.

The wife said, "Make another one. Use some more of the tree."

It was a long tree trunk so he cut out the best section and used it to make a smaller mortar.

The pestle was made from red birch. The wife held the red birch pestle and thumped it up and down like the red fish leaping the summit of Altay. Seeing how happy this made her, he gave her a flirtations pinch of the cheek producing a beautiful wide smile in response.

"You can harvest the crops now."

The crop waves galloped on the hillside like a herd of golden stallions. He harvested the crops overnight, by the light of a round silver moon; she could not bring herself to wait. She wanted to hear the thumping of the wooden mortar.

"Did you do this in your mother's home? You work as hard as an ox."

"I was an ox in my mother's home, but it's not like that in my own home."

"What are you then?"

"I don't know."

The new bride sprang up like a doe: "This is women's work. Get out of my way."

He lay down in their house, listening to the thumping of the wooden pestle. He also heard the rustling sound of the crops, the billowing waves of barley...! What would they become once they felt the touch of a woman's hands? He was wondering about it even in his dreams.

One day, he was riding his proud Yili stallion down the hill slope and noticed his woman pounding barley in their courtyard. That sturdy mortar he had made from the oak tree sat there, like a strong horse lying on the ground waiting for her to ride it. Why didn't she get on?

The horses we left behind were those owned by the Ubashi Khan. Our own horses came with us all the way.

Why do I have to get on? When you start riding, so will I!

The blushing face of his wife set all the sky aflame.

Many of life's troubles disappear if you have a good woman.

The Silver Doe

The old couple had time on their hands now. They had been busy all their lives, manacled and shackled to the pestle and mortar, to the cooking range, to their livestock and their land until many of their tools had worn out. Eventually their daughter-in-law had burnt them for firewood. Grandpa said, "The sun is smiling on us. It's pleased with us." Grandma was itching to try the new pestle and mortar but Grandpa tried to stop her: "It's OK just to take a look, but whatever you do, don't start using it. You'll never take your hands off if you do."

"I want my hands back."

"You're too old now. Save yourself trouble."

They were sitting in the courtyard, watching their daughter-in-law busy with this chore and that. Grandma admired her: "She's as graceful as a doe the way she works."

The tall daughter-in-law was deft in her movements and calm in her manner. Pots, jars, and all the utensils became compliant in her hands, as obedient as a flock of young animals. Grandma could not help herself: "I was like that once too."

"Back then you were just like her."

"What was I like?"

"A doe, a pretty doe in the forest."

Watching her daughter-in-law working only made Grandma feel sadder, so, in an attempt to distract her, Grandpa said, "Listen, the deer is calling out to you." Grandma heard a deer calling too.

They walked up the slope and passed an area of grass. The grass suddenly turned yellow.

"That grass is the 'gold' of the Altay."

Grandma was wearing a big gold bracelet. It was made from "Plum Blossom" gold Grandpa had gathered from the Gold Gulley when he was still a young man. Ten pieces of "Plum Blossom" gold had been melted to cast the gold bracelet that from then on graced Grandma's wrist. She took off the bracelet and set it on the grass, whereupon it bored quickly through the ground and plunged down it, like a groundhog diving for its burrow.

"Gold can walk, can't it?."

"It will return to the gulley where I found it."

But he could not remember in which gulley he had found the gold.

"It will go back home anyhow."

"To Ten Plum Blossoms."

"Right. To Ten Plum Blossoms."

As a young girl Grandma was a pretty silver doe. On her fine white body she wore ten lovely plum blossoms. Those blossoms had cost Grandpa ten years hard graft, ten years of backbreaking work until he had won ten pieces of gold from the gulley. As soon as the good woman wearing gold stepped into the wooden house, the house became a spotted deer, that some call plum blossom deer. Their house was surrounded by trees, but by trees that had followed them. Grandpa had not planted them. The trees had moved down the slope one after another. The scene had amazed Grandma.

"They were riding horses. They came over here to us."

It happened soon after their wedding, when their new wooden house was still giving off the clear scent of timber. Even the blue smoke rising from the chimney looked appealing.

White birch, small red birch, young poplar and oak trees moved down from the high mountain and surrounded the house in their embrace. By the time next spring arrived, their tops were hugging the roof. The white and red birch stretched out their limbs through the windows so that when she got up she often collided with their branches. Their cool, jade-like leaves slipped across her face all day long; she felt caressed by their cooling, silky breath. She felt like a fish swimming in clear water. "Our home is like a river."

"Yes, and now we are flowing out."

"Out of the Altay?"

"To Lake Hanas, old woman."

They walked away from the golden meadow and up the slope. The deer in the forest called every now and then. It was so peaceful there, they dared not raise their voices. The water of Lake Hanas appeared to touch the sky. The trees were enjoying their reflections in the limpid lake water. Grandma whispered: "We are back."

"That's the sky, not Lake Hanas."

They lived by the lake so they could never forget the mirror surface of their lake.

"Look at our reflections in the water. They're as clear as a photograph. Take a close look."

Images of them in their old age floated in the clear waters. It was hard to distinguish what was blue autumn sky and what was lake. Grandpa believed that their elderly images were reflected in both – in lake as well as sky.

"Where's our house?"

"Isn't that it?"

That big oak tree occupied several acres. Grandma looked at that far-away tree in all its luxuriance.

"That? That's our house."

The huge tree towered between the sky and the earth. It recognized the two old people. As a young man, Grandpa rode a proud steed and the image of him galloping through mountains year after year was engraved in each huge age ring in its trunk. Back then, Grandma was a skipping silver doe, happily picking mushrooms among the grasses in the forest groves. Such fine memories the old oak tree really treasured. With a thundering boom, its 22 stout branches seemed to fire off a huge salute. Its leaves took off, like a flock of startled birds, swiftly flying and whirling, obscuring the sky with golden wings.

"Pure gold is the best. I've searched for it all my life, but even though I've dug in the 72 gold gulleys. I've never found any"

As Grandpa was saying this, all the leaves showered down on him until he was knee deep in fallen leaves. There were gold leaves and there were red…pure gold so close to him! Grandpa jumped like a child, throwing himself into the pile of leaves in his excitement.

"Pure gold! Old woman, these are pure gold!"

Grandma picked up the gold and red leaves for a closer examination, putting them down and picking up more for another look.

"Such pure gold must come from heaven."

They hardly dared believe such a day would come... a day when leaves brought down gold from the sky as if they had been mined from the sun. "Only the trees could have such able hands."

Grandpa raised his own hands and said to them, "You should fall too!"

With this his hands did fall to the ground, no less brilliant than the golden leaves. His palms were covered with golden calluses. On the back of his hands, his blood vessels bulged like earthworms. Aided by blood and gold now, his hands could reach the sky.

"Forget it. Better keep your hands where they belong."

Grandpa got up and clapped his hands. Within the forest all was bright and brilliant. White birches spread the autumn coolness like columns of water spouting from the ground. Their leaves had all fallen and were carpeting the forest floor. As they should. The clouds should get back home too. The sky was as clear as if newly cleansed. The clouds had wiped the sky and clean and spotless but where had they all gone now?

"Back to Lake Hanas"

"They've turned into white fish."

The mountain peaks were capped by crystal clear snow. Their hair was completely silver-white too.

"The peak is so white."

"That's not fish but the doe you long for."

"Such a wonderful doe! It's run up the mountain."

"That's where Lake Hanas starts."

That was the famous Hanas Glacier, a crystal clear, translucent world of snow and ice, worshiped down the ages as their holy realm. Through the thin spread of trees they could make out the white light coming from the glacier.

The autumn was nearly at an end but the pine leaves were still deep green, as dark a green as the lake water at its deep center. These trees seemed not to acknowledge it was autumn. Squirrels scurried up the trees and dug deep into the insides of the pinecones, extracting all the pine seeds.

Pine seeds rained down like a storm.

The squirrels moved them home for food.

Women and children dried the seeds and took them to Bu'erjin to trade them for money. One bag of pine seeds could fetch over 100 yuan.

Grandpa said, "You could exchange one grain of gold for a whole sack of money."

The kids had no idea about what a sack of money might be worth; they just knew that pine seeds were not that valuable. And they knew that if they took a long pole and hit the pines hard enough, the pines would obligingly hand out money. Autumn was just like that: suddenly life became relaxed.

Their son turned over the soil, opening up the field's broad body to inhale the fresh air.

Leaves fell, denuding the trees. Wild creatures roamed the forest – wolves, bears, foxes and lynx. The earth sent them all out.

The lake was full of fish. The water set them all loose.

Every household in the village opened up their livestock sheds allowing their oxen, cows and sheep to graze the last pasture of the season.

Their final day arrived at last. The great red fish swam to the side of the lake and Grandma called her old man out to look.

They bent forward as if about to jump in. Scared off, the great red fish swam away.

"Why didn't it leap?"

"It's old now. Not a girl or young man any more."

The great red fish was moving in leisurely fashion, like a boat.

"It won't go down until it gets to the middle of the lake."

The great red fish swam right through the morning before reaching the middle.

"It's still there."

The sun was starting to fall in the west; suddenly the fish vanished.

"It's gone home."

"Let's go home too."

They lay down on the bed, buttons undone and belts untied. Their son and daughter-in-law opened the windows and door, the cabinet and cases, every drawer, bottle and jar even. A careful woman, the daughter-in-law even pulled out the wooden plug blocking the mouse hole behind the door. The souls of the old couple would soon be freed. The son removed the cross bar from the fence and the daughter-in-law pulled aside the tree branches at the windows. Their eyes cleared right away. They could see Lake Hanas. "The great red fish will come out," they said. Indeed they both saw the big red fish. And not just one – a whole group of them.

All the village children, wearing bright new clothes, gathered at the old couple's side, boys around Grandpa and girls around Grandma. Seeing all these red fish around them, the old couple laughed. Once the final laughter of their lives trailed off, their clear eyes became misty; their life shrank back into their throats with its final utterance, "Such a tall oak. We are happy!"

The kids told them. "The tree is budding. Feel the new buds." Under their old fingers the buds were tender and smooth to the touch. So many soft young hands were holding their old hands they began to feel they were their own. Life began to revive in them and they opened their mouths to eat. Their son placed grains of barley and of oats into their mouths.

They wrapped their bodies in white cloth and proud Yili steeds carried them to a level ground in the valley. Their son dug a meter deep pit to receive their bodies and covered it over with soil. Their children were told to jump on and tamp down the loose soil. Then came the horses. Breaking out of their enclosure, they galloped up the hillside, their hooves trampling the new tomb flat and solid.

The following spring, two clumps of oat and barley started growing in that spot; before long it had spread, forming a large stretch in the wild country. Gradually wild oats and barley totally colonized the area, ousting the spear grass and mugwort that had previously grown there. The horses would run there to feast before racing up the mountain, throwing back their heads and neighing. White clouds flew off into the distant turquoise sky. Hanas returned to the heavens.

The Glass Lake

"The husband and wife died together? How incredible!"

Marriages among the Tuvans were determined by Lake Hanas. The great red fish accompanied them throughout their lives.

"Just like the fish in the water."

"Just like the fish in the water."

As they talked about the fish in the water, the woman in Urumqi was looking at her fish bowl, a pair of small goldfish, red as it happened, a gift to her husband from someone or other. Since his promotion to school principal, there had been a constant stream of students and parents lining up to visit him.

She had began to calm down since the arrival of two small goldfish, becoming tired of her games. Even so, for quite a while, she kept up the habit of clandestine affairs. Although it was a hard habit to break, somehow, unbeknownst to her, the habit exhausted itself. Her last lover was a highly sensitive man who quickly intuited her inner secret. Without a moment's indecision, he removed his body from hers, his expression stiff and formal, "Has something upset you?"

"Ask yourself that."

"What have I done?"

The man dressed and quickly made to leave.

"What's wrong?"

"You'll understand soon enough."

The man withdrew from the battlefield before the insult befell him. Just as he had hinted, the frantic flame inside her had burnt itself out. The dry riverbed that lay beneath the seductive surface of her beauty was exposed. She stopped going out after work and returned home every day on the dot. From some point, her husband started a meteoric career rise, with one promotion following hard on the heels of the last. Now he needed a wife beyond reproach to care for their home and she seemed to have acquired that moral excellence immediately. She saw pretty roses growing from a dry stone bank.

The husband was teasing their goldfish; they were chasing each other around the fishbowl, and their swinging fiery tails looked like two dancing flames. She joined in the teasing. One goldfish suddenly leapt out of the bowl, splashing water onto her face. She burst out laughing, despite the water dripping down her face. She had never laughed that heartily before and immediately their home lit up. Husband and son whooped with joy to have their mom return to them, laughing and warm!

Her melancholy son gradually opened up. "The fish is a diver!" he said, and the little goldfish obligingly produced another leap.

Her husband stroked his chin and sighed admiringly, "What a beautiful parabola!"

Now at junior high school, her son no longer needed much of her attention. Since childhood he had got the good habit of self-reliance and had grown up without giving her much trouble. Thus she could devote herself entirely to the needs of her husband and of the two goldfish. But the principal was not used to being waited on, so her leisure time at home centered solely on the fishbowl.

She loved the pair of fish enormously. The two dancing flames were warm but not scorching. She wondered about the size of the great red fish in Lake Hanas and her old schoolmate told her, "As large as a boat."

"Is it like a flame?"

"It's like a sun that illuminates the mountain range and the grassland."

"It's hard for me to picture."

"In Urumqi you could think of it as a flame. That wouldn't be wrong."

"Do you think I am talking about the flame produced by a lighter?

"In Turki, 'flame' means 'rabbit'."

A terrified panic-stricken rabbit suddenly jumped into in her vision and she almost dropped the handset. The rabbit was desperately running and hopping in the wilds. She could hear him on the phone speaker: "Hello, hello. What's up? Are you sick?"

"I'm fine."

"I can hear you now. Are you all right?"

"How could you use such a vile image?"

"But 'rabbits' are good creatures, aren't they?"

"Good, you say?"

"Only a good being would possess the instinct to flee for its life."

"Thank you then!"

That was the best comfort life ever brought her.

She put down the handset and turned to look at the night sky. The window panes were inlaid with thousands of brilliant stars. She cleaned the window every day but never had she found it so clean, so profound. She gazed at the window for an age, as if trying to gauge the width of the glass itself. From the depths of the icy blue lake floated one white spot after another. Snow was falling on the Tianshan Mountains, on the Junggar, and on Urumqi…. The glass was now opaque, like a sheet of white paper. She could not believe that a vast lake could vanish in a blink of an eye. She drew her fingers across the pane. "It's iced over," she said. She believed that the great lake was freezing beneath a great layer of ice.

Araka

The great lake was indeed under a layer of ice or, as the Tuvans put it: "Lake Hanas is a jewel set into a big emerald." It looked unbelievably mystic and beautiful.

The long cold winter closed up the Tuvans' wooden houses. They took out their araka, the lovely name they gave to their home-distilled liquor. The araka was contained in crystal clear bottles, translucent and glinting like small emeralds affixed to the beautiful Hanas. They kept their lake in those bottles and when drinking their liquor, their mood turned mystical and magic. The men were drinking; the women were drinking and the kids were drinking too. Blazing flames danced across those mystical faces.

"Have I turned red?"

"Red!"

They all sat on the boat formed by the great red fish, and the boat swayed them to a distant place.

They were lying on their beds but their hearts were racing with excitement. They saw stars in the daytime sky, saw the moon in the face of a woman, saw the shiny black sun in the pupils of their children's eyes. They asked their women, "Where am I?" Their women would say, "You are in Lake Hanas now." They asked their kid, "Where's your dad?" The kid was honest even though he too had been drinking, "My dad's on the floor." Indeed, his father had rolled down off the bed. He said to himself, "Slow down, horse, slow down. Do you want to get me killed?" He thought he had fallen from his horse.

The Ögedei Khan, that noble ancestor of theirs, in keeping with his hurricane lifestyle, drank without a break and rode a thousand kilometers a day, alternating between each of his pair of horses. After he became khan, the hurricane inside him blew even stronger. He could not stop but went on gulping down his liquor; his heart beating like a drum tattoo, as urgently as ever. His heart jumped faster and faster; "Too fast, too fast! Stop! My steed! Stop!" At the precise moment his horse stopped, the khan's life erupted from his chest. His horse resumed its running. At the sound of horse hooves, Mongols sensed their blood rising. In spring they cultivated crops; in summer they grazed horses; and in autumn they went hunting or cutting forage grass. In winter, they survived by means of araka – one bottle and then another. Transformed into red fish through the power of the araka, they tossed and turned on their beds. In the bitterest depths of the winter cold, the fire ignited by the araka made the whole sky glow red, as if the whole lake was on fire. The ancient horse herds were stampeding in their veins.

Staying drunk was not the answer: Tuvan Big Brother took up his rope and went into the mountains.

In silence, he waited behind a snow bank, waiting for a miracle to happen. His ancestors had come into being through a series of miracles. He himself was part of a myth.

If the plant horses had appeared at Zaysan Lake, they would emerge on the snow ground too. According to their ancient legend, the plant horses had stayed on after carrying the Tuvans to Lake Hanas. Their elders told them how the plant horses had turned into the red pines, white birches and blue poplars, into the forage grass, barley and oats, into the squirrels, foxes and silver deer.... Generation after generation, they continued to grow and spread. All good things around Lake Hanas originated with the plant horses.

A plant horse came up. Snow white as a silver deer, it was as fast as lightning too, and hard to make out were it not for its plum blossom markings. He put down some bait grass in the forest clearing. Due to its equine nature, the plant horse slowed down as soon as it got the smell of grass and its entire body was clearly visible against the snow ground. This was the first time he had ever seen a plant horse. Even without araka inside him, his heart was jumping fiercely, so he undid a few buttons to sooth his drumming heart. The plant horse started eating the bait grass. The rope he had hidden beneath the bait flew up, entangling its hooves. Leaping from his hiding place he pressed its head down onto the snow. The plant horse had two legs as big as the braches of a tree and a temperament more gentle than the Yili horses. He untied the rope and mounted the plant horse.

The plant horse trotted so steadily, he didn't need to use reins, he could ride it just by pulling on its legs. Could it be a *kylin*? According to all the legends a *kylin* has legs. He was holding a beautiful legend right between his hands.

When he got home, his wife and son were still drunk. The plant horse rubbed their faces with its feet, so calming their breathing and steadying their heartbeats. Even the child recognized it as a plant horse.

The whole village was drunk so Tuvan Big Brother led the plant horse to each household to rouse them.

"Who'd have thought a plant horse would rescue us."

"If it could rescue our ancestors, why not us?"

He cut off its horns and set the plant horse free.

So time slowed down. Women and children could enjoy the araka without worrying. When they cut the plant horse horns they realized that time could be cut. Liquor could speed up time but horse horns could slow it down. Time was something that must be idled away.

Once the teacher brought some experts to the area and they stayed at at Big Brother's home. The teacher told him that the government planned to do something major for the Tuvans.

Soon the experts focused their attention on the river section where the lake water flowed out of Lake Hanas. That section was narrow and steep so they decided to build a hydro-power station there. They laid power lines to every household: electric lights were to illuminate the entire village. Some rich families even bought TV sets. The Tuvans were indifferent to money. The teacher said that these things signified modern civilization, so they took money from their pockets to buy civilization. Clever Tuvan Big Brother caught on sooner than everyone else that such things were built up to fend off the dark night. "Modern people enjoy a rich nightlife," the teacher added.

The villagers waited in excited anticipation for nightfall, for the time they could turn on their electric lamps and TV sets. The children saw the brilliant stars first as they appeared in the velvet dark sky, like mysterious flocks of sheep. Once the kids began exclaiming about the stars, the adults could no longer resist the enticement of starlight. Before long, they even turned off their lamps. The wind played majestic music in the pine forests. In the distance came the low, deep growling of bears; wolves howled with all their being; from somewhere close to the lakeshore came the calling of the deer…. Women could even hear fish splashing in the water. Old people heard the leisurely swaying of the oats and forage grasses. That is the earth breathing," they said. The moon did not show her face, but what might have happened if she had?

The teacher could only tell the water resource experts, "The Tuvans love mysterious things. The name Hanas means something mystic and beautiful in their language."

So the hydropower station workers had nothing to do: the Tuvans would not use the power they were generating but just treated them as their guests. They drank liquor, ate talgan flour and horse meat. When they discovered the horse horns hanging on the wall, they claimed that was an herbal medicine: the velvet antler of red deer. They offered money to buy it, so the Tuvans sold it to them with no idea that it had medicinal powers. The power station workers told the villagers, "Beyond the mountains and in the big cities men have weak horses," pointing to their nether parts in a gesture the Tuvans understood completely. It was painful for a man not to have his horse; but if it galloped too fast, that was no good either.

"This problem is the result of your lamps and TV sets."

Feeling a great sympathy for those beyond the mountains, the Tuvans asked the power station workers to stop producing electricity. So the power station ceased operations entirely; from then on its workers concentrated on dealing in herbal medicines.

(*Translated by Ji Hua*)

Ballad of the Bell Flowers

Kim In-Sun

Kim In-Sun. Born in 1970, in Baishan, Jilin Province, from a Korean community, she graduated in 1995 from the Department of Theater Literature, Jilin College of the Arts. Living in Changchun, the capital city of Jilin, Kim is a professional writer of Changchun Federation of Literary and Art Circles.

Kim has published works totaling over a million Chinese characters in literary periodicals such as *Writer*, *Harvest*, *Flower City*, *People's Literature*, and *Zhongshan*. Her works include the novel *Lady Chunxiang*; the novella and collections of short stories *Cold Current in Love* and *Moonlight*; and the collection of prose *Like a Daydream*. She has written the scripts for the films *Green Tea* and *Esquire Runway*.

Ballad of the Bell Flowers

Zhonghe's heart was thumping as he put down the phone, his hands numb. At the second pull he managed to draw a tissue from its box, to wipe the tears in his eyes.

He fished out a new shirt from the wardrobe and got a pin prick on his finger while removing the packaging. The thick drop of blood looked like a tiny red pea. The fold lines of the new shirt were really conspicuous and the starched collar pressed into the back of his neck, so he took it off and changed back into an old, everyday one. He bent down to put on his shoes in such a hurried movement that his head started swimming and his vision went a little dark. "Take it easy, take it easy!" he warned himself, leaning on the wall as he slowly straightened up.

Chunji was not at home. After retirement, she had formed a mahjong group with a few ladies in the neighborhood, taking turns to play in each other's homes for three or four hours every day. When the group came to her home, Chunji always treated her friends to a meal — cold noodles, wild herb soup, or dumplings. She would urge them eat this dish, press them to try that, with the greatest enthusiasm. It was as if even a mere dish of shredded potato, once stir-fried by her own hand, had been transformed into a rare and exotic delicacy.

Zhonghe could no longer envisage what Xiucha looked like. Back in the days they lived in Chaoyangchuan, his home and Xiucha's had been close to each other. There were dozens of pear trees around the houses. During the couple of weeks every year when they were in full flower, the pear trees would be covered in a heavy snow which the sun could not melt, and after dark he would look out of his window towards Xiucha's room. Sometimes she appeared like a fairy in the kingdom of snow, while at others the light in a lantern. Forty years had passed, his waist was many sizes larger, and his hair had turned gray. Fortunately, his back was still straight, thanks to many decades of exercising, walking for an hour every day.

At the entrance to the waiting room of the train station, amid the din, the indescribable smell and whirl of colors, Zhonghe spotted Xiucha even before he got out of the taxi. She was wearing a darkish purple suit, as slim as before, and her skin was still as white as bean curd. Her wrinkles had not made her ugly; rather, they made her look soft and natural, like old wrinkled linen. Zhonghe felt a weight pressing on his chest, like a millstone, the kind his family had owned in the courtyard at Chaoyangchuan. At dawn or at dusk, he and Xiucha used to sit beside it doing their homework. Even after they graduated from senior high school, they kept on reading there. Mostly they read novels borrowed from the county library, the content of which he had long ago forgotten, but he still remembered the song she liked to hum while she read:

Oh, white bell flowers and purple bell flowers.

Standing below the slope,

We see an ocean of flowers flowing down from heaven,

Covering the hills and wild lands.

We gaze transfixed,

Oh, white bell flowers and purple bell flowers.

"Zhonghe — "

Her smile was right in front of him, but it was soon submerged in a lake of tears. Zhonghe wiped his tears, and Xiucha's eyes also misted over.

Xiucha had joined the Sunset Glow Art Troupe of the city where she lived, and she had 29 travel companions in Waiting Room Four. "We're on our way back from a trip to Changbai Mountain and have to change trains here."

They only had just over an hour.

Zhonghe took her to a cafe adjacent to the waiting room, but the only coffee they served there was the instant coffee sachet variety. He summoned the waiter and ordered two cups of expensive *tieguanyin* tea, in addition to dried beef, dried squid slices and preserved plum. "This tea is too hard-tasting. Do eat something, or your stomach will play up."

Xiucha smiled, "So you're still that careful."

"How did you find me?" he asked.

"You can always find someone if you try," said she.

He felt rueful. He had never tried to find her. But nor had he ever forgotten her. For quite a few years, every night he had massaged his mother's arms, shoulders and legs for an hour before she went to bed. Time and again, the old lady would recall old anecdotes of Chaoyangchuan, and Zhonghe could see Xiucha in every incident and behind every person that mother mentioned. "Are you tired?" the old lady used to ask before he left. "You come to massage me day in day out, and have to listen to my chattering. You must be sick to death of it, eh?"

"I'd be happy to keep massaging you till you're a hundred," said Zhonghe. And he meant it from the bottom of his heart; this was how he got time with Xiucha, how could he get tired or fed up with it?

Zhonghe seldom lost his temper, except when Chunji scolded their daughter. Whenever she had been at the receiving end of a tirade from Chunji and turned to her dad in tears, what he saw was little Xiucha's grievances, and would respond to Chunji with a dirty look. He would then take the girl out to eat and buy her a present.

"I used to hate you when I was little," his son once told him. It was as if you loved little sister so much you wanted to eat her, but I was something you wanted to spit out."

"But you have to indulge girls a bit. It's only natural," he replied.

Right from childhood he had got accustomed to being nice to girls. When he went to school with Xiucha, if they came across a muddy section of road he would always give her a piggy-back across the difficult section. Up there, holding on to his back, she reminded him of a bird with folded wings. In springtime, he used to weave cricket cages for her. When splitting the dried cornstalks into thin strips, he cut his fingers many times and would grimace in pain when washing his hands. On one Dragon Boat Festival, he was bitten by a snake while gathering Chinese lantern plants for coloring her fingernails. Fortunately, it was only a grass snake, so not very poisonous. His mother was horrified; she held his leg and sucked out the venom until her lips swelled right up. Xiucha's parents just looked on flapping their hands, completely helpless. They blushed at what his mother did when her child was in danger.

A widow at the age of 21, Zhonghe's mother had raised him on her own and supported him until he graduated from senior high school. The boy's clothing was always spotless. Even though he had only one set of clothes, it was washed and aired dry overnight so he could leave home clean and tidy in the morning.

The one and only requirement the old lady ever had for her son was this: Marry Chunji.

"I like her big face. It means good luck," she said. "And she's got good hips for childbearing."

True to the old lady's words, Chunji gave birth to two healthy children. During the course of their growing up, Chunji grew rounder and plumper, like a mound of rising noodle dough; in her sleep she would snore, snore and snore, so he often dreamed he was standing in the autumn rice fields hearing the wind blowing the rice waves into booming surf; he was a straw scarecrow, dressed in rags with outspread arms, able to see Xiucha leaving along the field embankment, but unable to utter a sound.

In the first few months since his retirement last year, Zhonghe had started obsessing like one possessed about the soymilk Xiucha's family used to make. He thought back to that old dimly-lit bean curd room, where the newly churned curd was still trembling in its sack above the wet ground. The soymilk was contained in a coarse china basin. Every day he and Xiucha would sprinkle in a few grains of saccharin and drink their fill before going to school. When he hiccupped he got the taste of the soy again. Zhonghe had done the rounds of every shop in town that sold soymilk but that fresh, soft flavor was never to be found again.

"How's she doing, my sister-in-law?"

At Chunji and Zhonghe's wedding, Xiucha acting in the capacity of his younger sister had held a wooden dipper toward the bride across the wedding table – every inch of which was crammed. On it were a pair of wooden mandarin ducks (thought to be the most faithful lovers that never part with each other – *ed.*), a cooked rooster and hen couple biting a whole red pepper (signifying a wish to the newly weds to have a happy life – *ed.*), various candies, fruit, fresh flowers and a dozen varieties of cakes and cookies. The bride threw in a big handful of candies too. Later, Zhonghe heard that Xiucha had gone off into the woods and eaten every one of them. She had ironed out the wrappers and made an *origami* mandarin duck to display on her windowsill.

When Xiucha got married, Zhonghe rose before daybreak and beat rice cakes – a communal effort with a few other young guys. The glutinous rice was steamed hot and translucent, glistening like teardrops. Their wooden mallets weighed four pounds apiece, and they had to beat thousands of times to turn the teardrops into an inert solid mass.

Xiucha had married a Mr. Yin, a demobilized army officer, who, despite his youth, had a natural air of authority about him. Zhonghe had been at their engagement banquet too. The gentlemen were drinking away, but the ladies' tables were set near the bean curd room. During the banquet, Xiucha was summoned by her father to propose a toast to the guests. She bent her head low, her eyelashes like curtains, and trembled as she raised her cup. Never had Zhonghe drunk anything so hard to get down his throat; every cup of it had felt like the bite of a saw, inflicting pain with every gulp.

Xiucha told him that her husband, Mr. Yin, had had a stroke five years earlier, but that thanks to the prompt treatment he received, his ability to walk and so on had not been affected. Her son had hired a full-time nurse to help her.

"His name is Wanyu," she said.

"I've been out to meet up with Xiucha."

Zhonghe changed into his indoor slippers and went into his own room – they had slept in separate bedrooms since the children had set up their own homes. On the wall was a photo of his mother, taken on her 60th birthday. She wore a white Korean-style dress, the collar and sleeves trimmed with white satin and an immaculately tied butterfly bow at her bosom. Not one hair on her head was out of place. It was held together with a hairpin, which had taken him a whole week to fashion out of a wooden chopstick – carving it, rubbing it down, painting it, and rubbing it down again.

The old lady's deep eyes looked out at Zhonghe from the picture.

In the two years before she died, she liked to sit in the cane chair on the balcony, gazing at the long river in the distance through narrowed eyes. At sunset, the sunlight spread over the river like a splashed egg yolk, being consumed one mouthful at a time by that giant snake of a river until it swallowed up the sun in its entirety.

Zhonghe used to sit by his old mum watching the sun going down. It reminded him of a time long, long ago with Xiucha sitting beside him on a slope dotted with red physallis. With a thin straw she poked into the plant through a hole the size of a millet seed, so as to extract the fiber and seeds. The resulting empty husk, as thin as a cicada's wing, she placed on her tongue. She blew air into it, causing it to swell up like a little lantern, then squeezed the air out again with her teeth; then she repeated the process. She did one for him too. That lantern-like husk fell on the tip of his tongue, a bitter taste mixed with sour and sweet. He kept on blowing it up until he had no breath left at all.

"You've been out to meet up with Xiucha?"

Chunji was still standing at the door. Zhonghe turned his head toward her and she threw what she happened to be carrying at him with great force, but being light, it just kind of floated and fell to the ground way short of its target.

"I thought you got hit by a car. Had a heart attack, or a stroke! And you've been meeting up with Xiucha? Why didn't you call me? Or leave me a note?"

He looked at Chunji; her face was flushed and tear stained. But her rage did not touch him any more than the cloth bag she'd just thrown at him that had floated to the floor. Just like in the cab ride home, when the driver had kept on chatting, it took him an age to reply:

"I'm back now, aren't I?"

"You're back?" Chunji sneered. "Where's your soul then? Gone off with Xiucha?"

She was right. Xiucha's words had stolen away his soul like a dog with a bone.

Zhonghe did not want to quarrel with Chunji. There had never been any violence in the language between the two of them. Living with his mom for all these years, he felt all the more embarrassed if he scolded anyone. Besides, Chunji was also a good-natured woman. It was over a month since they last had words, when she served up barbecued beef to her friends, and the smell had lingered for hours. He had gone into the kitchen to boil water and really lost his temper when he found the kettle coated with a film of smelly oil.

At supper, Chunji cooked braised whole small potatoes and soybean sprouts in sauce, adding pine kernels, walnuts, sesame seeds and red beans in with the rice, which she steamed in a stone pot. As soon as the lid came off, a fresh sweet smell came his way and his anger evaporated at the first whiff.

Their children called: first one and then the other. Though Chunji was in the sitting room, the phone kept ringing so long he had to pick up on the extension, "Where were you? Mom was worried sick."

Once they'd talked with him they wanted to speak to mom. Zhonghe went into the sitting room to call her to the phone, but she just kept her eyes fixed on the TV, refusing to take the phone from him.

"Mom's still cross," Zhonghe told the children.

"Then you'd better find a way to make amends and get back into her good books," they laughed and hung up.

The local TV station showed three episodes of Korean soap operas every evening. The titles were different but the plots were much of a muchness: two brothers in love with the same girl; two sisters in love with the same guy; or two brothers in love with two sisters. These ridiculous stories easily moved her to tears.

"How old are you, blubbing at stuff like this?" Zhonghe laughed at her.

"What do you know?" she retorted.

Indeed, what did he know? And what about her? After leaving Chaoyangchuan, she had now and then contacted people back there but he had resolutely severed all connections with the place.

Even when the soap operas were over, Chunji did not go to bed; the light in the sitting room remained on, shining out under the door.

When Zhonghe went to the bathroom, he saw her take out of the fridge the fresh ladybell roots someone had given her the other day. They had knotty thick skin much like that of a crocodile, which had to be cut away bit by bit with a knife. As he was coming out of the bathroom she suddenly blurted out the question, "Has Xiucha gotten old too?".

"With eyes like hers, with age, her lids will droop and cover half the eyes."

Chunji was quite kindhearted, and Zhonghe knew he could cool her down by choosing words that would please his wife. Yet, this was Xiucha they were talking about! "She's quite good looking even now."

"She's too good looking, that's the problem," said Chunji. "That's why your mom was against her as a daughter-in-law. She said you could tell from what someone was like at the age of three what they would be like when they got old. And that Xiucha's looks and figure wouldn't bring her good fortune."

"And she also said you were a kind and honest girl."

"And what's that tone supposed to mean?" Chunji looked up at him. He had sharpened her knife a couple of days before, so that its cutting edge felt like a shard of ice. "Did I spoke ill of Xiucha?"

"I didn't say you spoke ill of her."

"Anyway, things didn't go that well for Xiucha," said Chunji. "Her husband was always beating her up, until she had a miscarriage. He gave her a broken rib once and she had to convalesce at her parents' place for two months until it healed."

Zhonghe felt as if had just drunk a big bowl of steaming hot chili soup, but he was shivering as if from cold. He tried to stare the lie out of her, so that she would retract her words, but she stared right back at him

"Don't you believe me? Everyone back in Chaoyangchuan knows it."

Everybody knew; but not him. But what would he have done if he had known? Would he have had the guts to take Xiucha away from that guy? When she got beaten up had she expected his arrival? Since even Chunji knew about what had happened to Xiucha, Xiucha must surely have assumed he knew about her situation.

"They rowed for years and years until they went to court and got a divorce. After the divorce Yin started drinking every day and on top of losing his leadership position he went on to lose the job he got demoted to. Then he had a stroke. But for some unknown reason, Xiucha went back to nurse the man rather than enjoying her quiet life!"

He doubted whether Chunji and Xiucha had been speaking about the same man. Today, Xiucha had talked about Old Mr. Yin as a cute, obedient boy, She had said their son would use his free time to take them to the zoo, the aquarium, the fun fair, and indulge them like children.

"Xiucha's son…," his mouth was so dry each word came out like a spark. "His name's Wanyu, isn't it?"

Chunji looked up, and they stared at each other, each one seeing something more.

"You could be right," Chunji looked down and started peeling again.

Zhonghe went back to his room and made straight for the balcony, where it was chilly. Many new apartment buildings had been developed on the bank of the big river. When they had first moved here, there had been stone embankments, with wild grass growing between the stones, but now those had been replaced by concrete dams and lines of lilac trees. As spring turned to summer, the lilacs came into bloom, creating banks of pink and white clouds that reminded him of the bell flowers covering every hill and valley at Chaoyangchuan. But nothing was visible now. In the pitch dark, surrounded by emptiness, the wind was feeling at his body, first a light touch, now a heavy one.

"Why did Xiucha go looking for you?" Chunji asked, having followed him over.

He was happy they were standing in darkness; it made it easier for him to speak. "Wanyu is getting married next month. Xiucha has invited us to the wedding."

"She didn't come to our children's weddings," said Chunji. "But she expects a return gift from us at her son's wedding?"

Chunji had had her daughter find her a famous beauty saloon for a perm. It cost several hundred *yuan* but even so she had it cut again within days, leaving only a few curls.

"Wasn't that a waste of money?" he asked.

Chunji said it was the normal course of events. She stood back to give him a better view. "This hairstyle makes me look slimmer, doesn't it?"

He could see nothing, but replied with conviction, "Much slimmer."

Chunji also had her daughter buy a pile of facemasks, to be applied every evening while she watched the Korean soap operas. Her whole face was covered with a whitish mask, with holes for the eyes, nose and mouth. The first time he saw it he got a shock.

"Are you crazy or something?"

Chunji gave him a dirty look from under her mask.

She had also bought clothes, shoes, and several sets of underwear even. "Dad, just how beautiful was your first love? Look at the state mum's got herself into." In came their daughter; she threw down several paper bags, lunged for the sofa and sprawled out, spread-eagled, "The old lady plays the young shopaholic!"

"I've spent all my performance bonus for this month – "

"Is it really such a pain to take your mother shopping?" Zhonghe said. "Lip service alone is no way to repay our efforts in raising you."

That said, he thought Chunji was taking things too far. She was skipping proper meals, just eating one apple a day, chewed

very slowly. And since she wasn't eating her meals, she cooked per-
functorily for him. In one week all she fed him was three meals of
fried rice with kimchi and shredded pork. She even suggested that
Zhonghe drink salted water with an apple just like her.

"Your stomach and intestines also need a good cleansing,"
she told him.

The day before they left, she dyed her hair. The name of the
color on the box was "Sweet Caramel." He complained that the
smell of molten wax on her hair had destroyed his appetite.

"More likely because you're nervous about seeing Wanyu,
eh?" she said.

These days of frenetic activity seemed to have changed Chunji
into another person — not only did she look different, the way she
spoke and acted was different too.

"It's your hair I 'm talking about! What's it got to do with Wanyu?"

"You don't like me?" she pulled a long face. "I won't go then."

She banged the door shut behind her.

"I didn't say anything," Zhonghe pushed it open. "Why lose
your temper?"

"It makes me mad to think about it," she started getting difficult. "You two had a good thing going back then, and now 40 years
later you put it out on public display. Am I supposed to come and
lead the clapping?"

He was just opening his mouth to reply when she roared back,
"I've never been so humiliated!"

There was nothing for it but call in their son and daughter,
who talked with her behind closed doors for two hours. The son
came out first, telling him in a low voice, "Agreed to go."

"I'll drive you both there tomorrow," he added.

They sat on the sofa for a while and the son suddenly burst out laughing. Zhonghe looked at him, "What's so funny?"

"Nothing."

Another half hour passed; the daughter came out, her eyes all red, "I'm coming tomorrow as well."

She went home with her brother. As Zhonghe was seeing them off at the door, she turned to look at him and whispered in his ear, "I can't wait to see this elder brother of ours."

She referred to him so naturally it hit Zhonghe like a thunderbolt, and his eyes moistened.

They set off early the next day, Zhonghe and his son sitting in the front and the women in the back. First his daughter praised mom from top to toe, like she was a movie star. Then she added that it was just like a spring outing, the four of them not having been out together on their own for ages.

"A fall outing, you mean," the son corrected her.

"Who cares whether it's spring, summer, fall or winter?" She took care of everything on the way there, what to eat and what to drink. She said that the morning mist rolling in the wild looked like cotton fiber, and suddenly pointed at a maple tree bathed in the sunlight, yelling , "Look at that tree, it's like it's on fire!"

"Don't be such an excitable child. You're a mother," Chunji admonished her. These were the first words Zhonghe had heard from her since the children had left the night before.

They went straight to the restaurant. The men got out first, while the daughter helped Chunji fix her make-up.

"Who's the older of us, him or me?" asked his son.

"You are, by a few months."

They took the elevator up, where even the daughter fell quiet. As soon as the doors opened, Zhonghe spotted Xiucha being led into the hall on the arm of a lady. Glimpsing them out of the corner of her eye, she stopped still on the instant. Chunji's face turned pale at the sight of Xiucha.

Xiucha came scurrying towards them. Her traditional Korean dress with its full skirt and trailing ribbons made her look as if she was treading on clouds. While still far away she stretched out her hands toward Chunji. The two women, with a combined age of over 120, hugged and cried like little girls.

The lady who had just been helping Xiucha came over, puzzled, "What's all the crying about? It's time to start. Come along in."

Xiucha ignored her, wiping Chunji's tears with a tissue. Glancing past Zhonghe, her eyes fell on his son and daughter. "You are so grown up."

Together they bowed to her in polite greeting.

Xiucha pulled them up, tears gushing again.

The lady pulled at Xiucha, "They're all waiting."

"We'll all go in together," Xiucha held onto Chunji and ushered them into the hall. At the entrance, they saw the bride and groom hand in hand.

Zhonghe felt dry-mouthed and a little shaky. Wanyu was quite tall, dressed in a dark suit and white shirt, with a pink rose pinned to his chest. He had single-fold eyelids, a high-bridged nose and thick lips – the very image of Zhonghe. When he caught sight of Zhonghe, his expression froze. Totally absorbed in giving Wanyu the once over, Chunji trod on Xiucha's skirt, nearly causing her to trip and fall.

"Hurry up," the lady kept on urging, pushing the whole group inside. Xiucha showed them to the reserved VIP seats, before sitting in her own seat at the table in the middle of the hall reserved for the parents of the bridal couple. Zhonghe saw Old

Mr. Yin, sitting in a wheelchair alongside Xiucha's seat. His hair was cut short and he was clean-shaven. He wore a dark suit, white shirt, and a handsome tie. One half of his body was completely immobile, while the other half trembled constantly. His eyes stared in a fixed direction, and his lips quivered. Zhonghe doubted whether he could get out a whole sentence.

The master of ceremonies announced that the auspicious moment for the wedding had arrived and the guests stood up to greet the new couple. The music started, a medley of Korean folk ballads rather than the usual Wedding March. The guests clapped along with the M.C. as they watched the new couple slowly progressing along the rosepetal-strewn carpet and up onto the stage.

The M.C. introduced the bride; his commentary was accompanied by photographs, projected onto a big screen behind him, showing the bride at every stage of her life, from infancy to as she appeared before them today. She was a teacher of dance at the art college, she was 28, she was the apple of her parents' eye, she was clever and sensible too, she'd had people chasing after her since the age of five, she had broken the hearts of at least a thousand gentlemen for the sake of Wanyu.... His words triggered wave upon wave of clapping, with frequent cheering from those tables where the young people were grouped. Then the groom was introduced: Wanyu was exceptionally intelligent as a child – Zhonghe stared at the images on the screen. The little boy was thin and frail-looking, staring at the lens in panic. After five or six, he no longer seemed as afraid of having his picture taken; in one shot he looked exactly like Zhonghe as a young boy. At seven or eight, he looked melancholy, positively taciturn. By his teens, sorrow and restraint had become permanent fixtures of his expression. At around 20, he became a man, with something cold and composed about his eyes. He was admitted to Beijing Textile University thanks his excellent exam scores, 10 years ago, he opened his own company, which now employed 600-700 full-time workers, their products did not just sell in China: they had gradually established a market presence in Korea, Japan and even Southeast Asia. "Why have you left it so late to get married?" The M.C. stuck the mike toward Wanyu.

"Originally I wasn't reckoning on getting married," Wanyu said, smiling to his bride. "But one moment of carelessness and I was caught."

The banquet continued for a very long time.

Wanyu brought over his bride to raise a toast to Zhonghe and Chunji. The bride looked prettier close up, and she toasted them in very graceful fashion, addressing them in the sweetest of tones as "uncle" and "auntie." After mingling with the other guests for a while, Xiucha came over, pushing Old Yin's wheelchair. Zhonghe shook Yin by the hand, a hand more forceful than he had imagined. Then the nurse came to take the old man home ahead of the rest.

The young people switched on the stereo and began singing and dancing whilst continuing to eat and drink.

While talking about Zhonghe's late mother, Xiucha and Chunji came to tears. Zhonghe heard for the first time that Xiucha almost died while giving birth to Wanyu. It was his mother who had purchased bear gall and sent someone to deliver it.

"You take after your granny," Xiucha sighed with emotion, taking the hand of Zhonghe's daughter.

Zhonghe went to the bathroom, where Wanyu was washing his hands. Their eyes met in the mirror, and Zhonghe nodded to him. Inside the cubicle, he trembled violently as he unbuckled. It took him twice as long as usual. He groped around inside his belt, and found the envelope containing 20,000 yuan which he had with-drawn from the bank – all of his private savings. In addition, Chunji carried with her 3,000 yuan gift money. He knew Wanyu was not short of money, but he didn't know how else to express his emo-tions, other than with cash.

As he came out, Wanyu was drying his hands on a paper towel, and pulled out two pieces for Zhonghe. They came out of the bath-room together, and Wanyu fished out a pack of cigarettes. He took one out and proffered it respectfully to Zhonghe in both hands, then lit it for him with his lighter.

"Sorry." Zhonghe took a pull on the cigarette. But as he started to talk he began coughing, so he doubted whether Wanyu had heard a thing he said.

Zhonghe touched the money inside his pants, was just about to take it out when someone, his face flushed with drink, grabbed hold of Wanyu and pulled him back into the hall. Wanyu only had time to turn his head toward Zhonghe and nod.

Back inside, Zhonghe saw a woman singing into a mike. She was standing on a round platform, around which dancers were swirling on three levels, first to the song *My Dear Lover*, then to *Bell Flowers:*

Oh, white bell flowers and purple bell flowers.
Standing below the slope,
We see a ocean of flowers flowing down from heaven.
Covering the hills and wild lands,
We gaze transfixed…

Zhonghe returned to his table. Xiucha and Chunji, now red with wine, were singing along: "Oh, white bell flowers and purple bell flowers." After that, they hugged, and whispered into each other's ears. Chunji laughingly pointed to the cups and told her daughter, "Fill them right up."

The daughter poured out wine for them, and grimaced to Zhonghe, "They've agreed on 50 plans: to pay homage at Granny's tomb, to make bean curd back in the bean curd room in Chaoyangchuan, to pick pears, to go and view pear blossoms next spring…."

(Translated by Wang Zhiguang)

Killer

Tsering Norbu

Tsering Norbu was born in 1965 to a Tibetan family in Lhasa. He was enrolled in the Tibetan Language Department of Tibet University in 1981. Tsering Norbu graduated with a bachelor's degree in Tibetan language in 1986 and was assigned to a teaching post at a county middle school in Chamdo. In 1995, he started work at *Tibet Daily*, his career there including various editing, translating and reporting positions. In 2005, he transferred to the editorial department of *Tibet Literature*. Tsering Norbu mainly writes short stories, which have been published in literary journals such as *Tibet Literature* and *Ethnic Literature*. His representative short stories are *The Boatman of Luozi*, *The Pilgrim*, *Incineration*, *The Rainy Season*, *Someone Is Waiting For Her*, *The Net* and *Killer*. He also writes novellas, including *Where Does My Love Belong?*, *The Legend Continues* and *The Boundary*. In October 2004, Tsering Norbu attended the Fourth Advanced Seminar for Young Ethnic Minority Writers jointly held by the Chinese Writers' Association and the Lu Xun College of Liberal Arts. In November 2007, he was invited to the All-China Young Writers' Conference on Literary Creation. In 2006, his short story *Killer* was included in *Selected Stories*, in *Chinese Short Story Collection 2006* and the Chinese Fiction of the Year List. *The Boundary* won the Fifth New Century Literary Prize of Tibet.

Killer

The truck, a *Dongfeng*, was speeding west across the boundless sandy land, a tail of yellow dust billowing behind it. I had a full load, tightly secured and covered under a grass-green tarp, I was alone in the driver's cab. Waves of fatigue kept threatening to overwhelm me and I yawned again and again.

I gripped the steering wheel with my left hand and pulled out a cigarette from the pack with my right. With fingers too podgy to see the knuckles, I clumsily clicked the lighter and lit up, leisurely exhaling a wisp of whitish smoke that spread indolently around the cab. Ahead in the dusk stretched boundless expanses of vastness, and I could feel exhaustion spreading through every fiber of my body. All I could do to fight it was to take long, hard drags of the cigarette. It was soon smoked to the butt.

Just as I was reaching into the pack for another, I suddenly spotted a small creeping black shape on the horizon. Wondering whether it was a human or an animal, I accelerated toward the small shadow. As the distance between us shrank, it started getting more distinct and I could make out that it was a lone traveler carrying a quilt on his back. A lone man traveling on foot like this must be a Buddhist pilgrim, I figured. I put on a bit more speed and drove on toward him.

Hearing the roar of the truck, the man stopped walking, stood still and turned to look east, the direction my truck was coming from. I peered through the windscreen to see what he was like. He stood in the howling wilderness, looking extremely tiny, miserable and helpless.

I felt an impulse suddenly to do something benevolent and give him a ride. When he saw my truck approaching, he stretched out his arms to wave at me. I could see the black tassels tied to his hair then. The guy was skinny but had a long knife tucked into his waist. I braked to stop the truck alongside him and gestured him to get in. He opened the cab door on his side, put his dirty quilt and a blackened aluminum pot on the passenger seat and deftly squeezed himself in next to his stuff.

"Move your things off the seat!" I ordered.

He moved the quilt off the seat, stuffed it under his feet, and then stamped on it hard. He was a Khamba man with a dark complexion and high cheekbones. Sweat had drawn white streaks on his dark face and his worn out leather shoes had holes at the toes. I started the truck and it galloped on again, speeding over the vast sandy land with its yellow tail of dust. The Khamba man looked out of the cab window woodenly, absorbed in the never-ending sandy wilderness all around. Occasionally, at the appearance of thorn bushes—tenacious to the last—a thin, barely perceptible smile crept onto his hardened face.

"Hey, Khamba guy. You making a pilgrimage?"

His numb eyes turned toward me. But he just swallowed and turned away his face, back toward the wilderness ahead.

"Are you on a pilgrimage or doing business?" I was a bit offended so I raised my voice a little.

"Neither. I just want to go to Saga County."

Showing him a smile to express my satisfaction at his response, I pressed on: "You've got the right truck then. I'm going all the way to Ali, so you can ride with me for a while." The Khamba man shot me a grateful smile. A harmonious mood warmed up the driver's cab. I lit up another cigarette and smoked leisurely, my drowsiness already over and gone. "What takes you to Saga?" I asked, on the road ahead.

"To kill someone."

I was gobsmacked. I tried to calm down and squeeze out a casual smile. "You're kidding me, right? You don't look like a killer. I don't believe you for a second."

The Khamba man tucked the few tassels fallen over his forehead into his hair, his gaze fixed ahead, and said, "If you don't believe me there's not much I can do about it." He swallowed again and I noticed how dry and cracked his lips were. He added, "That guy killed my dad 16 years ago. He fled after the killing. I've been searching for him for the past 13 years, hunted the length and breadth of Tibet practically but got nowhere."

I cast a glance at the Khamba man and a wave of sadness overtook me. In my imagination, an avenger should be tall and stalwart, dressed in black from head to foot, wearing shades and with a pistol at his waist. But the guy sitting next to me came nowhere even close to this description of a killer—well, apart from his silence, icy cold expression, the determined look in his eyes, and the long knife with a silver handle. A big disappointment! I turned my face again to gaze at the empty landscape ahead. The only sound in the cab was the sleepy humming of the engine.

"When will we get to Saga?" The Khamba man asked, keeping

his stare straight ahead.

I chucked the cigarette butt out of the window and answered, all nonchalant, "Should be before dark. You in a hurry to kill that guy, then?"

The Khamba man turned his eyes on me with a half contemptuous, half teasing expression on his face. I felt uneasy and my palms began sweating. Through clenched teeth he replied, "I've waited more than 10 years already. You think I'm going to quibble over half a day or a day?"

I didn't respond, just kept looking ahead.

Before long, a vague outline of a mountain range emerged on the western horizon. I stole a glance at the Khamba man sitting next to me. He kept his eyes ahead but his extraordinary tranquility, silence and tough look all worried me a little. To lighten the oppressive mood, I said, "We'll be there soon. Once we get to the mountain opening you see a highway, follow the highway and you get to Saga."

"Eh." The droning of the truck drowned out his short reply.

The truck dashed toward the mountains looming in the west, and we sped on, following the road as it snaked its way through the foothills.

"We're here." I said, in great relief. By now it was almost dark and a wild wind was howling. I stopped the truck at a fork in the road, the view ahead was indistinct already. The Khamba man fumbled open the passenger door, and a dark, cold blast howled in, sending shivers through the two of us. He pulled out his quilt and aluminum pot and loaded them onto his back. Taking the direction I'd pointed out to him he was soon out of sight, swallowed up in the endless black curtain of night.

Gravels, riding on the coat-tails of the wind, kicked and

pounded against the glass without a let-up. "Ka-cha, ka-cha," the poor windscreen was wailing pathetically; "Ke-da, ke-da," the tarpaulin cover groaned and danced. The sandstorm was truly frightening. I sounded the horn a few times into the pitch night but the sound was swept away by the howling wind again. I wondered why I done that, to embolden the Khamba man or as a farewell gesture? I could not explain why.

I drove on in the sticky darkness toward Ali. The headlight beams looked extremely miserable and lonely in the endless wilderness.

I was delayed for four days at Shiquanhe Town and returned without a load. That Khamba man and his revenge story occupied my mind all the way. I couldn't help worrying about what happened next and many a result flashed through my head. When the truck approached the fork leading to Saga, I made an unconscious decision that even alarmed myself: I turned the steering wheel and drove the truck onto the road toward Saga.

The high noon sun was burning hot, bleaching the highway into a deadly paleness. I ran the truck through a river. Seeing the water crashing white against the rocks and hearing the roaring torrent had an instantly cooling effect. The mountains flanking the highway were basically bare of vegetation apart from the occasional thorn shrub, and behind them perhaps a scrawny goat or two. A truly bleak area.

Low dwelling houses appeared along the highway. The dirt-gray houses had not a sign of life about them and exuded the stale air of a remote age. One long road ran right through the middle of the town. I parked the truck at the county boarding house and bought lunch at a teashop. It was an extremely basic kind of place, a bumpy earth floor, and a few wooden tables with ramshackle wooden stools set around. My meal was simple: one bottle of sweet tea and 15 steamed stuffed buns and my belly was full. Well fed, my mind returned to the killer. I couldn't wait to get on with it.

"Hey, miss!"

"What is it you want now?" She responded, her impression impatient, thinking I wanted to boss her around again.

"I want to inquire about a person."

"Who?" A smile appeared on her face.

"About a Khamba man who came here a few days ago."

"You mean that skinny guy? I took him for a beggar at first."

"Did he make any trouble?"

"No. He was looking for Madra."

"Did he find him?"

"Yes."

My heart jumped in my throat. I pictured the scene—Khmaba man pulling out his long knife and stabbing it into Madra's heart, blood soaking Madra's white shirt like the flowering of a red rose.

"Oh, I'll tell you all about it." The teashop girl obviously was keen to natter. Of course, there were just the two of us in the teashop.

"The sun was already high that day," the girl continued. "People suddenly noticed a strange Khamba man wandering along the street. He was carrying a quilt on his back, and was walking aimlessly even though the sun was burning hot. Our town isn't a big one. You can see through it from one end to the other. The buildings are spaced out along the main street and few pedestrians were around at the time. Probably he was tired of walking, I could tell that just from one look at his bloodshot eyes. He swaggered in and sat down by the window there. His eyes fell on me and I noticed his cracked lips and ragged clothes. But that knife he had on him was really beautiful!

"Holding a thermos bottle, I sized him up from across two tables. 'Do you know someone by the name of Madra around here?' he asked me. Then, I came to know that he was in town to look for that person. It corrected my earlier assumption that he came to beg. I turned round the tables and stools—my defense line, pulled off the lid of the thermos and poured some milk tea into a white glass for him. I said, 'There is a Madra living at the western end of the town. He runs a small convenience store.' 'Is he from Konjosaren? About 50 years old?' he asked eagerly. 'Are you here to look for a relative?' I chuckled and inquired. 'Is he from Konjosaren?' he pressed on.

"This was beginning to get boring, so I just told him, 'I've no idea if he is from Konjosaren or not, but he's in his 50s and he's run the store for nearly two years. He goes to the temple a lot to spin the prayer wheels. He's very devoted to the Bodhisattva. That's why everyone here knows him.'

"Suddenly the Khamba man was breathing hard and his face was burning red. 'Are you excited because you've located your relative?' I asked, standing at one side of him. Suddenly his eyes filled with tears and he started to sob. That cup of tea was turning cold. 'Finally, I've found him!' he said. I was surprised to see him get so excited so I sat down opposite him with the width of the table between us. The Khamba man gradually calmed down. He wiped his tears and turned to the window to look out onto the street. There were very few people about at this time and you could tell the idle, tranquil air of our town from the relaxed way they walked. The Khamba man turned round and saw me still watching him from across the table. He lowered his head and picked up the cup to drink. 'You are different from most Khambas,' I told him, and his stiff face gave a twitch or two. After a while, seeing him drip the last drops of tea in the glass onto his tongue, I poured him another glass. He asked, 'Do you sell Tibetan noodles?' 'Yes.' 'Bring me a bowl.' I lifted the curtain and walked into the back kitchen. 'Here come the Tibetan noodles.' The Khamba man stared into the large porcelain bowl containing the noodles. The thick noodles swam in a greasy bone broth with a spoonful of crushed red peppers sprinkled over the top. He swallowed hard and licked the edge of the bowl with his sickly yellow tongue. His saliva stuck to the rim of the bowl and the sight of it made me feel ill so I left him there.

"It took him no time to gulp down the whole bowl. 'Can I leave my quilt in the corner there for a while?' he asked me. I nodded, 'You can come and collect it once you've found your relative.' Then he left. Look, there're his quilt and pot. He's not been back since then. If he was still here in the town I'd have met him so I guess he's already gone."

Right, that was definitely his quilt and aluminum pot but where had he got to?

"Is that Madra still around?"

"Yes, he runs a little shop a little further up the street."

Wondering if it might actually be Madra who'd settled the matter of murder, I began feeling a faint uneasiness. That's me all over, as soon as I get nervous I get thirsty and every nerve in me stretches to breaking point. My wife often advised me with a Tibetan proverb: Don't squeeze yourself into a quarreling crowd but try to push into a team selling oil. She was so right.

"Get me a bottle of beer."

"Which brand?" the girl asked.

"*Lhasa.*"

The beer gurgled straight down my throat into my belly and my taut nerves relaxed at once. I had to go find that killer.

"Fill up my barrel with barley liquor," a man with a slight limp sat down at my table.

"Who's looking after your sheep?" the girl asked him.

"None of your business. Just get me the liquor, and get a move on." So I knew he was a herdsman.

He smiled at me so I handed him a cigarette. We started chatting. He had seen that Khamba man as well.

The shepherd told me, "I didn't know he was Khamba at the time. I was driving my cattle and sheep over when I felt the need to piss. You know what it feels like, pressing so hard you think your bladder's going to burst. OK, you know what I mean now. I stopped my herd and climbed behind that house that stands on its own at the foot of the mountain and then relieved myself. It felt so great after I pissed. Then I began to check around me and I saw this guy lying behind a rock sound asleep. You don't believe me? I tell you, this guy's snoring was really something. I thought he was a pilgrim so I didn't disturb him. But maybe when I walked down the slope and shouted to that hybrid ox of mine, I might have woken him up.

"By the time I reached the highway, he had gotten up and was standing on a rock. The sun had just poked its head from behind the top of the mountain and was pouring its golden rays onto the town and warming it up. I saw that Khamba man lazily stretching his arms and breathing out deeply. He kept on looking at me. There were dozens of oxen on the highway, ambling along at their own pace. I circled some rounds of wool on my left arm and twisted the wool coil with my right hand by then. My spirit was at ease and my gait leisurely. Occasionally, some high-spirited yaks tried to wander off the highway on their own. I had to holler hard, pick up some stones off the ground somewhere and threw them at the yaks that had wandered off the road onto the slopes. That startled them into a short trot, then ambled back to the herd, wagging their tails. All this time, the Khamba man kept watching me. Maybe he felt smug inside. Afterwards, I saw him pick up his pot and follow the boulder-strewn slope down toward the river. The river was flowing fast and its loud splashing drowned all other sounds. The Khamba man took off his shirt and bared his chest, then he quickly washed his face and neck and dried himself with the shirt. Scanning left and right, he finally chose a lime rock with a level surface. He filled the pot with river water and placed it next to the rock. Then he began sharpening his long knife on it, pouring water onto the rock and whetting his knife against the wet stone. The rushing river drowned out the sound of the harsh grinding. Afterwards, the Khamba man put the knife back in its sheath, refilled the water pot and climbed up to the highway.

"What happened next?" I asked.

"Next? There is no next. That was the last I saw of him."

The shepherd finished his story. He'd emptied three bottles of beer.

The sun continued its rule over the afternoon street. It was empty and deserted and I was a little drunk. The stony ground was tricky underfoot and it was all I could do to keep my balance. I aimed for Madra's convenience store at the western end of the town. His shop was by the highway, rented from a local. Next to it was a snack bar run by a guy from Sichuan.

The closer I got to the store, the more nervous I got. My face was burning like it was on fire and I was panting so hard I felt I might stop breathing soon. I pictured myself as the killer or that I was following the route he'd taken. Reaching the window of the convenience store all I could see was a woman in her mid-30s sitting to the right of the goods shelves. Her clothes looked ordinary and her face looked a bit withered and sallow. She smiled as soon as she saw me and asked, "What do you want to buy?" I stared at her like an idiot for a while until I calmed down, "Is this Madra's store?" I could hear a slight quaver in my voice.

"Do you know my husband?" The woman stood up.

"No, I don't."

"Oh." Madra's wife heaved a long sigh and said, "How come someone else came looking for him a few days back? He's been on edge ever since."

"Is he home?"

"He's gone to the temple. Should be back in an hour. Why don't you come in and have a cup of tea?"

I went around and entered the shop from its backdoor. Inside, a low Tibetan table stood between two wooden beds. There was a great heap of cardboard cartons piled up in a corner of the dimly-lit room; already no great size, it was divided into two by a large cabinet. On one side was the shop; this side was their living accommodation.

"You don't sound like a Khamba," I asked.

"I'm not. I was born here."

"How about the Khamba guy who came looking for your husband?"

"He sat here for a bit and left in tears."

"How come?"

Instead of answering my question, Madra's wife asked, "Are you a friend of that Khamba guy?"

"No, I am not. My name is Tsering Norbu. We came to Saga in the same truck."

Madra's wife busied herself pouring tea for me. My tense nerves began to loosen up.

"I'm back!" The clear voice of a child sounded from outside. The voice gave me goose bumps and quickened my breathing. Soon a little boy of about four years old was standing in front of me, staring at me with wide curious eyes. Then he turned around and plunged into his mother's arms. Madra's wife comforted, "He's here to see your dad. Where is your dad?"

"Behind me," came his timidly answer.

The door was pushed open again and a man walked in. His back was bowed and his hair was pepper-and-salt gray. His forehead was a mass of wrinkles, some deep, some shallow. He dodged back and stared at me in shock. His eyes were as large as silver dollars. "You, you, you are, you are…," he stuttered.

"Tsering Norbu."

His face turned ashen and his lips trembled.

"Are you OK?" his wife was concerned.

"I'm fine. Just walked too fast just now. What do you want from me?"

"I came to ask if you saw a Khamba man a few days ago."

"I did. He came here saying he was looking for me. But once he saw me, he shook his head and mumbled that it wasn't me. I gave him some tea and he ran off crying. I haven't seen him since."

"I have to go and look for him then. I'll say good-bye."

"What's all this about?"

I chose to ignore him, thinking I had not only wasted time but gas too. I got out of there fast.

As I drove the truck away from Saga I was thinking I might run into that Khamba killer again somewhere along the road.

I had a tire blow-out in the deserted wilderness, so I slept in the driver's cab.

I saw myself back in Madra's shop. His wife had taken the child out earlier. Madra and I were staring at each other and the air in the room seemed to freeze all of a sudden. I had the knife in my right hand gripping the handle hard with every ounce of my strength. In that instant, the one and only aim I had in mind was to avenge the Khamba guy and his father by killing Madra. The knife handle felt handy with its curling pattern. Madra admitted, "I am praying to the Bodhisattva every day to try to expiate my guilt. I have nothing to fear now but just failed to expect your arrival so soon. One who has killed must pay with his life. It is fair. Come, just do it!" I pulled out my knife and, by just one cold flash across the air, my knife was in his chest already. I pushed him to the corner with the cold blade. Red blood gushed out from his wound, dripping along my knife and wetting my hand. My hand felt warm and sticky. With a serene expression in his eyes, Madra grinned at me with difficulty and breathed his last. I retracted my long knife and saw him slide down along the wall like a bundle of hay.

I woke up. The sun was bright outside and it blinded my eyes. I told myself I must get out the driver's cab to change the tire.

(Translated by Ji Hua)

A Tale from the
Huolin River

Bai Xuelin

Bai Xuelin was born in 1954 to a Mongolian family in Beipiao City, Liaoning, and is a member of the Chinese Writers' Association. He has been Associate Editor-in-Chief at *Grassland*, a magazine under the Inner Mongolia Writers' Association, Director of Inner Mongolia Writers' Association of Theoretical Studies and Editor-in-Chief of the newspaper *Ethnic Minority Literature and Art*. Bai began writing in the late 1970s, and in 1981 published the series of poems *My Village Home* in *Spring Breeze*, a literary quarterly of Liaoning Province. In September 1984, his short story *Early Summer* was published in *People's Literature*, followed in December by *The Blue Valley*, published in *Grassland*. *The Blue Valley* won the 1984 All-China Short Story Prize and the All-China Ethnic Minority Literature Special Award in 1985. His novellas *To Grow Up* and *Ballads of Huolinhe* were included in the September 1989 and October 2007 issues of *Selected Stories*, respectively. Bai's other publications include: five poetry anthologies—*Searching For the Flying Birds of My Old Home*, *In Autumn, the Brain Sprouts*, *The Lake Water Tempted by the Moon*, *The Fox in the House* and *The Swinging Singer and A Tree in His Heart*; fiction—*The Emotive Poplar* and other works; and TV screenplays—*The Beauty Cove*, a 45-episode TV drama about to go into production. Bai is a three-time winner of the Suolongga (Rainbow) Literary Prize sponsored by the Inner Mongolia government, and has received an award from the Jerim League Administrative Office.

A Tale from the Huolin River

Midway down the Huolin River, along the eastern shore, is the small village of Hailisitai, populated by about thirty families. Their homes are sparsely scattered over four *li* of sand, nestled at the foot of Erdun Mountain.

Norima's home is the farthest south.

Early one winter morning, Norima came out from her low mud house, untied the brown bull from the front door and hitched it to her jigger cart. She stroked the bull on its hindquarters, and it began its slow clip-clop out of the village.

The breeze was gentle, the sun had yet not risen, and the grassland was covered by a thin layer of frost. Norima sat in the cart, allowing the bull to meander. She was in a good mood. The cart wobbled, so she was going to ask the carpenter, Dawa, to fix it. The axles were worn down, and the willow beams connecting the straps and the shafts were thinning. If never fixed, it would break down someday on the rough road. Like the cart, Norima's body seemed to need fixing. She felt sick all over, especially in her stomach. She missed Dawa's strong arms and itchy beard, and being touched and held by him. The nearness of him relaxed her. She had been a widow for a long time, and Dawa was single, too. Dawa was not willing to get married, saying he didn't want to be tied down. So he wanted to live together. It seemed to Norima that it wasn't just the young city kids who got the most out of being single. Dawa also enjoyed his independence. Men are clever, Norima thought. Dawa had no wife but he had never been idle, and he liked to flirt with women. Could such a man be a good husband? At least he was a good lover. Dawa was good at making cabinets and making love. If he weren't, Norima wouldn't have stayed with him for twenty years.

The cart lurched forward. Norima thought about sex with Dawa and grew sweaty and restless. The cart was moving too slowly.

Then the sun came out, the frost began to melt, and a light mist rose from the grassland.

Now few villagers use jigger carts, which are made entirely of wood. Wealthy families have bought cars, tractors and motorcycles, and middle-income families use lightweight donkey carts with rubber wheels – "donkey jeeps" as they are known in the village. For everyday purposes, Norima prefers the jigger cart because it is not as difficult to maneuver as a donkey cart. The rubber wheels of a donkey cart can be pried out of holes in the road, but the jigger cart can be be used for mountains, dirt and muddy roads, gravel, and even shrub-covered areas. When Norima was young, she had had sex with Dawa on a jigger cart. Making love on the swaying cart had heightened her pleasure. It was the first time they had made love. Men are all the same, she mused. Even at such special times, they can be completely indifferent. But then, she wasn't too impressed with the act, either. Why was that? When it comes to sex, maybe men and women are the same, she thought.

Few people use jigger carts and few carpenters are able to make them, but she still drove one. Was that because Dawa would be the one to repair it if it broke down? Her lightweight cart, made by Dawa twenty years ago, is still good-looking and sturdy, like Dawa himself. Thin men always had plenty of pee and stamina.

It was a jigger cart that brought her together with Dawa. Three years after her husband died, her family decided to buy a jigger cart and sent for Dawa. He came to her house and worked on the cart for seven days. When he finished, she was very pleased. She walked around it, carefully inspecting every inch. "The cart is finished," she said finally. "Is it time to pay you?"

Dawa wiped the sweat from his forehead. "You're the head of the family, you decide about the payment."

"Didn't we settle on it already?"

Dawa gazed at her steadily. "I am not only good at making carts," he said softly. "I'm also good at something else. Do you want to do something else?"

"Do something else?" Norima was confused. She was a serious woman and didn't recognize flirting.

Dawa chuckled. He moved close to her and patted her on the butt. "What fertile soil," he murmured. "Will you let it stay unsown?"

Then Norima understood. In those days, she had dealt with him respectfully, talking little. She never imagined that the carpenter had plans for them once his carpentry job was done. Angrily, she threw his payment at him and shouted, "Get out, now!"

Dawa had never met such a sharp-tongued woman. He gathered up the money and walked to the gate, then turned around. "Don't be angry, Norima. If you have any problems with the cart, please let me know."

"I can fix the cart myself. Get out!"

But Dawa lingered at the gate. "If you have any other work, let me help."

"Why are you so bothersome?" Norima cried, now furious. "There are no more jobs here. Get out!"

Dawa refused to leave. "You are young and stubborn. You don't understand what real life is."

Norima ignored him. After a few moments, Dawa left.

* * * * *

As Norima was a widow, many matchmakers had approached her, but she wasn't interested in any of the mates they offered up. She couldn't stop thinking about the thin carpenter who made jigger carts. So she decided to drive the cart to his place for a visit. She would tell Dawa that she needed him to make some minor repairs, but her true intention was to find out if he liked her. If he did, she was willing to marry him. Dawa was a good man, had a strong body, and could make sturdy jigger carts.

Unexpectedly, she met Dawa on the trail along the Huolin River. He was on horseback, carrying his tools on his back and singing. Norima shouted to Dawa to stop. Then the two of them sat down under a willow tree next to the trail.

Norima spoke shyly. "Dawa, last year when you made the jigger cart for my family, were you interested in me?"

"What do you mean by interested?"

"Did you want to do that thing with me?"

"Of course. My imagination was running wild."

Norima blushed. "I am serious. I want to know."

"I am serious, too."

"If that's really the way you feel, let's get married. You don't have a family and I only have a daughter."

"Get married?" Dawa's playful expression hardened. "That's silly. Look at me: I'm single, carefree, happy-go-lucky. It feels good. I don't have any stress in my life. But I'll go crazy if I have a wife, raise a bunch of kids, and have to work like a dog to support everyone."

Norima was taken back by this. She had never met a single man who did not want to get married. What was wrong with Dawa? She composed herself and asked, "Are you telling me the truth? You don't want to get married? Are you sick or something?"

Dawa thumped his chest. "Do I look like I have an illness? Look at the muscles all over my body. Do I look sick?" He unbuttoned his shirt to let Norima see his hard muscles.

This made Norima uncomfortable. She couldn't stay and watch Dawa unbutton his clothes. Flustered, she ran to her cart, intending to drive to Halisitai. But Dawa tied his horse to the back of the cart and then jumped into it. He sat there, serious and proud, and tried to reason with her.

"Look, Norima, we're both in our thirties, not kids anymore. Don't be ashamed," he said. "We can be lovers."

Norima hadn't thought about this. Though her husband was gone and she hadn't been intimate with a man for several years, she had never thought of having a lover. If Dawa truly liked her, he should marry her.

Silent and angry, she drove her cart. Dawa knew she was upset, but persisted. "Norima, my way of living is right and your way is wrong. Let me ask you something. Why do you insist on living for others?"

This caught Norima off guard. "What are you saying? That I should live only for myself?"

"Yes, of course. We have to live for ourselves and do whatever feels good."

Norima said nothing. She listened as Dawa continued to jabber behind her.

"Norima, did you come to me to ask me if I wanted to marry you?"

"You are so conceited. My cart is broken and I wanted you to fix it. I just happened to mention what went on between us last year."

"I see. You weren't only interested in fixing the cart. Your mind is calculating, too. Maybe I can help with that."

"You're crazy."

"Don't you desire a man? You not sick, are you?"

Now it was Norima's turn to be offended. She turned around in the cart seat and punched Dawa in the chest.

He snatched her wrists. "Don't hit me! I'm being honest with you, so let me finish." His face was close to hers and his warm skin made Norima nervous.

"Let go of me. Let go of my hands!"

Dawa looked around and saw no one. The touch of his big hands made Norima feel faint. Dawa's gaze burned into her and he pulled her close. She tried to struggle but Dawa pushed her down onto the cart. She wanted to cry, to shout, but her hands disobeyed her thoughts and grasped tightly around his body. Dawa made love to her so strenuously it startled the bull into a trot. Down the dirt road they went, the cart swaying from side to side.

* * * * *

Norima was thinking about the good times past with Dawa as her cart drew close at his front gate. Dawa came outside and smiled at Norima like a child catching sight of his mother.

"What are you doing here? Luckily I didn't leave, or I would have missed you. We should use cell phones," Dawa joked.

"Even if I had a cell phone, I wouldn't know how to use it,"

Norima joked back.

"Come on in and have a drink and something to eat."

"The cart has problem. Please fix it."

"I will fix anything you need."

Norima got out of the cart and walked into the house. Dawa seized the chance and pinched her round butt. Norima sternly brushed his hand away. Just then, a russet-spotted cow tied in the yard mooed softly to Norima. She stopped and looked at the cow. Its eyes were moist.

"What's wrong with the cow?" Norima asked Dawa. "Why don't you let it graze on the mountain?"

"It is old. I intend to sell it."

"Is it old?"

"Yes. Its legs are weak and it can't withstand a bull's pressure. When the bull is around, it kneels down on the ground. If it can't even stand a bull's playfulness, why should it be allowed to live?"

Norima glared at him. "Do you mean to say that it should die for not tolerating a bull's advances?"

"Life should be about fun, whether you're a human or an animal. If it is old, it should be sold." Dawa said.

The cow continued to moo at Norima, almost pleadingly, as if asking for help. Norima was touched and went over to pet it. She saw that the cow was indeed old. Even now, after a plentiful autumn harvest, it remained thin, so maybe it was right to sell it after all. Norima wondered if it would survive the coming winter.

Dawa saw all of this and spoke to Norima softly. "Listen, it's normal to grow old. If humans and animals never got old, that would be strange, wouldn't it? Could the grassland hold them all?"

Then his voice lowered to a whisper. "Come inside. I want you."

Norima reached out to the cow and it licked her hand tenderly.

Its tongue was soft and hot, making Norima feel warm and happy. As it licked Norima, tears rolled down its face.

"Don't sell this cow," Norima said suddenly. "I will take it home. It may give birth to a calf. "

"Done. It's yours."

Norima was pleased. She patted the cow's forehead and then went into the house with Dawa. Inside, Dawa pulled her to his chest, and she responded eagerly. They hurriedly took off their clothes. As they made love, Norima noticed that Dawa was crying.

"What's wrong?" she asked, surprised.

"You are so good, Norima. I don't know why, but I'm worried. How long will this last?"

"You're too old to have such worries. If the cow can get old we can get old. Maybe too old to do this again."

"But I want to stay on top of you for the rest of my life."

"To stay on top of me for life, you'll have to marry me."

"Why bring that up again?"

"All right, we won't talk about it. I know you don't want to get married."

After she and Dawa made love, they went outside and saw a middle-aged woman standing beside the cow. Norima knew her; a widow named Haijile.

With her head cocked to one side, Haijile watched Norima. "What are you doing here?" Haijile asked.

Norma was polite. "My cart is broken, so I asked Dawa to fix it."

Haijile turned to Dawa. "Did she come to fix her cart?"

Dawa hastily answered, "Yes, yes, her cart isn't working well."

But Haijile didn't believe him. "There are carpenters in every village," she said to Norima. "Why did you choose Dawa?"

"What are you talking about?" Norima asked, growing annoyed. "What business is this of yours? If Dawa were your man, I wouldn't look twice at him. But he isn't, so why are you questioning my being here?"

Haijile flushed then turned pale. She went to Dawa, who was pretending to examine the cart for Norima, and grabbed him by the collar. "Dawa, tell her what kind of relationship we have."

Dawa was flustered. "What's wrong with you? Norima came here to have her cart fixed. I have no relationship with her."

But the widow wouldn't let him off the hook. "Dawa, if you are in love with me, you can't be with other women."

Norima was red with anger. "Haijile, I know you. If you really wanted Dawa, you two would get married."

"I wouldn't marry that old thing," Haijile sniffed.

"If you don't intend to marry him, you can't stop him from seeing other women."

Dawa looked around anxiously, hardly knowing what to say.

"I still haven't fixed your cart," he muttered to Norima.

"Forget it," Norima said, not looking at him. "Don't fix it." She got in the cart and started to leave, but Dawa stopped her.

"Norima, do you still want the cow?"

Norima turned back to get the cow. But Haijile stopped Dawa from unhitching the animal. "Dawa, how can you let her take the cow away?"

"She likes this cow, so I gave it to her."

"How much will she pay?"

"Three hundred yuan!" Norima snapped. She took three hundred yuan from her pocket and gave it to Dawa. He was embarrassed, but took the money.

Haijile examined the cow from hoof to tail. "Wait a minute. How can you sell such a good cow for only three hundred yuan? I will pay you four hundred. Sell it to me."

This made Norima angrier. "I will pay you five hundred, Dawa. I'll give you the other two hundred the next time I see you." Clenching her teeth, Norima led the cow away.

Haijile shouted at her back, "From now on, stay out of our village! Because of you, Dawa's life is falling apart."

But Norima held firm. "You can bet I'll come back! I'll come back in a few days."

Norima sat on the cart, giggling as it rolled away. Though she had just spent three hundred yuan to buy a cow, she was happy. She rode along for awhile and then burst into tears.

* * * * *

When she got home, she tied the cow to a pole in her yard. Her daughter and son-in-law were pleased. They knew the cow was old, but if it was special to Norima it was special to them.

"What a beautiful cow," said her daughter Narengaowa. "It would be nice if it could have a calf next year."

Her son-in-law Namula spoke up. "Don't worry, Mom. I will take care of the cow."

"No, you have your own things to do. I will take care of the cow," Norima said firmly. "If it can live through this winter, I think it will be able to have a calf next year."

Norima named the cow Morigen, which means "smart." She believed the cow was very smart. If it hadn't approached her for help, it would have died.

In the days that followed her visit to Dawa's home, Norima busied herself taking care of the cow. She wanted to prepare it for the harsh winter. The most important thing was to let it build up fat; otherwise, it wouldn't be able to stand the frigid cold. Winter in the

Huolin River region was so cold that your butt could freeze when you squatted down to pee.

Norima gave cornmeal to Morigen every evening. Grain was better than forage grass, she reasoned. By the time the cold weather arrived, Morigen was heavier and her hide was glossy. Norima's fears were eased now that she knew the cow would survive the winter.

Before the temperature dropped much further, Morigen was in heat. This pleased Norima immensely. One evening, a bull wandered into the yard with Morigen. The bull was huge, with a big head full of curly fur, a body like a wall, and testicles as big as bowling balls. He was very intimidating.

Norima wondered if Morigen could withstand the powerful bull's advances. In front of him, Morigen was very timid; she blinked nervously and seemed shy. The bull snorted and swung its tail proudly, oblivious to everything but Morigen.

Then after thinking about it, Norima decided not to allow the bull to mate with Morigen. She tried to drive the bull away by waving a stick at it, but it paid no attention to her. She smacked it hard on its hindquarters with the stick, but it didn't budge. It glanced momentarily at Norima then continued to sniff Morigen's rear end.

"Are you blind?" Norima shouted at it angrily. "Can't you see that she is old? Do you think she can stand your weight? What's the matter with you, you willful thing? Go find a strong, young cow."

Norima ran toward the bull, brandishing the stick to scare him, but he ignored her. He was so determined that he arched its back and tried to mount Morigen while Norima was watching. Furious, Norima hit the bull on the head. That time he felt the pain and dropped to his knees, glaring at Norima all the while. He bellowed and lowered his head. Norima was terrified. If the bull charged at her she would be in danger. She ran out of the way.

Then the bull jumped onto Morigen again. Despite his bulk, he did so nimbly. Norima stared wide-eyed. But before the bull exerted its strength, Morigen collapsed to the ground. The bull stood there disappointed, waiting for Morigen to get up, but the pressure was too much for her to bear. Morigen was unable to stand up.

"She can't do it, so get out!" Norima shouted at the bull. She ran back home and called out to her daughter and son-in-law, "Come out here! Morigen has attracted a bull!"

Narengaowa was embarrassed. "Mom, why do you care so much about that?"

"Oh don't be so shy. Morigen can't hold up the bull, he's too big."

"Mom…." Narengaowa started to say something, but Norima had no time to listen. She hurried back to the animals.

The bull was stamping on the ground, not wanting to give up on Morigen, but Morigen couldn't bear his weight.

"Let's hold Morigen up for the bull," Namula suggested.

"How do we do that?" Norima asked.

Namula ran back to the yard, found a thick wood pole and shoved it under Morigen. Norima was to grab the other end of the pole, and thus prop Morigen up, but Namula shouted, "Give the pole to Narengaowa, you aren't strong enough!"

Narengaowa grabbed the pole, just as the bull again climbed onto Morigen.

"Hold on!" Namula yelled.

Before he could say anything else Morigen fell to the ground, pulling Narengaowa down, too. Namula and Narengaowa laughed out loud. Insulted, the bull bellowed and walked away disappointed.

Narengaowa sat on the ground, unable to stop laughing. She had never done anything like this before.

"Get up and stop laughing," Norima yelled at her. "What do we do now?"

"Don't worry, Mom," Narengawa said. "There is a breeding station on the west side of the river. They will be eager to help. This is too good a deal to pass up."

"A breeding station?" Norima shook her head in disbelief. She thought that cows were different from humans; humans could be in the mood for love every day, but cows were only in heat once a year, and then for just two or three days. Besides, using a plastic breeding device was cheating Morigen out of pleasure.

"What's wrong with a breeding station? It's a business," Narengaowa said. She pointed to Morigen. "Morigen, you can't blame us, you're just no good. Don't you know that the bull left unsatisfied? Only a breeding station can help you out now!"

Morigen seemed to understand that Narengaowa was mocking her. She shook her head angrily.

"You see, Mom, even Morigen knows she failed," Narengaowa said. "But she doesn't want to resort to a breeding station."

"This is the last time that Morigen will be a bride," Norima said. "We should seriously look for a bull for her."

Namula watched the bull's back as it moved farther and farther away. "This bull is too big," he said. "We need to find a smaller one."

His words spurred Norima into action. "You're right. I shall go to find a small bull for Morigen." And with that, she was on her way. It seemed she was more eager than Morigen.

Unlike a woman seducing a man, a cow has a window of only two days after she's in heat to effectively snare a bull.

"Mom, you don't need to go," Namula said to his mother-in-law. "Let me go. I know where to find a small bull."

Namula was a smart man. After awhile he returned with a small bull that obviously had just entered the mating season. Norima was very pleased; Morigen would now have a mate. Morigen was satisfied with the small bull. She rubbed against him, licking his body with her long tongue. Encouraged, the bull sniffed at Morigen's body amorously. Then he jumped onto Morigen, heaving with passion. Morigen trembled and nearly fell down. Worried, Norima and Narengaowa shouted out loud, but Morigen regained her footing and stood firmly, submitting completely to the bull. Seeing this, Norima breathed a sigh of relief.

Narengaowa blushed, embarrassed by the fervent mating. She thought a joke might ease the tension. "Why is Morigen crying?" Narengaowa asked her mother playfully.

Norima pretended to be shocked. Then she said to Morigen, "You can stop bellowing now. I know you're satisfied. Give birth to a good calf for us."

Morigen closed her eyes.

Norima thought to herself, "If we had sent for people in the breeding station, Morigen would have suffered unjustly."

The bull and Morigen were inseparable for two days. Then Morigen lost interest in him. Norima hugged Morigen around the neck and told her, "Morigen, this time you had better make a good showing. Bear a sweet little cow, okay?"

Morigen swished her tail and mooed.

*****

The days were growing colder. Norima worried that Morigen would freeze in the winter, so she went to the bend in the river to gather reeds to pad Morigen's stall. Now, the Huolin River is barren. Reeds used to grow as dense as fox tails; now they are as sparse and dry as the hairs on an old man's head. Norima searched and gathered several bundles of reeds. She arranged them throughout the small pen to block out the harsh cold. Cows should live outside. If she let Morigen live inside, the cow would be spoiled.

In winter, heavy snowstorms blanket the Huolin River area. Snow can pile as high as a man's leg, even on the plain. The cattle and sheep suffer terribly. The stored forage grass is limited in all households, so many strong cattle and sheep die. Norima was worried about the coming winter: what would she do with Morigen? Luckily, her daughter and son-in-law understood the problem, allowing her to feed Morigen as she pleased. Norima knew Morigen would only live a few more years, but she wasn't ready to give up on the animal.

By the time of the New Year, the sky grows overcast, the north wind roars, and people become numb with cold after only moments outside. The cattle and sheep hurry home from the fields by late afternoon. In the Huolin River area, the hours around dusk were the coldest time of the day. When cattle and sheep run from the mountain to the village, they lower their heads, mooing and baaing, as if to say the cold wind is painful and their heads are ready to burst.

Every afternoon Norima went to the highland outside the village, fearing that Morigen would be too cold to return home. But Morigen always appeared, running to Norima to lick her hand.

Morigen's belly was becoming bigger and bigger. Norima was worried that the unborn calf would get cold. On the most frigid days, she brought Morigen into the house and let the cow sleep in her room.

Norima's house had three rooms. Her daughter and son-in-law lived in one room, Norima was in another, and Morigen slept on the floor of Norima's room. Norima was getting old, so her daughter and son-in-law let her do whatever she wanted. After all, they were cowherds, accustomed to living this way.

Norima slept easy once Morigen was bedded down in the house. When Morigen lived outside, Norima woke up several times during the night to go out and check on the cow. Now, she could sleep soundly until sunrise.

Morigen always woke up earlier than Norima. After opening her eyes, she went to Norima and licked her forehead with her long tongue. Norima would waken with a giggle, and pat Morigen on the head.

Morigen pulled through the winter. The mountains in the distance were turning greener and greener by the day.

Cowherds dislike this season. Domestic animals can smell the fresh grass and see the faraway green mountains sooner than people do, and it is in their nature to seek the green. The cattle are stressed to death, running all the time in search of a bite of grass. Norima felt sorry for Morigen, who was too tired out to seek green grass day after day. Norima was unwilling to let Morigen go outside, but there was no forage near the house. So she let the cow outside; a bite of decayed grass is better than nothing, she reasoned.

One evening, Morigen didn't come back from the highland. Worried, Norima went in search of her cow. She looked everywhere but couldn't find Morigen, and she started to cry. Eventually, she saw Morigen at a small bend of the Huolin River, hopelessly stuck in the mud. When Morigen saw Norima, she mooed softly, her eyes bright with fear.

Norima took off her shoes and rushed to the cow, not stopping to roll up her trouser legs. The muddy water was very cold. Morigen tried again and again to move forward, but her struggling only sank her deeper into the mud. Norima knew that much more of this would be exhausting to the cow. She needed to go for help.

She looked up and saw Dawa standing at the river's edge. He was watching her, smiling at her predicament.

"You are heartless to watch me suffer!" Norima yelled angrily. "Don't just stand there, come down and give me a hand!"

Dawa's smile never wavered. "I told you that cow is old and useless. But you wouldn't listen."

Norima wiped the mud from her face. "Oh, shut up and get down here!"

Dawa took off his shoes and splashed into the muddy water. The water chilled him to the bone and his face contorted. "Look, the muddy water is so cold that my penis is shrinking."

"Your penis is shrinking? I think your head is shrinking. If you're too cold, leave."

"Fine, I will," Dawa said, heading back to the shore.

"No, wait! Come back!" Norima grabbed hold of him. "Now that you're here, you can't go."

"So what should we do?"

"You stand here and push. I'll go around and pull."

"Every time I ask you to do that you refuse…," Dawa said slyly.

"Don't talk nonsense."

Norima made her way to the river bank. She untied her red trouser belt and knotted it around Morigen's horns. She bent down so that her trousers wouldn't fall off when she tried to pull Morigen out. Dawa realized it would be impossible to get each leg out, so he simply pulled on her tail.

"You idiot! She has a calf in her belly. Don't hurt her!"

"What else can I do? You just pull hard. Don't worry about your pants falling down."

Norima pulled with all her might, sucking Morigen out of the muddy water. But in the course of this, her pants fell down.

Dawa came out from the muddy water huffing and puffing, his teeth chattering. He was too cold to laugh at Norima's predicament. Morigen was shaking from the cold.

Norima gently wiped the mud from the cow, and then suddenly took off her clothes.

Dawa was surprised. "What are you doing? Did I ask you take off your clothes?"

"I'm not doing this for your sake. Can't you see the cow is trembling?"

"Then you shouldn't take off your clothes. I'll take off mine. I don't want you to freeze."

"Fine. Take your clothes off. The calf will come out soon. Did you see the water bubble under Morigen's tail?"

Every cowherd knows that several days before a cow goes into labor, a water bubble will appear at the birth canal under a cow's tail. When the bubble is as big as an egg, the calf is ready to be born.

Dawa took off his shabby cotton-padded jacket and put it on the cow's back. Then he and Norima drove the cow back to the village. On the way, Dawa told Norima that he had come out to visit her, that his health was not as good as before, and that he had been lonely. But Norima was in such a flurry that she had no time to think about his needs.

When she got home, Norima put the mud-covered Morigen inside. She found a jacket for Dawa to wear. Their cotton-padded jackets were soaked through with muddy water. She fetched an old broom and asked Dawa to get a basin of water so she could wash the cow clean.

It took a long time but Norima and Dawa finally finished Morigen's bath. The floor was covered with mud. Norima ordered Dawa to get some straw to make a bed for Morigen. Morigen was standing quietly, and Norima, knowing that the calf was safe, was filled with relief.

She sat on the heated brick bed, preparing a pipe bowl of tobacco for Dawa. Looking somewhat woebegone, Dawa sat and smoked. "You old thing, you gave my jacket to the cow. What will I wear to go home?"

Norima giggled. "You can go back naked."

Dawa sat back on the bed. "Am I your slave now? Then order me about as you will. Tonight I won't go home."

"It's all right with me if you don't go home. What do I care? I'm an old woman. If it weren't for you, Morigen would have been stuck in the mud all night. That would have been terrible – it would have cost two lives."

Her daughter and son-in-law came in and prepared dinner. "Today we were lucky to have Uncle Dawa's help," Norima told them. "His jacket is wet all over, so he can't go back today. He's going to stay here."

Her daughter glanced at her husband, then said, "It's okay with me if he stays."

"No, I have to go," Dawa said, his face reddening to the ears.

Norima looked at him. "Don't pretend you don't want to stay. Your jacket is a mess and you can't wear it."

By this time, Dawa was very tired. He laid down in the dark. He did, in fact, want to spend the night. For an old bachelor like him, having a place for the night is very satisfying.

Norima took out two hundred yuan from her pouch and thrust the money at Dawa.

"What are you doing?"

"Remember when the widow Haijile meddled in our business? I still owe you two hundred yuan."

"Forget it. I didn't come here for money."

Norima took the money back. Dawa's words pleased her; for once, he seemed like a real man.

The family went to bed. Namula whispered to Narengaowa, "I think our mom and Uncle Dawa care for each other. Maybe they should live together. What do you think?"

Narengaowa moved close to her husband. "I agree. Tomorrow I will talk it over with Mom."

After midnight, Norima was wakened by the cow's heavy breathing. Morigen was in labor.

Norima gave Dawa a kick to wake him. "Get up! Get up! The cow is in labor."

As Dawa hurried out of bed, the head of a calf came out. Dawa reached out to catch it, and Norima smacked his hand. "What are you doing? Don't touch it. Let it come out by itself."

"I was only trying to help."

Norima lit a lamp and peered at the calf. "Is it male or female?"

"Female," Dawa said, shivering in the cold room.

Smiling, Norima patted the back of Dawa's head. "That's great, another female in the house."

*****

So Morigen gave birth to a calf, safe and sound, and everyone was happy.

Narengaowa said softly to her mom, "We owe a debt of gratitude to Uncle Dawa for his help. I think you should let him stay here. You two can take care of each other."

"That's a big issue," Norima replied. "Let me think it over."

That day they ate bean paste buns, lamb soup, brown sugar, white sugar, butter and lard. Dawa enjoyed the meal and was glowing with happiness. After he finished breakfast, he left. Norima didn't try to talk him into staying. She was sixty years old now, with grown children. All of a sudden, she had to consider whether or not to live with a man. She was slightly disconcerted and needed to think about this carefully.

Morigen's calf was brown and white, just like her. It was born after midnight, and by the next afternoon was up and running around. Morigen followed close behind her calf, frequently licking it until its hide was glossy. Norima sat on a pile of wood and beamed with joy at the two animals.

Morigen was an old cow, and Norima hadn't milked her since she gave birth to the calf. The important thing was to feed the calf well. The calf grew fast. Five days after its birth it was healthy, with brown ears, big eyes, sturdy legs, and a tail as strong as a newly braided rope. From its considerable size, Norima was sure that the calf would grow big. Whether a calf will grow big can be determined by the length of the bone from its hoof to the middle of its thigh. If this bone is long, the calf can grow big. Norima had raised cattle all her life, but she had seldom seen such a beautiful calf. She lovingly named it Chaganyina, which means "white girl."

After a crisp spring rain, grass grows all over the mountains and wilderness; the land seems to turn all green overnight. The bright green grass now covered the earth, providing the cattle with hearty meals. Norima watched as Morigen grew fatter and fatter, and produced more milk. Finally, she decided to milk Morigen and let Chaganyina eat some fresh grass, too.

Before Morigen's first milking, Norima tied Chaganyina to a pole right after she was fed. That first night, the cow and calf would have to be separated; Chaganyina couldn't be let close to her mother. If she nursed for a whole night, Norima's teats would be empty.

So little Chaganyina was tied a distance away from her mother. She was so agitated that she ran around and around the pole. Cowherds tie cattle and sheep in a particular way, tethering them with loose knots so that the calves can run around the pole without winding themselves tightly against it. They can run all night if they want to. Chaganyina mooed incessantly until midnight and then got tired, knelt down on the hay beside the pole and went to sleep. She was very cute when she was asleep, curled up with her head between her hind legs, forming a circle.

In the morning, Norima woke up and went to Chaganyina with a bucket in her hand. The little thing had already stood up, lowering her neck and trying to reach her mom. Morigen knew that being separated from her calf meant it was time to be milked.

Narengaowa walked up to the cows. "Mom, let me milk her."

"No, this is the first time Morigen has been milked. Let me do it."

Norima untied the rope on Chaganyina. The calf dashed to its mother, grabbed a nipple in her mouth and sucked hard, her small head batting against her mom's teats. Norima stood aside and watched, smiling. She knew though that Chaganyina wasn't yet getting much milk because her tail was still straight; when her tail swished from left to right it meant the milk was flowing fast. As soon as Norima saw Chaganyina's tail swinging swiftly, she pulled the calf away. But the calf planted her hooves firmly on the ground. Norima reached under Chaganyina's hind end and grabbed hard. Chaganyina didn't like that and followed Norima obediently.

Though Morigen was an old cow she had plenty of milk. Norima squatted under her, holding a full nipple with two hands and squeezing the milk out into a bucket. What a pleasant sound! Before she had squeezed all of the milk out, Norima stopped; she wanted to leave some milk for Chaganyina.

Norima let Morigen follow the other cattle onto the mountain. In the village there were two cowherds who drove the cattle from all of the households onto the mountain every morning, and then brought them back at dusk.

Chaganyina wasn't allowed to go with her mom. Norima took her to the sandy hill behind her house where there were good-tasting vines and grass. Chaganyina didn't like grass, preferring her mother's milk, which was sweet and thick with bubbles. But by noon she was hungry and had to eat grass. Gradually, grass tasted better to her. After many bites, her little pink mouth turned green.

Once Chaganyina was full she ran over the meadow, pulling Norima along. She liked to play on the meadow, running wildly about. But Norima was too old to run as fast as she used to. She just stumbled along, puffing and panting. She said to Chaganyina, "Don't run any more. Do you want to wear me out?"

Chaganyina seemed to understand. She looked at Norima and slowed down to a listless amble. Chaganyina felt frisky but Norima wasn't cooperating. Chaganyina watched Norima, then got mad and tried to butt the old woman with her head. Norima was nearly knocked down. She raised the rope to whip Chaganyina. "You brat! Why are you butting me?"

Before the rope could hit Chaganyina she grabbed it and ran away, mooing.

This amused Norima so much that she squatted down and laughed. She stayed there, waiting for Chaganyina to have her fill of nonsense and come back.

*****

Norima hadn't seen Dawa for a long time. Why didn't he come? The calf brought joy to Norima most of the time. However, on rainy days, Norima sat on the bed watching the raindrops fall and missing Dawa. When the sun came out, Norima decided to visit Dawa. She and her cart needed fixing.

Norima got in her cart and drove off. She arrived at Dawa's home at noon. His yard was quiet. Several oxen were let loose in the morning and would return after sunset. It was the typical dreary life of a single man.

The door was closed and Norima was unable to tell if he was home. She tied her cart and pushed the door open. A hoarse voice called out to her, "Who is that?"

A bad smell filled her nostrils. Mongolians along the Huolin River won't empty themselves inside the home even in winter; instead, they go outside to relieve themselves, for cowherds like to keep their home clean. But that day Dawa's home smelled unpleasant.

Norima saw Dawa lying on the bed. "What's wrong with you?" she asked him. "Are you sick?"

Dawa was quite ill, unable to speak clearly. He couldn't move one of his hands, and the other one was limp. He told Norima in a weak voice that he had been ill for two days and was afraid he wouldn't pull through this time.

Norima asked him how he got sick. He said that he had gone out drinking a couple of days before, and had slept a whole night at home after the binge. When he woke up the next day, he realized he was ill.

Norima was heartsick. It seemed that he was suffering from hemiplegia. Dawa was more than 60 years old. It would be difficult for him to recover at this age. She knew that he had five years at most to live.

Dawa started to cry and whispered to her, "Norima, I am dying." His mouth was skewed from the paralysis, and the crying made it look even more askew.

It was unusual to see Dawa like this. Norima looked at him for a long time and thought about their relationship. Dawa had had a lot of girlfriends. He was a carpenter with a personality that appealed to woman, and he was intimate with a lot of them. Norima was just one of many. She had chosen not to live with him simply because she disliked his weakness.

In a voice that struck her to the core, Dawa said, "You can leave now. You came to see me. I can rest in peace." As Dawa spoke, he pushed Norima away with one arm.

Norima patted him softly. "You're talking nonsense, you old thing. Do you think I am that kind of person? It is fate that I came here, and you will die with me at your side. Come, let's go to my home."

With that, Norima went to Dawa's bed, intending to carry him to the cart outside.

Dawa mumbled, "Let me stay here. Let me die here. It won't be long."

"Shut up," she whispered.

Dawa murmured something but Norima ignored him. She took hold of him but he was too heavy for her to move. Dawa continued muttering, which made her nervous. Soon she realized she wouldn't be able to move him by herself.

Norima went outside and put Dawa's mattress on the cart, threw two quilts on top, and drove to the village to get help. As soon as she arrived she met Haijile, who came swaying toward her. "Norima, why are you in such a hurry?"

"It's bad," Norima said shortly. "Dawa is ill. Half of his body can't move and I can't understand him when he speaks."

Haijile was stunned. "Oh my, that's terrible! He is in his sixties. An illness like that will be hard on him."

Norima looked at the old woman and decided to test her. "Haijile, you are his neighbor, and you have a good relationship with him. Why don't you take him home?"

But Haijile recoiled. "Are you joking? Keep an ailing man in my home? I won't do it."

Knowing Haijile's true intentions, Norima said, "Since you don't care about Dawa, I'll take him home. Please lend me a hand."

Haijile looked at her, blinking, then said, "I doubt if we can carry him. You go find two more people."

Norima went in search of help. She met two young men on the village road, and told them about Dawa. She said she wanted to take him home and needed help. The young men didn't know Norima, and asked how she was related to Dawa. She told them she was Dawa's wife.

The two men looked at each other questioningly. Dawa had been a bachelor all his life. When did he get a wife? They were reluctant to go with Norima. At that moment, another villager who knew Norima came along. After learning that Norima would take the ailing Dawa to her home, he was very touched and agreed to lend a hand.

When Norima got back to Dawa's house, she saw a cabinet had been pried open. Did Haijile do that? But there was no time to worry about such things now.

With help from the three men, Dawa was moved onto Norima's cart and she drove to Hailisitai. What a day! She had intended to ask Dawa to fix her cart and her body, and as it turned out, she had to fix Dawa.

Norima took Dawa home. Her daughter and son-in-law hesitated when they saw him, but Norima had already done it so there was nothing left to say. Uncle Dawa was ill, and if no one took care of him, he would die.

After the journey, Norima felt wearier than before. She lay on the bed, with a terrible knot in her stomach. After all, she was elderly herself; it would be difficult for her to take care of a sick man, especially a paralyzed man who would need special attention. Dawa couldn't move his body. Cleaning up after him would be exhausting.

* * * * *

When you're busy, time flies and the seasons seem shorter. Autumn arrived and it turned cool again. Norima still was exhausted. The autumn winds made Norima feel sentimental. Watching Dawa lying on the bed, she wondered what her own future would be.

Dawa was improving, though he still was paralyzed on one side and still couldn't speak intelligibly. One evening at dinnertime, Dawa started to cry.

"Uncle Dawa, why are you crying?" Narengaowa asked him. "Don't we take good care of you?"

"Even though you and Namula are not related to me, you care for me as if you were my own children."

"So why are you crying?"

"Narengaowa, there's something I want to tell you and Namula. Men should get married and have kids. When a man is ill, he realizes how good it is to have a family of his own."

Norima pretended to be angry. "You silly old thing. What are you talking about? I am not your wife, but don't I take good care of you?"

"Yes, you do, very good. You are a good woman. We are not husband and wife and you aren't obligated to take care of me. If you had left me alone, I would have no right to complain. So why *are* you taking care of me?" Dawa burst into tears. As he grew older, his emotions became more and more fragile – like a child's.

That night, Dawa couldn't fall asleep.

Norima fussed at him. "Oh, you old thing. Why can't you go to sleep?"

"Norima, I've thought it over and I think you had better let me go."

"Go?! Where will you go?"

"I have thought a lot about this. The reason I wanted to be single all my life is that I didn't want to be tortured by illness when I grew old. What is a man? A man lives to talk, to be strong and virile. But look at me, unable to talk clearly, unable to move. I'm useless."

"Don't worry. It takes time to get better. You'll be well soon."

"Don't lie to me. I know how sick I am and I know I won't get any better. This half of my body is warm and that half is cold. At least I can't cause you any more trouble."

Dawa's words broke Norima's heart. "What are you talking about? I don't care about trouble. Even if you were ill for twenty years, I would take care of you."

"I am not only worried about bothering you. I feel miserable, just lying on the bed doing nothing. I don't want to live. I am a carpenter, but I won't be able to work even if I recover," as he spoke, Dawa sobbed wretchedly.

Norima sat up and grabbed him by the ears. "Stop talking like this! Do you hear me? I won't listen to this any more!"

Dawa stopped crying and said weakly, "I'll do as you say. Go to sleep. Go to sleep."

Norima caressed Dawa's body gently and he gave out a long sigh, "It's good to be young. When I was young I was a real man. Now I'm not a man at all. I'm old and sick, which makes life even more meaningless. The best years of my life are finished."

Norima remembered that the last time she went to Dawa's

home, the time he made love to her, he cried. Now, the tears seemed like an omen.

Dawa continued to talk. "Norima, even though we aren't husband and wife, you have taken care of me for a long time. That makes me happy. But I want you to do something for me. Don't let me suffer. Find me some sleeping pills. If I take enough of them, I'll fall asleep and never wake up. Then the pain will be gone."

Norima was shaken by this. "What's the matter with you? I asked you not to talk about death. Why are you still talking about it?"

"You don't understand the feelings of a sick person."

"I know all about it. You go to sleep. I want you to live by my side. As long as you are breathing, I am happy."

"You may be happy, but I am not."

Norima covered Dawa's mouth gently and he stopped talking. He playfully bit at her fingers and she laughed. She remembered that when Narengaowa was little she often bit Norima's hand. Norima stretched her legs onto Dawa's quilt. Dawa touched her thighs and sighed deeply.

Like Norima and Dawa, the cow was aging. Morigen didn't look as good as she had the year before. She walked very slowly now. She no longer went into heat. Apparently Chaganyina would be her last calf.

Norima patted Morigen's head and said, "You've had a lot of children and Chaganyina is a fine animal. You have earned a good rest."

Morigen seemed to understand Norima's words and licked Norima with her long tongue. Norima put her forehead against the cow's. "Old. We're both getting old," Norima whispered.

By the first snowfall, Chaganyina had grown as tall as Norima's waist. Norima decided not to milk Morigen any more. She was an old cow and deserved to spend the winter in peace. Neither did No-rima allow Chaganyina to nurse from Morigen. She covered Chag-anyina's mouth with a strip of leather that had nails sticking out of it. If Chaganyina tried to nurse, the nails would hurt her mother. And if Morigen felt pain, she would shun her child.

Norima worried that Chaganyina wouldn't grow properly with-out milk, so every day she poured milk into a small basin and gave it to Chaganyina. "Chaganyina, your mom is too old for you to drink her milk. You're a big girl now."

Chaganyina closed her eyes and noisily drank the milk from the basin. She could eat a full meal of grass, plus the milk Norima gave her. She didn't need her mom for food anymore.

* * * * *

A stranger came to the village to buy cattle, as the price was very low that year. Narengaowa and Namula wanted to sell Mori-gen, but Norima refused. She loved Morigen and Chaganyina very much, and thought Chaganyina was too young to be without her mom. Norima explained this to her daughter and son-in-law. They didn't argue with her.

So Norima didn't sell Morigen, but that winter a sad thing hap-pened. Morigen's life ended tragically.

And on the third day after the first snow, Dawa died. Norima had looked after him week after week, changing doctors often, to no avail. Dawa didn't want to bother Norima, arguing that since they weren't married, she wasn't obligated to him. Added to that, he didn't want to live in that condition anymore, no longer a real man.

One night, he chewed up a towel and swallowed it. Norima had left a towel beside his pillow in case he needed it to sneeze into, never imagining it would be used for a different purpose. It is hard to swallow a whole towel, and before he could get it all in he choked to death.

When Norima woke that morning, she saw Dawa lying in bed, motionless. Not realizing what had happened, she spoke to him and got no reply. She lit the lamp and saw the towel stuffed into Dawa's mouth, and the gleaming whites of his eyes.

Norima grieved for Dawa. She didn't expect him to end his life in such a way. If she had known that he was truly determined to end his life, she would have given him sleeping pills, which would have allowed him to leave this world without such dreadful suffering. She had been so tired lately. She took care of Dawa every day, and at night fell asleep as soon as her head hit the pillow. When Dawa was swallowing the towel, she heard nothing.

Dawa had no children and he wasn't Norima's husband, but many people attended his funeral and paid their respects to Norima. Although times have changed in many ways, Mongolians living in the Huolin River area still keep the custom of drinking wine and eating meat after a burial service.

After hustling and bustling the whole day of Dawa's funeral, Norima's family was exhausted. That night they fell fast asleep. The family dog barked incessantly, but they didn't waken.

* * * * *

Hailisitai is located on the east side of the Huolin River, and to the east of Hailistai is the towering Erdun Mountain, the highest peak in Tuxieyetu Banner with an elevation of 800 meters and a circumference of fifty *li*. It is full of cliffs and precipices. During the "cultural revolution," all the trees were cut down but the grass was still very tall. Hidden within were many wolves.

In the winter of Dawa's death, the snow was heavy. Wolves

couldn't find food on the mountain and frequently roamed through the village in search of meals.

In Hailisitai, every family raises cattle. The public security is good, so there are no thieves. Mongolians have great disdain for thieves and let their cattle run loose in front of their houses. Many families don't even have pens for the animals.

One night a wolf sneaked into Norima's yard. The family dog barked furiously in its kennel, too scared to come out. Morigen and Chaganyina crouched under a gate outside the yard, but the wolf lunged at them. Wolves are especially cunning and fierce. This particular wolf targeted the fat and tender Chaganyina, but first it charged at Morigen, perhaps testing the mettle of the cows. Morigen stood up, lowered her head, and shook her horns at the intruder. The wolf stopped about ten meters away from Morigen and crouched tightly, like a drawn bow. This is an advantageous position for a wolf: it can either attack or run away.

The village dogs were barking wildly, which frightened the wolf and diminished its courage. Morigen was nervous; she wanted to attack the wolf and also protect Chaganyina, who was hovering behind her. The cow roared angrily and stamped the ground with her front hooves. Morigen's defiance unnerved the wolf. Morigen rushed at the wolf and it backed off swiftly. But as Morigen moved forward she exposed Chaganyina to danger.

Before Morigen could turn around, the wolf attacked. It hurled itself toward the calf's neck, but the nimble Chaganyina jumped close to her mom. Before Chaganyina's hooves touched the ground, the wolf lunged at her and locked its jaws onto Chaganyina's back, getting a mouthful fresh meat. The wolf was very hungry and the mouthful of tender meat caused it to shake with excitement. The wolf paid no attention to Morigen, regarding her as too old to fight back.

Chaganyina staggered, mooed miserably and ran to her mom. The wolf rushed toward Chaganyina again. The calf was trembling with pain. This time the wolf bit her on the neck, not seeing the furious Morigen coming toward it. Just as the wolf sank its teeth into Chaganyina's neck, Morigen gored the wolf in the belly. Flailing on Morigen's horns, the wolf scratched at Morigen's eye with its paw, pulling her left eyeball out.

With the wolf stuck fast on her horns, Morigen started to run and hit an aspen tree. The powerful jolt caused the tree to snap in half, its trunk and crown crashing to the ground. Morigen fell down and the wolf was squeezed against the tree. Its intestines spilled out onto the ground and died. Morigen crouched down and panted heavily. But soon her breathing stopped.

The family was wakened by the noise of the falling tree, and everyone rushed out of the house. The moon shone brightly on the snow-covered ground. Morigen had knocked down a tree as thick as a washbasin. Now she lay on the ground, silent. Chaganyina crouched by her mother's side, bleeding and shivering.

It broke Norima's heart to see Chaganyina bloody and alone. If Morigen hadn't rescued Chaganyina, the wolf surely would have killed her. Chaganyina was led into the house, still trembling.

No one who saw the pitiful-looking calf thought it would survive, because a wolf's mouth contains poison strong enough to end the life of any animal – an ox, a horse, a sheep or a donkey.

Norima held Chaganyina lovingly and spoke gently to her. "Don't be afraid, Chaganyina," she whispered. "Your mom is gone, but she died for you. Now I am your mom."

Chaganyina nuzzled against Norima's bosom, still shivering. Her wounds were still bleeding. Norima wanted to let Chaganyina lie down, but the pain was too severe for her to sit for any length of time. Norima knew she had to think of a way to save the calf. Suddenly it came to her.

Someone had once told her that bone from a human skull can absorb poison and stop bleeding. Norima knew where she could find skulls – on the hillside ten miles outside of the village. The hillside was known as the "black den," a place full of neglected graves. No one knew how many years the human skulls had been there, trod upon by oxen and sheep. People in the village thought the burial mounds had been left by lamas. Actually, there were not that many lamas in the villages; the graves probably belonged to the ancient Khitan people, who inhabited the place. There are remains of an ancient village to the east of Hailisitai, which was probably a Khitan town long time ago, but had now become Mongolian grassland.

Norima walked alone toward the "black den," arriving at dusk. She could still see the snow-covered grass, but the moonlight was swiftly fading and soon visibility would be limited. She thought she should go back home. If Chaganyina died that night, she wouldn't be there.

As she walked, she thought of Dawa and grew angry. "Dawa, you shameless old thing. I intended to go along with you. Why did you go by yourself? Why did you swallow the towel? You didn't have a good heart, you could have died. Why did you go and take my Morigen away with you? You caused the wolf to come. If it weren't for you, the wolf wouldn't have dared to run to my door. You are really hateful. You gave Morigen to me, and then you took her away!"

Norima scolded Dawa out loud as if he were beside her, and gesticulated to emphasize her anger. Anyone watching would have thought her mad. Suddenly she tripped and fell in the snow, which covered her face and filled her mouth. She struggled to get up, continuing her rant. "Dawa, you heartless old thing. I blame you for this. Why did you make me trip and fall?"

It was very quiet, windless night. Norima felt strange. What had tripped her? She bent down, carefully searching through the snow, and felt something: a human skull. At the sight of the thing Norima was overjoyed. She clutched the skull to her bosom and hurried back to the village.

* * * * *

Narengaowa and Namula waited in the dark for Norima to come home. They grew apprehensive. Their little child cried aloud. Narengaowa became more and more anxious. Yesterday they had buried uncle Dawa, and at night a wolf came to their door to cause trouble. Tonight, her mom was missing. She started to ask Namula to gather some villagers to help search for her mother. Then Norima appeared.

Namula ran to her. "Mom, it is so *late*! Where did you go?"

Norima held the skull. Her face was blackened with frostbite and small cuts. "I was searching for treasure," she said softly.

Namula looked at his mother-in-law in confusion. What was wrong with her? What sort of treasure was she talking about?

Norima rushed into her room and told Namula and Narengaowa not to follow; she didn't want them to be frightened by the skull. She closed the door and got down to work. First she found a board to place the skull on. Then she fetched a hatchet and pounded the skull into pieces. The skull had been blown by wind and washed by rain for several hundred years, and was as fragile as a bag of rice hulls. She pounded the bone into powder, then opened the door and asked her daughter and son-in-law to help.

Narengaowa and Namula didn't know what to make of the

commotion in the old woman's room, so when she opened the door they entered quickly. Chaganyina was still there, shaking with cold.

Norima briskly issued orders. "You two press the calf down and spread its legs apart, and I will smear medicine on it."

Narengaowa and Namula obeyed. Norima cleaned the calf's injuries with wet cotton. Every time she touched a sore spot, Chaganyina twitched and moaned. After the large wound was washed, Norima carefully dusted the skull powder on it, and on all of the other smaller tears in the flesh made by the wolf. Then Narengaowa and Namula released the calf.

Changanyina stood up and walked unsteadily into the room.

"Mom, what kind of medicine did you use?" Narengaowa asked, her eyes full of wonder.

"I can't tell you now, wait until Chaganyina gets better."

Narengaowa and Namula didn't ask any more questions. Norima was behaving so strangely, they thought. Had she lost her mind?

Norima decided she wasn't finished yet. Dawa's clothes, quilts and other belongings had been burned already. Only his tobacco pouch was left; she kept it to remember him by. Dawa also had a string of Buddha beads and a teapot which Norima planned to give to his nephew. The next day, Norima drove her cart to Maodaoailin.

When Norima arrived at Dawa's house, no one was inside; even the doors and windows had been taken off. Norima stood in the yard, remembering. Though the adobe was not good, the heated bed inside had brought her a lot of pleasure and happiness. Now all of that was gone.

The widow Haijile, Dawa's old neighbor, saw Norima coming, and quickly hid in her house.

On the ride home, Norima thought, Haijile is no good. What did she steal from Dawa's home?

* * * * *

Norima's unusual medical remedy was surprisingly effective. Chaganyina's wounds stopped bleeding, scabbed over and soon grew new flesh.

Chaganyina got better and better with each day. Norima was delighted, and told her daughter and son-in-law about the medicine made from a human skull. Narangaowa was dumbfounded. Chaganyina stayed in Norima's room where she was fed cornmeal, soybean powder and the best dry grass available.

That spring, when the mountains and fields were covered with green grass, Norima let Chaganyina go outside. But the lovely young calf didn't go far, staying close to the front door. Chaganyina had long thin limbs and stood a fist taller than a regular calf. However, after the frightening incident the previous winter, Chaganyina had grown timid. She was especially fearful of dogs and scampered away if a dog barked at her. She dared not sleep outside; every evening she waited at the door of the house until Norima let her back in.

"Chaganyina, you are a good-looking little girl, but too timid," Norima told her. "You were hurt once and had a stomach full of bitterness. But you couldn't speak out."

Chaganyina mooed at Norima. Norima laughed, thinking Chaganyina understood her.

Chaganyina continued to grow. It upset Norima that the calf was so timid. After all, a cow should live out in the wind and rain, not hide under a roof. Norima tried to teach her to be brave.

One evening, a heavy thunderstorm fell on the prairie, with gales and rumbling thunder. Even the thick old trees swayed in its force. Chaganyina hovered near Norima's door and tried to nose her way inside. Norima pushed her out firmly and closed the door tightly. Suddenly, Norima ran outside into the storm. Chaganyina followed her. Norima was running madly around the grassland. This made Chaganyina nervous and she followed Norima closely. Norima finally grew tired and stood still in the rain, panting. Chaganyina stood beside her, wide-eyed. Norima puffed and panted for awhile, then began to breathe evenly. Then she took off running again. Chaganyina was shaking all over, mooing in panic, trying to follow Norima.

Later that night, Norima tied Chaganyina outside in the darkness, refusing to allow her to enter the house. But to make Chaganyina feel better, Norima stood at the door, keeping a close eye on the calf. Her daughter and son-in-law pitied Norima and asked her to sleep inside, but Norima refused. She wrapped a shawl around her shoulders and continued her vigil at the door.

The storm stopped after midnight, exposing a sky full of twinkling stars. The night sky in Hailisitai is brilliant; the Milky Way is wide and long and studded with stars. Norima wasn't sleepy. Chaganyina finally stopped mooing and fell asleep. Occasionally she raised her head and saw Norima standing at the door. Then she mooed softly and went back to sleep.

Norima spoke to the calf softly, teasingly, lovingly. "Go to sleep, go to sleep. Why do you moo? I will never let you stay in the house."

Morning came. It was the first night that Chaganyina had spent outside since she was injured by the wolf. The next night, Norima again tied Chaganyina in the yard, standing at the door the entire night. After three nights of this, Chaganyina gathered enough courage to stay outside alone.

* * * * *

Two years passed and Chaganyina was three, a big, full-grown cow. She was tall with brown ears, brown fur around her eyes, and several brown spots on her body. She still had faint scars on her neck, and one ugly one on her groin, but they didn't dull her beauty. And one day, Norima discovered that Chaganyina was pregnant. She was due in summer.

Norima became extra careful with Chaganyina, who had suffered so much. What would her first calf look like? One day, Norima saw the water bubble as big as an egg under Chaganyina's tail. Norima knew the cow was ready to give birth. And sure enough, that afternoon Chaganyina bore a brown and white calf, also female. Norima cried with pleasure. How wonderful it was, she thought. The calf was of Morigen's blood.

But to Norima's surprise, Chaganyina showed no feeling for her calf. After the delivery, she walked away, paying no attention to the newborn. Norima was angry with Chaganyina. "You shameless thing, why are you acting like this? This is your child! Please lick her body clean!"

But Chaganyina just wandered away and quietly ate grass, wanting nothing to do with her offspring. Norima picked up the sticky calf and shoved it under Chaganyina's mouth, forcing the mother to lick her babe, but Chaganyina ignored this. Norima pressed Chaganyina's head down but Chaganyina got mad and tried to poke Norima with her horns. Norima smacked her on the head.

Norima had raised cattle for many years, but this was the first time she had seen a mother cow ignore her child. Norima had no choice but to clean the calf herself with a brush and a basin of warm water. Norima knew the brush wouldn't work as well as Chaganyina's licking tongue, which was soft and warm and affectionate.

After Norima had washed it clean, the calf stood up and walked unsteadily to Chaganyina, seeking the nipples under her body. Norima clapped with excitement.

"Yet, she is your mother! Feed yourself..." But, Chaganyina

raised her hind leg and kicked the calf far away before she finished.

Norima cried out, "Oh!" and ran to the calf, scooping her up off the ground. Luckily, she wasn't injured. Norima snatched up a stick and swung it hard at Chaganyina's buttock. "What's wrong with you? This is your child! Why won't you allow it to suck milk?"

But Chaganyina just grazed greedily, paying no attention to Norima.

Norima took hold of the calf and carried it close to Chaganyina. She pressed the calf's mouth onto Chaganyina's nipple. Chaganyina didn't kick the calf this time, she just ran away. Norima closed the gate of the yard quickly, preventing Chaganyina from getting out. Chaganyina had just turned three; she was still too young to know how to be a mother. She would need time to get familiar with her calf and develop a bond.

But Norima apparently was wasting her time. Chaganyina continued to reject the calf, kicking it away whenever it approached. And when the calf sought her mother's nipple, Chaganyina turned and butted her with her horns. Norima always intervened, carrying the calf off to safety.

Norima was growing angry at Chaganyina. "I understand your cold heart. You don't want your child at all!" Norima shouted. "What kind of monster are you? If you kick your calf one more time, I will peel off your skin and eat your meat!" Meanwhile Chaganyina behaved as if nothing unusual was happening, and continued to graze unperturbed.

*****

The red sun was setting; it was a beautiful evening. Norima was gloomy. Even though Chaganyina wouldn't let her calf nurse, it was no problem to raise a calf in the village, where milk could be easily found. She just couldn't understand how a cow could turn away from her own baby. Norima decided to talk some sense into Chaganyina, so she tied the cow to a pole, got a stool, sat beside it, and started in. But Chaganyina didn't listen.

Norima's heart was pounding and her face was getting hot. She wanted to share with Chaganyina what it was like to be a female. She believed that if she spoke quietly, the cow wouldn't listen.

Norima went back into the house, washed her face and combed her hair, changed into clean clothes and went back outside. She shortened the rope on Chaganyina so that the calf could not move easily. Throwing her arms around the cow's neck and grabbing her ears, she shouted that any mother who would refuse her own calf was cold-blooded and ungrateful. And if Norima hadn't saved Chaganyina after the wolf attack she would have died. She had rescued Morigen, too. If she hadn't, Morigen would have been butchered, and then Chaganyina never would have been born.

Norima was yelling to the cow, telling story after story and getting more and more excited. But Chaganyina paid no attention. Tears poured down Norima's cheeks. Then she started to sing. She sang louder and louder, drawing out the notes. Mongolian people are good at singing; the love of long songs is in their blood. Norima had a beautiful voice and was often asked to sing at celebrations. Her singing always brought joy to people, but that day her songs were especially moving, the notes lingering in the air above the village. The sun had set and it was dinnertime in the village, but everyone was silent and solemn. The old woman's singing had cast a pall over the place.

Norima was intoxicated by her own voice, singing about a Mongolian woman's feelings for the prairie, her lifelong hardships, the long, difficult path of a woman, the forces that inspire women, and the relationships between men and women. She added commentary to her songs, intending to communicate these important things with Chaganyina at all costs.

The moon rose high but few stars came out. The only sound in the village was Norima's singing. At first, Chaganyina seemed restless as Norima sang and tried to run out of the yard, but the rope was so strong she couldn't break loose. She had no choice but to stand there. As time passed, she became more and more docile. Norima's voice flew into Chaganyina's ears. Gradually she quieted down. Norima's maternal tone tamed the cow, and she began to relax. She stuck out her tongue to lick Norima, but it didn't reach far enough.

Norima was exhausted; the singing had taken a toll on her. Never in her life had she sung so sweetly and for so long. She sang about the whole course of her life, her loved ones, her feelings about the village, the coming and going of the seasons, the stars in the sky, and the ceaselessly flowing water. She sang about everything in the universe.

Narengaowa didn't cook dinner that evening. Her mom's singing had shaken her. She held her own child tightly, wiping her tears time and again. Namula didn't eat any dinner; his mother-in-law's singing made him nervous. He couldn't sit down or stand still, so he left home and went for a walk around the village.

Norima finally stopped singing. Chaganyina was finally broken down by the sound and she mooed to her calf to come. The calf was unsure; her mom's bad temper had taught her to be wary. When she heard her mom's call, she mooed again and again, as if to say, "Mom, I am hungry, don't kick me any more." Mother and daughter mooed to each other. Then the calf rushed to Chaganyina and hungrily took a nipple in her mouth.

Narengaowa leaned on a windowsill, looking at the scene in the yard. Hearing the calf noisily suckle, Narengaowa shouted and ran outside.

Norima waved to her daughter, "Come, come here quickly!"

"Are you all right?" Narengaowa asked.

"Hold me – I can't stand any more," Norima said weakly. Narengaowa caught her mom, who was ready to faint.

* * * * *

The river continued to flow, and the days passed.

After a number of years, Chaganyina had six calves and eventually became a grandmother. Wherever she went she was followed by several calves, all white and brown – the colors of Morigen.

Since the day she gave birth to her first calf, Chaganyina had developed a peculiar habit. Every morning before going to graze on the mountain, she stopped at Norima's front door and waited for her. When Norima came out, Chaganyina licked her hands slowly. Sometimes she tried to lick Norima's forehead and hair, but Norima pushed her away.

"Okay, okay, stop licking me! Go up to the mountain to eat grass," Norima laughingly told her. Every evening, Chaganyina returned to the door, licked Norima's hands again, tried to lick her forehead and hair again, was spurned by Norima again, and then crouched on the ground and went to ruminate.

It was all Chaganyina could do. She couldn't talk, only look at Norima silently, lick her softly and gently moo to her.

Early one summer, Norima had a sudden longing for *halahai* nettle leaves, which only were available in early summer. They are delicious when boiled and are good in salad and soup. They are favorites of the Hailisitai villagers.

Norima had lost most of her teeth by then and had a desire for soft *halahai*. After breakfast, she took a small basket up to the hillside to collect *halahai* from the fields.

Narengaowa tried to stop her mother. "Won't you let me do it for you?"

Norima pushed her daughter away angrily. "Why are you trying to stop me? It's not just *halahai* I want. I also want to roam around the mountain. When it gets hot, I'll come back."

Narengaowa was busy that day. Her child stayed at the high school in town and someone was intending to go to the town and she would ask him to take something to her child. So, she urged her mom to not stray too far and to come home early.

Norima walked a short distance, and then stopped at the foot of a hill in a big patch of nettles. She carefully chose the tenderest leaves to pick. All of a sudden, she had a sharp pain in her head, which steadily grew worse. In truth, the pain had started long ago, when she sang for Chaganyina. Norima sat quietly for a moment, watching the familiar sights of the village and hoping someone would come by. But there was no one around. She saw Chaganyina grazing nearby, and shouted to her.

As soon as Chaganyina heard the old woman's voice, she came to her. The cow didn't know the old woman had a headache or why she was calling out. Chaganyina walked up to Norima, stuck out her tongue and slowly licked her forehead.

Norima patted Chaganyina on the head. "Chaganyina, why are you a cow? It would be better if you were a human so you could carry me home or take a message for me. I have a headache. Do you understand?"

Chaganyina heard but didn't understand. Her big, gentle eyes watched Norima. The old woman stood up and started to head back home, but with her first step she fell heavily. Seeing Norima on the ground, Chaganyina nuzzled the old woman's body.

Norima was very tired; her strength seemed to disappear. She patted Chaganyina's forehead. "Chaganyina, if you can understand what I say, go back to get help. Get help. I have a headache…." Norima's face was growing bright red.

Chaganyina silently watched Norima. Norima shook her head and tried to stand up. She needed to go back to the village, but every time she tried to take a step she fell down.

Norima pushed Chaganyina's ears toward the direction of the village, and pointed toward the village over and over again. "You silly cow!" she cried in frustration. "Why can't you understand what I'm saying?"

Chaganyina didn't move. Lying on the ground, Norima took the scythe out from the basket, pretending to stab at Chaganyina to get her to move. But Chaganyina didn't budge. Norima could do nothing but shove the scythe at Chaganyina's neck, slashing into the skin. Blood flowed out slowly, but Chaganyina remained still.

Norima shouted to the cow, "Run and get help!" Norima stabbed at Chaganyina's neck again; this time, the cow moved off toward the village.

Chaganyina arrived at the house but nobody was home. She ran around the hosue and mooed incessantly. When Narengaowa appeared and saw the cow behaving so strangely in the yard, she knew something was wrong. The cow never came back home at noon, and now her neck was bleeding! Narengaowa grabbed Chaganyina's halter and tied the cow to the pole.

Chaganyina became irritated and mooed loudly, banging the pole with her head, trying to knock it down.

Narengaowa stared at her, speechless. What on earth had happened to the cow?

(Translated by Jade Meng)

Editor's Recommendations for Further Reading:

On the Right Bank of the Argun River, Chi Zijian
Land of Fusion, Fan Wen
Hard Snow, Wen Yajun
Gorlos: Penetrating Your Soul, Guo Xuebo
Worship of the Guardian Deity, Mei Zhuo

图书在版编目（CIP）数据

一双泥靴的婚礼：英文 / 施战军 主编
—北京：外文出版社，2009 年（21 世纪中国当代文学书库）.
ISBN 978-7-119-05940-2

I. 一… II. 施… III. 短篇小说—作品集—中国—当代—英文
IV. I247.7
中国版本图书馆 CIP 数据核字（2009）第 129948 号

责任编辑　邵　东　曾惠杰
英文翻译　孟凡君　纪　华　高文星　张光前　张晓蓉
　　　　　廉望舒　王之光　Yuvonne Yee　蒙雪琰
英文审定　Sue Duncan　Lisa E. Buckley　李振国
装帧设计　视觉共振
印刷监制　冯　浩

一双泥靴的婚礼

主　　编　施战军

出版发行　外文出版社有限责任公司
地　　址　北京市西城区百万庄大街 24 号
邮政编码　100037
网　　址　http://ww.flp.com.cn
电子邮箱　flp@cipg.org.cn
电　　话　008610-68320579（总编室）　　008610-68996177（编辑部）
　　　　　008610-68995852（发行部）　　008610-68996183（投稿电话）
印　　刷　鸿博昊天科技有限公司
经　　销　新华书店 / 外文书店
开　　本　787mm×1092mm　1/16
印　　张　27.5
版　　次　2014 年 11 月第 1 版第 2 次印刷
书　　号　ISBN　978-7-119-05940-2
定　　价　108 元